OVER THE MOON

ALSO BY THE AUTHOR

THE STARSTRUCK SAGA

Starstruck

Alienation

Traveler

Celestial

Starbound

Earthstuck

Inalienable

Dreadknot

AIX MARKS THE SPOT

NOVELLAS AND SHORT STORIES

Miss Planet Earth (Pew! Pew! - The Quest for More Pew!)

The Horrible Habits of Humans (Pew! Pew! - Bite My Shiny Metal Pew!)

Miss Planet Earth and the Amulet of Beb Sha Na

Head over Heels (Starstruck Halloween Short)

Lasers and Tiaras (Starstruck Short)

Study Night at the Museum (Unbound: Stories of Transformation, Love, And Monsters)

OVER THE MOON

S.E. ANDERSON

SEA BREEZE
BOOKS

OVER THE MOON

Copyright © 2022 by Sarah E. Anderson

All rights reserved. No part of this publication may be reproduced, distributed, or transmitted in any form or by any means, including photocopying, scanning, uploading to the internet, recording, or other electronic or mechanical methods, without the prior written permission of the publisher and/or author, except in the case of brief quotations for reviews.

This is a work of fiction. Names, characters, businesses, places, events, and incidents are either the products of the author's imagination, or used in a fictitious manner. Any resemblance to persons, living or dead, or actual events is entirely coincidental.

First published in 2022 by Sea Breeze Books

ISBN:
978-1-7344495-3-2 (Ebook – EPUB)
978-1-7344495-4-9 (Paperback)
978-1-7344495-5-6 (Hardback)

Copyediting by Madeline Statham
Cover Design by Sarah Anderson
Cover Art by Petyr Donat

SEANDERSONAUTHOR.COM

TO THE OTHER FOUR
OF OUR FIVE

AND TO ANYONE
WHO WAS EVER TOLD
THERE'S NO SPACE FOR THEM
IN SCIENCE:
YOU ARE WELCOME HERE
AND YOU BELONG.

PART 1

GIRL ON THE MOON

BEFORE

I'M SEVEN YEARS OLD THE FIRST TIME I SEE THE girl who wears my face.

Princess Jo'Niss Sylvarian of the Sister Systems waves to the crowd from her father's car, propped up by her mother as they drive down Mirah Memorial boulevard. I imitate the girl who has my skin, my hair, and I wave to the toys on the couch next to me, lined up to watch the coronation like the crowd on the screen. I wave out the windows, across the empty sea of corn. I wave like it's me in that little blue car.

The princess is matching her mother, wearing a dress spun in the brightest yellow—a beautiful gold that shimmers when she moves. She looks so poised beside her parents, the newly crowned king and queen of the Systems; she is the first royal daughter since the Great Exodus that began her line. She doesn't smile at the crowd, and instead keeps her lips a straight line, tight and dignified. It looks like she's found a sweet candy and doesn't want to seem too eager.

I try to do the same, but it feels like a frown, too hard and stiff. She must have practiced that look for hours.

"Oh honey, no, no, no!" Auntie rushes in, grabs the remote from my hands, and shuts off the TV.

Jo'Niss's face snaps into blackness, replaced by my own reflection—identical in every way, as if the screen is still on—a little girl with golden skin and hair black like the void.

"You shouldn't be watching TV." Auntie busies herself, fluffing the pillows on the sofa. "It's bad for your eyes."

"It's the coronation!" I say. My eyes prickle. "Everyone is watching!"

Television is a rare treat: we are so far out on the rim of the colonized universe, so we only get major events. For a second, I think the cost of the uplink made Aunt Emery angry. Everything is always too expensive for me to enjoy. Lemonade? Expensive. Ice cream? Expensive. Everything I read about in books is too expensive, even the books themselves.

"We..." She looks up as my uncle enters the room. "Waelon," she says to him, "I think it's time she knows."

"But she's too young," he replies. "She's not old enough to understand."

I don't dare say anything. I want to know whatever they're keeping from me, their grown up secrets. Begging for it is something babies would do; I am not a baby.

"She doesn't need to understand," says Auntie. "All the other children will be watching this. They'll have seen the royal girl. Tobis will be asking questions. We won't be able to hide it forever; she needs to be ready."

I don't want to make them unhappy. Uncle always is always reminding me that if I fail them, they can make me go away. "Did I do something wrong?"

They turn to look at me, and their features soften.

"Nymphodora," Auntie says with the gentlest voice as she reaches over to clutch my hand in her pale fingers. "We have something to tell you. That girl on the screen…she's your sister, in a way."

"I have a sister?" I ask with a flutter of excitement.

"Dora, when princesses are born, they're not born by chance," Auntie explains. "Princesses are born through science. They are born with star-shine and perfection. And they are born in batches."

"Like cookies?"

"Exactly like cookies. When you bake a batch, you know how some of them come out burnt? Or not perfectly round?"

"Uh-huh."

"When a princess is born, she usually has matching sisters. We call these sisters clones. They're all made with the same ingredients, like cookies, but each comes out of the oven with tiny differences. The king and queen want the most perfect cookie. The roundest cookie, the sweetest cookies, the one that's least burnt, the one that is just right. So, they only keep one. Of all sister clones, only one will ever be the princess."

"But what happens to the other sister princesses?" I ask, feeling a chill. Even the fields seem like they're getting darker, as if the giant blue planet in the sky has suddenly gone dim.

"They…" Auntie swallows, hard. "They are terminated, dear."

I only know the word from the other colonists, when we shut down equipment for the very last time. Can you shut down a person, the same way you would a terraforming droid? The thought makes my head swim.

"I thought you were just as perfect as the princess," Auntie continues, "so I took you away. And now that you know, you need to help us, too."

"The rules we put in place are for your own protection, Dora," says Uncle, his voice dry and hoarse. "We want to keep you from getting hurt, so we can't let anyone know who you really are. If they find out, they will take you away from us, and they will hurt you. Do you understand?"

I nod. I clutch my little stuffed dog against my chest. My mouth can't seem to form any words, as if the act of speaking was forgotten to make room for all the new.

"Rule number one," he says, "you must never tell anyone you are a clone. Rule number two: you must study your sister in order to look nothing like her. If she cuts her hair, you grow yours long. If she carries herself tall, you will learn to walk hunched over. You will let your skin dry and crack to stop it glowing like hers. And rule number three: You are not her. Just because you share the same DNA, it does not mean you are meant to be alike. Do not forget that she is a stranger, even though you will know her inside and out. And if they find you—run. Run to the end of the road and don't look back."

I don't know who *they* are, and I want to ask – but my mouth still hasn't remembered how to speak.

"And know that we love you," says Auntie, "not despite what you are, and not because of it, but *because* you are you. And we will always be your family."

I learn the rules like the back of my hand. Like the back of *Jo'Niss's* hand, all smooth and unblemished. The only rule that matters is the one that keeps me tethered to the world, that keeps me safe.

Rule three: she is not me, she is not me.

As years go by, I learn the rest, fill in the gaps. Clone batches are expensive, but it's worth it to receive the perfect child. I read about epigenetics, and how the same DNA does not always equal the same personality. How each clone needs to be carried by a different surrogate, and that this plays its own small role, too.

The books I read never specify how doctors know which child is the ideal one, but whatever magic genetic marker *she* has, I don't. I'm a Genetic Imperfect, a mistake who should have been terminated at birth.

I also learn that the process of clone-batching was made illegal long, long ago. So double whammy on the 'shouldn't be alive' part. If the Systems find out that the royals are still batching, it could rip society to shreds.

Which is why my face can never, ever be seen. Though my so-called aunt and uncle never mention the word in my presence, I come to understand that the Royals entrusted the ocugry—a genetically engineered race of beast-like mercenaries who are known to follow a scent halfway across the galaxy for the right price—with keeping their secrets in the dark. And an illegal clone of the princess is most definitely the right price.

So, I watch Jo'Niss—my sister, my clone—grow up on the interstellar broadcasts, basking in the love and admiration of billions. All the while I am raised on Nesworth, the barrens of the Sister Systems, the invisible farmer girl. Safe.

I despise the girl who stole my childhood and my life. Jo'Niss grew up gentle and graceful, while I grew up all rough edges, bold and brash. Maybe because of the farm work; maybe it was just encoded in my nature. That's probably why the royals wanted to terminate me in the first place—they saw that somewhere in my genes.

Until the night of Queen Maratha's funeral. The night Auntie, Uncle, and I crowd around the screen, turn on the uplink and down the volume so my sleeping cousins won't hear from way upstairs. It is the night I see the princess's face explode in a violent burst of reds halfway through the eulogy, while she's telling the Systems about feeding the ducks with her mother as a small child, and I'm too busy wondering what a duck is to process what just happened.

The night I watch her crumple by Queen Maratha's casket, dead.

The TV goes black. Uncle has ripped the uplink from the unit, shattering the image, leaving only my reflection in the black mirror. The same face as the *hers*, only mine is intact.

"Go to your room," he says, panting.

"But what just…"

"*Go*, Dora!" he bellows, his voice so loud I fear he's woken up my cousins.

Hours later, I tiptoe back into the living room, muting the TV before switching on the uplink. The pictures flick up on screen, accelerated through the simulcast from Apricus, light years away, yet instantly relayed to our pixels, burning the image of my own dead face into my retinas. Over and over, they play the footage of the princess crumbling to the stage, interlaced with interviews, sobbing as they recount the news I can't even hear.

With every breath, I see her face again: the moment she goes from being a person to a page in the history books. Her skin ripping, the blood. My skin would look the same if I was shot, my face would—

No. I have to calm down. *Breathe, Dora, breathe.*

She is not me.

I was seven years old the first time I saw my clone, and sixteen when I watched her die on live TV.

I'm not sad. Or scared. Unlike the people on the screen, I'm relieved. The day I watch the princess take a bullet to the face on live TV, I'm free.

But I was wrong.

She died, and my life remained exactly as it was— nonexistent.

1

THE SHIP DIVES THROUGH THE COTTON-CANDY morning, leaving a silver slice of sky through the clouds in its wake.

The harvest ship's arrival is always breathtaking. Its prow breaks through the pale pink skies as the ship settles in the atmosphere, half-obscuring the light of our blue giant. Hundreds of automated drones spill from its blade of a belly, swarming through the clouds and settling over the farms of our outpost. Months of farmers' hard work finally come to fruition as the drones alight on silos, grasp the full tanks, and hoist them into the sky, where they bring them to be emptied into the massive cells of the harvester ship in orbit.

I take another sip of my coffee, lean back on the porch swing, and gag before taking another to top it off. The drink is bitter, cut by the sharp artificial taste of synthetically processed grounds. We ran out of the good stuff months ago, but I put in a request with the last shipment and should—emphasis on the *should*; deliveries are always finicky—be receiving fresh roasted beans today. That would mean real coffee for a little bit, until we inevitably run out again. No matter how much we order, it never lasts long enough.

Our farm is up next, and I find myself edging forward on the porch swing, leaning toward the horizon and the drones. Even from this distance, across the vast expanse of empty fields, I can see one of them assessing how many legs it needs for the job. It grasps the metal rim of the silo before ripping it straight out of the ground and hoisting it up into the sky as clumps of dirt shower over the empty field. The harvest is fruitful—yielding as much corn as last year put together—proof our terraforming efforts are finally paying off.

The Nesworth colony exists for a single purpose; to provide the Sister Systems with corn. It's a baby among farming moons: families were only cleared for settlement less than twenty years ago, and Auntie and Uncle were among the first to arrive, with baby me in tow. I've shared this rock with them for almost seventeen years; seventeen years of growing corn, harvesting corn, and not much else. Growing and harvesting, over and over and over again.

A smaller ship drifts over the house, a gentle electric hum in its wake: the shuttle. Its underbelly is a glimmering pearly white, more pristine than anything on the entire moon. It shimmers blue as Thebos's light reflects off of it, then goes dark, blocking the rays from my face just long enough for me to feel a chill. Then the sun and the giant are back, and the light is too bright to follow the ship anymore.

Nothing on the moon even remotely comes close to the ship's magnificence. The most high-tech piece of equipment on Nesworth is probably Uncle's combine, and that's a Frankenstein monster I pieced together from scrap. The shuttle will also be bringing a few essential parts, providing the farm with a whole new season of working materials and the prospect of something mildly interesting to do while trapped on this dull moon. It's only when I have my head completely focused on a build that I can forget my baseline boredom.

I stand, flinging my messy braid over my shoulder. Usually, my cousins are happy to help me shape it, but this morning they're too busy getting ready for the fair to help, so

I made do. I'm better at weaving circuitry than hair, and I desperately want to cut mine, but even now, six months after Jo'Niss's death, I'm still not allowed.

The princess is ruining my life even from beyond the grave.

I'd give almost anything to go to the fair with my family. While it's true that travelers at the Landing are ten times more likely than the locals to recognize my face, I've spent my life perfecting how not to be myself. Even without a veil, it's possible that no one will see the late princess in my features. It's not like the imperial family hangs around the kinds of people who spend their lives on harvest freighters. The odds of the Coalition people picking me out for what I am are astronomical.

And I'm allowed to say that. I live on a moon.

I step into the house just as Uncle comes up from the cellar, buttoning his cotton shirt as he climbs. He usually wears the same overalls as me—denim softened by years of farm work—but today he's in a loose shirt and actual trousers, an outfit both elegant and casual for his grand day out.

"Is everybody ready?" he asks when he sees me. 'Everybody' means my five cousins—two sets of twins and the singleton, Duncan, in the middle. After the whole 'Hey, you're secretly a clone of this princess' spiel, Auntie and Uncle felt comfortable enough to expand their family, especially since the Nesworth colony was beginning to thrive.

My cousins are still far too young to understand my predicament, and I'm not exactly sure how Auntie and Uncle will go about explaining it, but until that day comes, I'm just happy some people exist that judge me for who—not *what*—I am. That, and it's nice having more than a handful of people to fill in my days.

"They're upstairs," I reply, grabbing some toast off the kitchen counter and nibbling at a crust, "but dressed, last I checked."

"What, all of them?"

"All of them."

"Stupendous day, indeed," he says, with a small chuckle. But I'm not in a laughing mood.

"So, I really can't…" I begin, but he cuts me off.

"No, Dora, I need you here." His lips form a taut line. "You haven't finished your chores."

"Only because you gave them to me last-minute," I say, balling my hands into tight fists in my pockets, "like every year. But I know the rules, Uncle. I know how to stay hidden."

"Dora…" He levels his eyes at me, holding my gaze. That patronizing gaze—both sorry and firm—is the bane of my existence. "Please. It's not safe for you."

"I could wear my veil?" I lift my gray shawl over my head, demonstrating how easy it is to conceal my features. "No one here has ever caught me out. I doubt any of the off-worlders will."

"No, Dora. I said, I need you here. With everyone at the Landing, the farm will be vulnerable."

"It's not like I can defend this place on my own, if it does come to that." It's true. The house is huge, and I'm just one girl. Old Tidbit, our hound, broke down last month, and no one's been able to repair him yet, not even me. If we're lucky, some replacement parts will come in with the shuttle shipment today.

And also—defend against what? There are two-hundred-and-forty-four colonists on this moon right now, and not a single one of them would put us in danger. And, unless the Farming Coalition has gone rogue in the last six months, there's no way their representatives are going to attack the farm while they're here harvesting, either.

"You won't have to." Uncle stands and shouts upstairs, "Emery? Can you wrangle the kids?" He turns back to me and lowers his voice again. "I've asked Tobis to come help keep an eye on the farm."

"You mean keep an eye on *me*."

Tobis is the neighbor boy who grew up too close to home to not be in on the great family secret, the only person my age for kilometers, and thus, the pre-approved friend who's been assigned to me practically from birth. The only other sixteen-year-old on the entire moon, and he happens to live right next door. Our friendship was written in the stars.

Until Uncle and Auntie told us to replace it with something a whole lot more, and with his instant yes and my disgusted no, it all came crashing down. Now, the two of us barely speak.

"Perfect," I reply. "Tobis can protect the farm, and I can go with you to the fair."

"That's not how this works."

"But I really want to see the shuttle. I've never seen one up close, and I just want a close look at their anti-grav nacelles. Please? You know I'll be careful. You know I'll be safe. Please. I've never gotten to go to a landing."

"And you will," he says. He's avoiding my eyes, the interstellar language for lies. "Just not today. Maybe next year."

"You say that every year."

He runs a hand through his thinning hair. "Well, one year, things will be different."

"Different how? She's already *dead*, Uncle. What else would it take?"

Before he can answer, the cousins come rolling down the stairs like boulders in a mudslide. Auntie does her best to keep up with them, grabbing one to fix his hair before rushing to another to adjust her dress, at which point, of course, the hair of the first one has to be redone.

The cousins are quaking with excitement. For them, Shuttle Day means eating candy and talking to someone other than our few hundred neighbors. If they're lucky, they'll meet a star child, like they did three years ago and haven't shut up about since. Though I'm not sure how much I believe their story about people born in space actually glowing white.

"Steady there!" Uncle throws out his arms, half to stop his children from running any farther into the house and half in an invitation to hug. "Behave or you'll be staying at home today."

"Is that why Dora's not coming?" Luce asks, in one of those kid whispers that isn't low enough to be subtle. "Cuz she's been bad?"

"Dora never comes," says Duncan. "She doesn't like people."

"Dora's staying because we need someone to keep an eye on the house." Uncle shoots me a look. "And she's the best person for the job."

"I can protect the house!" says Wallace, puffing out his chest and giving it a resounding slap.

"Fine. If you want to stay"—Uncle runs a hand through the boy's soft blond hair—"then you can stay. But there might not be enough stardust left by the time we get back…we might get hungry and eat your share…"

"Dora can handle it," Wallace says, letting out a breath as he deflates. I brush his ruffled hair, setting it back in place, smoothing it behind his ears. As obnoxious as my cousins can be, I love them ferociously.

"Dora can handle what?" asks Tobis, letting himself through the front door.

He's updated his hair with new designs since I've last seen him, laser etchings on the short, black fuzz. Its detailed patterning clashes with the sloppy sweatshirt he's thrown on over dusty jeans, though why he's wearing a sweatshirt in this heat is anybody's guess. As always, he's grinning, his smile an overburdened clothesline.

"Nothing the two of you can't work out," says Uncle. I cringe. There never *had* been anything the two of us couldn't work out until Auntie and Uncle interfered and played matchmaker.

"Come on," Posy whines, tugging at her dress while staring pleadingly at her dad. "Can we go yet? They're going to be out of all the best treats!"

"Right, yes," says Uncle. "Dora, Tobis, look after things, all right?"

"That's the plan." My hands are still stuffed into the pockets of my overalls, as deep as they can go without ripping the seams. So, their plan is to force me to talk things out with Tobis while the rest of them have a fantastic time at Shuttle Day? First, that ridiculous 'subtle' attempt at an arranged marriage, and now this. I'm already trapped on their stupid moon—I don't need to be trapped in the house with *him* on top of it all.

"I'm going to eat a whole stick of stardust, and that'll be my lunch, okay?" says Wallace, apparently oblivious to the tension in the air. "If you don't say no, then you think it's a good idea."

"No, definitely *no*," says Auntie, giving me an apologetic look as she shuts the screen door behind her.

I know they mean well. Auntie's cared for me my entire life, the closest thing to a mother I have ever had. She's made it her life's work to hide me: she taught me how to use makeup to alter the shape of my face and how to style my hair when it grew far too long for my frame. She's also the only reason I have books at all: despite the expense, she's always sourcing copies of engineering textbooks and manuals for me to devour, pushing me to follow my passion for circuitry. But even that push has limits. I know all my family wants to do is keep me safe, but I don't need them to help me anymore. I just want to be me.

My heart clenches as I watch them leave through the screen of the closed door. I've forgotten what real quiet sounded like. The cousins are always making some kind of ruckus, and a house without their rumble in the background hardly seems a home at all. The silence hangs in the air like dust in a sunbeam.

Somewhere over the moon, over the solar system, light years away, there has to be a better place than this. A place where I can show my face without fear of retribution. My family will probably be better off without me—certainly, they'd be in less danger—so why can't I just…go?

"So, what's the plan, then?" asks Tobis. He's grown again since last month when I repaired his father's generator. He stands over a head taller than me now, and his skin seems stretched over his lanky limbs, like his bones spurted but the rest of him hasn't yet gotten the memo. I have to look up to him now, and I'm sure he's just loving that. He's carrying himself like he owns the slagging moon.

"I've…got work to do." I push the door to the back porch open. I have almost a half day to myself, and I'm not going to waste it.

Well. So long as I can ditch Tobis.

I pick up my abandoned mug of synthetic coffee and sip the cold, bitter liquid, watching the harvest drones come and go as they scramble about their work with the silos. Once emptied, they mark them with heavy white paint, which washes off with the first rains of the season.

"Come on, don't be like that." Tobis is suddenly at my side. I flinch; I didn't hear him sidle up beside me until he's way too close. "I'm missing the fair, too."

"Only difference is that you get to go this afterclipse," I mutter, placing my now-empty mug on the side table. "Or sooner, depending on when my family gets back."

"Look, it's not like I asked for babysitting duty."

"So, that's what this is? So much for keeping up a pretense. I don't need to be sat."

I fix my gaze on the silos in the distance and try to push Tobis out of my mind. Good timing, too: one of the drones is acting strange. Even from this distance, I can make out the white mark on top of the already-drained silo—but there's a drone there anyway, trying as hard as it can to hoist the container into the sky with only two of its six spindly legs.

Something is terribly wrong. And I can't be more excited.

My shed is only a few steps away. Well, it's not exactly *my* shed; it's not as if Uncle gifted me the little square box in the back of the yard, a few feet from the out-of-use outhouse. It had once been a toolshed, but when I was twelve, I found myself making so many trips between my room and the shack that it just seemed like less of a hassle to set up my own workbench in there. What with the horde of noisy children in the main house, and the all-nighters when a project was too exciting to put down, I slept in that shed more often than not, until it became my bespoke bedroom. It's also where I hoard my collection of books. After all, you don't need a spaceship to see other worlds when you have a well-stocked library.

Uncle has strict rules, but when it comes to my fascination with all things mechanical and electrical, he gives me free rein and lets Auntie spoil me. It's probably because he actually finds my hobby useful. The more I know about engineering, the more I can help around the farm. And the less, in his opinion, I'll want to leave.

"Are you at least going to talk to me?" Tobis says as he trots to catch up.

"There's nothing to say." I run my thumbprint over the padlock and open my small domain. Instantly, Tau rises up from behind a pile of Tennyson manuals, making excited little beeps as he recognizes his creator.

"What the void?" Tobis stares at the tiny egg as it hovers around my face, looking for affection. It would be annoying if it wasn't for the fact I codded the behavior into Tau myself.

"Hey, buddy." I pat his top. "Tobis, I thought you'd met Tau before?"

"This thing has a name?"

Tau lets out a low beep, whizzing backward into the shed like a dejected puppy.

"*He* has feelings, you know. Sort of, since I programmed them. Tau is part of my portfolio. A pet project, quite literally, as he's the only pet I'll ever own on this rock."

"You…you made it?"

Tau chirps, rapid clicks of frustration.

"*Him*, sorry. You made him? What…what exactly is he?"

"An AI. If I want to be taken seriously as an engineer, I need to have an AI under my belt. Tennyson himself called it the pinnacle of robotics, combining the three points of artificial existence: maneuverability, usefulness, and personality."

"An actual AI? He's actually *conscious*?"

"No, that would be impossible," I reply. "Even Tennyson couldn't get a synthetic brain to understand the concept of 'self', and no one has gotten closer than he has since he died. But Tau does think."

Tau is my most successful creation, with an antigravity propulsion system to keep him hovering at all times and a chirpy interface that allows him to make his own decisions and share them with me. He might not be alive in the literal sense, but he's my buddy. And considering that I built him out of scrap material from the farm, he's a friend I can actually be proud of.

Beyond that, Tau isn't much use. He's primarily for interfacing with computers and other tech, but when there aren't any around to interface with, or without a task to do, he's just a floating egg. I did give him a few diodes, so he does make a fantastic flashlight, though I rarely need him for that—nights on Nesworth are lit by Thebos's reassuring blue glow, bright enough to walk the farm by. True darkness only comes during the daily 'clipse and it's never long enough to bother anyone—except me. Thankfully, Tau has my back. I love his company, even if his personality is my own programming and a whole lot of projecting on my part. I don't care. He is mine.

I only wish Tennyson was alive so I could ask him what he thinks. The father of modern-day robotics has been dead for over three centuries, and yet, every single facet of engineering still revolves around his principles. Physicists have their Isaac Newton; roboticists have Sylas

Tennyson. 'Genius' doesn't even begin to cover the man's mind.

"So, you're like…applying to university?" Tobis scratches his head, seemingly not daring to take a step farther into the shed. There's only so much space to move around the old, padded barstool I sit on when doing small, focused work, and I'm currently taking up most of it while I try to find my tools. I reach a hand out to the desk to grab for a book by Tennyson—the poet, not the roboticist, as the latter was a fan of the former, and frequently used snippets of his favorite poems as controls for his droids. I shove it out of the way so I can reach into a drawer, pulling out my toolbelt and buckling it around my waist.

"Of course I am. Aren't you?"

"Yeah but… never thought you would actually leave."

I freeze, one hand on the pommel of my screwdriver, the other squeezed tightly into a fist. Tau rises up and beeps a little tune by my ear. It's a series of questions: *what are we doing? Where are we going? What next, and how can I help?*

Thank the Sisters for helpful robot buddies.

"One of the drones is down, and I'm going to fix it," I proclaim, ignoring Tobis and grabbing my protective gear from where it's scattered around the shed in various forms of disarray. I slip on my worn, yellow spark coat, letting it bulk up my shoulders. My tall, lanky frame does the rest of the work: I have no chest to bind, no curves to hide. I wrap my shawl over my hair and chin, concealing my face in a half-veil. A quick glance in the greasy mirror tells me that I'm getting the exact look I'm going for: as in, not myself.

"What the void, Dora?" says Tobis, but I'm already shoving past him to get outside.

The heat is beginning to rise now, a dusty haze settling on the fields. I can practically smell my own sweat already.

Tau beeps again, another question. I focus on the little chirps, the dips between the tones. His language is simple, even if it was the hardest thing I've ever coded.

"Of course, they probably have their own people," I agree, "but I've never worked on a harvester drone before. I want to see what's going on inside that head."

Tau chirps once: *Impulsive.* I pat the bot on the top of his little egg-shaped body, making him dip and bob in the air.

"That's me, bud," I say. "Impulsive through and through. But at least no one is going to recognize me."

There's no one out there anyway: just kilometers of empty fields. No one except Tobis, whose heavy hand clamps down on my shoulder before I can take another step.

"You can't give me the silent treatment forever, Dora," he hisses. "You don't have to talk to me, but you do have to stay on your farm. Your uncle put me in charge of defending you, and I'll…"

"Oh, don't worry, I'm not leaving the farm—"

"Not without me, you're not."

"I'm just heading to the end of the field. That's fine, right? Still on family land."

Tobis's fingers tighten around my shoulder, releasing only as he moves to place himself between me and the barn. "Dora. I haven't seen you in weeks, and we need to talk. I know you're not one hundred percent on board with—"

"What? Getting hitched?" My heart clenches as I say the words, as if uttering them aloud will make them true. "I need time, Tobis. I have a lot of things I need to work out, and just…"

It's one thing to be best friends with a guy, quite the next for him to jump with excitement when your uncle suggests you tie the knot before even finishing high school. I hadn't put any thought into how I'd said the word, only reacted on instinct, shock, and my tone would have hurt anyone. He accepted my 'no' well enough, but I saw the look in his eyes. You can't go back to being only friends when you know how someone really sees you.

"It's not like you have many options. There isn't anyone else on Nesworth anywhere close to our age, and we get along—we used to get along so well."

"Before my aunt and uncle played matchmaker."

"Before you were forced to consider the fact that we could be more than friends, yes."

"But we're not. And we can't be."

"I still can't let you go, Dora."

"You can't stop me, either."

"I wasn't talking about your field trip."

Tau beeps a little ditty once more, moving to hover over my right shoulder—*let's get moving, already.*

"I don't have time for this, Tobis. Let's both agree not to tell my family about this and leave it at that."

I grab my bag of useless space parts, push past the boy whose heart I broke, and go on the hunt for an injured drone.

2

THE MOST VALUABLE PIECE OF EQUIPMENT I'VE built so far is the family quadcopter. The four propellers were so expensive we had to live off rations for a while, but the quad is the only way to cover the kilometers of farmland Uncle manages. It's my crowning achievement: well, except for Tau, who'll be offended if I don't put him first. And I know that because I programmed him to—not quite sure why I gave him an ego.

Flying the quad out to the middle of nowhere to fix a downed drone will effectively be taking away the most valuable piece of machinery on the farm; all I will leave behind is a sullen boy and maybe my common sense. Not that anyone local will ever steal from the farm: everyone is busy at the Landing and the Shuttle Day fair, and besides, there're less than three hundred colonists on Nesworth, so any theft and you'll never hear the end of it. When Duncan snuck a half-eaten jar of pesto from a neighbor's fridge, the entire moon branded him a thief: perpetual shame is a good incentive never to mess with your fellow colonists. It's a small moon.

I slide my bag across the seat and strap it down before storing Tau in the inside pocket of my spark coat, above my breast. I tighten my goggles and kick on the ignition, feeling power course through me as all four propellers spin alive beneath my feet. I rise a good half meter upward, the quad resting on a cushion of air, before I nudge the vehicle forward and burst out of the barn. I fly down the dusty road and across the empty fields, dirt spinning in my wake. I hardly notice the dust; at these speeds, my only focus is on flying straight and level. I'm a meteor streaking through the sky, even if I'm barely off the ground.

In minutes, I reach the foot of the silo. I switch off the quad and drop to my feet. High above me, the demented drone flails about, its legs scrambling as it tries desperately to pick up the empty container and bring it to its ship. Poor frightened thing. I let Tau out of my pocket and tighten the toolbelt around my waist. *Show time.*

The bot chirps a long, dull tone, and I smile a wicked half grin in response. He can call me impulsive all he wants to, but I'm not about to relinquish my one and only chance at seeing a harvest drone up close after all these years.

The sound of the drone's metal clamps hitting the roof echoes sharply through the empty silo. I grip the first rung of the rusty ladder and hoist myself up. It sounds like being in the heart of a storm, thunder resonating all around us. But I'm not afraid—at least, I tell myself I'm not. Power of positive thinking and all that. Fake it until you make it. I take the ladder one rung at a time, climbing the silo with excitement running through my veins like electricity.

A drone. I'm going to see a drone.

I only have three rungs to go when reality catches up with me. A silver leg, wielded by a confused and out-of-control drone, whizzes toward me and I duck just in time. If I hadn't, I would have lost my head—and life—entirely.

My grip tightens on the ladder. Maybe I've bitten off more than I can chew. The drone is much larger in person than I could have possibly imagined. From a distance, its body looked like the head of a pin; up close, it's actually nearer to a decameter wide. The poor thing is waving frantically, trying and failing to grab hold of the silo's rim. It doesn't take an engineer to see why: a fistful of cables has been ripped out, dangling from the gutted beast's body like discarded entrails.

My heart swells: I'm going to see inside a drone. I'm going to be able to hold the parts, to see how it really ticks, more than any book or virtual specs could ever show me.

I grab the next rung, but before I can hoist myself up another leg whistles past, missing my nose by a hair. My heart races, pumping a thousand beats per second. Part of me wants to run, but another part, the larger part, wants to be the one to solve this. It's the challenge of a lifetime.

Then, all at once, the drone freezes. Its light flickers and then turns off, legs growing stiff and heavy. Before I have the chance to gauge what's happening, the massive body topples forward, a dead hunk of metal plummeting toward the ground.

Having to fall through me, first.

I don't have time to scream. Out of instinct, I pull myself flush with the ladder, flattening my body against the rungs. The drone whips past me, hair dragged down by the vertices, and I clutch the ladder for dear life, squeezing my eyes shut.

Before I can draw another breath, cold metal tugs against my back. I'm ripped from the ladder and thrown into the air.

I feel every single heartbeat, the stretch and pulse of blood through my veins, as I fall. One, two, three beats, that's all the time it takes for me to sail through the air—but I live a lifetime between each one. My arms move as if through thick water, slugging slowly through the sky. There's nothing but blue above me as I plummet toward the earth.

I'm going to die. The worst part is, I know exactly what my corpse will look like: I saw it just six months ago.

I crash down only for the sky to freeze before my eyes. Suddenly, I'm floating atop a pillow of air, clumsy hands paralyzed, grasping at nothing.

"Are you all right?" comes an anxious voice from right behind me. A masculine voice. A stranger's voice. I try to turn my head, but it's as stuck as the rest of my body.

"I can't move!"

Well, at least my mouth isn't paralyzed, too.

"That's just the tractor beam." The stranger's voice is gentle, melodic even, despite the worry that fills it. "I'm going to turn it off, now. You're going to drop, but it won't be far. Don't panic."

I say nothing as he turns off the beam. Even though the drop isn't high, that last meter is a doozy. I hit the ground, all wind knocked out of my lungs in a single gust. *Guh.* I don't dare think about how I would be feeling after twenty times that drop.

"Are you all right?" There are footsteps beside me, and then there's a head, inserting itself between me and the sky. I blink, trying to make sense of the stranger's silhouette. I can't make out any of his features with the blinding sun behind him.

"You already asked that," is all I can say, gasping for air to fill my empty lungs as I push myself up into a seating position.

"And you told me you couldn't move. I fixed that. Are you all right *now*?"

I'm lying in a crater of my own making, just a few meters from the drone. That thing now lies—asleep or dead, I don't know—in its own much larger crater, a mess of legs sprawling out around it.

Tau drifts to my face, letting out a worried set of beeps.

"Yeah, I'm good," I say, making myself stand. My entire body is screaming, but I've had far worse injuries on the farm. I try to push the pain in my back out of my mind: there are much more interesting things to see, including—especially—the stranger.

In all my years living on this moon, my fear of being discovered has never been so present. This is a *stranger*: he isn't from Nesworth. If he recognizes my face, everything my family has done to protect me will have been for nothing. I tighten my scarf. Surely my eyes, hidden as they are behind the thick quadcopter goggles, are not enough to go on? And yet there he is, still staring. Staring at my half-covered face, so intently that I wonder if he too, like the drone, is malfunctioning.

I've never had a stranger to gawk at before. Judging by his face, he must be my age-ish, though I only have Tobis to compare him to. He's probably handsome: growing up on a spaceship does that to people. All the balanced meals, calculated portions, and regulated workouts; not to mention having to deliver heavy machinery to people across the Sister Systems. He's well built, with strong shoulders, his dark-gray uniform shirt clinging close enough to his stomach to show a bit of muscle definition. His hair is dark brown, matching his eyes perfectly. And his face…a kind face, soft and free of blemishes, and when coupled with a wink, enough to make a faint heart swoon.

I don't have a faint heart, though; I have guts of steel.

"Astrophel," he says, extending his hand.

"Nymphodora," I reply, turning away. "But people call me Dora."

By 'people,' I meant the seven other humans I share my house with, and Tobis. Tau just calls me 'beep.'

"I should probably tell you it's illegal to tamper with our material," he says as I hoist myself onto the drone's exposed underbelly. "I could have you arrested, you know."

"I'm not tampering!" I try to find the exact wires I saw dangling earlier, which is difficult now that the beast is lying on its back. "I'm fixing."

"Yeah, well, that's my job. If I hadn't been here to shut it off, you could've been seriously injured."

"Only I'm not."

"Thanks to whom?"

I groan, but he presses on.

"Aren't you going to thank me?"

"Thanks for saving my life. Now, can we please not talk? I'm trying to concentrate."

Tau lets out a sweet beep, and I turn to find him flicking his lights excitedly. He's found the wires for me, that little ball of perfection. I could kiss him if it wouldn't interfere with his circuitry.

"Have we met before?"

My heart clenches. Has he recognized me, under all my coverings? I try to keep my cool. Maybe if I sound aloof, he'll get the hint that I don't want his attention.

"Is that what you say to all the local girls?" I try to ignore him, but he's already at my side, lifting the exposed wires with the safety of his thick rubber gloves. I pull mine from my tool belt and let them shrink to fit my hands, averting my gaze from him. The sooner I can fix this drone, the sooner he'll leave, and take all his pondering along with him.

A small voice in the back of my head screams that *I* could leave, that every second he spends with me brings him closer to understanding what I am. But this may be my only chance to tinker with a drone, ever.

"First of all, this is my job, and you really need to get off this drone before you get in trouble." His voice is stern. "And second, I'm sure I know you from somewhere."

My heart is racing, but I keep my face sullen. "I'm sorry to disappoint, but I've never left my homestead, so you've definitely never seen me before."

"Well, maybe I have. Last year, at the fair, maybe?"

"I've never been to a Landing."

"You've never been to the…? No matter, it couldn't have been there. I would have remembered meeting a girl like you."

"Seriously, is that how you talk to all the little lunar folk?"

"No," he says, "only the ones who are trying to mess with my head."

"Screw you," I snap, and instantly regret it. He looks hurt. Actually hurt.

He hasn't recognized my face after all. He's just trying to flirt. *With me.*

"Um, sorry," I say, my cheeks boiling hot. Hopefully enough of my face is covered by the veil that he won't see me blush.

"You should go," he says coolly. "Or I'll have to exert my power as a junior engineer to have you arrested for tampering with Coalition property. We're in a rush, with the storm coming in."

"Fine, I'll go." My knees creak, and I stand too quickly, my back still throbbing from the fall. That's going to hurt for days. The mention of a storm is a little nerve-wracking—storms here are usually caused by distant impacts, the kind you'd wait out in the reinforced cellar under the house for fear of being struck by rocky ejecta—or worse—if you step outdoors.

"If you really want to fix this drone," I say, "you're going to need a new power converter. I have an old one I can fix up and set in place, which'll hold long enough to get the drone back to the ship. Saves the Coalition the cost of having to tow it all the way back to your freighter."

He shakes the loose cables in my face. "We don't need a new power converter. We need to get these back in place. Now, go."

"Why do you think they were ripped in the first place?" I hop off the drone's body onto the dry soil. "Cables don't just snap. You know better than most just how well the Coalition is supposed to take care of its machines."

"Accidents happen."

"Yeah, like an overloaded power converter surging, causing the drone to move too quickly and rip its own alpha cable by accident, completely screwing with its command core. But fine. Repair those cables and set the droid on its merry way. It'll just rip them right back out the next time it surges."

I turn to the quad and start off, Tau at my shoulder.

"Hold up."

I stop, a smile rising to my lips.

"How would you know that?"

"I'm used to heavy machinery," I say. "I can hear when a PC's fluctuations are off. Something you would've heard, too, if you hadn't shut the thing down so soon."

"I only did that so you wouldn't die, you know."

"I already thanked you for that." I turn to face him, glad my scarf hides my smile. I don't want him to know how excited I am that I'm going to be able to see the inner workings of a harvest drone.

"Well, if you're right," he says, slowly, "then this is going to be a two-person job. I wouldn't mind a little help."

"You sure? Not going to arrest me for tampering?"

He shrugs. "Maybe I will. Is that a risk you're willing to take?"

"Would I have climbed up there if I didn't like risks?"

I like it when he smiles, the way the corners of his lips lift, like a curtain rising over a stage, the performance those glistening white teeth. Not that I've ever been to a real theater, but watching him smile invites me to my first play.

I grab my bag and clamber back onto the drone, carefully avoiding the dead legs. My scarf is still up, my face covered, my eyes hidden. But the way the stranger holds my gaze through my goggles makes me feel as if he sees more. Seeing, without recognizing, but with an awe no one has ever shown me in my life.

Today is a day for new things.

I start work on the converter's chamber, taking my screwdriver to the hatch. I ignore Astrophel's look, afraid that if I pay too much attention to it, it'll go away for good. Not to mention it's slagging distracting. He watches my every move, saying nothing, simply holding the cables out of my way.

"Where are you from?" he asks.

My heart skips a beat: no, he's not prying, he's only making conversation. A thing people supposedly do.

"Oh, here. Born and raised on Nesworth. You?"

"I was born on the *Bountiful*."

"The *Bountiful?* That's the ship, right?" I point at the sky, at the silver blade above us, the drones flying their silos overhead. That's when the weight of his words comes crashing down. "Wait, you were born in space? You're a star child?"

"Yeah, I guess. You make it sound more exciting than it really is."

Well, that's a letdown. "I just thought star children were, you know, more…"

"Glowing?" Astrophel laughs as I pull open the small access hatch to the crisscrossing wires that make up the drone's brain. I've never seen them in real life, only in manuals. Gazing at them now is like looking at the sun: beautiful, making my eyes fill with tears. Happy ones, I think.

"My cousins saw a star child at the fair a few years ago," I say, carefully moving the wires aside to get to my golden nugget. "They told me that her skin was white like starlight, and her eyes were red."

"Oh, that's just Maru. She's got albinism. She wasn't even born in space."

"Albinism?"

"She doesn't have any skin pigmentation," he explains. "It's congenital."

No wonder I've never heard of it. Most people use some extent of genetic manipulation to ensure their children inherit their parents' selected hereditary traits. Even my cousins were born without genetic predispositions to most illnesses. Maybe Maru's parents are old fashioned, or religious: not everyone likes to tamper with their unborn children in the womb.

Finally, I feel it: the old, rundown power converter that drove the drone mad enough to rip out the filaments of its own mind. I pull my replacement out of the bag. It belonged to the combine at some point and broke down. Uncle Wae replaced it with new parts, but I took it upon myself to fix the old PC as a personal challenge. It was never meant to be used on a drone this big—but hopefully it will last long enough to get this one home.

"It's lucky you were around with the right parts," says Astrophel, closer than I expect, his sudden proximity making me jump.

I'm so focused on my job, I didn't hear him approach. Tau drifts up to inspect him, then slips quietly away. He has nothing in his programming to tell him what to do when faced with a stranger…but then again, neither do I.

"Lucky you had a drone that needed repair." I jam my screwdriver between clenched teeth, wiping my brow as I dislocate the old part and pull it out. I thrust it at him and go right to putting the new one in. "Not a two-person job after all."

"You're not very good at small talk, are you?"

I put down the screwdriver, bending down to reach into the drone's mind. Since the replacement converter is smaller, I have to stretch farther down to reconnect it and use quite a bit of jiggling to get it to fit. The challenge has my heart bursting with excitement, with the thrill of solving the unsolvable.

"There's not that many people to talk to on this moon, you know," I say. "I don't get that much practice."

"Well, have you ever thought about leaving?"

I glance up at him, warily. He's crouched over the hole, watching me work without trying to intervene. I must be doing something right.

"What kind of question is that?" I retort.

"I don't know, small talk."

"Not a very small question." I close my eyes, letting my fingers do the seeing for me. If I turn the lead this way, yes, it will connect. I just have to—

The converter snaps into place, and relief washes over me. I push myself up, gently brushing the wires back where they belong, adjusting one or two as I clean up.

"Yes, of course I have," I say. "Have you ever thought about settling down on a farming colony?"

He lets out a laugh.

"What? Is it that funny to you?"

"Not my place," he says. "Not my kind of world. But then again, I don't usually meet girls who put my technical expertise to shame."

"Then maybe you should question your technical expertise, not the moon."

Together, we reconnect the loose and broken wires, sharing tools and fixing all that's left. It only takes a few minutes and is nowhere near as big a job as I had thought it would be. I'm flooded with the overwhelming sense of pride of a finished project, knowing I have breathed life back into a collection of metal and wires. *You're welcome, drone.*

"Well, if you ever need a way off this planet, we sure could use someone with your expertise up on the *Bountiful*," says Astrophel, grinning from ear to ear. "You seem as nimble with a drone as Tennyson himself."

Well, there goes the joy. As much as that may sound like a compliment to him, to me it's a reminder that I'm stuck here just like a fly in a jar of honey. My heart swells with pride and sinks with fear all at once, making me feel like I did when I caught a sparkmoth as a child, only for it to die in my hands.

"I have to go," I say, a little too quickly. I only realize when I turn away that he was reaching for me—to shake my hand, I think?—but it's too late and too awkward to turn back now.

"Hey, don't leave yet!" he says as I rush to my quad, Tau following close behind me. "Don't you want to turn the drone back on?"

"You can go ahead." I toss my bag onto the quad and climb up after it. "I've been gone long enough as it is. Remember not to push the drone too hard; the converter is old. Replace it as soon as you get it up there."

"Will I see you at the fair?"

I desperately want to answer yes, that I'll be there, that we can talk freely without a drone between us. But that will never happen, and it's no use getting either of our hopes up.

He's still talking, but the rest of his words are muffled as the quad carries me back to my world.

3

I RIDE THE QUAD HOME, WATER WELLING IN MY goggles as I fly across the fields. I alight and chuck them in a corner of the barn, stowing the vehicle as I wipe my tears. My tools go back in the shed where they belong, as if I've never been gone at all. I consider putting Tau in sleep mode as well, but don't feel like being alone right now, even if *he* is an *it* and a flying, beeping egg. Instead, I slip him in the pocket of my overalls and head back to the house.

Tobis looks up from his book as I walk in, his smile fading to a frown as he sees the look on my face. He drops the book onto the table.

"What happened? Are you hurt?" He reaches for me, but I shy away, letting the screen door slam behind me.

"It doesn't matter," I say. "Don't you have somewhere else you'd rather be?"

"I told your uncle I'd be here for you, and I'm not letting either of you down."

But he *is* letting me down. Every day, flaunting his freedom. The only reason he's even willing to watch me in the first place is because he'll then be free to head off to the fair himself. No matter how he chooses to phrase it, he's agreed to be my jailer. I'm never getting off this planet, never even getting off this *farm*.

My life belongs to a dead girl.

Suddenly the house feels too small, shrinking with every ticking second, until it's tight around my ribcage, stopping my heart. I turn for the door and throw myself outside, gasping for air—and slam right into my uncle's chest. He's home early, his face red, chest raised. I spring back, knowing his anger means he has to have seen my dust trail in the field. *Void.*

"Uncle Wae," I say, trembling on the stoop. "You're home early."

The door opens and closes with the creak of hinges in dire need of oil, and Tobis appears behind me, casting a shadow over the porch. I silently beg him not to say anything about my disappearance.

"There's going to be a storm," says Uncle. "Coalition people saw it on the way in. Comet got reeled into Thebos's gravity and shattered into fragments that have been impacting the far side of Nesworth for the past few hours. It won't be long until the dust reaches us, so we have to prepare the cellar—and unload the new deliveries. You'd best be getting home, Tobis. Your pa needs you. I hear he's got some good news for you."

As if to punctuate the sentence, he thrusts a stack of crisp white envelopes into my shaking hands, each one the pristine color of the shuttle's belly, adorned with a different crest. All addressed to me. The first mail I have ever received.

"What. The void. Are these?" Uncle tilts his head like our hound used to do when we gave it conflicting instructions.

"I…I have no idea," I say, but that's a lie. I know exactly what they are, though I didn't dare hope. My hands shake as I try to open one, try to ignore the tightness in my chest, the walls closing in even on the porch.

I finally rip the thick paper and pull out the sheet. The words are printed in stark black on white, and for a moment I can't read them, can only see individual letters inked on the pulp. And there it is, the one word I care about: *Accepted.*

I tear open another envelope, and then a third. Dappled sunlight shines onto the paper, brightening the word on the crisp white pages. *Accepted.*

Accepted. Accepted. Accepted.

"I'll head out," says Tobis, sounding awkward.

"Thank you, Tobis," says Uncle, lowering his voice, though his face is still as red as topsoil. "There are some pretty thick letters for you, too. Now get home safe, before the storm hits."

"Thanks, sir."

I can't pull my eyes from the letters. All I want is for this moment, this single moment, to be about my own success.

Even if I know what's coming.

There's no point denying it or trying to avoid the inevitable argument. What had I expected, anyways? This day had been bound to come sooner or later, when these letters arrived.

Part of me never expected to get one response. Let alone five.

Uncle leads me inside, fuming, leaving me free to tear open the rest of the envelopes as I walk behind him. *Welcome. Accepted. Congratulations.* Every single letter is an invitation to follow my wildest dreams. Too bad I'm not allowed to feel excitement.

The door slams behind me. The sound echoes through the house, making the silence that follows even louder. I turn to face him, clutching my letters to my chest, pushing them against me like I can force them into the fabric of my skin.

Uncle is clutching his hands into tight fists, then loosening them. Tight. Loose. Tight. Loose. I find myself more focused on his fists than on his scowl.

"What can you tell me about these letters?" he asks, his tone even. *Tight. Loose. Tight. Loose.*

"They're acceptances," I reply, "from universities I applied to."

"You applied...to universities?" His eyes go wide—but I can't imagine he's actually surprised. There aren't much else these letters can be, and their crests are dead giveaways. Uncle can be thick at times, but he isn't dumb. I nod.

"But...how? You can't just...apply to universities! You've been homeschooled! You've never been tested! And not to mention that contacting other planets is..."

"I used the Network. Found everything I needed online. I knew there would be a delay, but there was no rush. Most universities have programs for students on rim planets; turns out my situation isn't as rare as I thought."

"You're kidding me, right?" Uncle looks like he's going to explode, his face getting redder with every passing heartbeat. "Your situation, *rare*? Have you forgotten who you are? *What* you are?"

"But she's dead now, Uncle!" The words burst like sparks off my tongue. "She's dead, and I'm who's left. Aren't I allowed to have my life back?"

"She never took your life from you."

"She never took my life?" Heat rises in my face, the blood rushing to turn my skin hot. Fury is a fiery thing, and I'm not going to put it out this time. I've been tending those fires for too long now. "I've been trapped here, on this moon, in this house, my entire life. I have talents, Uncle, and all these universities see it. I want the life that's rightfully mine, to see where I can go now that her shadow's not keeping me in place!"

Uncle glowers at me. "Do you really think your life would be all that different if you weren't in hiding? We'd still be here on Nesworth. We'd still have the farm to work. We homeschool all the young'uns, not just you. Don't blame the princess for this life just because you don't like it."

Hot tears well in the corners of my eyes. "Why won't you let me leave? I just want to build things, and these schools…they'll let me build my wildest dreams. That's how I got in without test scores: I showed them what I can do, and they want to see more. So why don't you?"

"Because I love you, Dora! I love you, and I don't want to see you hurt! This is a bad idea, and you're still a child under my care and my protection. I forbid it."

"You call that love? How is that love? It's the same kind of love that made chickens domestic. The same kind of love that almost kept the wayfarers from leaving First Earth. I want to be an engineer, and you can't stop me."

Uncle stares at me. Then he says, *"Fine."*

"What?" My face flushes. A breeze blows cold against my face, defusing me. "Are you really saying…?"

"You're right." Uncle falls butt-first into the soft couch, staring out the window at the expanse of his land. It stretches as far as the eye can see, still as a painting. "You're right, I can't hold you back. It's not my place. But you understand that I can't see anything hurt you, right?"

"But those are my risks to take."

"Did you really get accepted to all of your schools? Even Helmia Proper?"

"Every single one," I reply. "Some are even offering financial aid."

"I know you want to go," he says, "and I want you to, it's just...why didn't you talk to us first? We could have worked this out...your aunt and I, we need you for this next harvest. We have so many new parts, new repairs..."

"What are you saying?"

"I think you should wait a year. Wait a year, and your aunt and I will pay for everything. Wait until the boys can start helping on the farm. Wait."

Wait a *year*. The same words he says every time I ask about going to Shuttle Day. Every. Single. Year. His promise means nothing.

"I have to go now," I say, rubbing the soft fabric of my overalls for support. "I can't stay on this stinking moon, in this slagging town—"

"Language!"

"—a minute longer. I have to go, Uncle, I have to."

He rises to his feet. "I'm just trying to help, Dora!"

"That's what you're always saying!" My head spins, my ears ring. I want to drive my fist through the door, to make myself hurt outside like I feel inside. To make this house share my pain. "I just want to be free!"

"But you are free! I know it might feel like, sometimes, we're trying to keep you trapped, but we only want you to thrive. Dora…"

"Don't *Dora* me," I snap. "I'll be in my shed. Since I'm not allowed to go anywhere else."

"Dora!"

I storm across the painted lawn and into my shed—a little melodramatic, but I want him to see how furious I am—and slam the door behind me. I toss my acceptance letters on my workbench. This is my room, my refuge, the only place Princess-Slagging-Perfect can never touch. It's amazing how far Princess Jo'Niss can still reach from beyond the grave.

I'm not going to cry. I promise myself that. I look at the small picture of Tennyson I ripped from the page of a library book and tacked to the wall, admiring the features of a mentor I've never met. He's in his mid-fifties, long after the death of his wife and daughter, but he still has more smile-lines than wrinkles, blond hair swooping over his forehead and refusing to recede. He's staring toward the camera with a proud look on his face, holding in his hands a perfect synthetic mind of his own creation. I don't want *him* to see me cry.

I let Tau out of my pocket, knowing he'll at least keep me company even if he might not cheer me up. He whizzes around my face, worried, filling the shed with sweet little electronic chirps. I pat the top of his little egg point, and he dips, flying away to land on top of a pile of old technical manuals.

Those will be my life now. A year fixing tractor parts will probably be the next decade of my life, until I marry Tobis and settle down, expanding the colony with land and numbers.

I know I'm more than capable of handling myself—my work with the harvester drone is proof of that. I've done what even one of the Coalition's own can't do, all without revealing myself to the stranger, or even letting my uncle know I've been gone at all.

I know that there's something out there for me, beyond the curtain of space. All the stars in the sky can be mine if only I can get a ship to get me off this dead-end world.

There's a knock on the wood; a gentle, quiet knock. Not Uncle's fist.

"Who is it?"

"It's me," says Tobis. "Let me in? I have coffee. The real stuff."

Maybe the guy does know me, after all.

I get up and unlatch the door. Tobis slips in without a sound. I sit back on my stool as he places the steaming mug on the workbench, in the small free space next to Tennyson-the-poet's *The Wasteland.* Auntie gifted me a small book ages ago with all the vocal commands he'd ripped from the text, and I've been studying the poem to try and understand Tennyson-the-scientist's obsession with it.

"Don't you have a proud pa to get home to?" I ask, trying not to seem eager or too sold on the concept of drinking coffee just yet…even if it is the first fresh roast I've had in six months. "If there really is a storm brewing."

"He can wait. I asked what I could do to help you feel better, and he told me coffee always helps. I didn't even realize you liked the stuff."

"I don't, but I'm hooked on it now. And you really don't have to stay. The delivery will be here any minute, and I'll have to help unload. I've got my work."

"What you've got is a sucky lot in life." He nudges the mug closer. "But you're not letting anyone help make it better."

I snort. "My family's idea of help is a little overbearing."

"I'm so sorry about, you know, all the protocol. And I'm sorry you couldn't go to the Shuttle Day fair." He lets out a heavy sigh.

"Maybe next time, right?"

"Sure," he says, but his smile is noncommittal, pitying. "Did you really get into every single one of your universities?"

I wave at the stack of papers I've tossed on the workbench. "Yeah, not like I can go, anyways."

"Dora." He puts a gentle hand on mine. "It's still an accomplishment. You should feel proud."

"Who says I don't?"

"I'm just trying to help." Tobis looks sullen. He used to laugh all the time when we were together; that changed after I admitted I'd never see him as anything more than a friend.

"Where would you go?" I ask in an effort to redirect the conversation. "If you could leave Nesworth, I mean."

"I don't want to. Not forever. Wherever I go, it'll be to study colony growth. I want Nesworth to flourish; I'll do whatever it takes to make it a place for generations to grow. To thrive."

I nod, staring into the black void that is my coffee. I don't share his need to put down roots: I don't have any roots to put down in the first place. All I want is to discover and explore. I dream of meeting minds like mine, of joining them in creating something bold and wild and free. Anywhere but here.

"There's just so much to do out there," I say. "I've never heard a frog, you know that? I hear the first generation seeded a planet out there full of them and they've completely taken over. I just—"

The door hits my back, jolting me, making the coffee splash from the cup down onto my acceptance letters. Little pools of black soil on the crisp white.

"Tobis?" Auntie sticks her head into the shed. "I thought you'd left."

"We were just talking," he says, turning his winning smile on her. "I wanted to make sure Dora was okay."

"I am," I say. I'm not—actually, I'm still seething, and it's taking all my energy not to glare—but it's what Auntie needs to hear.

"We need your help with the delivery, dear," she says. "It's quite a big one this year, and we're in a rush to avoid the storm. You should probably head home, Tobis. It's soon 'clipse and I'd rather you not have to walk back in the dark."

He slips past me, giving me one last, pitying nod before heading out. I stuff my hands into my pockets, staring up at Auntie, who beams back down at me.

"Your uncle told me you got accepted everywhere," she says. "I'm sorry it's not safe for you, yet. Your uncle and I love you, Dora. And we only want what's best for you."

"You don't have to sweet-talk me, I'm coming to help," I say, switching to work mode. The farm is the farm, in the end, and I know better than to shirk responsibilities. "So long as I don't have to talk."

"You won't have to say a word if you don't want to."

"Thanks," I reply, following Auntie out of the shed. I watch Tobis trotting down the driveway toward his own family farm, and, in my heart, I'm grateful. Grateful for a family that loves me and a friend who's still trying to stick by me.

But in my head, the gears are turning, churning out plans for getting off this slagging rock.

4

A PLUME OF DUST SPIRALS INTO THE AIR, A LONG way down the lane. The delivery is here, and it's time to get to work.

I drape my scarf around my face as I walk to the barn, shoving my braid off my shoulder and covering my features like I've done each time deliveries arrive. I used to hide in my room when people came, but when I got old enough to help, the value of my extra hands outweighed the risks of being caught.

I don't speak. I don't make eye contact. I blend into the background and make myself forgettable.

Uncle and Auntie are already in front of the barn when I get there. Through the dust comes an old quad, easily four times the size of ours, made of chrome like the ship but dented and dirty, hauling a hovering flatbed big enough to carry my shed. Auntie turns to me, giving the scarf an extra tug to make sure it's firmly in place.

The driver is covered head to toe in fabric, with dark goggles over his eyes and a rag wrapped over his face to protect it from the dust. He pulls up the driveway and stops right next to the barn, exactly where we need him. Perfect. He turns off the quad and slides to the ground, unwrapping the ragged scarf and looping the goggles around his neck. Slag, it's Astrophel, the boy from the silo. The only stranger I've ever spoken to, and here he is, standing in my barn.

His eyes grow wide at the sight of me. My heart beats faster and more violently than it ever has before, even more than during my fall. Has he just placed my face from earlier, or is he seeing right through me, recognizing the princess beneath my veil? I move my head slowly, shaking it in a silent plea, hoping he'll understand and stay quiet. He doesn't say a word, but that's probably because Uncle is reaching out to him.

"Waelon Gale," he announces, shaking Astrophel's hand vigorously. "You're from the Coalition?"

"Yup," Astrophel answers, any sign of recognition on his face plastered over with a blinding grin. "Call me Astrophel.

I should have everything for you here—you wouldn't believe how tough it was to get everything on a single palette."

Uncle laughs, then jabbers on about who-knows-what as he follows Astrophel to the hoverwagon towed behind the quad. It's just as monstrous as the quad itself, large enough to carry the house if it tries hard enough.

"He's handsome," says Auntie, raising her brows at the boy. I hadn't noticed: my heart is pounding for fear of discovery, not out of any attraction I feel for him. Sisters, I'm too busy hoping he isn't seeing me that I haven't *seen* him at all. At least, not in *that* way.

My mind is all over the place, trying to keep track of all the ways he could ruin my life. If he gives any hint of having met me before, if my uncle and aunt learn I've been away from the homestead, alone, and talking to strangers, then I can kiss college goodbye forever and ever. And that thought is even more terrifying than the gruesome T-word. At least if I'm terminated I won't be bored.

Astrophel lowers the hoverwagon to the ground, turning to look at our little family. I feel as if all eyes are on me, even those of the cousins, who are watching from the porch, trying hard not to get roped into extra chores by being seen as possible helpers. His eyes hold mine in a vise grip. He clears his throat.

"Um, you probably should tie your hair up," he says, without a hint of ever having met me. "You wouldn't want it to get caught."

A warm feeling flows through my veins: I'm safe. My body unclenches, and I relax. He's understood me, protected me. I shoot him a look—a thank-you look, a look of relief—and he winks.

Auntie's right: he *is* quite handsome.

The fear of recognition melts away. He won't say a word, I can tell that much. Somehow, he's understood that I need our meeting kept secret.

He makes conversation with Uncle and Auntie as we unload the cargo. The trolleys are a little worse for wear, but they hold up, and, one by one, we unload everything into the barn and cellar. I feel myself getting excited: fixing things is what I do best, and the haul of new parts is Arrival Day for a mechanic who's used to making do with cheap. I can't wait to get my hands in there.

I shake myself. I can't get sucked in. I have to *leave*. There are many more interesting things to fix in the rest of the Sylvarian Systems.

"Want a beer?" Uncle asks as we unload the last skid.

Astrophel wipes the sweat off his brow. "I should be getting back, actually."

"Aw, too bad." Auntie looks at him, then at me, and I can practically see the gears turning as she plays matchmaker, frowning as she obviously knows it can never be.

They thank Astrophel and turn back to the house. I make to go with them, then stammer something about closing up the barn. The second they're out of my field of vision, I dart back to Astrophel's side.

I know what I have to do. And he must have guessed, too: he's waiting for me, pretending to adjust the empty pallets back on the hoverwagon's bed.

"Take me with you," I say, my voice so low even I can barely hear it.

"You sure?" Astrophel's eyes go wide.

"Did you really mean what you said earlier? About needing someone like me, on your ship?" He doesn't answer, so I go on: "You asked if I ever thought about leaving. The truth is, it's all I ever think about. Every day of my life, it's my first thought when I wake up, my last when I close my eyes to sleep. Please," I say, holding out my hands. They're smeared with grease and oil. "You know why you've never seen me before today? My family won't let me out on Shuttle Day. I'm trapped on this farm. I don't have money to pay for a trip, but you've seen what I can do, you know that…"

"It's okay," he says. I've never seen a face break into a smile so wide before, not even Tobis's. "People travel with us all the time. If you want to join us, we can ask the captain if he's willing to take you."

"You mean it?"

"Only if you can handle being in space," he says, a shadow crossing his bright face. "Hyperspace windows are always opened out of the way of any major solar system bodies, and it takes days to reach them on sub-light engines. Our trajectory will use a gravity assist from your Big Blue to get us out of the system, where we can then safely open our window and go to our next system before reaching the Core worlds. With two planets to harvest, we'll be busy for quite a few days. You'd have to be up for it."

I nod, my face hot with the thrill of it all. I don't know much about faster than light travel—not my kind of engineering, though I'd still love to take a look at the engines of the *Bountiful* if they'll let me. And a gargantuan ship like this one would need massive power to cross the vast emptiness of interstellar space fast enough to bring fresh goods to the core with days between Hyperspace jumps.

My feet have never left the soil, but I'm sure they can handle being in a ship. A few days doesn't seem that bad, for where it's getting me. I'm already imagining myself climbing the steps of Helmia Proper, wearing the crisp uniform, tablet tucked under my arm. In my mind, I'm already there.

"I'm up for it," I say. My lips are suddenly dry, so I lick them. I'm so deep into the vision that I almost forget he can't see me there, too.

"Then come with me, Nymphodora of Nesworth," says Astrophel, extending a hand, "The universe awaits. Do you need to get any things?"

I tap the inside pocket of my spark coat, checking on Tau. Him, my spark coat, and my overalls—the only things I need in the whole wide galaxy.

Without a second thought, I hop on the back of his quad and leave my farm life forever.

Town—which doesn't have a name, seeing as how it's the only place with more than a single house on the entire moon—isn't far from the farm. Then again, nothing is ever far from the farm. The colony started in one location and hasn't progressed much from there. Nothing is ever more than ten kilometers away in any direction, at any time. I certainly haven't gone any farther than that in my lifetime.

I clutch Astrophel's back, breathing in the scent of his uniform as he drives up the familiar road. The cloth is saturated with smells I have no notion of, so unfamiliar they're alien to me. Some are sickly sweet, like concentrated fruits, while others are harsh and metallic, reminiscent of my shed. I breathe him in deeply. I expected riding the quad as a passenger to be a pain in the ass, but it's so much better than expected: warmer, sturdier. Though maybe it's the fact that I'm clutching a stranger that makes my heart burst in my chest. My arms are wrapped around my salvation.

The streets of Town are empty, shops closed, everyone off at the fair or managing deliveries at their farms. We drive down streets that are usually packed—at least by my standards—now turned into a ghost town since the last time I visited, to mail off college applications through the library.

The street's emptiness is a relief. Despite the effort my family has put into concealing me, I'm sure everyone on Nesworth has a vague idea about my face in some way, shape, or form. So long as they don't have the full picture, I'm okay. It's impossible not to know each other when we have the entire slagging moon to ourselves. With the scarf across my face, I'm hoping my disguise will be enough to make my neighbors think I'm from the shuttle, and those from the Coalition think that I'm a forgettable local.

We pass the memorial to the lost colonists, and I shy away. It's its own small plaza: the ground, a disk for Earth, with the Lost Pilot, Mirah Sylvarian Tennyson, rising from the center, holding her Lost Ship in her hands. It's a gruesome reminder of the dangers of space travel, and I don't want fear to distract me now.

Three ships were launched from First Earth through the wormhole to settle the Sylvarian Systems, but only two arrived: the third swallowed whole when the wormhole collapsed on it. A million lives lost in one instant, along with the only way back to Earth, and the mind behind the wormhole device in the first place, Mirah herself.

Three great ships, commanded by three great women. The Sylvarian sisters, who would then give their new worlds their names. Mirah's twin sisters Lani and Eva Sylvaria, who had piloted the ships that had survived, went on to become our world's first royals. Sylas Tennyson, Mirah's orphaned son, carried on his mother's legacy after her death, his great mind engineering our fruitful worlds.

All in all, great memorial, five-out-of-five would recommend, just not when you're trying to escape via outer space.

Thankfully, while the wormhole technology that brought our ancestors here during the Great Exodus was lost with the Lost Pilot, enough tech survived to replicate it on a much smaller scale, allowing ships to open a pinhole just large enough to slip into Hyperspace. Which is a whole extra dimension—enough to do your head in, really. Wormholes are easy in concept: folding space in order to bring point B to point A. Meanwhile, you use Hyperspace to enter a dimension where points A and B are already touching, if you come at it from the right angle and with enough power. Without this technology, our ancestors would have been limited to a single solar system. Instead, they expanded over dozens, with hundreds of planets and moons to call home.

Except our real home: First Earth. Without the wormhole technology, we can never return. I don't think anyone even knows where it is.

The landing port is only used as a port twice a year; the rest of the time, it's just market space. I've never seen anything actually dock there until today. I find my breath catching in my chest. I've only ever glimpsed the shuttle fly overhead before, looking as if it was almost brushing the top of our homestead. Now, it's obvious the shuttle wasn't anywhere close to the roof: it's so large it must have always been hundreds of meters in the air. It's massive, taking up the entire length of the dock, long enough for one of Uncle's fields to fit in there without damaging a single crop. The entire back end of the thing is dropped down, and men and women are handing out goods to the crowd, all busy enjoying the festivities.

Streetlights turn on as Thebos slips in front of the sun, casting its shadow onto Nesworth and plunging us into the dark. It's a truer darkness than actual night, when Thebos remains overhead and the world is bathed in a dull, blue light. The daily eclipse only lasts a little over an hour and is more annoying than anything else. I don't like the true dark, and I use the excuse to clutch Astrophel tighter.

In the darkness, the fair is even more beautiful. The road is lined with tents with local food along with stands for the travelers to show their wares, all covered in bright lights. Music is playing: a weird, celestial song, one that rises and falls on the breeze as if it is the wind itself. The song is so new, I've not yet heard about it on the Network—even if our version of the music is distilled and slow, lyrics only, since we're too far out in the rim planets for heavy downloads. The air smells like a gentler version of Astrophel's uniform, all sweet fruits and cold metal.

Children fly past us in a swarm, some from Nesworth and some from the shuttle, playing like they've been best friends for years. I watch the mismatched space kids and farm kids excitedly trading stories: exaggerated, for sure, but part of a life I've never had a chance to experience.

"Coming through," says a man, carrying two huge crates on his shoulders.

The quad brakes, and I lean away, gaping—a *mod*. An actual mod. I've never met anyone with superhuman strength before, and I have so many questions. My jaw hangs as I watch him walk away, both crates sitting gently on his shoulders as if he's carrying pillows of air.

Astrophel lowers the quad until it's barely hovering off the ground, gliding us through the crowd with his toes. He's making a drone-line for the open doors of the shuttle's cargo bay, where neighbors talk with the travelers, arranging payment for all the parts they've ordered over the past few months, wrapping up quickly before the storm hits. There's going to be a whole lot to take back to their farms: it's been a bad year for rust, even if it's been a good year for crops—the cost of improving the humidity quotient of our air. But if the storm hits as soon as it sounds like it will, they're going to have to stockpile elsewhere.

The quad drifts up the cargo ramp, Astrophel politely asking townsfolk to move out of the way so we can slip inside. The white doors are so large they would dwarf the family farm. Inside, the cargo bay is clean and tidy, with rows of equipment stacked neatly against the metal bulkheads.

A ship. I'm inside an actual ship. Even if the captain might deny my request for a ride, this cargo bay alone is large enough that, if I hide, they probably won't find me for days.

I can be light years away from Nesworth before anyone notices.

"It's a shame, really." The voice is familiar—Harvey, a neighbor. He must be chatting with the travelers. I turn my head away. "That poor young girl. She had so much life ahead of her."

"My kids had nightmares for weeks after the fact," says a man I don't know. "We never saw it coming."

"I *still* have nightmares," says another one. "You see people getting shot in films, and it's nothing. We're desensitized by the violence, when we know it's part of a narrative. But seeing someone's…flying out of the back of her head like that…cut off mid-sentence… I never thought I could cry so hard."

"Our ship's counselor has had her hands full treating all these new cases of PTSD. Up 'til now, most of her cases had been, I don't know, cabin fever and space madness. Now half of the crew is seeing her every day just to try and get past it."

"It's been the same on the moon," says Harvey. "The worst is by far the children who saw it happen."

"The entire galaxy saw it happen," says one of the travelers. "No one can unsee it."

Chills run up my spine. *Rule three, she is not me, she is not me.* My mantra to ward off dark thoughts. *Rule three, she is not me, she is not me.*

"Did you watch it, too?"

Astrophel's voice cuts through the low hum of the quad, and I shake myself back to reality.

"I think we all did." Do I sound nonchalant? I sure hope I do. "But that was months ago. Why are people still talking about it?"

"You don't understand," says Astrophel, hands shaking as he turns the quad off and lowers it to the ground. "Everyone loved Princess Jo'Niss, and she just…"

He shudders, and, for a moment, I see the ghost of something else flicker before his eyes. Recognition? Slag. I hope I'm just imagining it. But he says nothing, turning away from me.

The Sylvarian Systems have taken the death of their darling to heart. The first princess born in over three hundred years definitely counts for something. Even as far on the rim as Nesworth, we all mourned her death, laying wreaths and candles on the memorial to the Lost Ship. But they were cleared away months ago. Here, we don't talk about the trauma of that night. Forgetting is the best we can do. In the rest of the Systems, it seems everyone is still openly grieving.

"Are you coming?"

I'm frozen halfway off the quad, zoned out as I stare through the cargo bay doors at the only town I've ever known. I turn to Astrophel, forcing a smile as I call Tau back to me, putting him back in my pocket for safe keeping. *We're on our way out of here, little buddy.*

"Of course," I reply. "I'm ready."

5

WE DIVE DEEPER AND DEEPER INTO THE CARGO bay, past rows and rows of crates, people—some even modded, powerful muscles rippling up and down the lengths of their bodies—chatting as they prepare the wares for a rushed delivery. At the very back are stairs as steep as a ladder, and we climb them quickly, our footsteps echoing through the massive, emptying hold.

Upstairs, my guide throws open a door and leads us into a large sitting area, cozy as my living room. A few people are lounging on stuffy couches or sitting on the long benches around metallic tables, laughing as they grab a meal. They look up as we enter, then avert their gazes. The only person who keeps her eyes riveted on me is a pale woman, who stands as soon as Astrophel leads me through the door.

"Giving a local the grand tour, are you?" she asks, brushing corn-silk white hair away from her face to reveal her stunning red eyes. Maru, another star child—the girl with albinism.

"Seeing if we can pick up a hitchhiker, actually," he says. "Have you seen cap' anywhere about?"

"I haven't," said Maru. "But Abril probably has. Abril?"

A girl with cropped dark hair and a rebreather covering most of her face turns to meet us. Instinctively, I shrink back: her eyes are piercing. My scarf is still wound tightly around my face, but I'm not going to be able to keep this disguise forever. Eventually, I will have to remove the scarf or deal with questions that can't be answered. I need a rebreather like her, something to cover my face that raises pity instead of questions. She must have damaged her lungs terribly if she needs to wear it all the time.

Her smile reaches her eyes, the only part of her face that I can see, and my heart skips a beat. I should have been counting my exits, planning for an escape the second I set foot on this ship: anyone here can recognize me at any time and ruin my entire escape plan.

"He's been working with navigation to plot our next course," she tells Astrophel, never breaking her gaze from mine. What is she waiting for?

"You off to see the universe, sugar?" asks Maru.

"I need a change of scenery," I reply. "Have you seen this moon?"

Maru laughs at that, giving Astrophel a playful punch in the shoulder. "Where did you find this one? She's a hoot, man."

"Maru, this is Dora," he says. "Dora, Maru."

We shake hands.

"I'll get to know you later. Sorry, sugar, they need me up front," she says, before dashing off toward the cockpit.

There. A perfectly natural interaction. I'm better at this than I thought.

"And I'm going to find the captain," says Astrophel. "Abril, want to give our guest the grand tour?"

"Not much grand to a shuttle, but sure," she says. "She'll be more impressed with the *Bountiful* itself if Hardi lets her board. He's in the astrometry room. I'll loop around and join you."

"Perfect." Astrophel turns back to me, giving a brilliant grin. "Abril's gonna take great care of you. In a few minutes, you'll be one of us."

He dashes off before I can say another word, slipping into one of the dark corridors connected to the lounge. Abril watches him go, hands on her hips, shaking her head and tutting under her breath.

There's something oddly possessive in the way he passes me off to her, like he's guarding me, making sure I stay. I'm probably being paranoid, but even so, it makes my hair bristle.

"Is he that nice to all the local girls he meets?" I ask, dismissing those pesky alarm bells.

"Girl, he's nice to anyone who can stand him," says Abril. "You can't imagine what it's like being stuck in interstellar space with him. But then again, *everyone* is exhausting when you're stuck with them for weeks on end. You sure you can handle it?"

Sisters, I know that well. Being stuck at the same farm with the same people my entire life has given me a literal lifetime's worth of experience in that department. "I can handle anything if it means getting off Nesworth."

"Is this place that bad?"

"Have you seen any of it?" Abril shook her head. "Exactly. You've been in space for weeks, get a chance to walk on terra firma, and still you don't want to—that's the power of Nesworth."

Abril laughs. "Come on, I'll show you around. I have a feeling I'm going to like having you on board."

She loops her arm through mine, and, together, we stride toward the cockpit. Slag, am I blushing? I haven't ever made physical contact like this with anyone outside the family before. This is weird. Is my stomach meant to feel so fluttery?

I'm blown away by the cockpit. Never before have I seen so many controls and displays in one place, so slick and clean. Everything back home is always covered in a thin layer of dust and/or cobbled together with parts from here and there. I want to tear up the pristine console and pull it all apart, just to see how it works. I would stay here all day, but Abril pulls me away.

She gives me a quick tour of the shuttle, explaining that this was just her first season with the crew, and she's still settling in. By the time we finish the short loop and find our way into the astrometry room, it's empty save for Astrophel. He stands with his back to the doorway, admiring a holographic display projected off the table in the middle of the space.

"Can we keep her?" asks Abril, giving my arm a tight squeeze. "Pretty please? She's got a good sense of humor, which will help make you more bearable."

"Cap' says he'll have to meet her first," he says, turning his head to grin at us. That grin seems to be perpetually baked on his face now that we're in this shuttle. "But I think he's going to love her."

The astrometry room isn't as impressive as the cockpit, though I'm pretty biased when it comes to gadgets and gizmos. At first glance, this room has none, save for the holographic table Astrophel is leaning over. I've seen these at the library and already know how they work, so it's not all that exciting. All in all, the room is dull compared to the rest of the shuttle. It doesn't even have a window.

I cross my arms over my chest—it's colder in here—and wander to one of the walls to inspect a chart, trying to look casual. I'm not sure how I'm meant to behave, how anyone is supposed to act in the presence of potential friends. There wasn't anyone my age on Nesworth while I was growing up except for Tobis, and social skills are not something that come naturally to me. But I'm on a roll today, and I don't want to ruin it.

"So where are we in all this mess?" I ask. I'm starting to sweat despite the chill, small beads of water trickling down my back under my heavy spark coat. I feel Tau's small body in my chest pocket and press him tighter to me.

The holographic display in the center of the room brightens, and Astrophel threads his fingers through the light. I drift toward the blue spheres, which hang lazily in the air above the table.

"Well, we have the settled worlds around here," Astrophel says, his lips curling into a smile when he meets my gaze. Abril rolls her eyes. "The original worlds the Sisters settled are contained to this space here, the core, with Apricus right in the heart. And we are…here." He reaches out to the very edge of the table. With a swift set of motions, he makes the holographic spheres grow, reeling them in until they take up the entire surface. And there it is, a little cheerful label popping up: *Nesworth, Corn, 244.*

Farmland. Prison. Home.

I've seen maps before, but something about seeing the small blue dots form the only home I've ever known, here, now, in the navigation room of an actual ship, makes my heart soar. I trail my fingers through the projected light, letting it catch on my blackened nails. How small it is.

"Have you seen the rim planets before?" asks Astrophel.

I shake my head. "On paper. Printed maps. Charts. Never like this."

The planets shrink again and begin to swirl around the table in a dizzying dance of lights. Thousands of stars flash by, hundreds of habitable planets and moons, all at the very beginning of being settled. The human race is expanding, spreading throughout the galaxy, making the odd rocks their homes despite the loss of their birthplace.

I want to see them all.

Suddenly, the map skips. Without warning the entire span of stars goes dark, text fizzes out, and then comes back again, somewhere completely different from where we'd been seconds before.

"What just happened?" I'm slightly nauseous from the display, the universe spinning too fast for my body to follow.

"Oh, we just skipped over the Outer Zone." Astrophel shrugs. "Not much to see there anyways. Our charts don't carry that kind of detail."

"What do you mean?"

"You have heard of the Outer Zone, haven't you?" He scoffs. Abril shoots him a glare. "What? Everyone's heard of it."

"Yeah, but I thought it was a Core myth," I say. "I mean, ships disappearing, alien species in hiding…"

"*Those* are myths," says Abril, before Astrophel can say anything else. "By our estimate, half the legends about it are true and the other half are only partially so. The truth of the matter is that the Core has no real control over it, what with the globules disrupting transmissions."

"Globules?" I ask.

She glides her hands over the table, twisting her fingers to bring it to a halt, having now brought the holochart back a few light years. If she hadn't warned me, I would have thought the map was shorting out—a whole patch of space is flickering, as if one of the projectors was loose. Some stars are stable within the patch, but otherwise, it's as if a ghostly hand is trying to pull them from the display.

"Bok Globules," says Astrophel. "You know, small nebulas, only a few light years across? Unfortunately, they're the unbearably dusty kind, completely absorbing visible light as it passes through. It makes communication and navigation a nightmare. The Outer Zone is full of them since it's at the edge of the Smudge Nebula."

"And people live in there?" I say, awestruck. "Inside the nebula?"

"Not exactly." Astrophel smirks. "Planets can't form *inside* nebulas, not since the stars are still in the process of forming themselves. But some of their stellar siblings outside or on the edge were lucky enough to form a few planets. They just happen to be hidden by a big 'ol interstellar dust pile."

"This isn't a seminar on the interstellar medium," says Abril, rolling her eyes at Astrophel. "If this is your game, I get why you're single."

She flashes me a grin—or what I'm guessing is a grin from the twinkle in her eye, seeing as how the rebreather is hiding her mouth—and I feel myself flush. Maybe he really is flirting with me, if someone else is picking up on it.

"A few colonies were seeded when they were found at the end of the Great Survey," he continues as if she hadn't said a word, "but they were so cut off from the core that any real semblance of law was impossible. So now it's more of an…autonomous region. Freight ships like ours avoid that space like the plague. Our nav systems struggle to get a fix on the right coordinates for a Hyperspace window."

Can Astrophel be any more impressive? I thought he was just a junior engineer, but seeing him spin the controls of the map, pointing out every star and planet without waiting for the index to name them for him, I realize he must be much more. He's so at ease with the shuttle, far more comfortable than he'd been on solid ground. He has space legs, like a true starborn ought to have. At least some myths are true.

I'm going to like it here, I know. These people are so warm. If the rest of the crew is like Astrophel, Abril, even Maru, maybe the rest of the galaxy can be as well.

We're deep into a conversation about the mythical position of First Earth when the Captain finally arrives. He doesn't look like a captain; he isn't bold and imposing, but drifts into the navigation room, barely a paper doll of a person. He's tall, as if overstretched, without a gram of fat on his bones. His uniform seems to cling to his skeleton, but it's tight and crisp, elegant even in its gauntness. From his frame, he must have been born on a ship, or at least a planet with a gentler gravity.

The man does a doubletake upon seeing me, just as I did when I saw him. I gulp audibly—probably not the best way to make first impressions, especially when first impressions can mean freedom or life stuck on my backwater moon. The way he looks at me is no better, though: all wide eyes and an unblinking stare. He probably hasn't expected someone so young to have repaired his drone in lieu of one of his own people.

"Ah, you must be the new recruit," he says, looking from me to Astrophel and raising his eyebrows. "I'm Captain Hardi. My boy here tells me you're quite the mechanic."

My boy? Is the man Astrophel's father? I look for some kind of resemblance between the two, but can't spot any.

"I try to be, sir," I reply, hoping that isn't too forward. He reaches to shake my hand, and I clasp his, trying not to focus on the sensation of the bones squeezing my flesh. "But I'm nowhere near the level of your people."

"I sincerely doubt you've had the chance to test your skills against all my people," Hardi chuckles. "But if you think you can keep up with them, you're welcome to travel with us for as long as you'd like. A' says you helped him out with a downed drone earlier. They're quite technical. You enjoy working with bots?"

I helped *him*? More like he played the assistant while *I* did all the heavy lifting—but it's not worth losing an ally and potential friend to a technicality.

"I'd definitely like to work in robotics someday, yes, sir."

"Oh, stop calling me *sir*." Hardi has a surprisingly hearty laugh for such a slim frame. "My crew calls me Cap, or Hardi, or Captain when they've majorly screwed something up. You're welcome to use any of those."

I smile, and Hardi smiles back. Suddenly, everyone in the room is smiling, and I have never seen so many teeth before in my life, even when I was teaching the twins to brush theirs.

The twins. My cousins. If I leave now, will I ever see them again?

No. I don't care. I *can't* care. My family has been holding me back since the day I was born. The dumb rules spin in my head, and I put them all aside. I spoke to strangers today, strangers who took me in when I needed help, who didn't judge or pry or ask many questions.

"We'll take off in a few minutes," says Hardi, turning to Abril. "You three should strap in. We want to leave before the storm, and the ride will only get bumpier every minute we stand around here. Takeoff in fifteen."

Fifteen what? I want to ask, but already I'm being swept from the chart room, away from the dizzying planets and moons, and Abril is taking me back to the mess hall, her mouth running faster than her feet.

"You can share my room! And we can talk bots together every night until we're so tired we fall asleep mid-sentence! I can't believe we get someone new on the crew! I can't wait to show you my workbench!"

I can't wait either. I bob along the waves of a budding friendship, bubbly inside, unsure of what to say to make Abril mine forever. I take a seat between Abril and Astrophel—they are my friends now, no doubt about it—and strap in.

I lean back, head resting on the fake velvet of the launch seat. The ceiling above me is made of panels with bright LEDs, and I wonder if the rest of the ship will be lit that way. In just a few minutes, I'll know the answer.

No paperwork. No begging. Accepted right away. Has this easy escape really been within reach all these years?

"Are you ready for your new life?" asks Astrophel, grinning.

"You have no idea," I reply, closing my eyes and sinking deeper into the warmth of freedom.

A hand slips into mine, warm and soft, fingers delicate. It squeezes mine, and I peel my eyes open again.

"I'm so sorry," says Abril beside me, her voice barely a whisper.

"What?"

"You have to run." A tear runs down her pale face, catching around the edges of her rebreather.

"I don't understand."

"They know," Abril says. "Run!"

What kind of heartless joke is this? I shatter into a million pieces as Abril's eyes remain steady, all signs of excitement gone. I sink into the floor, a quad run out of juice.

"Didn't you hear me? I said—RUN!"

With that, she punches me square in the chest, popping open the seatbelt. I topple forward, falling off the couch and onto the cold floor, gasping for air. Astrophel reaches to grab me, catching me by the ankle.

His smile, too, is gone.

"Don't you dare, Jo'Niss, whatever you are," he hisses, glaring at me with such animosity I could swear he's about to snap my neck. All eyes are on me, and in an instant, I understand—

A trap.

I thought my heart broke when Abril told me to go, but now it's blown to cosmic dust. There's nothing left of me but *fear*. My chest goes hollow and cold. I should have listened to the alarms in my head: everyone truly is out to get me.

They know who I am. *What* I am. And how much I'm worth.

"RUN, SLAGGIT!" yells Abril, pouncing on Astrophel. He screams as she jams a finger into his left eye, sinking deeper than any finger has the right to.

His grip on my leg loosens just enough that I can kick free, stomping on his foot as a reflex. But he isn't the only member of the crew who knew my value: the room is filled with a chorus of echoing clicks as the crew members' seatbelts release.

My instincts take over. I've had enough drills to be ready for this moment. I'm already far deeper than I should ever have gotten, in the belly of the ocugry—almost literally.

Rule three rings through my head like a chorus. Not the part I've recited to myself for the past eight years, the part that keeps me separated from the princess who owns my life, but the part that comes after, the part I've barely cared about before: Auntie telling me *if they find you—run. Run to the end of the road and don't look back.*

I throw myself at the stairs that leads down to the now-empty cargo bay, dodging the crew and flinging myself off the railing to land on the ground below. I hit the metal hard, a shock rushing up my legs, threatening to snap my knees, but I'm already numb. Every action feels like it's rendered in slow motion.

I have only one thought: run.

Escape.

"Don't let her leave!" a voice bellows from above. Hardi's? How does he even have the lungs for it? "She's only worth the bounty if we bring her back alive!"

"Run, sister, run!" screams Abril. "I'll hold them off! I'll…"

A shot cuts her off mid-sentence. No time to think about what just happened. I have to run—already the cargo doors are closing, so, so far away. I'm never going to make it.

The ship lurches forward, and I slip on the floor, now tilted to such a degree it could be one of the walls. The shuttle is taking off and taking me with it.

I have to get off this ship.

Run to the end of the road. Run and don't look back.

I don't think, I leap, sliding down the cargo bay floor faster than I ever could have run. The doors are closing, closing, the ground outside rushing away. The darkness of 'clipse makes the doors below look like the gaping maw of a wild animal, waiting to devour me. An ocugry in wait.

Better this beast than the one behind me. The possibility of death is better than the certainty of termination.

I close my eyes, and at once I'm falling, the wind thrashing around my face. Wind—outside air, free air. In an instant, I crash into the recently tilled farmland of my home world, alive, unbroken, the shuttle sailing ever-upward without me.

I'm ahead of them—for now. But they have a ship, and I have a moon—a moon with no place to hide.

A low rumble in the distance. The worst is yet to come— the storm is well on its way, and it's not going to wait for anyone, not even me.

6

MY BRAIN SHUTS OFF AND MY LEGS TAKE OVER.

Trying to outrun a storm is an impossible task, but I've seen the impossible already today. There's nowhere else to go but forward: away from the storm, away from Captain Hardi and his crew, away from those who would turn me in for a bounty, even if it means sending an innocent girl to her termination.

Execution. Death.

With any luck, the storm will make it impossible for the shuttle to land again, at least for some time. Us mooners spend hours, sometimes days, preparing our homes for events like this. We live on the near side of Nesworth, forever facing Thebos, in order to protect ourselves from asteroid showers. But accidents do happen, and, if I'm lucky, this impact has been enough to send detrimental weather barreling down upon us, keeping the ship off planet, unable to send anyone down to the surface.

The sun slides out from behind Thebos, casting weak light. I glance up, my gut sinking deeper as I take in the thick haze covering the sky. The storm is moving faster than I would like, dust from the impacts whipping around the moon. Shocks of lightning spark through the sky, flashing menacingly downward. Sisters, this is going to be a doozy.

Auntie, Uncle, and the cousins will be shutting themselves in their bunker right now, sliding metal shades down every window of the house. Are they looking for me around my shed? Have they even noticed I've left the farm at all?

I run the two kilometers in a daze. Heart pounding, lungs burning, I reach the farmhouse completely out of breath. The windows are already covered by the heavy metal shutters we only use at storm-time, the door barricaded shut. Not a single way in or out of the house. The doors to the storm cellar have already retracted and sealed: my family has not waited.

Right, so they've literally shut me out—I deserve that and more. But I have much more pressing things to panic about: the winds are rising, a whistling, howling sound echoing through the barns. I dart to my shed, keeping my scarf wrapped tightly around my face to keep from being flogged by the dust, but my sanctuary is already locked down as well. Reinforced steel keeps the door tightly secured, the one window invisible under the heavy covers. The barns are the same, expensive equipment protected against the harsh weather barreling down on us.

My training floods back as I rush back down the road, years of reminders flowing to the forefront. *Run to the end of the road, and don't look back.* It's not the best idea—but it's the only option I have right now.

I don't have any endurance. There's never much need for running on Nesworth, never a rush to get things done, or something so urgent there isn't time to grab a quad. I struggle, lungs scorching as I force them to *breathe, breathe, breathe.*

I have to stop. I can't take another step. I topple against a tree, breathless, grabbing its thick trunk to keep from toppling over. I've run clear past the small radius, the safe, terraformed farmland I grew up in for my entire life.

Tau chirps from my pocket, probably wondering what all this commotion was about. Slag. The only thing I have with me is the useless egg robot I built as a pet project. Fan-slagging-tastic. If only I'd loaded him up with weapons—not that guns or explosives would be any good against the wild chaos of nature or a shuttle hot on my tail.

The winds pick up, stronger with each minute. I clutch the spark jacket tighter, glad for the thick, insulated material. I zip up, fully muffling Tau's chirps.

How long will it take the Coalition to find me out here, supposing I even make it through the storm? There are only so many places one can go on foot on a little moon like Nesworth, and even fewer places to hide. That's if the shuttle can land at all. They'll probably search the house first, so that gives me a small window to work with. But they'll only find my corpse if I don't find shelter fast.

The now-howling wind whips off my scarf, sending it back up the road and far into the air. Slag, I love that scarf. It's been the easiest way to hide my face for years. Now it's gone, along with any hope of ever being hidden again.

I might as well have run right across the world. The land beyond home is sparse, never farmed, still practically a desert. So much has to be done to the soil to make it ready for farming, it isn't worth working it unless someone is settling and expanding the colony. There are patches of trees here and there, an asphalt road put in place for when the colonists are ready to spread out, but not much else.

At least, now, I am alone.

I have yet to get off the road—I'm much too exposed on this empty path to the middle of nowhere. But where else can I go? I have to run until the road ends. It's the only instruction I have to go on.

The temperature is dropping fast, trails of gooseflesh raising where the brutal wind rasps against my skin. As I look back over my shoulder, my braid whips around my face to slap my eyes. I stuff it into the collar of my coat—and that's when I see the line of dust clouds coming my way.

The entire sky behind me is aflame with lightning. *Flash, flash, flash* all along the horizon. The world is dark, a nightmarishly eerie twilight, cast in sharp contrast by the bursts of electricity.

I flee down the road, shoes hitting the asphalt faster than a jackhammer. *Bam bam bam bam bam.* I pump my arms and try to keep my breathing steady, as if panic isn't rising in my stomach, dread tying it into knots.

The wind is screaming now, rushing wild through the empty expanse and whipping dirt against my skin. The farther I get from the settlement, the sandier the soil becomes. It burns as it rips at my cheeks. I've never missed my scarf so much. Tau chirps from my pocket, smart enough to compute my panic from my sky-high heart rate but unsure what to do. I keep running, the storm fast on my heels and gaining. All that panic welling up inside me is now leaking out my eyes, hot tears running down my face.

My foot sinks as it hits sand rather than road. I've finally reached the end.

I spin around. Where's the salvation I was promised all these years? But there's nothing: whatever Auntie had insinuated would be here simply doesn't exist.

I'm royally screwed.

Then the world goes silent. The wind stops: the air is more still than I can ever remember. No sounds, no movement, a heavy stillness.

The storm is about to hit.

Slag it. I dash toward the closest blotch on the horizon: a thicket of native trees, barely more than bushes, the only shelter I can see. Not enough to save me outright, but I'm not going to go down without a fight, even if it means cowering under twigs. I close my eyes against the thorns and throw myself into it—

I collide with metal.

I blink. It's the hull of a small ship, old and dented. *A ship!* All alone, all the way out in the wastes, but who gives a slag? This ship *is* my salvation. I run my hand over the hull, hunting for a latch. A door slides open, and I clamber inside just as the winds pick back up and threaten to tear the thicket from the ground.

The ship is a small transport vehicle, bigger than my shed but smaller than the kitchen back home. It could have fit in the shuttle's cargo bay ten times over, if not more. Two dark chairs are planted in front of the control panel, but the rest of the tight space is cozy, with cushioned chairs and what appears to be a separate bathroom on the side. And the best part: it's entirely unoccupied.

The door slides shut behind me. Sand has blown in with me, but it settles now that I'm inside, red static on the dark floor.

The silence is a relief. I hadn't realized just how loud the wind was until the soundproof hull cut off the screams. I take a deep breath of stale, breathable air and shake myself, letting the captured sand fall out of my clothes and braid.

With shaking hands, I undo the zipper of my coat. A rattled but undamaged Tau rises out of my pocket, chirping at me like a worried mother. I find myself laughing with relief as I dump myself onto the sofa.

"I'm fine, lil buddy," I tell him, giving him an appreciative pat on his little top. "I'm fine."

I lean back onto the sofa. The ship is small, but so cozy, the temperature perfect and toasty. I lift my legs onto the cushions, feeling myself drifting, my racing heart slowing.

Yes, I can sleep here. I'm safe. Ships are built to withstand the worst conditions space can throw at them—what's a little storm going to do to it?

A quiet beep is enough to pull me out of the lull of sleep. Lights are on. The low hum of a motor coming to life fills my ears. The ship has woken up.

"No." I sit up so fast that all the blood rushes out of my head. "No, no, no… Why are you turning on?"

I fly to my feet, fighting off the bout of vertigo. My head spins as I race to the console, fingers fumbling over the panel, but the ship doesn't need my consent for takeoff. I crash into the pilot's seat, grabbing wildly at the controls. The dashboard in front of me has more lights, buttons and readouts than there are stars in the night sky. None of them happen to be big, round, red, and have *abort* printed on them.

"Tau." I call over the little bot, who drifts to my side and chirps. "Tau, can you interface with this system?"

"*Bi-nuuuur,*" he beeps back. Access denied.

"Can you tell me how to shut it off?"

"*Bi-nuuuur,*" Tau beeps again.

"*Calibrating,*" comes a calm, female voice from the dashboard in front of us. "*Please find your seats. This ship is about to depart.*"

"No!" I bring my hand down firmly on the dashboard. Nothing happens—the ship must be on automatic, ignoring my commands. "No, abort launch!"

I'm practically sobbing now—the exhaustion from the run, the fear of the storm, the men at my heels, the terror of this ship leaving with me still trapped inside it; there's only so much a girl can take. I can't fly any ship on a good day, let alone through a storm of this caliber. I can't even see the ground through the sunshield anymore. The air is murky brown—I can't go back out there even if I want to.

So, I have another choice to make. Between dying a certain death in one of the worst storms of the decade, or riding this ship out to safety, wherever it will take me. Trusting the ship is sounding like a better idea by the second.

The door latches with a heavy clang of metal against metal, the hiss of the ship pressurizing the air. *Too late now.*

Tau beeps a low, worried beep, hovering near my face. He's sensing my distress; I probably shouldn't have programmed him to do that, seeing as how he can tell if a person's panicking, but can't actually do anything about it. He has an encoded concern I put in there to make *myself* feel better, which I really regret right about now. Right now, what I need is someone competent to take the wheel and shut this all down. I don't even have my toolbelt with me to rip open the console and take control manually. I have no choice but to let the ship take over and hope it's able to weather the storm.

With a shudder and creaking gears, the ship lifts off the ground. It rumbles as it rises, vibrating violently in the blistering winds of the storm, breaking away from the pull of the little moon and lifting me from the only home I've ever known.

The ship takes off without warning, shooting forward like it's spring-loaded. The winds are strong, and the little craft spins as it fights to stay steady. I clasp my hands tightly over my ears as the dust batters the sides of the ship, the acceleration pushing me deep into the seat and threatening to throw me into the dashboard if it stops too quickly.

With fumbling hands, I belt the seatbelt over my lap and pull the strap tight, just in time for another gust to send the craft spiraling over its own nose. My skull slams against the headrest, hard, and now I'm seeing stars, faces forming in the clouds in the spiraling dust outside the window.

There goes Auntie, smiling gently as she hands me a new Tennyson textbook. And there's Uncle, hanging washing on the line, clips clutched between tense, tight lips. Cousins all squeeze together on the master bed, waiting for us to read them a story. There's Tobis, a year ago, when we were still friends who told each other everything, carefree and smiling, before I knew how he really saw me.

Abril is there now, telling me to *run, run, run, run far away.* I reach out a hand to clutch at her image, but it fades before my fingers touch hers. Astrophel replaces her, gritting his teeth as he reaches for me instead, threatening where Abril was soft.

I scream.

I'm having trouble distinguishing if he's in the dust outside or in the air inside the ship, with me, before I realize he shouldn't be here at all. My mind is playing tricks on me; the longer I stare into the dust, the more faces I see, faces of everyone I know, even if I've only seen them once in a crowd. It's making me sick. My stomach lurches along with the ship. My head is spinning, rattling from the shaking. I force down vomit.

I can't see Tau anymore. I can't see anything but the faces flashing in the dust in front of me. I squeeze my eyes shut, hoping, pleading with the universe to calm my rising panic. My hands grip the armrests for support, digging into the synthetic leather.

And then, all at once, the shaking stops. It's as if the ship itself has frozen mid-flight. There aren't any sounds other than the small whirring noises from the console itself—that and the heavy panting that must be coming from *me*.

I fling my eyes open and am greeted with darkness. The sunshield is velvet-black, dotted with tiny pinpricks—stars, more than I've ever seen before in my life. They stretch out like dust on a blanket in every direction, getting brighter as my eyes accustom to the gloom.

My jaw hurts from hanging open so long.

The ship has saved me from the storm. From Hardi and his crew. From Nesworth, even. A hiccup escapes my lips, and then another, and another more rapid than the last. I'm laughing, giggling nervously as I drift in orbit around Nesworth. I've wanted a way off that slagging moon for so long, and now that I have it, I don't know what to do with my freedom.

I'm in a spaceship. I'm in orbit. I'm in space!

I'm laughing louder, guffaws growing as I realize there's no one here to stop me. I'm alone, the most alone a person can be. I've wanted to be free—well, here I am. *Hello universe,* up close and personal, my own front-row seat to the stars.

Eventually, I'll have to figure out how to get back down from here. But that's for later. I lean back in the seat, letting out a huge breath of relief, the giggles fading away. Stale, recycled air rushes through my lungs, tasting almost fresh on my sand-coated tongue.

"*Calculating,*" says the female voice from earlier.

I stir. Okay, good feeling gone. "Calculating what?"

The voice doesn't answer. It doesn't seem to be all that concerned with me. I lean forward over the dash, note that my chair is too far back, and try to feel around for a handle. I find it, but it's jammed, of course.

"*Hyperspace window has been allocated. Please ensure all seats are buckled.*"

Hyperspace window? So now my ship has delusions of grandeur.

"That settles that," I mutter, ripping off my seatbelt. Or, at least, trying to—the thing is stuck. Everything is stuck. Whatever process is happening, it's already engaged, and I'm going to be sucked along for the ride.

Ringing electricity in my ears sets my hair on end. I turn my head back as far as it can go, staring over my shoulder at what I thought was the bathroom, which is now powering up. No. That's an engine. A Hyperspace engine, on a tiny ship that's barely a planetary lander. I know enough about the tech to see how impossible this is. In a ship this small, I could be ripped to shreds. And if I do survive, a Hyperspace jump could take the ship light years away from Nesworth— anywhere in the Sister Systems, or beyond. And I have absolutely no control over the destination.

Oh. Slag.

"Please, no!" I bring my fists down hard on the dash, sending shards of pain up my palms. "Stop this! Stop this now! Tau, help me!"

"Flight plan locked," the voice intones. *"Engaged. Activating hyperspace drive in ten…nine…"*

Hot, frustrated tears roll down my cheeks as I listen to the countdown, pounding my fists on the console so hard they turn purple. I gaze out into the expanse of space, without even the sight of Nesworth to give me anything to hang onto. My entire life I've wanted nothing more than to leave this world and build my own life, but not like *this*. Not chased by people who want my head for bounty, kidnapped by a *ship* I've never even seen before. I'm finally getting my wish, but it's sour and rotten.

Pop.

One second, there are stars. The next, clouds. Clouds and fields of yellow.

And a sickening crunch.

PART 2

NOT ON NESWORTH ANYMORE

7

I COME TO WITH MY FACE INCHES FROM THE console, loose strands of hair escaping my braid to brush the dark knobs and buttons. I'm dangling, limply restrained in my seatbelt, feet nowhere near the floor. The lights before me, once red and furious, are now lifeless and dead. My body, however, is awake, screaming needles running up my arms and legs.

Emergency lighting switches on, helping my eyes adjust to the gloom. It flickers feebly. The entire sunshield is covered in rich, dark soil. There's no way to tell how deep the ship has driven itself into the ground.

This has to be a dream. No, a nightmare. They say when you fall in a dream, you wake yourself before you hit the ground; but this dream has crashed me into dark soil and isn't letting me go, even though my mind is screaming in pain. If I really am alive, I'm waking up cold and alone in the dark.

I know only the basics of Hyperspace travel, but at the very least, I know it's completely ship-slag crazy for a jump to take me right into the atmosphere of another planet. What if I'd come out in the heart of a mountain? Or kilometers deep in an ocean? Human beings don't survive trying to share the same space as pure stone. In space, you never have to worry about knocking anything out of your way. Exiting hyperspace right in the atmosphere of a planet is dangerous, not to mention potentially suicidal.

But I'm not dead. I survived being kidnapped by an out-of-control spaceship to be stranded who-knows-where without my toolbelt anywhere in reach. And I've left my family at the mercy of people who will stop at nothing to collect the bounty on my head.

So. This is it. It's just going to be me, alone. Me and—

"Tau!" Realization hits me like—well, a ship crashing through atmo'. My eyes dart from side to side. "Tau, buddy!"

With three small chirps, Tau rises from the pillows of the sofa, drifting back to my side, his frantic beeps sounding almost relieved to see me. I chortle as he wobbles over. My only friend in this big, wild world.

Time to see where we've ended up. Then, figure out how to get back.

Wait—why do I want to go home? An hour ago, my only wish was to leave forever. But there's a difference between leaving to go to University and being chased off by ruffians and swept away by a mad ship. I want to be free, but not like this: not at the expense of everyone I love. I thought leaving would make them safer; instead, I've thrown them into the ocugry's maw.

The seatbelt snaps open, and I fall face-first onto the console, breath ripped from my lungs. I barely have time to throw out an arm to protect my face. Tau lets out a mournful, drawn-out beep as I groan in pain.

"I'm fine," I tell him, hoisting myself over the console and onto the sunshield. Ship glass is built to withstand micrometeorite impact: a little bit of dirt won't make a dent. How the mystery ship has survived who-knows-how-long at the end of the Nesworth road is beyond me. Had Auntie and Uncle known about it? Was this what their vague instructions were meant to guide me to?

I brush off my hands, though there's no dust on them—force of habit from working on the farm. It's all going to be an uphill battle from here, literally: the ship has come in at an angle, and I'm going to have to climb my way out if I ever want to see sunlight again.

Tau drifts upward, turning on all his LEDs to the brightest settings. It's the oddest obstacle course I've ever crossed, hoisting myself up and over the pilot's chair—which keeps wanting to spin—then using the bolted-down couch cushions to get up to the level of the exit. From there, I stretch, bracing myself with one leg on the outer bulkhead and the other on the not-bathroom door, and pull myself up with my arms.

"Lights," I order, and Tau switches off the LEDs. "I need to see what's out here."

I know I don't have to explain anything to him; it's not as if he's going to reply. But Tau is the only ally I have here, and it's better than talking to myself.

I squint against the tiny window in the door. Fluffy gray clouds drift along, promising rain. Where there is rain, there's water, and where there is water, there could be life. I don't want to end up suffocating in a methane atmosphere five seconds after opening the door.

"Think it's safe?" I whisper. Tau says nothing. This is far, far outside of his core programming. "All right. Here goes nothing."

I reach for the emergency release handle, the one kindly painted a bright, friendly blood-red, pulling it with all my might. I expect the door to open, but it completely falls out, toppling down the mound of dirt outside. But now here I am, standing in a gaping hole in the hull, staring up at gray clouds, which slowly part to reveal a brilliant blue sky. A patchwork of sunlight flickers down on my face, warm and comforting in the chilly breeze.

I take a tentative whiff of the air, picking up notes of dirt and rain. Then, a breath. Nothing feels like it's burning, so I take another, and another.

I grip the doorjamb and hoist myself out of the ship, sliding down the dirt mound until my feet touch solid ground. Outside the ship it's hot, the air thickly humid, and I slip off the spark coat, tying it loosely around my waist, while I gape at the sky. *No planet.* Without Thebos's constant presence, it feels as if the sky is just going to let me drift up and float away.

The ship has landed on the very edge of a road, a dirt path wide enough for two hovercarts or a reasonably-sized quad. I stand in a field of bright gold grain—wheat, if I remember the almanac correctly—bordered on every side by a forest, with tall, pointy trees stretching in every direction. I've never seen this kind of vegetation before in real life.

But more than that, in the distance, I spy objects I've only ever read of in books.

Actual mountains.

They reach up into the sky, taller than anything I've ever imagined. More massive than the harvest ships that visit my moon. They're enormous even from this far away, behemoths ready to rise and make the world kneel. I feel incredibly small, as if even from this distance they can crumble and crush me.

Well, this isn't Nesworth anymore.

I take a step forward on wobbly legs. Solid ground is a sister-send. I never want to get in another spaceship again: both attempts at flying have been absolutely disastrous. From the looks of it, my little ship shouldn't have survived at all. It's in awful shape, though I didn't have a chance to inspect it before I claimed it as shelter, so I'm not sure how much of the damage is new, and how much was there when I found it. Either way, the ship looks older than I am. It's scuffed and rusted, large dents on the sides, the entire thing half-buried in a crater of its own making. I can't believe it got me this far, let alone alive.

I also can't believe there's a pair of stockinged legs sticking out from beneath it.

A scream rises skyward, sending a drove of black wings into the air, startling me almost more than the corpse itself. I stare at the feet, ankles, calves. My hands cover my mouth without command. They're shaking, trembling, altogether being awful at being hands. Oh slag, the scream was mine.

The legs. *Oh, Sisters, there's a body under there.* The ship rammed into some stranger and killed them, crushing them into the ground.

I force myself to swallow the bile surging into my throat. Tau chirps wildly, gliding up to my shoulder in an effort to ease the panic. But it's no use: a little robot isn't enough to distract me from the fact that I've become a murderer, unwittingly or not.

I hadn't been piloting the ship, but I'd been the only one inside it when it crashed. I triggered its takeoff. And by some cruel twist of fate, this stranger was walking on the road, minding their own business, when the shuttle appeared out of nowhere and crashed right down on their head. Not the best way to go, if there even was one.

The stranger's shoes are heavy black boots, made to intimidate, with a solid two-inch platform and studs along the gleaming gold buckles. They're clean, despite the mud surrounding the crash site. Whomever this person was, they were too important to let their feet touch the ground—but without a quad in sight, the boots themselves must have been keeping them afloat.

Even with the sun behind the clouds, I'm beginning to melt. Maybe it's the exhaustion, as I come down from the adrenaline rush. I don't know, and I don't care: all I care about is the person I've just killed.

Tau chirps, and I shove him away with a flick of my hand.

"This is bad, buddy," I mutter, "really bad."

"*Beep.*"

"Can you figure out where we are? What planet this is?"

"*Bi-dum.*"

"I thought not." My panic is rising. I gave Tau an internal compass and a pretty brilliant gyroscope—if I do say so myself—so he has a pretty good sense of his location… but even if he does have GPS, it probably won't work on this planet. I don't exactly have the spatial coordinates, after all. I'm worse than lost, and I have a corpse on my hands.

Tau chirps, a reminder that I need to get my stress levels under control.

"Stop tracking them, then," I snap, "I have a feeling they're going to be high for quite a while."

Chirp. Vitals are off his checklist.

I crawl up the pile of dirt where the ship splits the soil, and I reach for the legs. Can you even take a pulse on legs? I don't know what to expect: a sign of life, so I won't have to feel so guilty? A sign that claims the body was already dead before I crashed into it? But when I reach the corpse, it's just that—a corpse, and a very dead one.

The legs stick out at an awkward angle, and the rest of the body is crushed deep under the dirt and the ship. There's no way they could have survived. So, it's true: I'm a murderer, on top of being an illegal clone. Life is just getting cheerier by the moment.

Tau spins wildly around my head, chirping a jaunty tune. I glance up: there's movement down the road. Off in the direction of the mountains, there are *people.* And they're coming right at me.

"Should we hide?" I ask the bot.

Tau says nothing: it isn't like he knows what to do in these situations either. Am I fast enough to make a mad dash for the tree line? Then I'll have to survive in an alien forest, which doesn't sound all that appealing.

Hiding is my only option. Not only have I just killed a local, but if this planet is part of the Sister Systems, the strangers will recognize me immediately with my face exposed like this. They'll probably have the opposite of help on their minds: best-case scenario, they'll have me terminated for the whole illegal royal clone thing. Worst case, they'll pummel me to death for killing their friend. Try telling the people who've just watched you crush someone to death with a spaceship that you're not the galaxy's dead princess. I'm pretty sure it won't go over well.

Their voices are louder now. Their language isn't foreign, even if their accents are. They're speaking Salvi, the unifying language of the Systems. It could mean anything: maybe this is an autonomous planet. At least I crash-landed on a civilized world.

It's too late to run: they're already here. *Please*—I beg anyone or anything that's listening—*let my training have been for something.*

Despite the heat, I slip the spark coat back on, bulking up my frame as a disguise. I risk another glance at the legs, my teeth digging into my lip hard enough to break the skin. What an awful way to die. If I'm lucky, these people won't follow the doctrine of *an eye for an eye.*

I clutch my wrist to stop it from shaking. There's bile in my throat, a sharp, metallic taste. All I can do now is wait.

Then the rock behind my left heel gives way, and I tumble backward, my head hitting the dirt before I roll over again. I land face-first on the field in front of the crater, wheat and grass surrounding me. *So much for being inconspicuous.*

I lie still, hands on my head to stop the pulsing, trying to breathe through the dust that clogs my nostrils and makes me cough.

When I look up, I'm surrounded. The people standing over me are dressed the same way I am, in loose farm clothes. The only difference is in their height: they can't be more than a meter tall. Relief swells in my heart—these are colonists, just like me. Farmers expanding the Systems. United in our respective isolation.

But my relief is short-lived. Their faces are stern, judgmental. They stare at me, like, well, I'm an alien.

Then again, aliens don't exist. In the three hundred years since the wormhole brought us to this corner of the galaxy, there hasn't been a sign of extra-terrestrial existence, not even a peep. No amount of digging will bring up remnants of a civilization that has never existed. If aliens do exist, it's certainly not here—though 'here' could be farther from home than I think I am.

"Did you kill her?" asks one of them, a man with a bristly red mustache. He clutches his pitchfork tightly, like he plans to hold it to my throat.

"She's a child, Julius," says the woman beside him, placing a hand on his shoulder. She gives me a warm smile, so foreign in the sea of frowns. "Hello, girl. Are you all right?"

"Answer the question!" Julius barks, pushing himself in front of her. "Were you the one to crush the bitch?"

"The what now?" I ask.

"The techno*bitch* of Night," he sneers. "Did you kill her?"

"The ship… I… it took me, we crashed, and…"

"The technowitch is dead!" The voice comes from the ship, where a short man in yellow overalls is tugging none too gently on the dead woman's leg.

Julius throws the pitchfork in the air, raising his hands in victory. His expression transforms, his snarl relaxing into a smile, beaming brighter than the sun. "She's finally dead!"

My ears burn with the rush of the roar. I've never seen so many people at once, and the *sound.* They mold into a dizzying mass, their shouts and screams melting together, the cacophony making me nauseous. A metallic clang joins the cacophony—someone throwing rocks at the legs and hitting the ship instead. My hands fly to my ears.

With a deafening snap that rises over the roar, a man in bright blue breaks the leg of the woman at the hipbone. It comes off easily, and he raises it high, parading the boot at the end of a long strip of pale skin and stripy sock.

I turn and vomit into the grass. No one is paying attention to me anymore, which is a relief: I'm still trying to figure out their excitement, why they aren't mad at me, why they aren't disgusted by the severed leg, how they even managed to rip it off in the first place. I close my eyes, breathing deeply. My hands grip the grass and weeds.

My fist closes around something cold and metallic, like a piece of the ship, though it's too smooth to be debris. I open my eyes again, bringing the tiny object to my face. It's a locket: a small, silvery circle latched shut on the side, with a dangling chain.

Tau presses himself close to me, trying to dive back into my pocket. I tap him lightly, not having any safety to offer.

"What is this place?" I ask, more to myself than to him, closing my hand around the silver. He doesn't respond.

A hand comes into my line of vision, a soft and clean hand that can't have seen a day's work. A dour woman is smiling down at me, tears in her eyes.

I scrunch my features the way I've practiced with Auntie, forcing my facial muscles to contract. Where the princess is soft, I'm hard. A lifetime spent learning how not to be myself has led up to this moment.

"What is your name?" the stranger asks without a hint of recognition.

I have to force myself not to smile in relief. Instead, I clutch the locket tighter, letting it dig into my skin, letting it hurt, the pain grounding me. "I'm Nymphodora" I reply, voice suddenly hoarse—a perfectly-rehearsed line wasted on a dry throat. I need water so badly. "But you can call me Dora."

"Dora!" the woman shouts to the crowd, taking my hand and hoisting me to my feet. "Her name is Dora!"

"Dora!" the crowd cheers, clapping and hooting as if I've just won some kind of award.

Two of them boost me onto their small shoulders, high above the rest, waving me around like I'm a victory banner. I clutch the locket, fearful of losing it in the tumult.

How are these small humanoids holding me so effortlessly? Unless—no—

Droids.

Android farmers. Built to look human, to work human. It shouldn't be possible for them to be so complex, so independent. Sisters, they're magnificent—all the strength and cunning of a human, built out of wires and circuitry. It would be rude to ask if I can look inside their brains—I'm sure I'd get the shuttle-day treatment for that kind of probing question. Seeing as how much they seem to love me, though, maybe not....

"Dora! Dora! Dora!" The chant spreads through the crowd until everyone is saying my name. They parade me forward, droids reaching out to touch my skin, calling for me, trying to clutch my hands as I'm passed around.

Maybe I really have died in the crash and gone to engineering heaven—but if this is the afterlife, it's definitely a letdown. I only wanted to study freely, and now I've toppled an alien tyrant, and while I'm somehow the queen of the droids, it isn't exactly the paradise I've been promised.

A collective shudder ripples through the crowd, and everyone quietens, turning slowly to face something far behind. I squint, trying to make out what it was that has quieted them all, but all I see is a far-off bubble, a trick of the light. It's heading right for us, drifting purposefully on an imaginary wind. As it grows, rays bouncing off the iridescent sphere and casting rainbows on the wheat field, I decide that the crash must have at the very least given me a concussion, and this hallucination is the result. But the droids are turned toward it, too, drawn by the sight—which means it *can't* be a hallucination ... unless they are, too. Which, honestly, would make sense.

By the time the bubble reaches the field, it's larger than me. It alights gently, stalks of wheat bending under its weight. It's not a bubble. It's a ship, a small pod with smooth, round windows mirrored to hide the pilot. A perfect, silent sphere, the kind of engineering that almost makes you believe in magic—a masterpiece.

And so is the woman who steps out of it. For a split second, I think she must be my aunt, come to take me home, to tell me it's all right and all a bad dream. But then her shimmering silver jumpsuit catches the light, and the illusion is shattered. The fabric clings on her tan skin and reflects the rainbows that bounce off her ship. Her black hair is thick and wavy, held back with a bright pink-and-yellow scarf. As she steps onto the dirt, her red sneakers sinking in the loose mud, she slides the sunglasses from her eyes and zeroes in on me. She purses her lips as she marches over to meet us.

The crowd goes silent, the droids lowering me until my feet touch the ground before shrinking back.

"What kind of ginny are you?" the stranger asks me, without any kind of introduction. Her face is as flat as the gray sky above us. "You a good one?"

"A ginny?" Here go my hands again, failing at being hands. "I don't think I'm any kind of ginny. I'm a farm girl. From Nesworth. I'm Dora." I pray for her—and the crowd—to believe me. My face is on display for everyone to see, to recognize. For the first time in my life, I'm completely uncovered before strangers. If this is a planet of the Sister Systems, then this is the end.

"That's odd." The stranger turns her appraising gaze back on the crowd. I worry she's about to expose me—but what she says next horrifies me even more: "Because I was definitely told a ginny dropped from the sky and crushed my sister."

"Your *sister*?" My heart sinks to the core of the planet. "Oh stars, I am so, so sorry, I—"

To my shock, the woman laughs. The crowd joins in. Tau presses into my back, cowering. My hands clench into fists, the locket squeezed in my palm. I slip it into my overalls. This way, at least, I won't lose the thing.

"My sister was heartless and cruel," the stranger says, placing a silvered arm around my shoulder. Her touch is warm and gentle, like sitting by a fire on a chilly night. "You did us all a great service, ridding us of her. She prevented these hardworking folks from reaching their full potential. You should feel proud of what you did today."

"But… it was…" A shiver runs through my body again, despite the warmth of the stranger's touch. "It was an accident."

"So what?" the woman laughs. "You still saved the Expedee, and for that we're all eternally grateful."

I have no idea what an Expedee is … or why this woman is so happy that I've done her sister in. For all I know, I've crash-landed right in the middle of a family feud big enough to affect an entire planet.

"Who was she?" I ask, nodding in the direction of the crashed ship and the severed legs. "Your sister? That you could want her…"

I can't finish the sentence. But it doesn't matter. The stranger carries on.

"The Technowitch of Night. Or, as some might call her, the *technobitch*." She addresses this last bit to the audience, and they let out a whoop of glee.

"We were going slagging feudal over here," Julius says. "She forced us to farm these lands, but when we told her we wanted more, she claimed it *wasn't part of our programming*. Fifty years I've been working with wheat, wheat, nothing but wheat."

Hearing this doesn't make me feel any better. I've killed a horrible person, sure, but I've still killed a *person*.

Like Hardi and Astrophel had wanted to kill *me*. A fate from which Abril had rescued me. Now, she's probably dead. Death follows me around like an unwanted stray.

"Come with me," says the stranger, warm and inviting. "It looks like you need a drink."

She doesn't wait for me to reply. With a strong hand on my shoulder, she guides me to the ship, away from the crowd, who are still ripping apart the earth to pull out the corpse.

"Dora, right? I heard the chants when I was flying over the forest. It sounded like the entire planet wanted to thank you."

"I don't think I deserve that," I say. "Thank you for helping me, um—"

"Gleïa," she says, waving her hand over the smooth surface of the bubble. "Gleïa, the Technowitch of Dawn."

I can see myself distorted in the convex curve of the bubble: shabby denim overalls, face dirty and streaming with tears, wearing the gaunt expression of a girl who isn't sure what to think.

"Pardon my ignorance," I say, watching a door take shape and open, sliding back to reveal two plush red chairs. "But what's a technowitch? And a ginny? And who are these people, and where—"

"Shhh." For some reason, her voice calms me, like a warm blanket being wrapped around my shoulders. "You need to breathe. One question at a time."

The woman helps me into the ship, buckles me in like a child, then climbs into her own seat as delicately and gracefully as a ballet dancer. She picks up a plastic cup and sips at a straw, frowning when it makes the universal 'empty' noise.

"There's just some things science can't do," she mutters, closing the doors.

I gasp: while the outer surface was reflective, inside is a totally different story. Every wall is transparent. It's like being belted into chairs in the middle of a field.

"You want to know what a technowitch is?" Gleïa, says with a sly smile. "This is a technowitch."

And then, as if by magic, without sound or sensation, we're *flying*.

8

IT'S LIKE A DREAM, THE WORLD RUSHING BELOW my seat, a whole new planet to discover, to explore. My fingers dig into the armrests as I stare at the scenery below, nails poking through to the foam as I try to still my racing heart.

As incredible as this is, dangling a thousand meters in the air can make anyone queasy. The fact that there are no engines to hear, no wobble to feel, only makes the experience more surreal. Further evidence I passed out in the crash and am hallucinating all of this.

Gleïa glances over at me, giving me a wide, beautiful smile. "So? You like it?"

I'm awestruck as we fly over a mountain—an actual mountain! I hadn't really believed they existed until today. A sharp, massive rock just jutting out of the ground like that … it doesn't even look real.

Tau buzzes nervously around my neck, his guidance system probably going haywire. I twist him, putting him to sleep, slipping him into my coat pocket. There, at least, he'll be calm.

"Did you make that bot?" asks Gleïa, looking me over.

"Yeah," I say. "His name is Tau. He doesn't really do much, but he's good company."

"Then you are a ginny! I would expect no less, with a ship like that."

"It's not my ship, though. I found it. It kinda… kidnapped me?" A short way of saying that this day has been the worst one in my life so far—but my curiosity keeps me going, as it usually does. "What exactly is a ginny?"

"A damn good engineer. What do you mean, it kidnapped you?"

"I mean I climbed inside, and it took off with me in it. I tried to stop it, but it somehow flew me all the way here. I couldn't pry open the control panels in time."

"Interesting," says Gleïa, returning her eyes to the skies. The ship flies too low to mingle with the clouds, which drift ominously above us. "If I'm not being rude—I assume it isn't a coincidence that you look identical to the late princess?"

Slag. I freeze, fingers so deep into the foam that the seat starts to rip. I want to kick myself. I haven't been careful enough. I haven't…

"Don't worry!" Gleïa smiles. "I'm not affiliated with the *Sylvarian* systems. At best, I'm … a subcontractor for them. If they need me, they have to reach out to the Technomage Superius first, and he rarely asks little old me for help. I have my own projects, like trying to wrench the Expedee lands from my recently departed sister's grasp—those droids you met in the field, her own cruel pet project. Father made them decades ago as part of an experiment, one which she took over in order to try her hand at playing the oppressive monarch. Thank you again for saving me the trouble of actually killing her. She keeps too close of an eye on me for me to be a step ahead. Or, I should say, *kept.*"

Who is this woman? A talented Engineer for sure, but in all my years studying the subject I haven't heard half of the jargon she's throwing at me now. She has to be light years ahead of me, a true genius. But as overwhelming as it is to be in her presence, I can't let my guard down. I don't know what she means to do with me. Or how far her powers go.

"In any case, I know you're not Princess Jo'Niss," Gleïa says, as if hearing my unspoken question. "I've met her, and you're nothing alike. I'm just trying to figure out who you are in relation to her." She says the words so casually, like it's the most natural thing in the world to stumble upon a dead princess's doppelganger in a field.

I don't answer her. I can't figure out what to say. Why would she want to help me, the girl who just outright admitted to murder? Who is this Technomage Superius, and would he be as accepting as she?

We start our descent, drifting down toward a large complex on the edge of the mountain: pristine, white structures pressed together where the rock levels into a natural terrace, a few small fields, and an herb garden dotting the landscape. It would look quaint, if not for the sleek, modern shape of the buildings. The house itself is massive: while my family's homestead was tall and sturdy, this one stretches out on the mountain terrace, making use of all the available space.

"Home sweet home," says Gleïa, as the craft alights on the bright green grass. She steps out onto manicured lawn and stretches her body toward the sky, yawning. Then she turns, raising her eyebrows at me.

I still haven't moved.

"Come along then," she says. "I'm not going to hurt you. I have no reason to."

"But…" I swallow again. I'm going to run out of saliva at this rate. "I don't know you."

"I'm the most technology-savvy person in this hemisphere. Believe me, you'll want to know me."

It's not as if my life can get any worse right now. I reach down, undo the strap that holds me to the chair, and slide onto the grass like a sandbag, with none of the grace of my host. Gleïa smiles, displaying her perfect, white teeth.

"Come along, I bet you're hungry."

She leads me inside her house, all white walls and floor-to-ceiling windows—so crisp and bright, compared to the faded wallpaper of the house where I grew up. The furniture is sparse, but the few pieces look brand new, surrounded by green plants that shouldn't exist outside of jungle worlds—which this one isn't, from what I've seen of it so far. I follow her past the living room—the huge sectional sofa could fit all those indentured droids—and into her kitchen. The technowitch has gadgets everywhere, all stainless steel and chrome on top of black granite countertops and a kitchen island large enough for my entire family to sit twice over. She ushers me to take a stool there.

I'm too busy admiring my surroundings. Nesworth doesn't have homes like this. This place is a designer's wet dream; the only time I've seen anything like it is in Tennyson's designs for a smart home. Even centuries after the roboticist's death, his creation had been too modern to realize. This technowitch must be richer—and more talented—than I can imagine.

Gleïa opens the fridge, the door as large as our barn's. "You like my house, hmm? I take it there's nothing like this where you're from?"

I shake my head, before realizing Gleïa can't see it while drowning in the refrigerator. I clamber up on the tall stool, accidentally muddying the suede in the process. Now *that* looks a little more like my home.

"No, ma'am," I reply. "Nothing like it at all."

Gleïa nods, pulling out a glass bowl filled with a smooth white yoghurt and adding bright fruits to the counter beside it. Red and pink berries. Yellow and orange cubes. Green wedges. She sets two bowls on the granite countertop, and shoves the yoghurt at me, followed by a spoon—a wordless invitation for me to help myself as she goes to grab glasses.

"Smoothie?" she asks.

"What now?"

"You're really not from here," Gleïa says with a laugh, then turns on a blender and fills the room with thunder. She brings over the flask of purple pulp, pouring it into both our cups. "Not sure what flavor profile you're looking for, but this will be refreshing and full of vitamins."

"Cheers," I say. Being confused is no excuse to be rude to my host.

"Cheers." Gleïa chugs down the fruity drink.

I follow her lead: the sweetness is thick and overwhelming, but amazingly refreshing. I didn't realize how hungry I was until I took that sip. Suddenly, all the yogurt and fruit in the world can't satiate my aching stomach. I slam the empty glass on the counter and dive into the bowl, taking bite after glorious bite of the fresh fruit.

Fresh fruit. And all I can eat. I must somehow be on a core planet. My heart races.

"So, what exactly does a technowitch do?" I ask in between bites. Small talk, to keep her from staring.

"Bit of everything." Gleïa beams, drinking from a glass of water so pure and clear, her glass almost looks as if it's empty. "First and foremost, we're engineers. Our job is to make people's lives better by creating things they need. Repairing tools they can't fix. But when you've had over two centuries to perfect your trade, sometimes your science looks a little bit like magic. Our inventions can be more impressive than useful."

"Like your ship."

"Flies like a charm," she says, "but not worth distributing to the public if they can't afford it. In any case, we're not just scientists. We're also diplomats, in our own way. We might have to travel to settle disputes farther out in the system, like my sister Noon is doing right now. She's much better at foreign affairs than I am."

"So you… create things. And solve problems."

"When I can, which is always." She smirks. "We're the highest level of authority here, other than the Technomage."

I'm confused: if this is the core, then where are the royals, their forces, their ocugry? One question at a time. "And he's like… another engineer?"

"He's more like a wizard. He can do *anything*. And I mean anything. He's wonderful."

So, I guess that's all I'm getting about him, that he's wonderful. "Glad to hear it."

"So, what's your story?" she asks, putting down her glass. "You said a ship kidnapped you? Is it because of your face?"

I freeze mid-bite. The woman laughs, a weird laugh, like the cackle of a witch—which I suppose she is. Combined with the cold smoothie, it throws her into a coughing fit. She shakes it off and turns back to me.

"Don't fret, sugarplum. Your secret is safe with me. So, what are you? A droid?"

"A clone," I reply. A chill races down my spine: this is the first time I've uttered those words outside of my family home. The first time I've admitted it to a stranger. I just threw rule-slagging-one out the window.

Gleïa coughs again. Her smile is gone. Better reaction than Hardi's crew, but not promising.

"A clone? A clone of Jo'Niss? I had no idea the princess was engineered."

"That's what my aunt and uncle told me." I stare down at my empty bowl. "The princess was the perfect one. My adoptive Aunt and Uncle hid me away on Nesworth to keep me alive."

She puts her hand on mine, her touch gentle. "Oh, you poor child. Oh, kiddo, it must be awful, knowing you're an imperfect, being hidden away... I've never even heard of Nesworth."

"We're new." This entire conversation is surreal. "Settlement started about twenty years ago."

She shakes her head. "Well, here on Haven, people have been farming for ten times that. We might be one of the first independent planets, but we're not completely cut off. Others might recognize your face, and some may not be as nonchalant as I."

Independent planet? I'm lost. This world is far too old to be a rim colony, but if it's not the core...

"Are we in the Outer Zone?" I ask, frowning.

Gleïa's face is a mirror version of mine, equally confused and somehow just as disappointed. "You sound surprised."

"As I said, the ship kidnapped me, I didn't exactly have any choice in the destination," I say. "Forgive me, engines aren't my area of expertise, but my ship shouldn't have been able to find its way here, what with the dusty nebulas?"

"Your ship must have been following a homing beacon," she says, almost to herself. "That's... curious. We don't get many visitors from the System Systems, but there must be a reason your ship returned here. It's probably my sister's fault."

"Your sister, the Technowitch of Night? The ship came to her?"

It would make sense, but no one would have programmed the Hyperspace window to drop me literally right on top of her. Even if my ship was set to return to her, it should have exited the window somewhere in high orbit, or better yet, at the edge of this solar system. Something went terribly wrong. Maybe that's what you get for calculating coordinates through a dark nebula.

"Or one of the others." She gives me a tight smile. "I now have two living sisters. We were a clone batch, too. We're lucky my father wanted us all in the end, but we still know that one of us is the perfect one, so I can empathize with you..."

"A clone batch?" I stare at her. I've never met another clone before. "Is that why you're in the Outer Zone? Are you in hiding, too?"

She laughs. "Honey, we were born long, long before the ban was in place. The technomage, our father, invented the technology. We're the first."

"The first? So that would make you..."

"Over two centuries old, yes," she says. "Haven't you ever heard, it's rude to ask a woman her age? Actually, you might not have, people don't say that much anymore. Though I'm told I don't look a day older than a hundred and twenty."

An *Immy.* Sure, it isn't real immortality, but unless anyone stabs or poisons her, she isn't going to drop dead anytime soon. Technology that was outlawed around the same time as clone batching. Hard to imagine what the Systems would be like if they hadn't been: maybe every planet would be overrun with towering, perfect people like her.

"We're the four technowitches of the Outer Zone," she continues, as I pick my jaw back up off the floor. "Dawn, Dusk, Noon, and Night. Noon is abroad right now, doing business for the royal family, but Dusk—*Eve*—is going to call soon, and she's not going to be too keen on her favorite sister being murdered."

I drop my spoon, which clatters in the empty porcelain bowl. My head snaps up to look at my host so fast a few vertebrae crack.

"I shouldn't have said anything." Gleïa's expression falls.

Of course she should have—how else will I know what to watch out for? Is Gleïa setting me up—is this a trap?

I leap off the chair, fingernails digging into my scalp. "Oh Sisters, she's coming? Here? What will she want with me, what…"

"Don't worry. Breathe. You're here under my protection. Eve knows what our dead sister was up to and never did anything to stop it. The consequences are for her to bear."

"Slag," I mutter, at a loss, but the technowitch just laughs again. I frown at her. "How is this funny? I didn't mean to kill her, I swear I didn't, and she…"

"I told you, child—there's no need to worry. Eve's our youngest sister, and the least rational. I'm the oldest, and my word goes. She'll have to listen to me."

"You're clones, though. Shouldn't you all be…"

"The same age?" There's a twinkle in her eye. "We are. Our surrogates went into induced labor the same exact minute. But Eve took an entire day to be born, like Night. They both came out sour. Noon and I were easy, so we're more…"

"Don't say sweet," I groan. "What do I do?"

"You stay with me." She laughs again, sounding more and more like a cackling witch. It's starting to seriously get on my nerves.

She gets to her feet in one swift motion. Gleïa just stares at a wall and straightens her silver jumpsuit, adjusting her hair nervously. If something is making Gleïa nervous, then I should probably be terrified. I remain standing, too, on nervous, wobbly legs. Without a word, Gleïa marches me out of the kitchen and into the sunken living room, gives me a gentle push, and I land softly on the oversized sofa.

Eve has arrived. How she can tell, I have no idea.

The front door opens, then slams shut. The Technowitch of Dawn bites her nails staring out the floor-to-ceiling window at her turquoise swimming pool.

"Sister, did you hear the news?" The voice comes from the atrium. A voice that rings out like little bells on Harvest morning.

I thought Gleïa was beautiful, but her sister redefines the word. Though she wears the same face, Eve is somehow more elegant, more graceful, gliding into the living room like using feet is beneath her. Her long, black hair ripples down her back, in sharp contrast with her white, chiffon dress, which drapes over her body like an expensive silk cloud. She wears a headdress of silver stars linked in a row across her brow, sinking into her hair as the darkness absorbs their light.

Gleïa called her sisters clones, but they're not identical. There's something in their faces, even in their skin, that makes them look more like cousins than sisters. I could slip easily into their family reunion. Auntie too, come to think of it. Then again, if they're two centuries old, who knows how clone batching worked way back when they were created?

"Oh, sister, isn't it awful?" Gleïa steps forward to hug Eve. "Our own sister. Taken from this world far too young."

My heart skips a beat. This isn't the Gleïa who had been talking to me for the past hour. Her tone has shifted so quickly it's thrown my footing. I brace myself, unsure of her intentions.

"So, you've heard," Eve shakes her head, "and by some snot-nosed child, on top of it all. Some kid, with a…" She turns, following her sister's gaze. I'm too scared to move. The woman's eyes bulge as she finds me.

I should probably say something. But I can't, even if I want to; my mouth stays stuck shut.

"I know," says Gleïa, "I know."

And then Eve is flying right at my face.

I don't have time to react, not an instant to defend myself. Even so, impossibly, a burst of electricity crackles up between me and the terrifying wall of witch. Eve shoots backward across the room, landing at the foot of Gleïa's floor-to-ceiling bookshelves. She looks up at her sister, stunned, her jaw quivering.

"What is the meaning of this? Why is she wearing our sister's shield?"

"Your sister's…?" I scramble back on the couch, hand flying to my throat. My fingers find soft silver, a smooth disk that definitely wasn't there a few minutes before. The pocket where I'd stashed the locket is now empty. I clutch the metal in my sweaty palm, giving it a sharp tug. The chain burns against my neck, digging into my skin as I pull, but it holds fast. Gleïa stares at me, just as shocked as Eve.

"What the void?" I spit, pulling harder. I slide my hand around the chain, hunting for the clasp, but the necklace is infinite. "I swear, I swear I didn't put this on!"

"Do not take me for a fool, girl," Eve screeches. "Not only do you kill her, but you rob her corpse! Sister, how could you let this happen?"

Around my neck is a dead woman's locket, a necklace I only picked up out of curiosity. I don't want it for myself, but it wants me. Like the ship, another inanimate object is taking control of my life. I didn't even feel it cinch around my neck.

"Take it off, if you don't want to become a stain on Dawn's couch!" Eve raises her hand, and there's no doubt in my mind that this threat is valid. Women who can create bubble drones are probably able to make death rays if they want to.

"It's stuck!" I insist. I lift it, trying to pull it over my head, but the chain is too short. "I'm sorry, I'm sorry, I'm—"

"Oh, stop your sniveling," Eve spits. She turns to Gleïa. "It looks like Night's safety features locked onto her before you could get there, Sister. Now this child is biometrically bonded to her locket, and along with it, her protection field. I know you and Father have had your eye on it for a century, but what on First Earth?"

"Don't ask me how that thing works," Gleïa responds, her calm starting to waver. "You knew Night better than I did. If anything, it's good Dora has the locket to protect her. I was a little worried you'd come here, seeking vengeance."

"*Worried?*" Eve takes a step toward her sister. "Of course I want vengeance! The question is, why don't you? Did she promise you the locket?"

"It was an accident," I squeak, my voice coming out many octaves higher than anticipated. "I didn't mean to!

The ship, it kidnapped me! I tried to stop it, I swear on the Lost Pilot!"

"Very likely! An accident, you say? Well, I can make accidents happen, too, you know."

"Eve, stop!" Gleïa grabs her sister's arm, clutching it tight enough for the skin to pale. "Let her go! She's just a child, and Oona was just in the wrong place, at the wrong time. It happened. Let us mourn her, but not create anything else to mourn."

The Technowitch of Dusk calms, but turns to glare at me, fire burning behind her eyes. I shrink back even farther into the couch.

Oona. The woman I killed had a name. She had a family. Gleïa can stand up for me all day and night, but it doesn't change the fact I'm a killer. I have to tell Eve I'm sorry, have to beg for her forgiveness and tell her I'll do anything to make things right. But my mouth is still dry, sewn shut.

Eve grabs Gleïa by the collar of her jumpsuit. "You make a poor sibling, sister of mine. If this wasn't your heath, I would smite you both down." She drops her, and Gleïa stumbles back, breathless. "Very well. I know my limits. But that locket is rightfully mine. Oona would never have wanted you to have it. None of you ever knew her like I did."

She turns to face me, one hand on her sister's shoulder. "As for you, Discount Jo'Niss, I can't attend to you here and now as I'd like, but just try to stay out of my way. Wherever you go, I will be watching you. My sister cannot protect you forever."

With that, she disappears in a little cloud of smoke. I watch the spot where she'd been standing, my eyes wide with terror.

Eve *knows*. She knows what I am. The technowitches have seen right through nine years of training—twisting and tweaking my muscles, changing my posture and hair— shattering the illusion in an instant. All my life I've been living in the princess's shadow to stay safe, and it still didn't amount to anything in the face of real danger.

I've wasted my life for nothing.

"Well, that's Eve," Gleïa hisses, rubbing her sore neck. Her suit is stretched in the front, and she sighs as she forces it to lay flat again.

"Why didn't you tell me I had this locket thing around my neck?" I want to scream, demand answers. But Gleïa is my only ally on this mad planet, so insulting her won't get me very far. That, and I'm still too breathless to ask much else.

"I thought you knew." Gleïa shrugs. "It's not easy to miss."

"My ship had just killed a woman, I doubt I would have noticed…" Gleïa's face falls, and I snap my mouth shut. Murdering a woman's sister isn't exactly a conversation starter. I take a deep breath and continue. "So. What is this thing?"

"It's Night's locket," she replies, still avoiding eye contact. "A personal force shield she made for herself. If you wear it, no physical harm can come to you. Only you can take it off."

My hands lift, trembling, to the back of my neck. The clasp is there now, as it should have been all along. Amazing tech: able to read my stress levels—like Tau can—so the necklace can't be removed under duress—and capable of rendering a locking mechanism invisible.

But what had Oona been protecting herself from? Was this planet dangerous? Was she protecting herself against the angered androids she'd created, or even against her clone sisters?

I settle for a simpler question. "Why is it around my neck?"

"That's a question only Night could answer." She shrugs.

"Night, who you claim is your sister-clone? But you're not identical. You look similar, but even your skin…"

"Oh, that's just good ol' Dad," she says. "While we're cloned from the same person, he played with the dominance of the genes, trying to create the perfect combination. I guess it worked too well, because we all came out perfect in his eyes. I'm honestly shocked you look so much like the late princess: any tinkering with your genes in-vitro was bound to result in more physical differences. Didn't anyone ever explain to you how clone batching works? Oh, well. It depends on what your parents paid for."

My parents. It's hard to even think of them as such, though yes, biologically the king and queen of the Sylvarian Systems are my mother and father. But seeing as how they tried to terminate me at birth, I don't linger on them long. I don't daydream of us being the perfect family, not anymore.

Gleïa stares out the window, frowning.

"Looks like you won't be able to stay in the O.Z. for long," she says. "The sooner you leave, the better, especially since Eve has her greedy eyes on that thing. I don't know why she wants it so badly, but whatever her reason, it won't be good."

"Can you get me back to Nesworth?" I ask, trembling. "Please? I don't know what happened to my aunt and uncle. There were some bad people after me, and if they hurt them… or my cousins, or Tobis…" His face swims in my mind, this morning's conversations cast in a whole new light. He cares. I can't let him die, too. "I just have to get home."

"I can build you a ship, yes, even repair your old one. But I don't have the coordinates for anything beyond the globules. You're going to need to see my father for that."

"Your father? The… wizard?"

"The Technomage," she says, marching into the kitchen to put the fruit back in the fridge. I hand her the plates, trying to help any way I can. "He lives in the moon above the capital. You'll have to walk since my bubble doesn't have the range—don't worry, it's not far, and the road is safe. Especially with Oona's locket protecting you. You'll be absolutely fine."

"You're not coming with me?"

"Stars, no. But I know someone who can."

9

BEFORE I CAN UTTER A WORD, GLEÏA STRIDES OUT the door, retying her cloud of dark hair back from her face. I dart out after her. She ignores the slew of questions I throw at her and keeps going, not even bothering to see if I'm following. She's already halfway down the asphalt road by the time I reach the door, and I have to run to catch up. She doesn't slow as I reach her, and I match her stride.

"We're leaving now?"

"There's no *we*," Gleïa says curtly. "I told you, I can't go. This place will fall into a panic if I'm not here to pick up the pieces. The Expedee have been under Night's control for so long, and now, with her gone, either someone else is going to take over that role, using the droids for their own means, or the Expedee will try and expand their parameters, and maybe—oh, the horror!—self-govern. Either way, total devastation. Night's absence is going to create a power vacuum that might destroy the balance of the whole planet. I'm sorry, but you're on your own."

"But you said…"

"Don't worry, as safe as you are with Night's personal shield, I'm still getting you someone to accompany you," she continues, her pace somehow, impossibly, quickening. "Someone a little more useful than your little flying bot. No offense."

"None taken," I reply, but yeah, offense taken. I know Tau's useless, but I'm the only one allowed to actually say it. Not some *stranger*. Tau's weight in my breast pocket is a constant reminder that I'm not alone. A reminder I sorely need. "And you said he lives on the moon?"

"In the moon, is the moon, but… semantics. You can get there from the capital."

Okay. This woman is unhinged. I have so many questions I feel I might explode, but every answer I get is just more confusing than the last.

"Can't I just go alone?" I ask. Just because I have to trust her doesn't mean I have to do so blindly. "You said it yourself, with this… thing around my neck, I'm perfectly safe, right?"

"Safe? Yes. Being a force field, it will protect you against any fast-moving object. But what about if you need to talk your way out of a situation? It won't do that for you. It's always safer to walk in pairs."

The driveway winds down and away from Gleïa's small plateau, splitting into two roads—one drifting down to the valley far below and the other threading through the mountains. Hopefully wherever I have to go won't require too much hiking.

Away from the sprawling house, we come upon small fields with grazing cattle—cows, actual *cows*, which I've only ever seen in books (they are larger, cuter, and smellier than anticipated)—along with goats, chickens, and even a smattering of sheep. There are also a few parcels growing wheat or corn, and we veer off the asphalt into one of them.

Why does it have to be corn?

The corn stalks—so familiar to me they make me ache for home—are waist-high, planted in perfect rows. Gleïa strides right into them, straight into the middle of the field. I have to force myself to follow her—on Nesworth, stomping into the middle of someone's field like this would be a grave offense.

I walk close behind, careful not to step on the rows. I'm so engrossed in my analysis of the stalks and comparing them to the ones at home that I don't notice when Gleïa stops—quite suddenly—and I slam right into her back. There, in the middle of the stalks of corn, sits a tall, metal cylinder, covered in a thick coating of dirt.

Gleïa doesn't waver. She wipes her hand across the cylinder, revealing a face. Any feelings of comfort I found among the stalks vanishes. I can't contain my gasp—it's a *girl.*

"What is that?" My jaw drops to the tips of the growing corn.

"It's a cryogenic cell." Gleïa runs her hand along the side, brushing away more dust. Diodes flicker to life under her touch. Near the top, a string of numbers appears—121575—a designation for whoever's inside? "Don't be afraid, you can come right on up."

"I'm not afraid. I'm just… who is she?"

"I have absolutely no idea."

"What?"

"She was around before I was born." Gleïa pats the number.

Not a designation: a date. Divide by 389—the Apricus year and thus, the standard everywhere else— and the girl has been frozen for over three hundred years, give or take.

"She was sitting in the Mage's den for absolute ages," Gleïa says. "He said he'd been keeping it for someone, but they never came back for her."

"That's awful." I find myself drawn to the girl's cold, frozen eyes. They're the only part not covered by frost, and they're *open*. A soft coffee-brown. "Is she still alive?"

"I sure hope so," says Gleïa. "Or else you're going for a long walk on your own."

"But how? How is the cell even still running?"

"Solar power." Gleïa points to a plaque on the roof. "Using the sun to keep her frozen. Seems like the perfect blend of science and irony. *Scirony?*"

I ignore her. I'm not quite sure that was ironic in any way, but there's no use arguing with her now, not with a frozen girl in a field waiting to be thawed.

"I was used to seeing her in the corner of the Mage's lab," Gleïa continues. "He must have thought I liked her, because he gifted her to me on my one-hundredth birthday. I didn't complain. Even though we were all born on the same day, I was the only daughter he remembered."

A red light blinks above the chamber door. Gleïa claps her hands in glee. "She lives!"

"But how did she end up in your field?"

"Well, I don't have any use for her, and the Mage's gifts aren't something you can return," she says. "She was my pet project for a while, but she was taking up too much room in my lab. And since the corn was attracting crows… I needed something to scare them away."

"So, you just put her in the field?" I look at her, take her in. *Nope, too surreal,* says my mind. *Wake me up when things make sense again.* So far, the Outer Zone is really living up to its reputation.

"Well, I did hook up the solar panel first." With a flick of Gleïa's hand, the cylinder falls to its side, stopping short of hitting the earth. It wobbles, then holds its position, floating a meter above the ground. Gleïa rests her arm on the glass window.

"So, what's the problem?" I ask. "Why can't you just wake her up? What were you and this Superius fellow doing all this time?"

"Come here." Gleïa waves me forward with a long, elegant finger.

I take a tentative step to her side. She's pointing to a small slot near the bright red light, the size and shape of a data drive. "What is it?"

"That, dear girl, is where her entire personality went." She taps it thoughtfully. "Her essence, if you will. Her soul? It's much easier to freeze the body and digitize the mind. That way, if any part of the body gets damaged, the personality is intact."

I remember this from my notes on the Great Exodus. The three colony ships used the same technology. I start—the age of the cylinder, the old fashioned, obsolete technology… could this girl be one of the first colonists?

But the emptiness of the slot dims the excitement. "Only nothing's here."

"Nope."

"So, what'll happen to her if you wake her up now?"

"She'll be fine." Gleïa waves her hand absentmindedly and begins the short walk back to the house, the cylinder following her like a dutiful pet. "She'll have no memory of who she once was, but she'll do. All you need is a companion. There's strength in numbers, on the road."

"Are you sure?"

"Of course." She nods. "I think."

This time, we don't enter through the front door. Instead, we take a left, toward the large building across the asphalt from where the bubble craft is still parked. From the outside, it looks like one of the barns on Nesworth, stocked full of tractors and quads. Then Gleïa pulls the wooden doors open.

I gasp as the trickery works, and my mind is blown. The room isn't what I expected: the building must have been shrouded under a hologram. It gleams like the rest of Gleïa's perfect home, with large windows invisible from the outside. This barn is Gleïa's lab: her clean, pristine, fully-stocked lab on top of a mountain. The floors are paved and gleaming, the workbenches split between chemistry tables on one wall and robots in different stages of assembly on the other. Everything is top-of-the-line, the best quality in the galaxy. The room is bright, with warm sunlight filtering through shades, keeping the glare off the marble worktops. The sunbeams beckon, saying *welcome, welcome.*

This room is my dream come true. My jaw drops again. I'm going to have aches tomorrow if this keeps happening.

Gleïa guides the cylinder to an empty spot on the floor, and I follow, the doors sliding closed behind us.

I run my hand over one of the workbenches, and a shiver of delight passes through my soul. Gleïa's lab is a mansion compared to my small shed, a dream to work in, if I ever have the chance. Maybe she takes interns.

Then again, one of her sisters wants me dead—for killing another of the sisters.

But right now, Gleïa's attention is on the girl in the cylinder. Gleïa's running her hands over the controls faster than I can follow. The defrosting sequence has already started, sweat beading on Gleïa's brow as she focuses on her work.

"What do we do when she wakes up?" My voice is a whisper. I am on hallowed ground. "Will she need time to recover?"

"She'll need to drink water, if she even wakes up at all. We should prepare ourselves for the moderate outcome—that is a healthy body, but her mind a blank slate."

The red light flicks green. The door depressurizes with a hiss. Steam rises from the chamber as Gleïa pulls the hatch away, like dry ice meeting with air. She waves her hand to part the mist, revealing the face below. My heart catches in my throat.

The woman is beautiful—in a way that's far different than that of Gleïa and her sisters. Her face lacks perfect symmetry, speckled with acne scars and freckles. She has frost burn on her tawny skin, taught and dehydrated in patches down her arms. Her long, black hair looks shiny under the sunbeam, coated in a thick chemical that's been slowly soaking into her body for three centuries.

And yet she radiates an aura of peace and well-being so profound I can't help but be drawn in. I want to bask in her presence until the end of my days.

Then she wakes up, and all slag breaks loose.

With a scream, the girl bolts upright, grabbing the sides of her chamber like it's a life ring. She gasps for air like she's drowning—long, rasping breaths, followed by short, panicky ones. Then she breathes heavily, again and again.

"You're all right," says Gleïa, putting a motherly hand on her back. "It's all right. Breathe, child, breathe."

The girl appeared so much older under a layer of dust and frost. Now she's awake, I realize there aren't so many years between us—other than the obvious 'few centuries being frozen' ones. Sunlight trickles onto her face, revealing every tiny freckle, speckling her cheeks like constellations. I want to draw them, to chart the skies with them.

I shake my head. Slag, I must still be in shock.

"Where am I?" asks the stranger, clutching a hand to her chest. "Where… who…"

"Hello, darling. My name is Gleïa, and I'm here to help you. This is Dora. We just woke you from a long sleep. How do you feel?"

"I feel…" She holds out her hands, stares at her palms, then her knuckles. She turns her hands over to see her palms again. "I feel like I… like there's something on the tip of my…"

Her brown eyes widen. She rises to her feet and sprints to the door, but before she can reach it, she's out of breath. She collapses on the floor, winded, arms outstretched.

"Calm down," says Gleïa, her voice smooth as honey and twice as sweet. She's already at the girl's side, crouching low. "Let me help you. Would you like a drink of water?"

"No. No." She pushes herself back up, shakes her head. "I just need to know. Why can't I remember… who… I…" She topples over again, collapsing into Gleïa's arms, and Gleïa holds her, as if she's no weight at all. Then, quite suddenly, the girl takes a deep breath, stands, and folds her hands behind her back. The transformation takes place instantly: one second, the girl's petrified, the next, she's pacing the room.

I watch her, awestruck. While her endurance might be thrown out of whack by her long sleep, her muscle functions are not. There seems to be no atrophy in her body at all. Impressive technology. Somewhere in the back of my mind, I recall one of Tennyson's first sketches for a cryogenic chamber that could hold a person indefinitely, a step up from the ones that brought him and our other ancestors through the wormhole. He'd given up on it when the wormhole technology had been lost—but it was a revolutionary idea, and obviously one that works in practice as well as theory.

The clothes the girl wears are unlike anything I've ever seen before: loose red-brown trousers and a mustard-yellow shirt, under a brown leather jacket that covers her shoulders and arms. Her boots are knee-high brown leather, a shade darker than the jacket, and thick. They make small creaking noises as she paces the workroom floor.

I only watch her feet for a moment. Every second staring at anything other than her face is a second wasted. I watch her lips, and wonder who the last person she spoke to was. How long ago that person died. Maybe their words to her had been a promise for when they were going to wake her up. A year? Ten years? A hundred?

All the people from the girl's natural lifetime are dead; yet she is not. And she won't remember any of them.

"There was an accident," says Gleïa. "Your mental data was compromised. I'm very sorry, um…" She runs her eyes over the stranger's chest, shoulders, frowning.

"Well, don't look at me," snaps the girl. "I have no idea who I am, but, somehow, I'm absolutely certain none of this is my fault. Didn't someone think to put my name on the tank?"

"No. I'm so very sorry. It was before my time," says Gleïa. "Believe it or not, this is a fantastic outcome. It seems only the long-term memories are affected. You still remember how to walk, to talk. So other than a lack of personal experience, you should be entirely yourself."

"Myself, minus my memories?" The girl frowns. "Even without them I know that's not right. You woke me up, you screwed me over—you fix this."

"That is beyond my abilities. But I do know someone who can put everything back the way it was. All right? The

Technomage Superius. He can dig into your brain and get your personality back."

"He can?" The stranger's eyes sparkle. "Good. A girl must know her name. I am a girl, right? I have that feeling." She looks down at her chest and nods.

"Stupendous!" Gleïa claps her hands. "The two of you both need the Mage to get out of your predicaments, so you can keep each other company on your walk to see him. It's not far—should take two, three days on foot."

"Company?" I start. "You said the way to the Mage was *dangerous*. Isn't she meant to be protection?"

"A Mage?" The girl is indignant. "You lost my memory, and you're sending me to a wizard, and with a stranger?"

"I would point out that since you don't remember anyone, everyone you meet will be a stranger."

"Good point. Look, I have no idea who you are, why you woke me up, or if you have my best interests in mind. Put me back in there and freeze me until you have a good idea of who I am, please."

"I don't have time for this," Gleïa hisses. "The Mage is a technical genius. The smartest mind in this entire galaxy. If you want to trust anyone, trust him."

"Like we're trusting you?" I say.

"And who are you meant to be?" asks the girl, finally looking in my direction. Her glower makes me sink deeper into my skin.

"Dora?" I should probably elaborate, but what else do you say to a centuries-old, recently reanimated stranger?

"She's the reason you need to go quickly. The Expedee are out of control, and I need to step in before they attempt to take over the planet." She turns to me. "Not to mention they've seen your face, Dora, and it won't take long for even them to realize who you happen to look like. You're going to have to act fast, before word spreads that Princess Jo'Niss is alive and back among her people."

I cringe. I can almost feel Auntie glaring from across the space between the stars, lecturing me on how this was exactly what she had always warned me would happen. "You're sure the Mage can get me home?"

"Positive. It's what he does. For a man with his power, helping you would be trivial."

The girl crosses her arms over her chest. "Can't come cheap. What's in it for him?"

She has no memory except for the concept of money, but she does make an excellent point.

"Yeah, why would he want to do anything for us?" I ask. "He has nothing to gain from helping us, and I have nothing to offer."

"He's the most powerful being in the galaxy. He's beyond mortal concepts of wants and needs. Nothing anyone can do for him will add to his current existence. Why would he help? Why does he do anything? Because he's *bored.*"

I sneak a look at the girl, but she's not having any of it. She's already done with this conversation, arms crossed over her chest, eyes darting to the door like she's itching to get going. The only thing on her mind is getting her memories back; anything else isn't worth her time. *I'm* not worth her time.

"That, and he wants the locket."

The shoe drops. Nice, Gleïa.

"I thought *Eve* wanted it," I say, "Why can't we just give it to her, if it will get her off our backs?"

"We can't," says Gleïa, shaking her head. "The shield isn't to protect the wearer, but what's inside the locket. Night has—*had*—been safeguarding the thing for centuries. She called it her secret weapon. The Mage needs to know what it is, what she's been hiding, and what she's been plotting with Eve."

"If it's so important, can't you just take us in your… bubble thing? If he needs it so badly?"

"It doesn't have the range, my dear." Gleïa flicks her hair off her shoulder. "That, and it would be incredibly easy for my sister to shoot out of the sky. Not to mention I'm the only one who can fly it. And have you already forgotten the army of small droids who are currently testing the limits of their programming? Now go! There's no time to lose. Any moment wasted is a moment where Eve's plans move forward. She's incredibly dangerous, and she wants what she thinks is rightfully hers. Do *not* let her get the locket." She turns to the girl, whose hand is now on the door handle. "Are you all right?"

"I would say I've seen better days." The girl slips her hands into her pockets. "But it's a little hard to be sure, with all my memories *fucking missing*."

"Great," says Gleïa, ignoring the girl's attitude and bizarre curses. She's speaking like she's in a historical video. "Together, the two of you should make it to Anchor easily.

I'll send a message ahead, so that the Mage knows you're coming."

"But how do we even get to this… Anchor place?"

"It's easy: just follow the road. It'll take you through the city of Anchor, straight to the Mage's moon."

"Right," the girl pipes up. "I've been conscious for what, two minutes? And you tell me to follow a strange girl I don't know down a road? Shouldn't you be giving us guns? What kind of dangers are we supposed to avoid?"

"Who are you calling strange?" I snap, but Gleïa is already answering.

"Solitude," she says. "Trust the road. Follow it until the end. Don't ask for directions, don't eat food that's not from a tavern. Be careful who you meet on the way. Don't tell them where you're going. And above all—Dora, don't you dare take off that locket. If you do, Mage help you, because I won't be able to. Now go!" She makes a shooing motion with her long fingers.

I hold out my hand to shake Gleïa's, but she keeps shooing us away. "Thanks, Gleïa," I say, trying to keep my fear at bay. "You might have just saved my life."

"Oh, trust me, child," she laughs. "I know I did."

10

AS WE LEAVE THE MOUNTAINSIDE COMPOUND, the road ahead seems infinite.

The girl hasn't said anything to me since Gleïa set us on our path. Maybe she doesn't have anything to talk about: after all, her memories only go back as far as what, half an hour? And I've been around for all of that. There isn't anything to talk about. I can't even ask her name, since she doesn't know it. I'm not here to make small talk and be her friend, anyway; we're only walking together for convenience.

I shove my hands deep into the pockets of my spark coat. It's the first time since the crash that I've actually had time to think, and my brain is spinning in circles like a quad with a broken rotor. I can't stop replaying my uncle's anger this morning; the look on Abril's face as she told me to run; Astrophel's hand grabbing my ankle, knowing he was going to be the literal death of me as he grinned at the thought of his reward.

And Tobis, sweet Tobis, just trying to ask me what was wrong. Always trying to be there, but never really listening.

I pull my coat tighter as I start to shiver. Tau's small casing presses into my breast, reassuring even in sleep mode. My mind is light years away, on Nesworth, on my family. Huddling in the storm cellar, waiting out the danger only for Hardi's crew to find them, if their ship survives the storm. What would Hardi do to Auntie and Uncle in order to find me? What was the ransom for turning in a royal clone? Was it worth killing innocents?

I need to get home. To save my family from the mess I've put them in. This Technomage Superius has to be incredibly powerful if he can make that happen, must have technology at his disposal that's beyond my wildest dreams. Maybe, just maybe, he can even teach me.

I stop. The girl's footfalls have gone silent. The field to our left, the last one on the mountain terrace, is full of crows. They peck at the ground, pulling up seeds. The stranger watches them, crossing her arms over her chest and hugging herself tighter.

"This place feels familiar," she says. She lifts her hands to block the sun as she turns to face it. It's much lower on the horizon than when I arrived, peeking out from behind the clouds.

"We found you in a corn field. Gleïa had you out there as a scarecrow."

"As a what?" She drops her arms and flies into the field, kicking the dirt up as she goes. The birds take to the skies, filling the air with angry cries. I run after her, but she's too fast, and I can't keep up. She chases the crows as if she has a personal vendetta against each and every one of them.

Finally, she stops, breathless.

"She kept me in a field," she says as I come up beside her, her face red and covered in sweat. "She kept me in a field to scare away birds."

"She did," I say. "It was wrong."

"Ya think?" She spins around to face me, her brown eyes brimming with fury and tears. "She kept me in a fucking field! When I needed help! And now I'm awake and can't remember who the hell I am. Fuck this shit, I'm out."

"Wait! Wait..."

What am I meant to say? I don't even have a name to call her by. She's already storming back to the road and down the path, and she's not waiting for me.

I do the only thing I can think of, and rush after her.

"Hold on!" I shout. "We need to stick together if we're going to find the Mage."

"Yeah? What if I don't want to find him? What if I don't want his help? That woman only woke me up when it was convenient for her. She kept me captive so she could grow some corn. And you trust this asshole?"

Her words sting. I don't know why I trust Gleïa about the Mage; all I know is that I have to. Without her, I would still be lost on this planet. The fullness of my belly reminds me of her generosity.

"Then get your memories and come back to get justice for yourself!" I hate that she hates me when I'm the reason she's even awake at all. "Come on! If you give up now, you'll never know who you are. The Technomage can help you, right? I don't trust him either—I don't even know him—but he's our only chance at getting to where we belong."

The girl stops, squeezing her eyes shut. She clenches her fists at her sides, breathing in and out so deeply I think she may deflate and fly away. Then she opens her eyes and brushes back her hair.

"Fine," she says, "but I'm not here to make friends. We'll get to the Mage, and then I don't need to see your face ever again. All right? The less time I need to spend with you, the better."

"*Fine.* I'm not here to make friends either. But you don't have to hate me. I haven't done anything."

"I don't hate you. I don't even know you, and I really don't want to," she says, crossing her arms over her chest. She looks off into the distance, nose turned up, brushing me off. Her 'holier than thou' vibe is starting to make my blood boil. "I hate the fact I have to blindly follow you across this planet on the off chance it gives me my life back. It's messed up that I'm so reliant on a total stranger, more than on my own brain. Literally the only thing I know about you is that you've got a necklace that everyone wants, and I want nothing to do with any of this drama."

She's right, this is messed up. Her memory is minutes old, and she's expected to come with me without question. But I didn't get much room for questions either. "I'm just trying to get home."

"At least you know where home is," she mutters. "All right, let's go."

"Just so you know," I continue, "I don't want the drama either. I accidentally crash- landed on Gleïa's sister, and—"

She lets out a sigh so sharp it could be a hiss. "I don't want to hear it. So please. Let's just get to their mage and try not to make a mess of it."

I shut my mouth. If that's what she wants, it's all right by me. I don't want to talk with her either. I trusted one stranger for five minutes, and that put my family in jeopardy. Home needs to be the only thing on my mind: friends are the furthest thing from it.

I have to believe in Gleïa to ensure my survival.

Tired, frustrated, and needing a friendly face, I thrust my hand into my pocket and retrieve Tau. The girl can laugh all she wants; it doesn't matter. I twist him awake and launch him into the air. Finally out of sleep mode, the little bot zips around, taking scope of the landscape. He flies back to me, beeping an all-clear, and hovers right over my shoulder like a trained parrot.

Sue me, I had a pirate phase.

"What is that?" the girl says, her eyes wide, seemingly transfixed by the little bot.

Tau hovers over my shoulder, scanning her and humming quietly.

"This is Tau. Don't worry, he's harmless. Just a computer with a programmed personality."

"Yeah, I know what a *bot* is. But what is it supposed to be? An egg?"

Tau beeps something that sounds way too close to a scoff. Maybe I programmed him better than I give myself credit.

I'm still trying to work out the full effects of the extended cryo-sleep on the girl's mind: she can communicate fine, remembers what a bot is, but apparently nothing about her own past. In any case, she's not up to sharing and neither am I.

"His housing was a kitchen timer," I reply. "Don't tell my aunt. She still hasn't put two and two together."

"What? So you're a ginny, too?" She lifts an eyebrow.

"I thought you didn't want to know anything about me."

"I don't," she says, "but if you're an engineer, that changes things. I'm not really liking them that much right now."

"Well, don't worry, I'm not," I say, patting Tau, who lets out a chirp of appreciation. "Gleïa called me a ginny, but I'm not there yet. I'm just Dora, a girl who likes circuits and gears."

"Well, good for you, *Dora*," she says, emphasizing the name like it's an insult. "Glad you have a hobby, Buttercup."

"Buttercup?"

"Your coat," she says, and I rip it away before her prying fingers can touch it.

"My spark jacket?"

"It's an *awful* shade of yellow, Buttercup. Washes you out."

"Stop that. Are you just sour because you can't remember any of *your* hobbies? Come on. Don't take it out on me. I'm the reason you're not still in that field right now, chasing off crows."

"At least *there* I didn't have to make conversation."

"Did I say I wanted to talk?"

The girl says nothing. Instead, she looks at the ground, stuffing her hands in the pockets of her jacket, and keeps on walking. I watch her go a few steps, then follow.

"Look, can you at least give me a name to call you, even if you have to make it up? I have to call you *something*."

"Call me Crow, then," she snaps.

"Crow?"

"It's the only thing I know about myself: that I've been scaring away crows. Well, screw that witch, *I'm* the crow now and I won't be scared off. Besides, crows are smart, resourceful; if I get to be anyone, I'd chose to be more like them. So call me Crow and that's that."

"Fine, Crow," I reply, "it's nice to meet you."

And we keep walking.

The asphalt is turning out to be less of a driveway and more of a lone road through a winding mountain. Once we leave the safety of Gleïa's compound, a peak blocks the sun, and the temperature drops like a rock in a pond, fast and heavy.

I'd been so excited to see mountains, but now that excitement is gone, replaced by a chill. I clutch my spark coat closer. The thing is insulated against flames, so it should be able to retain my body heat. Still, my hands are frozen stiff.

Tau lets out a sad little chirp.

"Did I program you to comment?" I hiss at him, and he flies away, retreating behind my shoulder. Guilt tugs at my gut; Tau has nothing to do with any of this. I can't fault him for trying to reach out. Not when it's my programming that made him do it.

"What's wrong with you, Buttercup?" Crow juts her chin at me. "You cold?"

"Yeah. I live on a moon, and we don't get that many seasons."

"Ah, well, suck it up. It's going to get a lot colder before it gets warmer."

I'm about to ask how she knows that, but it's not worth it. Instead, I stuff my fingers deeper in my pockets and trudge on.

Luckily the road is all downhill so far, and the path is steady. We slowly see more and more trees, until we're surrounded on both sides and walking through a thick forest. Nesworth doesn't have forests yet, just a few decorative trees here and there. I can't believe how fragrant the air is, and I suck in the warm, woody scents, trying to burn them into my mind.

Some of the trees have needles instead of leaves. *Needles.* I want to stop, to touch them, see if they're as sharp as they look, but Crow is keeping a steady pace, and I know she won't wait for me.

After two hours or so of walking, we finally reach the base of the mountain. At this point I wish I'd asked Gleïa to pack us a field snack. Not to mention the thirst! I'm so focused on my empty stomach that I don't notice how far ahead Crow is until she stops at the top of a ridge, pointing. I run to catch up, my stomach growling as I go. I need to get some food in my stomach soon, or I won't be able to go much farther.

"Would you look at that?" she says, pointing at the valley below.

The forest is fizzling out, and not a kilometer away there's a massive theme park, the kind I've only ever seen in books. One with roller coasters and carousels, with rides and, hopefully, concession stands.

"What do you think?" Crow smiles, teeth peeking out between thin lips. "Food?"

"I was thinking the same thing." My stomach rumbles again, loud enough that Crow lifts her brows.

"Great. We'll get food and get out. We're not staying to ride any rides."

"I don't think we can, anyway," I say. "It looks like they're closed for the night. Nothing's moving."

"A little early, don't you think? It's not even dark out yet. Anyway. We should still have food. We'll take it if we have to."

"Seriously? We're on this planet for all of five minutes, and you want to start stealing?"

"Exactly." She nods. "We're new here. They've got nothing on us."

"I'm not sure I like this plan."

"Well, too bad." Crow starts walking away. "I don't need your permission. Feel free to go hungry."

I follow her—reluctant but starving—down to the park. It's much farther away than it appeared from higher up. The place is monstrous, sitting in the middle of the empty valley like a pimple on otherwise perfect skin. Eerily perfect, as if nothing dares grow anywhere near it. The setting sun casts long shadows, black gashes on the landscape, stretching the park out and making it more impressive. Maybe leaning more toward oppressive.

"I think we should avoid this place," I say with a shudder. "I'm getting a weird vibe. Plus, it's not on the road."

"What?" Crow snaps, "and you think the technowitch cares about all the local hotspots? We eat where we can, when we can."

"She did warn us."

"Screw her," says Crow, gathering speed so she's trotting. "This is the woman who couldn't remember to find my brain. We're getting dinner. I can't remember the last time I ate."

The towering gates of the theme park are nowhere near as attractive close up as they were from the ridge. Though the rows of empty ticket stands and turnstiles beckon like the entrance to heaven, the large, welcoming letters above the park's entrance have long since turned silver as the red paint peeled off. Pieces still cling to the facade as if the place would fade from existence were they to ride off on the breeze. Beneath the old paint, the rusting words '*The Enchanted Forest*' somehow still gleam. First Earth stories have been at the heart of a lot of cultures since the exodus, since we lost the way back and the fear of losing the stories forever brought them back into the light. Even I'd grown up listening to them on my little isolated moon.

We look at each other and grin, the first smile I've seen from Crow since we met.

"We've got ourselves a theme park!" Crow exclaims, and before I can ask how she knows what a theme park is, she's already leaping over a rusty turnstile, throwing her hands up in the air with the pride of a royal gymnast. "Tadaa! Freedom!"

I follow behind, wary. The place looks like it's been abandoned for decades. There won't be anything to eat here.

I want to be excited about the park: it is, after all, the first time I've ever set foot in one. Seeing the monstrous frames of the roller coasters looming above me sets my heart aflutter. In another life, I might have ridden on them; me and my mother and father, screaming as we dropped over the highest hill and let gravity pull us to the ground, racing the wind.

But, even if I'd been chosen as the ideal daughter, I doubt the king and queen would have brought me to a theme park. I shake my head. Neither that life or my own would have brought me here.

Tau glides over the turnstile, following Crow. She notices and rolls her eyes in her signature wide loop.

I'm tired of her already.

Maybe I can leave her here, make it to the Mage by myself: perhaps the planet isn't as dangerous as Gleïa's made it out to be, and I have a slagging *magic locket*. I have absolutely no obligation to put up with an obnoxious stranger.

Crow might be useful. If she can find us food, it might be worth keeping her around.

But that, I remind myself as I follow her into the deserted park, has yet to be seen.

CLAUSTROPHOBIA SETTLES OVER ME AS WE walk along Main Street, as if the park is going to fall on top of us any second now. It isn't just empty, it's downright abandoned. The wood-and-stone fairy tale houses closing in on us are sad and drab, the paint flaking to dust. The silent streets are covered in a thick layer of dirt that must have blown in and was never swept away. Glass from broken windows reflects the golden rays of the setting sun.

I can't shake the feeling someone's watching us from the dark windows. There are faces in each of their shadows. An uneasy tightness climbs up my spine and settles in the back of my neck.

Crow, however, seems to have the opposite reaction to the park. She runs into buildings with their beat-down doors, then dashes across the street to another, as if exploring is all part of the fun. Sometimes, she comes out with empty jars, shrugs, and drops them where she strands. They break in a cascade of broken glass and prop food.

"I don't think we're going to find anything to eat here," I say, but Crow is already kilometers ahead. She jumps over the counter of an old hut-shaped concession stand and rips open the doors to their stock.

"Paydirt!" She pulls out little plastic bags filled with pink and tosses them onto the weather-beaten counter.

"Is this edible?" I ask. The plastic feels as if it will crumble to dust if the wind decides to pick up. In any case, the pink cloud inside the bag is too bright to be anything edible.

"It's on the sign, innit?" says Crow, ripping the bag open. The perfectly suspended pink cloud inside dissolves into nothing. She holds the bag up to her nose and inhales deeply before it can get away. "Sweet, sweet sugar, come to me."

She's giggling to herself now. I've never seen this look before: seeing without seeing.

"Are you high?" I don't know what to do with a druggie, don't know how to handle a stranger when they're not entirely themselves, either. But Crow wipes a sharp hand over her mouth, turning the smile to a frown.

"What the hell kind of question is that?" she asks.

"I don't know, you look high."

"Do you even know what someone high looks like?" Crow laughs, tossing the plastic bag on the ground. "It's kinda cute how sheltered you are."

"I'm not." I stuff my hands deeper into my pockets and try to hide the heat that rises to my face. "What about you? You've literally been sheltered for centuries!"

Her expression hardens.

"In any case, we're not getting full on this crap. It's pure sugar! I'm sure we'll find an old storeroom if we manage to track down a restaurant."

"And you think any food there will still be good?"

She doesn't answer, already trying the next abandoned storefront. I shuffle down the road after her. She's a complete mess: the sooner we part ways, the better. Just being around her makes my hair stand on end.

"*Universe of food,*" reads Crow, "*presented by the Farming Coalition.* This looks promising?"

"I think it's an attraction, not a restaurant, though?"

I had no idea the Coalition ventured this far into the Outer Zone. Astrophel said they avoided it, didn't he? But

Crow's already pushed through the door, her handprint lingering on the golden duck embossed on the frosted glass.

Wood panels cover the walls and floors of the large room inside. Shiny round tables surround heavy chairs, like an old restaurant from the archives of First Earth. The door swings shut behind me as I step in.

"See what I mean, Buttercup?" says Crow. She trots down the rows of empty tables toward the bar in the back and takes a seat. The wax figure in front of her is the aged bust of a man in a lederhosen—or at least, the top half of one. She slaps the counter in front of it. "Barkeep, I need jalapeño poppers, *STAT*. And one of every slider you have."

The figure, predictably, says nothing. Crow roars with laughter. I turn away. Even here, I still have that distinct feeling of being watched. It has to be the lifeless old glass eyes—a few more figures litter the restaurant, dressed like fairytale peasants, slumped over the furniture in various states of disarray.

"Um, this is just the room before the ride." I point to one of the flashy signs nailed to the walls, giving Crow the most deadpan look I can muster. "This isn't a real restaurant. It's a façade."

"You sure know a lot about theme parks, for a mooner," she scoffs, hopping off her barstool.

"Says the girl with no memory."

"Precisely. If I'm the one saying it, what does it say about you?"

I sigh, following the signs toward the ride, pushing into what should have been a kitchen in a real restaurant. Instead, it's a windowless room with its own river, complete with cutesy rowboats docked in a line.

"Well, this isn't how I would store my food, but then again, what do I know?" Crow brushes past me into the docking room and hops into one of the rowboats. "Are you coming, Buttercup?"

"Can you stop calling me that?"

Crow pretends to think about it while hunting down an oar, and, finding none, scrunches up her face. "Nah."

"The boat's on a track, anyway," I say, "so we wouldn't get far."

"Fine then." Crow steps out of the boat into the ankle-deep water.

"I want to make this very clear: I'm only here for the food. Not you."

"Yeah, yeah."

Tau leads the way. His light isn't strong, but it's enough to illuminate our next few steps. The dark has never been my friend, and, today, it feels like it's going to devour me. I never outgrew that little anxious voice that piped up when I stood at the top of the cellar stairs, telling me that anything could happen when there was no way to see. I hate the dark: it isn't something you can defend yourself against with your wits—not unless you have time and scrap tech on your hands. I'd built Tau to also be my torch in the night, stuffed full of LEDs wherever his casing allowed.

We slosh through the stale water and under a blackout curtain into the next room of the ride. The river that hides the track flows in a zigzag through the building, around raised sections and decorations. This first room is filled with stars and planets, each one painted with a cartoonish menu item: a planet for wheat; a planet for corn; bread and chocolate; and a laughing, happy cow. They're made to look like they're hanging in space, but they're bolted to the back wall.

"It's an educational ride," says Crow. "Dammit, we're not going to find anything to eat here."

No kidding. My heart sinks in time with my growling stomach. Maybe the only way Crow will ever be useful is as a source of protein.

What the void: I could just eat her.

I shake my head, pushing the thought away. Skip one meal, and suddenly I'm ready to resort to cannibalism. Then again, Crow was the one to suggest the detour, to stuff her nose into a bag of dissolving pink gas without fearing the consequences. Maybe this is what she deserves.

"You coming?" she asks. Tau drifts between us, trying to figure out where he needs to be to light us best. *Good bot.*

"Whatever," I mutter, and follow Crow through the next blackout curtain.

The next room is a patchwork of cultures from First Earth, each represented by a half-scale model of a human being, all clustered on tiered platforms. I cringe: the tiny humans are creepy with their larger-than-life eyes stuck open, mouths poised to speak or launch into song.

"Ugly bugger, ain't he?" says Crow, giving one of the more ostentatious dolls a shove in the face. It topples backward, stiff as a board, ceremonial headdress toppling off as it tumbles into the water.

An unsettled feeling spreads through my body as I watch it fall. That same feeling of being watched. "Don't touch them!"

"Why not? I'm not going to break it any more than it already is." She opens her arms wide and gestures to the expanse of the room around us: maybe a hundred little dolls with half-open smiles stare down at us. They look so much like the Expedee droids except that I can't help but see disdain in these eyes.

"I don't know. I don't like it." But I do know. Now I've seen the resemblance, it's so obvious. These are just smaller versions of the Expedee—an earlier generation, perhaps, but crafted by the same hand.

"Take a chill pill, Buttercup. No one is high and no one is going to arrest us for molesting the dolls. Shit!"

The doll's hand is wrapped around her wrist, holding fast. Crow rips her hand away, but the doll holds on, its arm ripping right out of the socket. Crow stumbles backward onto the floor, the doll's hand still clinging to her, its fingers twitching.

I watch in horror as the now-armless doll begins to sing. *"Come and see the world with me, a whole wide universe of food!"*

A chorus of voices join in—the other dolls, slowly coming awake. Their eyes light up, riveted on the intruders.

Slag. They're not just dolls: they're tiny, pint-sized droids. Little robots only half my height but twice my strength—walking programs with arms and legs and a deep-set need to ward off intruders.

"I take it back! I *am* high. I'm tripping! I'm tripping!" Crow screams and stumbles back into the water before the droids even reach her. They're advancing in a tight row, still singing as they march.

"Moons for sugar and moons for spice, comets with grand fields of ice!"

I open my mouth to scream, but a hand clamps down on it, stifling the sound. Cold synthetic skin presses against my face. The droids grab my arms, pulling them down. I try to shake them off, but they're so much stronger than I am. I've never been a fighter: Auntie and Uncle taught me to hide, not to fight. If I'd been discovered, it would already be too late for fighting.

"Dora!"

My name bounces off the walls as Crow sails through the air. Her foot misses my ear by half an inch. It slams into the head of the droid holding me and knocks over the plinth it's standing on. We crash backward into the water with a splash, and I expel the air from my lungs in one blow.

Crow punches the droid in the face, cutting it off mid-song as I surge to my feet. There are straight up *dozens upon dozens* of brightly dressed, culturally exaggerated little monsters marching toward us, all with singular determination, like drones to a hiveship.

"And to keep the systems fed, we must work to bring you bread!"

"Run!"

I feel Crow's hand tighten around my wrist a split second before she gives it a yank. I'm still winded, and it's all I can do to follow, let alone keep up. Crow's gait is long and powerful, so much stronger than just hours ago, when she couldn't make it across Gleïa's barn.

She's clasping a still-wriggling arm she must have ripped from one of the droids and is wielding it like a club. She has the reflexes of a fighter, a warrior. She seems to know exactly what to do.

We burst back into the fake restaurant only to come nose-to-nose with the upper half of a bartender. He's propelling himself forward using nothing but his arms, swinging off the bar. Two angry-looking peasant girl-droids in brown smocks flank him, their blank stares fixated on us. Unlike the droids from the ride, they're all human-sized—except for the barman, who is technically the size of half an average human. Crow seems quite happy they're regular-sized opponents and thanks them each with a brutish kick to the sternum. The bartender opens his mouth to say something, but maybe he's actually a beer tap, because instead of sound coming out, he splashes us both with a sour drink.

I might have once found that funny—but the mini-droids are still in hot pursuit. They're pushing us out of the restaurant, still singing off-key: *"We feed the universe! We feed the trillions!"*

"Now that's going to be stuck in my head for the rest of the year," Crow mutters as we flee onto Main Street, Tau beeping the alarm as we race for the park exit.

"How can you make jokes at a time like this?"

"If I'm going to die, let it be with a bad pun on my lips," Crow says—then freezes. "Wait. No. I don't want that at all! What am I saying? I don't want to die!"

Well, we have one thing in common at least: I don't want to die, either. The dolls are spilling out from the restaurant and into the street, locked on us. I was hoping that once the droids had chased out the ride's intruders, they'd give up … but instead they march grimly after us, still singing that stupid song. I should have known better: droids stuck on defensive protocols can't be deterred. Our hound Tidbit was the same before he broke down. When I turned him on for the night, I'd slept soundly knowing *no one* could ever get past him.

The park might be abandoned, but the droids will defend it to their last spark of power.

"We need to get to their central processing unit," I pant as I run. "Since they're part of the ride, if we shut that down, they should all go back to sleep mode."

"Are you out of your mind? You want us to go back in there?"

"They're tiny display units! Walking is the most complex thing they can do!"

"So? They seem to be walking pretty fast to me!" Crow huffs. "And kicking the shit out of us is a rather complex process!"

Droids don't get exhausted; as we slow—neither one of us in the sort of shape that can outrun an out-of-control mini demon droid horde—the tiny creatures are quickly closing the gap.

"We need to go back to the ride," I insist, "find the back door, the staff entrance. From there we can shut off all the residual commands lingering in their shared mindframe."

"I hear you saying words, but none of them make sense. And I'm not going back through that horde."

Crow's being *impossible.* But this isn't up to her. I brace myself, taking a deep, frustrated breath.

Then I rush at the droids.

Before I even reach the horde, Crow flies past me, punching her way through the first row. She swerves, dodging and kicking every one of their small forms. All of their eyes are fixed on her, turning me invisible.

"You sure you know what you're doing?" she spits, slamming a severed droid arm into another's head, smashing its casing.

"We'll find out!"

"You're the ginny!"

I sprint toward the far end of the street, where the wood-and-stone facades mask the hidden staff areas. I pause when I reach the restaurant, looking back to make sure the battle isn't already lost, instead seeing the impossible. Crow is an artist painting a swath of destruction. Shattered droids fly away from her as she whittles down the massive, chanting horde to fragments of plastic, metal and dust. I've never seen anything like it. Her memories might be gone, but her muscles haven't forgotten. Who was she in her past life?

I slam through the back door into the darkened passage beyond the ride. Two small windows overlook the ride's interior on one side and the street outside on the other. Sure enough, the control panel is right there, stretching across the desk that sprawls the entire wall, as if waiting for me.

I run my fingers over the dusty controls, reveling in their artistry, imagining how beautiful the park must have looked in its glory days, with droids left and right entertaining the crowds. I would've loved to see it like that. Instead, I bring my hand down on the kill switch—and absolutely nothing happens.

My hand instinctively slips to my hip, and I curse. I left my tool belt light years away, on a workbench I may never see again. I'm going to have to do this the old-fashioned way.

"Tau, I'm going to have to shut you off, bud," I say, plucking him from the air, "or you'll be toast like the rest of them."

I throw myself on the floor beneath the control panel, my heart rate slowing as I slip into my natural routine—pulling off loose panels by hand, finding my way around the wires by touch. Finding the relay to the backup generator. Taking away safety switches.

I rip my hands away, scramble out from under the panel, and watch in awe as power surges through the old device. Sparks fly, sure, but I'm counting on that. The entire panel blows up with a muffled boom and a blast of heat that pushes me back against the door. I'm grinning wildly. I've never tried making an electromagnetic pulse before, and yet it's worked perfectly on my first try.

I tilt my head, listening. Though my ears are still ringing—and probably will be for a while—I can still hear the silence outside. The dolls' creepy chanting has finally stopped.

"I got them before you did!" comes a shout from down the street.

I peer out the tiny window at Crow, who is standing in a circle of dead-eyed droids. She smiles back at me.

"Now," she says, "did you happen to find any food in there?"

12

NIGHT FALLS, AND WE PICK A HOUSE ON Main Street to call our own, settling in front of the fireplace. It would be much nicer if there was an actual fire—instead of Tau's dull glow—but like everything in this place, it's fake. I think it was once an old-timey souvenir shop, since there are empty racks on the walls, but nothing has been left behind.

Still no food.

Every few seconds, I think I see movement in the shadows outside. Without Thebos to cast its comforting blue light, I'm sure there's something lurking in the dark. The hair on the back of my neck is raised. Even if I was tired—which I'm not, a combination of shorter days and planet-lag making this early evening in my head—I wouldn't be able to sleep as I still haven't lost the feeling of being watched.

Because I'm not sleepy, I can devote one hundred percent of my focus to a particular problem: I've never been this cold before in my life. Nesworth has always been muggy: corn sweats during the day, expelling a sticky humidity, and the nights are long, so we've always had terraforming heaters going in the fields. My teeth won't stop bouncing off each other, chattering in a way I can't control no matter how hard I try.

"What the hell is wrong with you?" Crow has her arms wrapped tightly around her knees, clutching them to her chest. Her teeth, at least, are silent.

"My teeth, they're…" I start, but of course that only makes them start up again, a drill through bedrock.

"Chattering?" Crow lifts an eyebrow. "It's cold out, Buttercup. That's what happens when you're cold."

"How would you know?" I glare right back at her. "You're not supposed to remember anything."

"Stop asking. I don't remember, I just *know*. Where are you even from anyway, where you don't get cold?"

"I could answer you, but it wouldn't make much of a difference. Do you even remember what the Systems are like?"

"Probably not. My question was mainly rhetorical."

I groan, staring into Tau's light. My mind is trapped in a subroutine, trying to make sense of what we've just survived: the demented droids, singing and attacking, without impunity. I shudder.

I have to stand. I thought I could sleep on this floor, but it's way too cold for that. My spark coat is zipped tight, but it isn't doing anything for my denim-clad legs. I brush the dirt from the seat of my pants.

"Where are you going?" asks Crow, looking up.

"I'm going to start a fire," I say, realizing as I say it that this is exactly what I need to do.

"How?"

"I dunno." I shrug. "There's tons of wood around here. And maybe someone left matches, or, even better, a lighter. I'm going to find out."

"In the dark?"

"Tau will come with me."

"But then… I'll be in the dark."

"I never said I had to do it alone."

It's Crow's turn to groan, but she says nothing more as she gets to her feet. She ties her wild hair back with a strip of fabric she pulls from her pocket, brushing her curls from her face and framing it in a halo of black.

Crow's freckles stand out even more under Tau's dull glow. They form a bridge from one side of the face to the other, a galaxy of stars from cheek to cheek and across her nose.

"What are you looking at?" she snaps, brows furrowing, and I stare at my feet.

"I'm just thinking," I reply hastily. Slag, was I blushing? Why the void am I blushing? "I don't want for us to go far."

"Why?" Crow taunts. "You scared of the dark?"

I don't care what this strange girl thinks of me. I swear I don't. "On an alien planet, in an abandoned theme park? Void yes."

"Good." Crow nods, as if I've passed some kind of test. "I guess I am, too."

Tau leads the way again, and the way he's bobbing makes me think he's got the hang of smugness now. He reminds me of Tidbit, the way he nodded his head slightly after a job well done, like he knew he was essential even without personality programming. And Tau is definitely essential. The gloomy, oppressive feeling the park gave off earlier is ten times worse in the dark. I stop, closing my eyes. *At least for the moment, all is fine. I have Tau. I have Crow.*

"You coming?" she asks, impatient.

I open my eyes again. The street is still empty—save for Crow, who stands swathed in Tau's blue light. Drawing a deep breath, I look up—and freeze in awe.

So many stars.

I had clear skies back home. I had a beautiful view of the Milky Way's span, from end to end, but only for the hour where Thebos and the sun hid each other in the sky. But these stars are not my stars; none of these constellations are anywhere close to what I know, and the sky has empty patches of darkness from the dusty nebulas that surround us, like someone has forgotten to place any starlight there, or a giant has thrown a veil over half of the atmosphere. It's beautiful, and yet so wrong. The galaxy stretches above us, brilliantly bright, and I wonder which pinpoint of light might be Nesworth's, if it's hiding behind one of the dark smudges, the nebulous Bok Globules absorbing our sun's light.

Crow gasps.

When I tear my gaze from the stars to look at her, I see her hands are glowing. A dot on her left palm. Three on her right. A thin line around her wrist like a bracelet.

I take a step closer. "Crow?"

She unfastens her coat with trembling hands, shrugs it off, and lets the leather fall to the ground. The glowing marks continue up her arms, more circles, with rings around rings around dots. Big circles around bigger circles. Small dots in lines.

"They look like… navigational maps," I say, stepping even closer to her, reaching a hand up to touch the beautiful glow.

Crow flinches. I pull my hand back, as if burned. Still, I can't help but stare. It's as if the maps I saw on Hardi's ship are printed on her skin. They glow the way a hologram would, shimmering bioluminescent lines written on flesh.

"No shit," says Crow, grabbing the hem of her long shirt. She rips it off in one swift motion, apparently impervious to the cold, her radiance breaking the darkness.

"Tau, turn that light off," I tell my bot, and he goes dark.

In an instant, Crow's brightness doubles. Her marks glow with a light even Tau can't emit; concentrated concentric circles stretch around large and small dots on her chest, connecting with the dotted and dashed lines that cover her stomach and continue around her back. They both reach as far up as her neck and push down under the band of her pants.

Crow pulls the waistband away from her body, seeing for herself how far down the marks go. She lets it snap back into place and holds out her hands for examination, staring intently at one wrist, then the other. She touches the smoothness of her stomach, dimming the marks there for just a second. Her mouth is agape.

"My face?" she asks.

I shake my head. "No. None there."

"Are you a traveler?" Says an unfamiliar voice, male, high but masculine, rising from the darkness like a breeze from once-stagnant air.

Crow looks at me, and I back at her.

"Who's there?" Crow lifts her hands as if ready for a fight. Confidence replaces her delicate beauty, her strong, lean muscles going taut in sharp contrast with the smooth circles on her skin. What does her body remember that she can't?

"No idea." I keep my voice low, trying and failing not to sound as panicked as I actually am. "Tau, light!"

"Do you need a beacon?" the voice asks. Before we can reply, a flashlight flickers on. "I apologize. I thought you had one."

The man standing before us is a prince.

A very ragged one: tall, rail-thin, and pale as mayonnaise. A drab velvet hat perches on his dust-coated blond hair and frayed satin robes drape from his wiry frame. The robes must have been regal and lush once; now they're tattered and threadbare, his body so frail that I can see his ribs. The mud on his pants is so thickly caked, it's as if this ruined prince trudged through a swamp to get to us. Or maybe it's more passive than that: the mud spreads up his side and back, as if he'd been sitting in it for years.

He holds a large floodlight, the kind Uncle used to check on the fields at night, when he thought something might be getting into the corn. The torch blazes with power. As the newcomer takes a step closer, I finally get a look at his face. While her looks young, as young as we are—well, as young as Crow's meant to be—his face is as battered as the rest of him: gaunt, pale, and smeared with dirt. But he's smiling—smiling with the eagerness of a dog whose master has returned home just after he'd given up all hope.

"Are you a traveler?" he repeats, looking at Crow. He doesn't seem at all bothered by the sight of her standing half-naked in the street, or the glow that emanates from her skin.

"I don't quite know." Crow juts her chin at him. "Why? Are you?"

"No, no." He seems confused by the question, as if the answer is evident. "I only ask because of your markings. I've never seen that on a guest before."

"A guest?"

"A guest of the enchanted forest," he says with a smile. "I am Prince Florian. Greetings, dear travelers. You must be tired and hungry. Let me host you for the night in my castle."

"Your what?" Guys who have castles don't wander around theme parks covered in mud, asking young women if they need a place to stay.

"My castle." He gestures back down the path. "We don't have many guests anymore. I am sorry to say we haven't had time to prepare for your visit. But no matter! I will put my staff to it right away!"

Crow and I share a look, but the prince is already striding away, without waiting for our response. His joints must be incredibly painful, because he lets out a creak with every step he takes away from us, the sound dimming as the distance grows. His back is so coated in mud that if it were frosting, he could have coated ten wedding cakes.

"What do we do?"

"I say we follow the prince." Crow scoops up her clothes. "If there's food, then I'll go anywhere."

"What about Gleïa's warning?" My stomach rumbles, but I can't give in. Some survival senses are stronger than others. "She said anyone could be working for Eve: it could be a trap. We can't trust a strange guy just because he claims to have food."

"True, a random guy claiming to be a prince isn't entirely right in the head." Crow lets out a heavy sigh, shaking her head even as she pulls her shirt back over it. "That's one hell of a long wait for a trap to spring. From the looks of him, he's been taking a mudbath for a century. I say we follow him and if anything seems fishy, we've got each other's backs, right?"

"He could be like the other droids back at the Universe of Food, you know." I shudder. My skin is already starting to show the bruises the droids inflicted, and the ache reaches down to my bones. I don't want to go through that ever again. I'm not made to fight.

"Then I punch him, and you work your ginny magic. Good?"

I nod. It's a good compromise. "Stay alert."

"Stay alert," she agrees.

We catch up to the prince, who's now marched straight into the dark thicket of trees. He's not hard to find: his light is the brightest thing around, and his pace is slow.

There's an old brick road in the forest, weeds pushing through the cracks. We follow Florian down the unnecessary zig-zags. Crow reaches for my hand, and I take it without hesitation, feeling reassuring warmth flood through my skin.

The forest opens into a clearing. The break in the trees reveals an actual castle—albeit one the size of a house, with forced perspective to make it look larger than it really is. It's straight out of a storybook, with walls of chiseled white stone and high, vaulted windows. The flags that drape over the large wooden doors certainly need some love: like the stranger, time has not been kind to them, tearing large gashes in the fabric.

Florian turns off his light and pushes open the door. A gust of stale air rushes against my face, a mix of mildew and fresh pine. In an instant, the entire palace comes to life: fake torches in their sconces light themselves, as does a roaring fire in the old stone fireplace.

Unlike the park, this room has been spared time's ruthless touch. The plush couches near the fire beckon our sore, tired frames. There's barely any dust on them or the heavy carpets on the stone floor. Portraits hang on the wall: the prince's painting is right in the middle, above the roaring fire, showing him in his mud-less glory.

"Ah, my family's ancestral home," says the prince, waving his hands wide. "It has been quite a long while."

"Oh? Where have you been?" asks Crow, gazing longingly at the fire, then back at our host with a little apprehension. Her skin has suddenly lost its glow, as if switching off a light.

"In the ditch down the path. I had no guests to invite over, so I waited."

"You waited… in the ditch. And how long has it been?"

"About six-thousand, five-hundred and fifty-six days," he says, oh-so-casually, making his way to the sofas that are angled around the large fireplace.

Crow meets my gaze, apparently as baffled as I am. This prince is no prince at all: the mud, the frail frame, the years of solitude… this prince is another droid. A programmable host.

But the droids I've met so far have nothing on him. He's an authentic, flesh-and-bone droid—well, synthetic flesh-and-bone, but still fiercely real—like I've been dreaming of meeting my entire life. He talks like a human, thinks like a human, *thinks* he's a human. It's the pinnacle of engineering, the kind of science worthy of being confused with magic.

"Florian," I say, putting a hand on his shoulder. The skin is cold under his tattered robes, a little damp. "Thank you so much for your hospitality. We won't impose on you long."

"It's my absolute pleasure," he says, plucking my hand gently off his shoulder and planting a kiss on my fingers. Even knowing he's a droid, the gesture sends butterflies fluttering in my stomach. It's the first time I've been kissed. And it's by a *droid.*

"*To Sleep,*" I said softly, gazing into his eyes as deeply as I can. "*I give my powers away; My will is bondsman to the dark.*"

The prince falls heavily into the cushions of the couch.

"What did you do?" Crow dashes forward, taking one look at him before plopping herself down on the ground in front of the blazing fire. "Are you a hypnotist?"

"He's a droid," I say, unable to take my eyes from him. *It,* I should have said, but it feels so wrong when his face is so real. "I used one of Tennyson's key cues on him. There is no Prince Florian."

Tau drifts up close to Formerly-Florian's frozen features, letting out a small beep of understanding. I shoo him away.

"Oh. He's just part of the park, then? Like the creepy little tykes that attacked us earlier?"

"He was probably abandoned when they shut the place down, most likely. How he survived—what, twenty years?—alone out here, I have no idea."

"And he just kept on going, thinking he's some kind of prince and waiting to lure fair maidens to his castle?" She chuckles. "A little iffy, don't you think? What's to say he won't try to rip us apart like the other ones did?"

"I think his narrative arc stops him. The little creepy ones were guarding their ride, but he… he just wants to continue the story."

"And you know this… how?"

"I like robots. I've been reading about these places since I was a kid. I always wanted my aunt and uncle to take me to a park like this, but they said no."

"Why? Because theme parks all like this? Creepy, with dead robot Don Juans running around?"

"No," I say. "Mainly because I wasn't allowed to leave the moon. Then there was the question of crowds, both in the park and in the ship, and anyone could see my face."

"See your face? What's wrong with your face?"

And then, with a resolution I didn't know I had in me, I blurt out my truth. "Because I'm some kind of genetic freak and my face is the same one as Princess Jo'Niss's—the dead princess of our universe—and so people would recognize me on sight as an illegal clone. But that's neither here nor there."

Why-oh-why did I say that? Throwing out rule one again? Maybe because Crow is the only person who truly does not—cannot—care. I thought letting the words spill out would make me feel lighter, better, but Crow blinks, uninterested. Yeah, that didn't help at all.

"Now that's a can of worms," she says. "Anyway. You shut the prince off with your knowledge of theme parks? Why didn't you try that on the freaks that tried to kill us?"

I push aside the hurt, staring into the fire instead. Huh, that's what I get for trying to open up to a stranger. Still, she did say she didn't want drama. "He's a *Tennyson* model. Tennyson always makes his models inhuman underneath the clothes, to discourage them from being passed off as real people. Just a little precaution he put in place so no one would try to… sully his creations."

She makes a face. "Still doesn't explain your magical knowledge of droid key words. Or why you couldn't do this to the eighty-odd creepy singing dolls who tried to kill us."

"Tennyson likes Tennyson." I find myself grinning. For once, I'm the one who knows things and who gets to show off. "All of his key-cues are from *In Memoriam*. The pint-droids weren't as sophisticated, probably not even made by the same engineer."

"This Tennyson sounds like a prick," she scoffs. "And who designs droids with such an easy shut-off system? What keeps randos from shouting out poetry and having droids shut down constantly?"

My attention's piqued; she's got a point. I've never questioned the fact that the droids all have the same, easy-to-remember key-cues. I'd read about them in an ancient Tennyson manual Auntie gave me. She bought me every book on the man, feeding my obsession. She loved how much I loved robotics.

Pushing away how much I miss her, I do my best to focus. I assumed—until now—that anyone could get their hands on the book Auntie gave me … but maybe not? Is it possible she—unknowingly, of course—gave me access to knowledge about Tennyson's commands that most people don't have?

Surely not. That's ridiculous. A book like that wouldn't randomly be for sale on Nesworth. Still… I wonder.

"Nothing," I say slowly, still pondering this "Nothing's stopping them."

Crow raises an eyebrow. But she must see or sense what kind of state I'm in because she changes the subject rather than asking me to elaborate. "So, what now?"

"I dunno," I say, trying not to dwell on the old Tennyson books in my shed, or on Auntie, for that matter. "He mentioned having food?"

"*Prince Florian* mentioned having food," Crow says, holding up a lone index finger as if to scold. "It could just be—what did you say? *Part of his narrative arc?*"

"True. Maybe we need to wake him up again."

"No," she groans. "I don't quite like him. Something shifty in him."

"He seemed, I don't know, charming."

"A little *too* charming, if you ask me." Crow turns to stare into the fire. "A little too on-the-nose delightful."

"Well, usually the original droid under the narrative is still able to communicate. The one without the storybook personality. Maybe if I can wake just that part of him, he can find us some grub."

"You work your ginny magic," she says as she pulls her legs up onto the couch along with her, mucky boots and all. "I'll just stay here."

She holds her hands in front of the fire, staring at them. She flips them over, again and again. Palm. Knuckles. Palm. Knuckles. Her marks are still gone, as if they'd never been there to start with.

"For words," I say, turning away from Crow and staring into the prince's cold, dead eyes, drawing up the verse from the back of my mind. *"Like Nature, half reveal, and half conceal the Soul within."*

His eyes flare with life, miniature suns—bright enough to take me by surprise—as he boots back up. He looks at me for a second and they dim again, like he's mildly shocked to see me, then he shakes his head as if trying to rid himself of a bad dream. His hands lift ever-so-slowly to his face, his palms pressing into his eyes, pushing out the artificial sleep.

"Gah," he groans, loudly. "My joints, they're so…" He pauses, raising a hand, moving his arm forward and back, making the elbow squeak. It's even worse than his knees.

"You need some oil, don't you?" I say, cringing at the sound.

"Yes." He pinches the bridge of his nose between a thumb and forefinger. "That wall over there. If you pull the second torch from the left, it will open a supply cupboard. You should find some in there. Oh, if you are hungry, there should be some shelf stable rations. Unless someone has come back to take them."

Food. My stomach gurgles in excitement. "Got it!"

Crow's been ignoring us—right up 'til the mention of food. She flies to her feet, beats me to the sconce, and pulls the torch. Lo and behold, the wall fizzles out of existence, nothing more than a convincing hologram.

The storeroom behind has none of the theming. It's nothing but shelves, stacked full of silver packages. There's a tub of joint lubricant, which I pull down as Crow grabs a shiny mystery pack of food and greedily rips it open.

I stack the vat on top of a box of meal packets and haul them back to the fireside all in one go, because screw it if I'm going to make two trips across the cold castle floor. I slide the lubricant to the prince.

"Yum," Crow shouts from the fireside. "PB&J!"

More mysterious words. "What?"

"Peanut butter and jelly? What, have you never had a PB&J before?"

"We don't have peanut butter on Nesworth," I say. "It's one of those imports that costs way too much to get."

"Damn, girl," she says, tossing me the sandwich. Caught off guard, I only just have enough time to throw out my hands and grab the thing before it hits the floor. "Eat it. Everyone should experience this at least once in their lives."

"How do you even know if you've had one before?" I ask, and Crow glares at me, taking out another silver packet of shelf-stable food.

"In my mind, it's something everybody's had. So, I must have, at some point. The flavor isn't new to me."

"That sucks," I say. "if I ever lost my memory, I'd hope to get to experience the things I love for the very first time all over again. This kind of defeats the purpose."

"Well, then I hope you never lose your memory," says Crow, cold again.

I take a bite of the sandwich, and yes, it's good. But it isn't anything to lose my mind over. I'm so hungry that I don't really care, and Crow doesn't seem to want validation, so I'm glad to not have to give it.

"Are you all right back there, Florian?" I toss the empty wrapper back in the box and scoot over to where the prince is sitting, narrowly avoiding the clots of mud that cover his sofa. The stuff peels off him as he rubs the oil over his joints.

"Florian was my character's name." He puts the lid back on the lube and rolls it shut. "But yes. Thank you for your help."

"Oh? Sorry. What's your original name, then?"

"I don't think I have one," he says, finally meeting my gaze. His electric-blue eyes are brimming with life. If I hadn't seen him shut off minutes ago, it would be easy to believe he's fully human. "I have a serial number, but it is not exactly colloquial."

I nod. "I'm Dora. This here is Crow. Thanks a bunch for having us for the night. We're just passing through, so we'll be out of your hair soon."

"You are not an imposition," he replies. "It's been quite a while since this park has seen visitors."

"Yeah, looks that way."

"Where are you headed?" he asks, his face lighting up. "Maybe I can be of service!"

"The Technomage Superius," says Crow, waving her hands mystically in the air. "Dude supposedly can fix any problem you've got."

"Really?" The droid lets out a howl of excitement. "How fantastic! I know the man. He is my creator!"

"The Technomage Superius is Tennyson?" My heart surges so fast in my chest I feel like it might jump out of my mouth. "*The* Sylas Ignasi Tennyson?"

Crow scoffs. "Please. Didn't you *just* say he's been dead a few hundred years?"

Realization hits, sending my heart plummeting. Of course. I'm not the only person infatuated with Tennyson's designs. I'd been so excited to see a Tennyson-model droid that I forgot how patents worked. The Mage is most likely just another student of Tennyson's work.

"We all just call him *Father*," says the prince, and he shrugs an actual *shrug*—a lovely little detail his creator wrote into his personality matrix. The prince might not have been made by Tennyson himself, but his programmer is a comparable artist. "He will be able to repair my protocols, I just know it. He will make me whole again."

"Wait, what's wrong with you?" asks Crow, turning to stare at him with squinting, shifty eyes. "You seem fine to me, especially now that you're not, you know, lying in a ditch somewhere."

I cringe. You can't just ask someone what's wrong with them. Even I know that.

"I am without purpose," he says, unperturbed. "As Florian, I was a prince. I wanted to make all feel welcome—oof, did I really speak like that? I was built to love, but now I have no idea what that even means. Without Florian's personality, I cannot feel complete. I am nobody, I am no one. I am Nemo."

My heart breaks for the droid who has none. But I stop myself: I don't need anyone else slowing me down on the way to the Mage. I've already wasted too much time here.

But this isn't a person—he's a *droid*. A Tennyson model droid. Strong, smart, and with a personal connection to the Mage. Not to mention, this might be the only time I get to pick the brain of a digital man. And one who seems so alive at that.

"Well," I say, "it *would* be good to have a droid around. What do you think, Crow?"

"A droid with an existential crisis?" says Crow. "What could possibly go wrong? But then again, we might need the protection." Her shrug turns into a nod.

I let out a resounding *whoop* in my head. If nothing else comes out of this slag misadventure, at the very least I'll be able to say I met a Tennyson droid.

"Did you say protection?" Nemo frowns.

"We're being chased by a woman named Eve," I say, "or at least, we're in her sights."

"Eve?" He tilts his head.

"The Technowitch of Dusk," says Crow. "Dora killed her sister, Night, and accidentally stole Night's magic locket. Now, Eve wants her dead."

Nemo lets out a low whistle. His programming is exquisite, his every reaction a symphony. I want to tell him random things and watch how he reacts to them. I'm too enamored with his face to worry about him dumping us before we even leave.

"We'll leave at dawn?" he asks.

"Fine by me," says Crow. She stretches out in front of the fire, and within seconds she's already asleep.

I should get some sleep, too. But while my mind is light-years away on a little moon in the middle of nowhere, on a farm that may not still be standing, I can't tear my eyes away from the silent droid.

13

MY NIGHT IS RESTLESS. I SLEEP—OR RATHER, attempt to sleep—on the couch by the fire. My dreams quickly turn to nightmares of my family in agony. I wake, sweating, believing for a moment I'm at home in my own bed and this nightmare was nothing but just that, a nightmare, that Auntie will run in and embrace me and tell me it's all a bad dream.

But Auntie never comes, leaving me sitting in the dark in my new reality. The first thing I'm going to do when I see her—*if* I see her again—is sob into her shoulder and tell her that she was right: the universe is a cruel place and I should never have doubted her. But even if I ever do return, nothing will be the same. If my family even *is* alive. And, if they are hurt, or worse, dead, it will be all my fault.

So, I sit here, awake, staring at the ceiling, jumping from one terrible thought to another. I need home, yearn for it, but it's no longer the place I left this morning. I'm not the same person who left this morning. I'm a murderer.

I fall back on the couch, rolling on my side so the fire can keep me warm. All that's left are glowing embers. Across from me is Nemo, the Tennyson model droid, the closest I've ever been to meeting a celebrity. The peak of robotics I'm dreaming of reaching one day. Being in his presence is like soaking up starlight.

"Still awake?" he asks, and I almost jump out of my skin. Of course: he doesn't need sleep. "Having trouble sleeping?" His voice is calm, quiet enough to not wake up Crow.

I nod.

Tau nudges me nervously. The poor little guy has no idea what's going on anymore. Everything is beyond the scope of his programming. I reach up to pat his plastic form reassuringly before turning back to Nemo.

"You're in rags," I say, as my eyes adjust to the low light. His pale skin looks gray, old and barely alive, though his eyes burst with life. Unlike him, the rags he's wearing haven't withstood the test of time: years of water and sun damage have weakened the fabric making it brittle to the touch, so his every movement rips the material. "Will you let me help you?"

"You need your sleep," says Nemo.

"It's too late for that now. Please, let me help you."

The two of us silently raid the storeroom. Luckily, it once held changes of clothes for the staff, all nicely protected from the elements, so Nemo has something to wear—even if it is a bright green T-shirt with the park's logo on it and loose-fitting khakis.

"How do I look?" he asks, turning around. "Passing for fully human?"

I can't hide the awe I felt simply being in the presence of a true artificial intelligence, and the more time I spend with Nemo, the more the lines between human and technology blur. I have a hard time believing that his personality left though when I wiped the prince's engram from his digital brain. He almost seems conscious. At the very least, he looks more human than most people I know.

Then again, I don't know many people.

More than Crow, at least.

She wakes soon after with the sun, grunts, grabs her bag, and that's enough to let us know she's ready to go. I still haven't put my thumb on what exactly her problem is but still don't care enough to ask. Whatever's on Crow's mind probably has to do with there being little else in there with it.

We stuff a bag with shelf-stable rations and we're off, marching out of the dying park together, Tau proudly drifting ahead. The little bot glides along the asphalt road out and away from the theme park through the dry and dusty valley. The sun is barely up over the mountains, but it's already scorchingly hot outside, though we're somewhat protected by a layer of clouds. There are no fields like where I'd first landed. Instead, it's arid and dry like the un-terraformed sections of Nesworth. The old road is straight and narrow through this desert, leading to rolling hills and mountains that never seem to get closer no matter how far we trudge. There's nothing but the Enchanted Forest around for kilometers. The expanse looks endless, but it's nothing new to me: beyond the fields of Nesworth there isn't much to see either. What's different from home is actually seeing a destination in the distance.

With Crow determined not to speak unless spoken to, and Nemo not programmed to fill silence with words, the walk is a quiet one. It doesn't bother me: my mind is filled with diagrams and plans for how I could create a brain like Nemo's. Not that I can: a technowitch like Gleïa could, and maybe one day I could gain enough skill to be considered a ginny, but unless I can make it to university, there's no chance I can ever reach that level.

Thoughts of university lead to thoughts of Uncle, of my Auntie and cousins, and my heart sinks again.

"This is pointless," Crow says, after what might have been hours.

"What is?" I ask.

"Following this stupid road." She throws her arm toward the dusty expanse. Very dramatic for someone who's been asleep for three centuries. "I mean, look. We can see where we need to go. The city is that way. So, let's go that way."

Tips of Anchor's skyscrapers break their peaks above the distant hills where she's pointing. But the road we're on seems to pull to the left before swinging back toward the hills. What Crow's suggesting would cut kilometers from our trek.

"Tempting." My hand flutters to the locket around my neck, my thumb tracing the smooth silver surface. "But Gleïa said not to leave the path, or her sister would be after us. I think staying on the main road must somehow hide me from her."

Crow raises an eyebrow. "Is that really what she said? Because it sounds to me like her sister is after the locket, and I'm not the one wearing it."

"Oh, come on," I say. "You don't really want us to split up, do you?"

Crow lifts the corner of her lip in a sly half grin. "I'm going this way. You're free to follow."

She steps off the path and onto the dirt beyond. One foot, then the next. Nothing happens. "You see? The path is more like a guideline. You don't have to follow the whole thing if you know where you're going."

Nemo says nothing but follows Crow. Lightning doesn't rain down from the sky to smite him, either.

"We probably should stick to the path," I say, repeating what my gut is already screaming at me. "I'm all for shortcuts, but Gleïa said…"

"Gleïa this, Gleïa that," snaps Crow, "are you really going to take advice from the woman who forgot me in a cornfield?"

"She's the only person who cared to help me since I got here." I clutch the locket tighter. I barely know the technowitch, but I do know her a whole lot better than I know Crow. A whole hour or so better.

"Have it your way," Crow turns on her heel and storms away in the direction of the distant city.

"Meet you on the road?" I ask, but if she answers, her words are swept away by the wind.

I don't like how my gut sinks as she leaves.

Nemo glances at her, then back at me. I let out a heavy sigh. "You can go with her, you know," I say half-heartedly. "Eve isn't after you either."

"All the more reason I should probably stay with you," he says, "since you are the one in need of most assistance."

My heart swells. The droid, the logical mind, is choosing me. "Is that you talking, or Florian?"

"I am unsure," he says with a slow blink, "but it feels right. In here." He presses two fingers to his sternum and steps back onto the road.

We walk together down the road, and the wind picks up slightly. I shiver, zip up my spark coat. Crow is ahead of us, making a drone-line for Anchor, her trajectory slightly at an angle from ours, so that while we seem to be walking parallel, every time I look over, she's a little bit farther away. When the wind blows, I see her pull her leather jacket tighter, too.

I know I'll see her on the other side. She can't be leaving us for good, she just can't. It's not like I need her—I have Nemo now, rational, Tennyson-brained Nemo—but I'm uneasy without her, and I don't know why.

I decide to make small talk. Nemo is a cheerful companion when prompted, and I fill him in on both our stories. His own life is less exciting than expected: built to fill a role in the park, he was Florian for almost a century before the place shut down, and he was left behind. He doesn't know why—something about war expenditures, but if there was a war with the Outer Zone, I've never heard of it.

What scares me is that the park has been closed for at least six-thousand, five-hundred and fifty-six days, according to Nemo. And even that rough division puts the date of its closure nearer to my birthday than I'm comfortable with.

I glance over to the desert. I can't see Crow anymore. All of a sudden, I'm filled with a dread that I can't name. I scan the horizon for her—the wind picks the dust up, causing a low haze so thick that I can't see through it. And while I know I should feel safe with Nemo around, as I get to know him and the border between what is droid and what is human blurs, so does my unwavering confidence.

I need to stop anthropomorphizing him.

"Nemo," I say. "I don't like Crow being alone in this weather."

He scans the horizon as well. "The weather is changing."

Tau zips up and down, visibly agitated.

The wind really is picking up now: the haze is becoming such that I can't see Anchor in the distance at all. I can't see anything other than the road before me. The hair on my arms bristles.

Nausea fills my gut. This feels too familiar, too fresh. It's just like the storm that swept me off Nesworth. It's been only a day and I'm going to have to weather another one, and this time, no ships are conveniently stashed nearby.

"We need cover." The locket grows colder against my skin, and heavier. Not good signs.

A gust sweeps up, ruffling Nemo's hair. He sniffs the air. "The pressure has dropped significantly since we left the Enchanted Forest."

Tau flits around my head like a little bird in a cage. I'm feeling the pressure drop, too. My heart is starting to race, the memory of my escape, Hardi's crew in pursuit, still raw and fresh in my mind.

"Nemo," I say. "Do you see anything?"

A drop of water plops down from the sky, heavy and hot. It hits the ground near the road, and the dust begins to sizzle. Tau lets out a high-pitched beep—practically a squeal of terror—before throwing himself into my hands. I catch him and stuff him into the breast pocket of my spark coat just as more drops come down harder around us.

"Run!" I scream. I tear off like a quad up the road ahead. The dirt around us is sizzling, steam rising where every drop lands. If it can dissolve dirt, then what will it do to my skin? The sound is a thunderous roar that fills my ears and blocks out anything else.

But I don't have to run. The rain is coming down around us, but not on us: the drops break above my head, a clear tunnel of protection. There's no sense in running: we're already safe where we are.

The road is protecting us.

"Crow," I gasp, staring out into the wilderness. Somewhere out there, she's in the middle of this. She's going to die in the wastes if I don't get her to safety.

"Stay on the road," says Nemo, before doing the opposite.

He's cool and composed, even as he runs, just as his maker intended. If he truly is a Tennyson model, he's programmed to protect human life at all cost.

But the weather doesn't care that he's on a rescue mission. The second the rain hits his skin, it sizzles and puckers, leaving red in its place. He's going to corrode into nothing if I let him go.

Then a thought wriggles through my mind, a totally unexpected thought, the kind of thought you have when staring into nothingness for too long, or when you've looked too hard at the meaninglessness of your own existence. I fully expect to be furious with Crow: here she is, properly dying, despite the fact we're meant to be protecting each other. But I'm feeling fear, a great and terrible fear, fear of losing this woman, a stranger who doesn't know or care about my face. Somehow, in this instant, I realize I don't want to ever be alone again.

Even if I don't particularly like her company, Gleïa was right: I don't want to walk this path alone. I need help if I ever want to get to the Mage. If I ever want to get home.

And I don't want to be without Crow.

I can't just wait here. I don't know much about myself outside of the scraps Jo'Niss left me, but I do know I don't want to be the kind of person who waits idly by when someone else is in danger. I shrug off my spark coat and throw it over my head. There: makeshift umbrella. My coat can handle anything thrown at it—sparks bounce right back, hot solder rolls right off, never leaving a mark—but I've never put it to the test with *acid* before.

I step out into the acid rain. And I start to run.

Nemo scoops me up in his arms before I can make it three steps. The locket around my neck burns with the heat of a thousand suns, but I can't rip it off. I cringe in pain.

"Stay on the road," he orders. "I cannot carry both of you safely!"

"You'll dissolve into sentient goop before you reach her!" I cry. "My coat!"

Awkwardly cradled in his thin arms, I try to shift the coat to cover him as well. I'm not thinking—not about myself, really—and my hands are exposed. But the burning never comes. I'm awestruck as the raindrops stop an inch above my skin, rolling off the air as if they've hit glass. Steam rises around my body as the rain simply refuses to stick.

The locket. The burning around my neck is nothing compared to what I would be experiencing if rain touches my skin. Gleïa had said it was a personal shield. For once in my life, I have the upper hand.

"Take the coat," I order Nemo, tossing it over his head. "We're saving Crow."

"I cannot—"

"I know it's not rational, but I'm going to save her, with your help or not. You can't make me stay."

"We have no time to argue," he concedes, and we run.

He carries me almost like a shield as we fly forward. The locket makes me invulnerable enough that, with his speed, I'm basically creating a forcefield around him as well. And while I can't see squat through the breaking raindrops, Nemo seems to know exactly where we're going, because we find Crow in mere minutes.

I hear her before I see her. She's screaming in agony, loudly enough to be heard over the roar of the rain. Nemo swings me on his back as we come upon her crumpled form. She's curled up in a ball, back toward the heavens, her leather jacket foaming under the rain. Her face is protected by her hands, which are bright and red, boils the size of coins taking over her flesh.

Nemo plucks her up like a sack of flour, placing her not-insignificant bulk against his chest, and starts to run again.

He holds my coat over her head, covering as much of her body as he can.

She lets out only the smallest of whimpers.

I've got one arm around his neck—he doesn't need to breathe, thank the Sisters—and one palm-down on his head, sharing whatever protection the locket gives me with his crown.

I never thought I would be so happy to see asphalt ever again. Relief washes over me when we step back onto the road and into a new forest. Nemo gently places Crow on the ground, then shakes me off his back, before allowing himself to collapse.

"Are you all right?" I don't know who to ask first. Crow is slowly unfurling, while Nemo stares blankly ahead.

"I must regenerate my essential functions," he says through gritted teeth. "The corrosive element was… a lot."

"Tell me about it," says Crow, panting, as if this is all in a day's work. She looks terrible: her hands are covered in boils, and her leather jacket is pretty much gelatin held together by zippers. "You could have told me you had alien skin."

Eyes still fixed on her, I tap the locket. If I can't get a thank you, then Crow won't get a verbal response. Though Nemo needs the bulk of our thanks.

"Friends," he says, before I can speak. He wipes the residual water from his arms, leaving behind trails of quickly fading red. He must have some killer regenerative cells if he can clear up this fast. "I think you should take a look at this."

I turn to where he's pointing, away from the forest and back into the desert. The horizon is still blurred by falling rain, but it seems to be tapering off now. We found shelter precisely as the storm was ending.

Or, the storm ended simply *because* we'd found shelter. Because, as the rain recedes, the clouds do not. And if I look closely enough—though it isn't difficult to read at all—letters glare brightly from their depths.

Return it to me.

"Return it to me." Crow turns to look at me. Not look— *glare*. It's a feature I'm beginning to think is permanently baked onto her face. "So that Eve lady wants the super immortality necklace back."

"It's not an immortality necklace," I snap, clutching it protectively. "It's a locket."

"That protects you from acid rain? And what else? Are you laser-proof as well?" Crow spits, holding out the backs of her hands for me to see. The boils are red and so full of pus they're at the point of bursting. I feel nauseous at the sight of them.

"I'm so sorry," I say. "But if you'd stayed on the road…"

"Is this really time for an *I told you so*?" She glowers, her eyebrows pulled so tightly together they're a single line. "God, I can't deal with anyone on this damn planet."

"I am sufficiently recovered," says Nemo. "All I am lacking now—if my database is correct—is a *thank you.*"

"Thank you, droid man, for saving my ass," says Crow. "Can we go now?"

The rain has stopped entirely, not that we need to worry now we're back on the road. I can't see anything through the trees above us. Their branches are tightly knit together, so closely bound, that the road only leads to more darkness.

It's a relief to be in a forest again. Even having grown up with trees few and far between, seeing them up and down and all around just feels right somehow.

"You're not glowing," I say suddenly to Crow, the realization hitting me square in the face. No bright eerie glow from the invisible lines of her skin. There's nothing but angry boils on her hard-calloused hands.

"Nope, I guess not," says Crow. She shrugs off the remains of her coat. The boils, thank the Sisters, seem limited only to her hands. And she's letting curiosity take over from her anger. "I guess it has to be nighttime."

"Starlight," says Nemo, gently inspecting the skin of her hands. "If those were traveler tattoos, it would be starlight that draws them out."

"So, you know what they are?" I ask.

"Yes."

Figures. While Nemo's programming is doubtless excellent, droids do not elaborate unless asked. Crow crosses her arms, taking her hands away from him and glaring. *"Then can ya tell me?"*

"Traveler tattoos," he says. "For people who follow the stars so far away, they know the only time they will return home will be in a coffin. Their homecoming and their funeral are celebrated together, in equal measure."

"That's gruesome," I mutter. Tau lets out a low, sympathetic tone from my pocket. "When did you learn to do that?" I open my coat to ask him, but the bot doesn't respond.

"What do they mean?" Crow asks Nemo.

"It's a map to your home system," he replies, "so that anyone who finds your body could get you home, even if they don't share your language."

Crow stares at her hands and clutches them into fists, hissing as the boils stretch. She opens them only to wipe her sweaty palms on her thighs, tracing marks down to her knees as she sighs. "I'm not a corpse quite yet."

"Was my answer not satisfactory?" asks Nemo.

"On the contrary. It was pretty fucking informative."

The air in the grove is heavy. Silent. I don't know if it's connected to the rain somehow, but it's so humid it feels like it's pressing down on me. Maybe it's because I can't see the sun through the trees.

In that instant, it pounces.

One moment, Crow was glaring at Nemo, bristling with frustration, and the next, I'm dangling in the air from a tree, trapped inside a net, the rope digging into the flesh of my arms. I don't even have the chance to scream.

My stomach churns as the net swings in small circles. There's a lump on the back of my head, and it aches, fogging my mind. I peer into the jungle's depth, seeing nothing in the darkness.

I reach for the locket, hoping for some kind of sign, but it's ice-cold. I don't know what I expect—that it can somehow warn me of impending danger, as it seemed to when the storm was brewing earlier? But the dead piece of jewelry hangs limply around my neck, no more mystical than the tip of my little finger.

As the net turns slowly, I catch sight of another body hanging from a tree. Blond hair sticks out through the woven contraption, the frail figure within still and silent.

"What in the void? Nemo!" I stick out the toe of my boot to brace myself against the tree and stop the spinning. My gut is writhing.

"Dora?"

"Yeah, hey. Is Crow here, too?"

The droid slowly wriggles around to face me. He's no worse for wear, but his face is carved with worry.

"I have not seen her. Are you injured?"

"I don't think so. What happened to us?"

"We were abducted, though I surmise you guessed as much. By whom? No clue."

I groan in frustration. I have to stay focused, rational. Panic won't get us anywhere, but it's proving impossible to convince my body otherwise. Ropes and nets don't have wires and gears. They can't be tricked into helping me escape.

My chest buzzes, sending a wave of relief washing through me. "Tau?"

The bot chirps what could be either a confused jingle or a birthday song. It doesn't sound much like he has any idea what's happening either.

The net presses tightly against my body. I have my foot jammed against the tree to stop the spinning as I fight to wriggle Tau out of my coat. He slips out of the net to sweet freedom.

The dark forest is silent. If there were birds before, they don't make a sound now. The bot hovers between me and the droid, glowing softly.

"So, um, any idea how we get out of here?" I say, eyes fixed on Nemo. He doesn't look worried at all, his face stoic as a statue. Still, he's used to remaining motionless for years on end—life imprisoned in a net is closer to his default setting than the frenetic activity of our past day. "Do we even know where here is?"

"We are approximately one-mile northeast of our initial position," Nemo said, "according to my internal GPS. However, I am not quite sure how accurate it is after all these years."

"Not that far, then," I shudder. We're off the path, making us vulnerable to Eve, whether or not she's working with whoever put us in these nets. And Crow has either been taken somewhere else or has outright abandoned us. Lovely.

Eve will do anything to get her locket back and won't stop at killing me. Now that she has an idea of where I am, I bet she's sent her people after me—if she even has people? Maybe she's hired someone to take me off the path, serve me up on a platter ripe for the Technowitch's plucking. I clutch the cold locket tightly in my fist. It might just be a hunk of mysterious metal, but it's all I have right now.

Or maybe this has nothing to do with the locket at all: maybe someone knows who I am.

"Might I suggest we call for help," says Nemo, interrupting my terrible thoughts, "as I am unable to be of much assistance?"

"But whoever took us will know we're awake, won't they?"

"We are stuck, so we need to change the parameters of our situation. Either we get help, get ignored, or our captor comes back. Any which way, we will be more informed."

"Fine. CROW! Anyone! Help!" I scream, but the forest remains empty and silent. I squint into the darkness, but there's no movement in the trees, no sounds to track. We're completely and utterly alone.

Tau nudges my shoulder and lets out a low, sad tune. It's been a year since I last opened his casing and tweaked him, but all this time, his program has been learning and growing on its own. Can Tau *feel* empathy now? Is he as scared as I am?

My net shakes as the branch that holds me trembles. Heavy footsteps approach. I shoot a terrified glance at Nemo, who stares, eyes wide in shock, at what emerges from the darkness and stands before us.

At full height, the creature must be over three meters from the base of its giant furry paws to the top of its mane. Like the lions of First Earth, everything about it screams vicious ferocity. Every centimeter of it, face, muzzle, and body alike, is covered in a short gray fur. Its mane is thick, made up of stiff quills and tied back from its face with coarse rope. It wears body armor on its lower half, a utility belt strapped around its hairy waist, and a gun the size of a small tree is lashed on its back. Its feet are large, padded paws, bare despite the rest of the armor. Every muscle ripples as it breathes.

But its face is the most terrifying thing of all. Human eyes stare out from lion flesh. A beast ripped right out of legend.

An ocugry.

Years ago, when the Sister Systems had yet to unify, the colonists of First Earth needed a way to keep the peace. Scientists brought the genetic material they needed from their home planet to recreate its biomes. A group of them manipulated the gene fragments to their own designs. Hence the ocugry, among others—hybrid beings made from Earth's fiercest beasts and its strongest soldiers. Supposedly the best of the best.

There had been a war, a terrible war, the only war since the Exodus that I knew of. In the aftermath, the ocugry gained their own independent world, and hybridization was banned. It was the same genetic war that made the use of clone batching techniques illegal.

Two centuries later, the ocugry are mainly self-governed. They have a home planet, laws, schools. But they are still a military society and rent their soldiers out to the highest bidder. You can't get a better army than that made of creatures bred for war, trained to fight until their last breath, their bodies weapons of controlled destruction. Though a single ocugry can take down an entire mob, they work— hunt—in packs, each pack enough to keep a rebellious colony under control.

If one is here, there must be more. Odds are they're working for someone powerful—like the Technowitch of Dusk.

Then Crow strides up right behind it, arms crossed over her chest. And the creature starts sobbing, mewling like an injured kitten, its hands pressed against its eyes. It wipes its huge hairy hands across its face, eyelids squeezed shut, to stop the well of tears from streaming down.

What the void?

I press my face against the netting, straining for a closer look. I must be hallucinating: the creature from my nightmares is bawling like a baby.

"Nice net work," coos Crow, and the beast stifles a sob. She looks perfectly healthy, except for the bright red boils from the rain. "No, I mean it. I don't think anyone could have strung up people as quickly as you did. You can stop crying, you know."

It only sobs harder. Crow cautiously reaches up to pet the creature's hairy back. This only seems to make it sob, somehow, impossibly, louder.

This is the beast Auntie and Uncle had warned me would tear me to shreds at the sight of my face?

"Stop making a scene," says Crow. "I'm sure both of your victims find you terrifying and were impressed by your show of force capturing them. Weren't you, Dora, Nemo?"

My eyes meet Crow's, and her look isn't helping make any more sense of the situation. Crow is expectant, apparently waiting for me to say something. She keeps shaking her head in the direction of the beast, the same way Auntie used to do when she wanted me or Uncle to pay attention to a cousin.

"So, so terrified, you have no idea," I say. "I thought I was going to die up here."

"You see? You made her think she was going to die. You are a powerful beast. I would offer to have you talk about what's bothering you, but seeing as how you just kidnapped and almost killed my two closest allies, I don't really have the patience for an emotional heart-to-heart."

The beast sniffles. "Just kill me now. Put me out of my misery. I am a failure."

"You want to die?" Crow asks. Of all the things, the beast *nods*. "Fine. I'll kill you, just as soon as you bring Dora down, all right?"

"You mean it?" The voice is soft, like runny honey. It has a rumble to it, like the beast is speaking with its stomach, from somewhere deep, deep inside. It sounds warm. It doesn't fit at all with what I'd expected—something military, sharp and cruel.

The thing is a mountain all to itself. I shiver as its massive hands, each larger than my torso, reach up to loosen the knots that hold up my net. It lowers me gently to the ground, depositing me in my net at the base of the tree.

"What even was your plan?" says Crow. Now that the beast is no longer a sobbing mess, it's beginning to look terribly intimidating and a lot more like the stories I've been told. "For us, I mean."

"I wasn't planning on hurting them," it mumbles, fumbling awkwardly with the knots still. I sit deathly still, in case a brisk move means death. "I was going to use them to barter my way off this hellish planet. But failing to capture humans is the ultimate show of cowardice."

"What's that? Can't even keep a girl hostage? Despicable, you coward. Despicable."

"Don't taunt the thing!" I angle myself closer to the tree that holds Nemo. But the beast is cowering in the presence of Crow.

"Why not? It needs to be ashamed of what it is. An ocugry that cannot fight."

I shoot her a look of terror. Crow only shrugs. The girl has a death wish.

"I mean, it's an educated guess," she says. "It has no idea who or what we are. Target or civilian? Its HUD is obviously down. That's how I managed to get the upper hand in the first place. He was a pushover. Tell me, ocugry, did I hit the nail on the head here?"

It must feel awful inside Crow's head. Knowing details of the ocugries' creation and purpose, and not of her own life. Even I don't know any of this about the beasts.

"Yes," it grunts, "and no. My HUD was damaged when we landed here. It was a pit stop, not an away mission, but we were ambushed with weaponry, the likes of which I'd never seen before. My pack must have got the reading I was dead."

"Your pack left without you."

"Their HUDs must have displayed me as KIA," it says, "but as you see, I am very much still alive. Not that it matters. When one of my kind is disconnected, they may as well be dead. Death is preferable to life outside our unit."

"Why don't you just, I don't know, shoot up a flare or something?" I ask. It takes all my courage just to address the thing.

Maybe I'm feeling pity for it after all—abandoned on a planet far from everything it's ever known? Oddly relatable. But the calm I'm starting to feel in its presence is scaring me more than the beast is, and I tense back up. "Aren't ocugry known for their stubbornness? Never giving up and so on?"

"Easier to do when your HUD has instructions for you." The beast towers over us, yet Crow stands tall by its side, chatting as if they're old farming buddies.

Then Crow starts… walking away. Tau drifts after her, then whirls to face me, emitting a low, sad beep.

"You coming?" asks Crow, not turning back to check. "I didn't go through all that just for you to sit back and admire my backside."

"Wait, we're leaving? Just like that? What about Nemo?"

"Well, yeah," says Crow. "He's just a droid who caught feelings. The only reason he wanted to see the Technomage at all—*wanted* being a stretch, here—is because *we* gave him the idea. We're better off without him slowing us down." She turns back to the beast. "Ocugry, keep the toaster, it'll probably fetch you a pretty penny at market. Enough to get off this rock."

"Slowing us down?"

"Why do you insist on repeating what I say? Yes, slowing us down. We don't need him."

"He's our friend," I say.

She raises a bushy eyebrow. "Is he really? Because he is an *it* and doesn't give a shit about anything or anyone. Case in point, you both got captured."

"So, his programming's a little glitchy, but that doesn't mean he's not useful. Since when does usefulness determine whether or not you let someone get kidnapped?"

"I don't know, since we're on a quest?"

"A what?"

Crow rolls her eyes, still marching forward, pumping her arms like a sullen toddler. I turn around, forcing her to follow me back. "You know, a quest! I mean, it's either that or a very long, purpose-driven hike. Have you ever read a fantasy book?"

I haven't since I was ten, after the princess had shown a sudden affinity for fantasy fiction. From then on it had all been tractor manuals, Tennyson textbooks, and Aunt's secret stash of hard, futuristic sci-fi she keeps under her bed.

"Do you want this Technomage to send you home, or not?"

Crow stops. Our eyes meet with such intensity I have to look away, my stomach tying in anxious little knots.

"Do you want to save your aunt and uncle and all those little cousins of yours, or the droid you met in a ditch, Dora? Because I don't see a way we can do both."

"You realize said droid is right there?" I gesture at the tree, where Nemo hangs silently in his net. I'm sure he can hear us, but he's not complaining. I'll complain for him. "This is the rudest crap I've ever heard."

"I am not offended," Nemo says. "I am incapable of taking offense."

"You hear that, Buttercup? The droid is incapable of taking offense."

The ocugry stomps its way between the clearing and us, blocking our way with its massive frame. It's a wall of solid muscle. "Now would be a good time to kill me, please."

"Hey," I say. "You tried to kidnap me. That's not cool."

"Well, I failed, and you probably want revenge. Why don't you drive the dagger through my heart?"

It hands me a long-curved blade from its hip. Crow takes it instead, twirling the weapon with no obvious intention of stabbing it through the beast's chest. Instead, she swings it high over her head and with a swift motion, slashes the rope that suspends Nemo from the tree. The droid crashes to the ground in a tangle of limbs and net, but doesn't utter a peep.

"You're not going to kill me?" The beast's voice is getting harsher now.

"I'd rather not," says Crow. "But I'll still keep the droid, which may or may not have its uses."

"Wait what?" I turn to the ocugry. "You really want to die?"

"I am a failure. I deserve to die."

Nemo stands, disentangling himself from the netting. He looks up at the beast, who is almost twice his height. "Hello there. My name is Nemo. You seem to be under some form of mental duress. Would you like me to play some soothing music?"

The beast glares down at Nemo, then turns back slowly to face me, lending Tau the smallest of glances as the little bot flits around it.

"Ah. My music library is corrupt. I'm sorry, I do not have any soothing music to play. I can sing, if you prefer?"

The ocugry sighs. "Both your friends are free. May I request the sweet release of death now?"

"You have been disconnected from your pack," says Nemo.

"A little late to the party, Nemo," I mutter.

"Are you going to slay me, or not?"

Crow clutches the hilt, sweat dripping onto the worn grip. She holds it confidently before her, the blade unwavering.

The beast strips off its body armor, exposing a dense network of muscles. "You might not have the strength to break the ribcage the first time," it says. "Just keep trying until you get through. I'll try not to move."

"All I mean to say is that there is the possibility of reconnection," Nemo interjects.

The beast drops the body armor, reaching instead for the droid. It lifts him by his neckline a good ten feet off the ground.

"What did you say, Metal?" it snarls. "You had better not be lying to me."

"We are heading to the Technomage Superius to ask for help," Nemo explains, unperturbed by his altitude. "Since the Mage provides most of the maintenance for ocugry HUDs, he should be able to help you, too. Dora is looking for a way off-planet as well."

Nemo flashes the beast a warm smile. He's been programmed as a host droid, after all, to keep the guests of his park happy no matter what. This programming must have stuck with him even after the prince persona was wiped clear, though how or why I don't know. Degraded pathways? I desperately want to figure it out. Between him and Crow, I have a case study. Maybe I could pick this topic for my thesis if I…

I freeze, mid thought. If I ever get home, I'll never leave Nesworth again. Nowhere is safe for a face like mine. I see that now.

The ocugry's face lights up. "So, there's a Technomage here?"

"A really good one," says Crow, "or so they say. He's going to get my memory back. And he's going to fix Nemo's programming. He can probably get you a ship, like he will for Dora."

Two seconds ago, Crow was ready to run a sword through the brute. Maybe some bolts knocked loose when it put the sword in her hand. Or maybe she wants an ocugry friend for herself. I don't know, but it's freaking me out.

I can see the benefit of having the beast as an ally, which is way better than having it as an enemy. Though with its blubbering and crying, I'm not quite sure what it—he?—is actually good for.

"We have to call you something other than ocugry," says Crow. "This here is Dora. He's Nemo, and I'm Crow."

"I am Nekkan, formerly of the 48th Battalion, Dispatch 6," says the beast. He lets out a heavy sigh. "My HUD is down. My brothers are no longer with me. I no longer have an assignment, a target. I don't know who is friend or foe."

"Isn't that for you to decide?" asks Crow.

"Not in my line of work. I obey orders. When I don't have orders to obey, I don't know what I'm meant to do."

"The Technomage should be able to help with that." Crow pats his hairy hand.

"I hope so," he says. "I've never been alone. It's not a feeling I enjoy."

"Well, we're here. We have the same mission—to seek out the Technomage Superius of the Outer Zone. We have the same goal—to ask him for our help. We have the same enemies—anyone who wants to stop us. The Technowitch of Dusk already tried to kill us for being allied with Dora. Isn't that enough of a mission for the time being?"

And then, Nekkan does something that baffles me more than the sobbing and pleas for death.

He *smiles.*

"That will do," he says, a growl rippling through his chest. "For the time being."

"Perfect, big guy," says Crow. "Let's go find this Mage. Together."

The beast nods vigorously. Crow squeezes his arm in response.

My anxiety is so high it's reaching orbit. This is the beast who's meant to terminate me. And he probably would have already, if his HUD was up. He kidnapped me as an easy hostage, not knowing who or what I was—would this alliance change if he did?

The creature hasn't recognized me yet, hasn't attacked me for my face. Compassion urges me to accept him into the fold, but part of me knows the second his HUD is working again, he will see me as the target I am.

I can't say anything, though. If I tip him off, I might as well be signing my own termination warrant. I'm stuck with him no matter what I do.

14

I WALK WITH TAU IN THE SHADOW OF THE ocugry, teetering between relief at having a shield and absolute terror of being found out. Nekkan cradles the gun in his arms, a weapon unlike anything I've ever seen before, larger than my own body. Part of me wants to touch it, to take it apart, to see how the killing machine contains so much power—but that isn't something you can ask of the most dangerous beast in the galaxy.

Now he has agency again, Nekkan can't stop smiling. The rows upon rows of titanium teeth are so unnerving, I keep up the rear just to avoid looking at that grin. This creature is shaped for battle: I don't want to think of the action he's already seen, the kidnappings that haven't ended well, the throats those teeth have ripped right through…

I've pictured my death at the hands of his kind so many times before. It's hard to get the images out of my head.

But, whenever I try to focus on something else, my thoughts flow back to the plan I need to enact: Step one, get to the Technomage. Step two, go home. Step three, save my family.

Easy when you put it that way.

I don't dare think of what comes next. What if, Sisters forbid, I reach home and they're in trouble? What do I do then? Turn myself in to bounty-hunting thugs so I can save them?

And, even if I do miraculously make it back to my family and find them safe, I'll never be able to leave Nesworth again. I'll be forced into a life with Tobis, a brood of children at my feet. In order to stay safe, I'll have to put myself back in a cage. And that isn't going to happen without a key to get back out.

The only life I want to create is artificial.

"What's up, Buttercup?" Crow's elbow finds its way to my ribs.

Tau chirps, and I swear he's chiding her... though I might be projecting.

"I'm not sure I'm… comfortable being this close to a beast like that," I say, jutting my chin at Nekkan's broad back. "Crow, if you hadn't done whatever you did…"

She shrugs. "Now we're even."

"Even for… what?"

"The acid rain rescue service? Don't tell me our new friend hit you hard enough to knock that out of your head. I'm pretty sure you were there for that."

"You didn't even say thank you."

"Well, now I did. Happy?"

I don't point out she hasn't exactly said those words because I *am* happy, actually. Crow came back for me when she could have just as easily continued without me, without the locket holding her back.

"How did you overpower one of the most dangerous beasts in the galaxy, unarmed and all?"

She shrugs again, but there's a hint of a smile on her lips this time. A pinch of pride. "You heard what he said, his HUD was down. He didn't know what to make of me when I came at him. Took him by surprise, and he was so embarrassed by the defeat he turned into a housecat. No big deal."

"I'd say that's a pretty big deal."

"Do you think it's going to be a problem? Having him with us? We could use the extra muscle, but with you being Princess of the Universe and all…"

"Oh. That. I thought you had forgotten."

"My memory goes back what, a day?" Crow taps a stubborn finger to her temple. "I remember everything since then."

"Then you'll remember I'm not *the* Princess of the Universe. I just wear her face."

"What's up with that?"

I bite my lip. "These days people are *really* into genetic manipulation. The richer you are, the more tries you get so that your kid comes out just right—through cloning. But that process was banned ages ago: technically, I'm not allowed to exist."

Crow lets out a low whistle. "That's tough, Buttercup. Is it going to be a problem when we get into Anchor?"

"Maybe. I'm not sure yet."

"Then stop talking and figure out what you're going to do about it."

Ahead, light shines through the thick foliage; the end of the forest finally in sight. We step out into a clearing, and I blink in the brightness, forcing my eyes to adjust. There's a whiff of roasting potatoes on the breeze.

My stomach rumbles: real food.

A building sits at the intersection of our road with another, two stories high, sheer and metallic, strikingly like the hull of a ship with windows cut haphazardly into it. And a ship it must have been, at some time: it appears to have been built from repurposed materials from the first colony ships that landed here, judging by its apparent age. Purple ivy clings to the structure, like parts of it are being claimed by the forest. Smoke rises from one of the many chimneys, carrying with it the promise of roasted meat.

And so many more potatoes.

"Oh thank God, a tavern," says Crow. Her nose is high in the air, nostrils flaring. "I haven't had a warm meal in over three hundred years. No offense, Nemo, but your ration packs were shit."

"You know I am incapable of taking offense," says Nemo, "and I do not think I need to remind you that those packs were in no way mine to begin with."

Nekkan lets out a huff, setting the hair on the back of my neck on edge. The sound is triggering the most primitive part of my brain, the one that controls survival, the one telling me to *run, run away from this killer beast*. I force myself to look up, noting that his uncomfortably chipper smile has been wiped clean from his face. I don't know what's more terrifying: the smile, or the lack of it.

"We must remain on task," he says. "What is our plan?"

All eyes turn to me. *Slag.* In a panic, I toss my responsibility out of the window. "Why are all of you looking at me? How should I know?"

"You had prime time with Gleïa," says Crow. "Didn't she tell you what to do?"

Nekkan shifts on his feet. "And Gleïa is…?"

"She's one of the technowitches of this planet, though I guess she takes care of the entire Outer Zone, too. She said the Technomage Superius was her boss, so…"

"All these nonsense terms are getting on my nerves," Crow mumbles, rolling her eyes in yet another wide circle. "Just because you're a good engineer doesn't make you magical. You shouldn't have to have a fancy name just because you can wave a wrench around."

"Have you *seen* Nemo?" I ask.

The droid in question waves.

"He thinks for himself, decides for himself, is conscious of himself. It shouldn't be possible. That's *life*. And not just anyone can give it."

"He also lived in a ditch for decades and thought he was a prince until yesterday," Crow replies. "Any sufficiently advanced technology is indistinguishable from magic, right? He's still tech."

"Exactly. If you're so advanced that whatever you created is basically magic, shouldn't you deserve to be called a Mage?"

"Can you please stop bickering and make a decision?" Nekkan growls. "Are you stopping for sustenance, or are we to continue on?"

"I say we stop for a drink," says Crow, raising her hand high. "I haven't had one in a couple of centuries. You got any coin?"

"No," he says. "All my systems are offline, and that means my daily allowance, too. All my earnings have probably been liquified at this point. Perks of being legally dead."

"Then why go back at all?" I ask. "If you're dead, that means you don't have to fight their wars anymore. You could do what you want."

He looks puzzled. "I was quite literally made for this; I belong with my pack. My people. My family."

I open my mouth, then close it. I know why *I* have to go back: I've abandoned my family to the consequences of *my* mistakes, and I have to make things right, to save them. But once again, questions of what happens after I save them are bursting at the floodgates I've put up in my mind. I love my family, but I don't *belong* with them.

"Wow, touched a nerve there, Buttercup," says Crow. "I sure hope *you* have coin. You do owe me a drink for coming with you this far."

"Shut up about your drink," I reply. "I don't have any money. Slag, I don't even know what currency they use here. And who the void calls it coin?"

"Well then, I suppose we just have to hope this is worth something." Crow pulls her hand out of her pocket, retrieving a smattering of small gold coins. "I vote food. Or rather, my stomach votes for me. So long they're cool with an ocugry, a droid, and two humans chilling together…"

"There's no reason that anyone will have a problem with the four of us together," says Nemo. "Most in the Outer Zone are quite multiracial. Except for the odd separatist world."

"Great. Food it is."

Crow doesn't wait for us. She just skips down the road toward the tavern. This is the moment of truth, my testing ground: if I can't even handle a tavern, how will I be ready to walk through a city? I have no choice but to follow, biting hard on my bottom lip to keep my nerves from taking over and forcing me to run back from where I came. I pluck Tau from the air and twist him into sleep mode before he can complain.

The building is so old that the sign has completely faded. The lack of a visible name doesn't seem to bother the clientele: the place is bursting at the seams when we enter. There are so many people that I doubt Nekkan is going to fit. I find myself shrinking into my skin: I've never been around so many strangers before.

I close my eyes and pull every thought of the princess to the forefront. I can't help it: it's what I've been preparing for my entire life. I switch my gait to my practiced shuffle.

I've been to the lone bar on Nesworth less than a dozen times, always early in the day when it was empty, wearing my scarf and clinging to my uncle's side. It was never to sit and eat, always for some errand or another: most recently, to repair the dispensary, for which Mr. Solomon was very grateful. He'd let me take home all the old spare parts he had been keeping in his storeroom, not just the ones I'd replaced.

Crow waves down one of the silvery waiters, who points to the back of the room where an empty table miraculously waits for us. The hosts are droids, like Nemo but far less sophisticated—cheaper and less refined, their skin is nowhere near the quality of his even after his decades in the mud.

We order stew and ales and stuff ourselves into the booth. The atmosphere inside is warm and the smells heavenly, and, for a second, I think I can actually get comfortable here, even sitting at the end of the booth as I am, pressed against Nekkan's titanic torso.

But now, people are staring.

In the two days I've been on the road, not once have I had to worry about my face being exposed—well, other than that hot minute when I thought Nekkan might have wanted me dead. Crow doesn't care who I am, she's been frozen for centuries. Nemo? He's been sleeping in a ditch for as long as I've been alive. It's incredible how quickly I've gotten used to being able to show my face. Capture's been the last thing on my mind; all I can think about is my family.

I reach up and tug my braid tighter, pulling the spark coat high on my shoulders to let it bulk up my frame as I slouch into the booth. I let the muscles of my face go slack, puffing up my lower cheeks to make myself pudgier.

Rule three: she is not me, she is not me.

"You severely misrepresented the iconic nature of your face," says Crow, reaching for her ale as the droid returns to serve us.

"I didn't think they'd care this far out in the Outer Zone," I say with a shudder. "The real princess is dead."

"Which is all the more reason for them to see you for who you are."

I turn to face the intruder at the table and y blood chills. It can't be him—I left this man back on Nesworth, as I escaped the ship that had turned my hope of freedom into the dread of capture. His thin blond hair glistens like wet straw under the ambient lights, bracing himself on his fists on our table.

"Friends!" said Nemo. "How exciting!"

"A-astrophel?" I stammer. "What… How did you get here?"

"Do you really think we'd let you go so easily?" he says through his grin. "You can't imagine how much you're worth. We found your Hyperspace window. You have no idea how fast the *Bountiful* can be when it doesn't have to haul moons' worth of grain."

There's a vibration running up my spine—Nekkan is growling, the sound deep in his stomach. Between the beast and the boy, I find myself pressing deeper into the rumbling, monstrous chest.

"What have you done to my family?"

"Oh, them? They're no one," he scoffs, "and not even your true family, I should add. Though you already know that, don't you? We left some of our people behind, in case you were unwilling to cooperate."

My family is alive, but it's just as I feared. They're in danger because of me. "And Abril? I heard her scream."

"She betrayed us," he said. "She… *fell* out of the shuttle during the storm. It's unlikely she survived. We didn't hurt her, we're not monsters. What she did, she did to herself."

Dead. Abril died, saving me. I want to scream.

His eye whirs as he blinks, pupil shrinking. It wasn't bionic when I'd left him. Abril's last act had been to maim this ass forever. The fact doesn't make me feel any better.

"Who's this dud?" asks Crow. "Didn't realize you were this popular, Dora."

The rest of the tavern has gone eerily silent. Watching. Now, I know there was no one watching us in the park, because this is what it feels like to have hundreds of eyes locked on you. I'm shrinking deeper into Nekkan's fur.

"Yes, introduce us, Dora. Let me know who else to charge with harboring a clone."

"You have no jurisdiction, boy," growls Nekkan, "this is the Outer Zone. There are no law-keepers here."

"And what would an ocugry be doing so far from his pack?" asks Astrophel, his grin retreating into a sly smile. "You have no power here, either. Alone, as you are, it's easy to conclude you've been disconnected. Now, am I wrong?"

Nekkan stays silent, but I can feel his growl against my back. It's charging me, slowly filling me with the energy I need to stand my ground.

"Dora—if that even is your real name—you should know that things will be much easier if you just come with us," says Astrophel. "We have no reason to mistreat you. Quite the opposite: you are worth so much more alive."

"To whom?" I spit, drawing strength from Nekkan's warmth.

"The Coalition," says Astrophel. He takes a swig of his ale—*my* ale. "Clone-batching has been banned for centuries. The royal family would give quite a pretty penny to keep the news of your existence from ever getting out."

"You intend to blackmail the royals?" Nemo scoffs. "They're more likely to blow you out of the sky than respond to your demands."

"And how would you know that, toaster?" Astrophel snarls.

Nemo cringes. "I know royals: I was a prince for centuries. Just because it was programming doesn't mean it wasn't real."

"Sure, keep telling yourself that." Astrophel turns back to me. "And in any case, you've been marching across this planet completely exposed. *Everyone* here can see you. They know who you are. *What* you are."

"Then what makes you think you're the only one who gets to blackmail the royals?" asks Crow. "Hell, I could do it myself if I wanted to—I just can't be bothered. You're just one man; I'm pretty sure everyone in this room has already worked out how much Dora's worth, and if they haven't, you just gave them the blueprints to a perfect crime. So let me ask again: what makes you think you're getting her first?"

Ale flies at Astrophel's face. Nemo slams a now-empty glass down on the table and shoves Crow out of the booth, though she's already on her feet, bringing her fist between Astrophel's eyes.

The wind is knocked out of me as an extremely hairy arm wraps around my waist, lifting me into the air and slamming me down onto an armored shoulder. Nekkan pushes off against the wall, sliding us into the fray, though I'm high above it all, perched awkwardly on his shoulder.

The tavern has exploded. All the people who have been so hungrily sizing me up are now on their feet, stumbling over each other in order to reach me first. Nekkan bolts toward the exit.

We're not fast enough, not with so many people blocking our way. Astrophel is already standing, wiping the ale from his eyes. He lunges at me, managing to grab my hand before I can pull it away. I yipe, but Crow is faster, swinging a chair against Astrophel's back, like slapping a mosquito off a friend. The boy howls, but spins his leg under Crow, tripping her. She falls as Nekkan makes it out the door. He bolts out of the tavern and rushes me to the safety of the forest.

"We can't leave Crow!" I stammer, but my words are ripped right out of my mouth.

Astrophel slams the door open, dragging Crow out by her hair. She screams, a sound so shrill it makes my heart go still.

"Give me the clone," he spits, blood staining the grass at his feet. "Give her to me, and I won't report your desertion, that you're an unmuzzled beast to be put down. Give me the girl, and I may even give you this one back."

He lifts Crow by her scalp, forcing another scream out of her. A shiver runs through Nekkan, ferocious as an earthquake. I feel the world shift under me, and I'm shaken off balance. I tumble to the ground. There's nothing left in my lungs. I struggle to stand, but Nekkan's foot presses into my lumbar, keeping me pressed hard against the ground.

I should have listened to my gut—he's going to give me up.

The only things I can lift are my eyes, and I meet Crow's gaze across the damp grass. She's struggling against Astrophel's grip, and when she looks at me, I see the fear of death there. I've never seen anyone so scared before. Something in my gut twists, and I realize I'm more scared for her than myself.

"What makes you think you have the power here, pup?" Nekkan's voice rumbles. "You're a child of the Coalition. I may be removed from my pack, but even your entire family could not take me alone."

"You kill me, and you may as well have the entire Coalition on your heels," he replies. "I am the son of Captain Hardi. Heir to the entire enterprise. My family has maintained the rim worlds for centuries. Without us, the Core starves. Do you have any idea how powerful that makes my people? The Coalition is mine, and I can so easily make you public enemy number one. You mark my words."

My pocket squirms. It makes no sense—I turned Tau off, I'm sure—but, somehow, he is pushing himself against my chest, painfully begging to be released. As Nekkan pushes down on me harder, Tau pushes back, and I want to scream, but I still don't have the air.

The bot bursts from my collar like a wasp from the hive, and before anyone can make sense of him, there's a flash, so bright my eyes tear up. They burn, but it's a small price to pay to hear my would-be-kidnapper scream.

Flash. Flash. Flash.

My eyes are sewn shut against the light. I've never programmed this behavior in the bot, have no idea where Tau has gained the skill. Even through the pain, I'm bursting with pride at his tiny rescue.

I always knew he was brilliant.

There's a human scream and then a roar of anger and pain. His paw lifts for an instant, just long enough for me to roll out from under its clutches. Air fills my lungs so fast I feel they might burst, but I *can* breathe, slaggit. I push myself to my feet and scamper away from Nekkan as the sweet taste of air runs over my tongue. My back is screaming as I run, eyes still blinking out the residue of Tau's light. My fingers reach for my ears to block out the roaring, but they're too thin to make a difference. The only way to escape the sound is to run from it.

But I can't leave Crow. Though I can't save her if I can't see her.

There's a new roar—a *human* roar. Hope flares in my chest, and I find myself spinning on my heels even before I fully open my eyes. I speed back toward the tavern.

Astrophel is back on his feet: he's not waiting around for a rematch, and already he's sprinting off into the woods away from the tavern. Neither Crow nor Nekkan are strong enough to give chase. The massive beast is forcing his eyes open, but I can see they're red even from here, and he won't shoot where he can't aim. Not without his HUD. And Nemo—I'm not even sure where he is.

Crow is panting heavily, her forehead a crown of red. I don't stop running until she's in my arms. The move surprises us both: I find myself crumpling into her, holding her against me just to be sure she's real.

"Well," she says, panting. She doesn't outright reject the embrace—*what am I even thinking?*—but she holds me at arm's length. "Never a dull moment with you."

Tau drifts back to my side, chirping proudly. I clutch him in both hands and kiss the top of his tiny egg-timer body, causing him to emit a gentle pink light. Also not a behavior I've programmed. When did he even get red LEDs?

"I truly am a failure to my race," Nekkan grimaces, still wiping his eyes. "I could crush that bot in my fist. Yet it won."

"Anyone seen Nemo?" asks Crow, glancing left and right. "We need to get out of here before the creepy kid or his cronies catch wind of where we went."

"They have my family," I say. The words sink in my gut like a stone in a pond, slow and heavy.

It's worse than I feared: they have my family hostage.

And it's all my fault.

"We're so close to reaching the Mage," says Crow. "He'll get you home. You'll save them. Your witch lady said he can do anything, right?"

It sounds more like she's trying to convince herself.

My heart jolts as the tavern's back door flies open. Nekkan has his gun pointed at it in an instant, but it's only Nemo.

"Fat lot of help you were," grumbles Crow.

"Apologies," he replies. "I was ensuring that we were not followed. And I paid our tab. It seems your money was more than enough to cover the damages we made."

"*We?*" asks Crow.

Nekkan lets out a hearty laugh.

"Do they program all the princes to throw down like this in the Outer Zone?" asks Crow, peering into the tavern. The eerily silent tavern. "We should get going. Not that we're going to be followed for a long, long while. Not if the droid can keep pulling this off."

"Unfortunately, this was a… one-time only kind of situation," Nemo says. "Had some defensive gas left over from the enchanted forest. You know, to calm an unruly crowd. It must have gotten a little… stale while I was in the ditch."

I'm surrounded by the impossible.

And I think I'm loving it.

PART 3

STAIRWAY TO SPACE

15

"WHAT ARE WE LOOKING FOR, EXACTLY?" asks Nekkan. "A geocache? Some kind of handler?"

We're standing on an outcrop of rock that overlooks the sprawl of Anchor city below: a jumbled mash between original colony homes—old metal barracks assembled from the hulls of the first ships to have landed, back before planting colonies was privatized by the Coalition—and cold stone bricks. From our vantage point, I can see highly modern patches with sleek chrome and glass, intermingled with rougher barracks, all built together into what seems to be a crater.

"We don't know," I say, eyes fixed on the point where our single road diverges into many. "Gleïa just said, *Don't give up the locket, stay on the road, and find the Technomage. Avoid my sister and have fun!* before pushing us out the door."

Crow stares down into the crater. While she says nothing, I can feel her trepidation. Even I'm trembling slightly, hands stuffed into my pockets for their own good. I've never been to a place so big and so dense before. We're two-hundred and forty-four colonists on Nesworth, and this city has at least a hundred or even a thousand times that. I can't tell, I have no sense of scale. I'm not sure if I'm excited or terrified, especially after the near miss at the tavern.

"So, I take it we are going to the 'vator, right?" asks Nemo. He points to the center of the crater, where the skyscrapers cluster around what can only be a *space*scraper so tall I can't see where it ends. But as I stare, I realize it's not a building at all: four massive coils rise straight into the sky, reaching from the earth to the clouds and beyond.

"What's that?"

"The space elevator," he says, "which links Anchor to the moon? Well, it is not exactly a moon, but it is less of a mouthful to say than 'artificial satellite.' Since that is where the Mage lives, it is probably where we're headed, correct?"

I follow Nemo's finger to the sky. I haven't missed a celestial body hanging above us—I'm so used to Thebos I would be relieved to see one again. Instead, there's only a great green gleam, like a star in the middle of the day. So *that's* the Mage's moon. What makes it so green, so bright, I don't know, but it's glorious.

"The emerald moon." Nekkan lets out a low whistle. "The crown jewel above Haven."

"Damn, is the station really made of emerald?" asks Crow, staring at the thing in awe.

"No, I believe the name comes from the color of the solar panels," says Nemo.

"But how do we get there?" asks Nekkan. At least one of us is thinking proactively.

"We ride the 'vator, of course," Nemo replies. "We will ask for passage. If the Technowitch of Dawn is your sponsor, then I am sure they will allow us."

"I sure hope so," I mutter under my breath. Reaching the Technomage suddenly feels like a whole other insurmountable mountain. We've walked so far, and now it looks like we'll have to walk all the way to space. "Can I borrow a scarf?"

No one has a scarf, of course. Fashion isn't our forte. Nekkan offers his rebreather, but it's so big, it covers my eyes. He sifts through his belongings until he finds a paw brace, which, when stuffed over my head, passes for a balaclava.

The city grows up around us quicker than I anticipated. First, a house here or there; then, streets on either side. Some fly flags out windows, others—most of them, really—hang their laundry to dry instead. For a heartbeat, it reminds me of home, of wash days. But the image shatters as a woman slams her shutters shut, loudly ripping me from my thoughts.

Nekkan was right: the people here don't give a shipsslag about the four of us walking together in the street. We're striding side by side, and no one seems to care about the gigantic ocugry, or the battered droid, or the woman with a centuries out of date sense of fashion. But what they might care about, if they could see me, is their beloved princess strolling down the street in broad daylight when she's supposed to be dead.

Rule three: she is not me, she is not me.

But as I walk, my confidence leaks out my pocket. I shove my head into the collar of my spark coat, face hot under the balaclava.

Rule three: she is not me, she is not me.

They're not looking closely enough at my face to make a fuss, and the makeshift balaclava hopefully makes me look like a mine worker at best. I know that, and I know I have a small army beside me, but I still can't shake the feeling this will all end in an instant.

> *"Children, Children, you're not alone,*
> *They watch over the Outer Zone.*
> *Four for the Witches, One for the Mage,*
> *Five for the Immys who never do Age."*

There are children in the street ahead of us, singing as they skip between hovering pads. It's a game I played with my cousins, little stepping stones drifting a few centimeters off the ground that we jump between while singing. But this isn't any song I know.

> *"Witches, Witches, Spark and Wire,*
> *Can make whatever your heart desires.*
> *Dawn and Dusk and Noon and Night,*
> *Don't come between them as they fight."*

Tau lets out a low, long note. He senses my distress. I pluck him out of the sky, whisper for him to hush, and put him in my pocket again. There's no point turning him off, knowing now that he can switch himself on at will. He's learning so much so quickly: he's a real AI, just like I built him, but it's a little scary seeing how independent he's become from my programming.

"Are they going to come at us with pitchforks?" Crow asks, pushing herself close to me as if her added frame can help mask my recognizable face.

"Not if we reach the Technomage first."

"Oh, gotcha." Crow grins.

"I thought the practice would be enough," I say, staring at the paving stones as we walk. "My entire life I've been preparing for this, but none of it was worth anything."

"Well, no one is trying to outright kill you yet, so I'd call that a victory."

I let out a small laugh, remembering to force the harsh and guttural one rather than the sweet tinkling of the princess's cheer which is natural to us both. Still, I don't take my eyes off my feet.

Rule three: she is not me, she is not me.

It's too late to turn back now. I slow my pace, marching closer to Nekkan, his monstrous form reassuring. All we have to do is make it to the elevator, and then this will be over.

The street slopes slowly down into the heart of Anchor. Now, there are shops and restaurants and cafés, and the world feels alive in a way I've never felt. The rich tapestry of people's lives twisting and turning around each other fills my gut with anxious and excited flutters. They brush past us on their 'scoots, weaving down the streets like we're just part of the crowd. The roads are filled with the *ding ding* of streetcars and the smell of fried treats.

I don't know any of these faces, and they're not giving us a second glance. I try not to stare too long at any one person, but it's hard not to become engrossed by the novelty of the whole experience. Anchor's center is a beating heart. While I know this is just a small taste of what a city on Apricus might offer, I'm enthralled all the same.

And there, at the very center of this crater, in the middle of a shockingly empty plaza, stands a magnificent building, all marble and ornamental edifice, bright and glittering white. From it extends huge cables, wider than a house: these must be the cables that carry the elevator to and from the Mage's moon.

Now this is some serious engineering.

I've never seen something so technically perfect before. The space elevator was a thing of science fiction until quite recently, and I never believed I would lay my eyes upon one. I hold my breath, staring wide-eyed at the contraption.

"Why is everyone stopping?" asks Crow, poking Nekkan in the ribs.

Before, I wondered if the girl had a death wish before; now I'm absolutely certain of it.

"Nemo, come off it, you don't give a shit about the 'vator," she says.

"I stopped because the others stopped."

"You see? You're messing with the droid," she says, storming ahead with Nemo by her side, neither of them apparently taken in by the inspiring scale of the thing. "Come on, the sooner we get to this guy, the sooner we all get what we want and never have to see each other again. Isn't that great?"

At once, a chill runs through me. My fingertips turn cold at the thought, as if Crow's words have brought an ice age crashing down.

"Yo," says Crow, snapping her fingers in front of my face. "You a droid, too, Buttercup, glitching out the way you are? Come on, then."

"Huh," Nemo stuff his hands into the pockets of his khakis. "I think *glitching out* is considered a slur. It certainly… feels…wrong. Please refrain?"

"Oh, sorry," she says, and she seems to mean it. Then, she turns back to me and waves me forward, flustered. "Come on, let's go."

There's nothing quite like the entrance to the 'vator. The building looks even more imposing up close than it did from up the hill: the great white columns out front, topped with fleeing birds frozen in stone, are the work of a master craftsman, something rarely seen on small outer colonies like Nesworth. My little farming moon isn't worthy of such impressive artistry. Even the other buildings give it a wide berth—no patio seating on this plaza. The sounds of the city seem distant as we draw closer. The only stores are selling souvenirs, with postcards and replicas of the 'vator displayed outside the shopfronts.

I can feel the others' excitement thrumming in the air like electricity. The charge runs through my skin, inching deeper, until it's a buzz inside my bones, in my very core. We've sped up; I can no longer hear anything other than the pounding of our feet on the marble steps or the beating of my heart inside my ears.

When we finally reach the double doors to the 'vator, we're out of breath—well, I am for sure, and Crow's trying very hard to hide it. Nemo doesn't need to breathe to survive, after all, and Nekkan probably can run up the 'vator wires and back without breaking a sweat. He's the one who lifts the gigantic silver knocker and slams it on the door, announcing to the world that we have arrived.

Nothing happens.

He knocks again. And again. Soon, he's pounding on the door with the metal knocker, thunder echoing from his hands.

A round window in the door flies open where before there was smooth metal. Out pops the head of a man. Red and puffy, he's glaring at us with an anger so hot and dense he could turn the entire planet into a star. His face matches the velvet of the tiny red hat he has perched on his black hair, held secure with a strap that's tight under his chin.

"Will you be quiet?" His gaze is dagger-sharp. "There are ways of getting my attention which do not disturb the peace, you miscreants."

Nekkan steps forward immediately, puffing his chest so that he appears to grow another head taller. The man, however, does not look impressed.

"Did you never learn the rules of etiquette?" he sputters. "Do you have no respect for anyone? What do you want here?"

"We need a ride in the 'vator," he says. "We are here to see the Technomage Superius."

"Do you have an appointment?" ask the man. His face is no longer red; it's gone purple. Hopefully this is just a medical condition. And if it is, that it's not contagious.

"No," I say. My voice breaks over that single syllable, but I tighten my fists and step forward anyway. "But Gleïa, the Technowitch of Dawn, that is, she said…"

"No appointment, no ride," proclaims the man, "no exceptions. Look." He points to a sign hanging just to the left of the door, which repeats his exact words in gold-green lettering.

I knew it. I just knew this would happen: luck always runs out. Nothing can ever be simple in this chaotic slag-hole of a universe. I taste bile on my tongue and swallow it down along with my pride.

"But… it's an emergency," I sputter. "and Gleïa…"

"Is not the Mage," says the doorman, "and she is also not in charge of the Mage's schedule, either. So, take your redefined notions of entitlement and please leave. Come back when your name is on the list."

"But can we make an appointment?" asks Crow, pushing forward. "We just crossed an entire planet to get to him. The least he could do is see us eventually, if not immediately."

"Well, I can pencil you on Tuesday at ten," he says, "six years from now. The Mage doesn't see just anybody."

"Please," she continues, nonetheless. "We really need to see the man. As my friend said, it's urgent."

"Then you should have made an appointment last year!" he says, and, without another word, slams the window shut.

16

THE SILENCE BETWEEN US IS COLDER THAN A comet. I stare at the ground in shock and shame, my mind racing too fast to think of a way out of this mess, gears clogged and stuck in place.

"Well, that went well," says Crow, "didn't it, Buttercup?"

I could rip her head off. "Don't give me that look. I thought Gleïa made some kind of, I don't know, a booking, seeing how she sent us this far. She *said* she'd call ahead."

"Well, you thought wrong." Crow crosses her arms over her chest, fuming. I avoid her gaze and admire my own shoes again, knowing what I'll find in her eyes. There's accusation, sure, but that isn't nearly as powerful as the hurt I feel radiating off her skin. My heart gives a single, almost painful, *lurch*. All the warmth Crow's shown me has been out of self-preservation, not kindness. There's no kinship here now I'm not useful.

"Let us not accuse Dora of things she cannot control," says Nemo, clapping a hand on my shoulder. "She wants to see the Mage as much as any of us. We'll get to him; I know we will."

"It's getting dark," says Crow, changing the subject as swiftly as only she can, "so we need to think fast."

"Or," suggests Nemo, "we turn in for the night and deal with this tomorrow. Best not make hasty decisions that could impact us in the long run."

"True!" I say. Nemo is giving me time to think, to plan. I want to hug him. "Nekkan?"

"I say we break down the door and take the building by force," he growls. "We could storm the 'vator and ride up before they know what hit them."

"Well, that sounds great to me," says Crow. "We doing this now?"

"No!" I didn't know my voice could get so high-pitched. The trio stares at me as if I've just sprouted wings—but I feel like I'm wearing lead boots, bolting me to the ground. "I mean… we don't want to end up before the Mage as criminals, you know? What are the odds of him actually filling our requests if we storm in there by force?"

"Quite high," says Nekkan, muzzle twitching.

"Hey, if it gets us face time with the Mage, I'm willing to try anything," says Nemo. "Technically, he *is* my father. And I have not seen him in years."

I'd want to confront my father, too, if he'd left me in a ditch for over sixteen years. Though technically my dad tried to have me killed, so mine might not be the most objective opinion.

"Yeah, not me," I say. "I doubt us *getting arrested* is going to get us a consultation. We're going to do it right, okay?"

Not to mention, if we fail, the all-knowing Mage will probably refuse to take pity on this illegal clone and give me up to the authorities without hesitation. And that's not exactly the conversation I want to be having with my only allies.

"You're pretty naïve if you think that's going to work," Crow snaps. "That Farm mafia is after you, and as much as I want to believe we can do without you, you are our only link to the Mage."

The thought of Astrophel finding me again twists my gut. "Anchor's a big city, right? How easy would it be for him to find me? Let's *please* try to go through the official channels first. And if it doesn't work, we can always fall back on the use of force. All right? Just as a last resort."

"I can see the logic in this," says Nekkan, his hands twitching by his side. "But plan B is that you follow my lead and we take this 'vator by any means necessary. I'm the only one here with any experience in that department."

"Oh, I like that plan," says Crow. "You sure we can't just lead with that?"

"Not unless we have to," I say.

"I agree with Dora," says Nemo. "It is quite logical: if we use force and fail, then we shall never get an opportunity to see the Mage. If we try the official way and fail, nothing happens to us. Worst case scenario, we start over. So let us begin by trying to find the legal course of action, and resort to violence later."

I throw up a hand. "I said *force*, not violence."

"And I never specified." The look on Nekkan's face is brutal, his lips lifting to reveal sharp teeth. And it's not a smile this time.

"Great," I say. I rub my hands together—I need to get them warm, they won't stop shaking. They're doing a lot of that lately, and it's getting harder and harder to keep them under control. "I say we find a place safe for the night. A real bed is going to feel amazing for all of us."

"Sounds good to me," says Nemo.

I don't say anything about how he's the only one in the group with no actual need for a bed. The two others don't reply, but they don't object, either.

"I think I saw a hotel on the way here. Shall we?" Nemo asks.

"Well, I'm not paying this time," Crow mutters. Nonetheless, she follows me back down the white marble steps into the plaza below, Nemo and Nekkan close behind.

"We can—"

I'm cut off mid sentence. The stones beneath us give a low rumble. It's as if the earth itself is humming, the note rising as a shadow falls upon us. I reach for the railing as the stairs tremble and shake, turning my head toward the sky, my vision blurry as I adjust to the sudden darkness. Then the block passes, becoming more defined.

It's a metal box larger than my Nesworth home, carried upward by cables thicker than the columns themselves. The 'vator rises into the sky, returning to the Mage's moon, carrying with it those worthy of earning an audience with the most powerful man in the Outer Zone.

"Screw them," says Crow, stuffing her hands deep into her pockets. "You were saying?"

"I think we can do without," I finish.

"Without what? The 'vator?"

"I wish." I say. "I meant without money. Though I have to get cleaned up first."

There's a public fountain in the plaza, and I dunk my face under the running stream. The water is cold and harsh, burning my skin with its icy fingers. I wash two days' worth of mud and crud off my face, watching it hit the street below and forma mess at my feet.

"And this is meant to accomplish… what?" asks Crow. "If someone kills you over your face, then none of us are getting on that elevator."

"I agree," says Nemo. "It is unwise to show your face in Anchor if the farmafia is after you."

"Farmafia is not a word," I say.

Crow's eyebrows knit together as she meets my gaze. But I know what I have to do. My entire life I've been raised to hide my face, to stop others from thinking—even for a second—that I share even a passing resemblance with the princess.

Genetic imperfects are not terminated because they remind people of the measures taken to keep royal lines pure: They're terminated because of what they can do. *Who* they can *be*.

I have the princess's face, and I'm going to use it.

I reach back to my braid, twisting the long train of ebony hair through my hands, wrapping it up to perch it delicately on the crown of my head. The twist is not as elaborate as the princess's, but it will do in a pinch. Off comes my beloved spark coat—Tau still waiting for action in the breast pocket. Crow takes it from my hands. I bring the princess to my mind again, but this time let everything I know about her overpower me, tightening my face, my back, my neck, until I'm tall and graceful as a girl born of starlight and perfection.

"This face won't mean anything to you," I say. "But it means something to these people. My entire life I've been hiding it because my body belongs to someone else. But it's *mine*, slaggit, and, tonight, I'm going to show it."

Nemo is the only one to nod. His analytical brain has presumably already processed the situation, weighing risks against the possible outcomes, and has most likely come to the same conclusion I have: this is the best course of action, consequences be slagged. Auntie always called me impulsive, but, really, I like the possible results better than the risks involved.

Not that it turned out so well the last time I made a bold decision.

The sun is sliding behind the crater walls as we reach the silver slab marked *hotel*. We choose it because it looks clean, reputable, and nondescript—and it still has its memorial to the dead princess in the window.

The concierge's eyes bulge as we step in, but that's to be expected. We must be an odd assortment, even in the Outer Zone—Nekkan barely fit through the door—without taking my face into the equation.

"How are you…" she gasps. "You're not… but I saw…"

"We need your help." The lie spins itself together on my tongue, and it's too late to stop it from spilling out. "We're here to see the Mage, to make things right. I need to get back. The systems need to know the *Truth*. With a capital T."

"This—this is impossible!"

"Please, keep it quiet!" I shush her. The words are rushing now like a torrent. "Do you want them to find me? The people who killed me think they were successful, but I've been laying low, trying to wait until they drop their guard and reveal themselves. If they know they've failed, and I'm still alive, they'll come after me, and we'll lose all the work I've been striving for the past month. Not to mention I could die *for real* this time. So please. Help me. Help us."

"Anything, your Highness, anything." She points a trembling finger at Nekkan. "We don't cater to his type in here."

"He's my bodyguard," I say. "My last line of defense. I need him with me at all times."

The concierge is silent for a second, then nods. She reaches out to touch my face, then pulls her fingers back. I try not to flinch as they almost feel my skin.

"I can't believe you're here," she says. "You're alive. My heart broke when I watched… what happened to you…"

"But I'm safe," I say, reaching over the check-in desk to clutch her hand. "Or I will be, with your help. Now, for payment—"

"I wouldn't hear of it," she says, shaking her head. "You can stay here as long as you need. I won't tell a soul."

"Thank you," I say, "but you can always put it on the tab of the Technowitch of Dawn."

The shower is heaven on a plate.

The second the hot water rains on my skin, every muscle relaxes. I'm the calmest I've been in days, the ringing in my ears washed away by the rush of the shower. I close my eyes and let the water run through my loose hair, feeling it catch in the knots and tangles. I'm cocooned in heat and steam.

I can almost imagine I'm home, turning up the water pressure to drown out the shouts of my cousins banging at the bathroom door. I thought I would relish the silence, but the lack of their voices feels heavy, and the good feeling is gone. When I'm finally overwhelmed by the heat, I wipe myself dry with big, fluffy towels. I feel like myself for the first time in days.

The room itself is small: it's all that was left in the hotel. We technically have the top floor all to ourselves, though it's just two interconnected bedrooms with two beds each. It's incredible to be in a house with floors and a ceiling, with air conditioning, with a television and access to the Network. This is luxury, made even more incredible after two days of wandering in the wilderness.

I've never even been in a house other than my own before, not until two days ago when Gleïa invited me into her home.

Now, I'm in a hotel, a Sisters-sent hotel, and I'm so excited I don't know if I'll be able to sleep: even the very idea that hundreds before me have slept in this one bed somehow excites me, when I know it should gross me out.

Anything to keep me from thinking about my family.

I wrap a towel around my hair and balancing the fabric precariously as I walk. I'll braid my hair in the morning. I have to put my old clothes back on, and they smell ripe, the grime rubbing up against my clean body. I haven't yet decided how I'll be sleeping; there aren't many options.

I step out of the bathroom and right into an intervention.

Three bodies take up my room. And all the room in my room. They've been waiting for me. Nemo's taken the chair in the corner; Crow's stretched out on her own bed, and Nekkan's sitting on mine, as it keeps him from hitting his head on the ceiling.

"We need to talk," says Nemo. Despite his frail frame and soft tone, it's as if he's looking right through me. I feel every speck of dirt from my clothing reaching for my clean skin.

"Your face," he asks, tilting his head slightly. "*Whose* is it, exactly?"

"It got us our rooms." I reach a shaking hand to pull through my hair, but it only hits the towel. The precarious pile falls, and I catch it awkwardly, trying to pretend I took it off on purpose. Every second that their eyes are on me is a second I feel more vulnerable, a bug under a microscope. "Does it matter more than that?"

"I'm meant to be your *bodyguard*, yet I don't know who I'm protecting," says Nekkan. "You'd better believe it matters."

"I didn't tell them anything," Crow interjects, more frustrated with every word. Her face is even getting redder as well. "I don't even know the other girl anyway."

My knees have gone weak. I crumple to the floor, catching the bed for support. The world is spinning, and I can't will it to be still.

If this is an anxiety attack, it's chosen a wild time to manifest.

"It's easier for you," I say. "None of you have anything to hide. You're all looking for yourselves. But people immediately think I'm someone I'm not, someone I'm not allowed to be."

They say nothing. Even Crow keeps her mouth sewn shut. They're all waiting for me. I let out a heavy breath.

"I'm not the princess," I say, the words coming out barely louder than a whisper. "I was just… part of her clone batch. A genetically imperfect. The princess's genetically imperfect double, if you will. Her sister clone. I'm not meant to exist."

Crow nods slowly. Maybe she understands, probably she doesn't. But at least she has the decency not to interrupt.

"Most of you have apparently missed the parts in the history books where they talk about royal births. To ensure the royal line is the highest possible standard, each one is a batch of engineered clones. The one deemed the most perfect and with the highest potential for success is kept by the family. Jo'Niss was perfect. I wasn't. The others are terminated, so I've been told. So there."

"How barbaric," says Nemo. His eyes seem at the edge of tears, not that he can possibly cry. "They kill the children?"

"It's supposed to be illegal, now." I shudder along with him. It's one thing to know it's happening, another to speak of it aloud. "I've been kept in the dark about this, all of my life, for my own safety. All I know is I'm not even supposed to be alive right now. My uncle and aunt raised me on a farming moon, far away from the monarchy and the core planets, where I could be safe. But I am not the princess. Just because I am her clone doesn't mean I'm anything like her. Tonight was the first time I used her face, and I'm still trying to not think about it, I…"

I see the concierge's face so vividly in my mind. The adoration of a perfect stranger. Astrophel's hunger in the tavern. The locals there, swarming, swarming. And there, in the back of my mind, the face of Captain Hardi, a hunter chasing his prey. Astrophel as he reaches for me on the ship. Abril as she screams.

My face is not my own, and whenever I forget, I put others in danger.

Rule three: she is not me, she is not me.

I tell them all the sordid details. How trying to get off Nesworth resulted in being discovered and putting my family at risk. I tell them about the mysterious shuttle, about accidentally crushing the Technowitch of Night, about the locket appearing around my neck.

"I told you I needed the Technomage to take me home," I finish, "but I don't know what will be there when I get there. Or if he even can get me back to Nesworth in the first place."

Crow nods, slowly. "You're much more interesting than I pegged you for, Buttercup."

"That's it?" I don't know if I should feel relieved or terrified by her obvious lack of reaction. "No, *how could you keep this from us?* No, *you put us all in danger?* No, *we never want to see you again?* Nothing?"

Crow looks to Nekkan, then to Nemo, and shrugs. The three of them look as nonchalant as a stack of toast.

"I'm sorry for your loss," says Nekkan, the rumble of his voice filling me with warmth. "Jo'Niss was a light in the darkness. She will be missed."

I can hardly believe my ears. "You knew?"

"I couldn't place it until now," he says softly. "Without my HUD to run facial recognition, people are just people to me. No names or aliases or crimes or anything. But Jo'Niss's death is a tragedy for all of us."

My hair stands straight on the back of my neck, muscles coiled and tense. "This is one bounty you will not get."

"I've known you for less than a day, and in that time, you promised to kill me, reneged on that promise, witnessed my shame, and became a danger to yourself and others," he says, hoisting his massive shoulders into a shrug. "But if this is my first decision without my HUD, I would rather not kill you, Miss Dora."

Mercy from an ocugry is a rare treat. He's even my *friend*, in a way. Not many people can say that about their kind. My nightmares made flesh, sweet in the light of day.

"You are not, and never will be, my bounty." The room rumbles as he speaks. "The death of innocents is something I stand against."

"And yet ocugry go where they are told."

"Then call me a conscientious objector," he says. "I don't need a HUD to tell me you're no threat to the galaxy."

"Thank you," I say, and I mean it. Part of me knows that if his HUD is repaired, then things might change. But for now, I relish the fact that I have an ally like him.

"I have no idea who this princess person is, and I don't need programming to know that infanticide is beyond criminal," adds Nemo. "I don't care who you're supposed to be. I quite like who you are, Dora. You've treated me like a person despite the fact that I am anything but."

He reaches for my hand, and I take it, squeezing it lightly. When he smiles, I don't have to wonder if it is genuine or simply programming. It's part of his nature, whether that be mechanical or natural, just as my own instinct is to smile back.

My eyes turn to Crow, who just… shrugs.

"I'm sorry about this 'jaundice' girl," she says, "but this makes you a liability. So long as you're around, we have a target on our backs."

"I'm also the only one with the bargaining chip," I say, fingering the locket. "The Technomage wants it. And we need something in return. If you help me reach him, you all get that piece of you back. So, it's up to you. Whether or not my face is a deal breaker."

I'm proud of myself, of my little speech. But Crow is still frowning.

"I'll think about it." She stands and turns to the ocugry, all softness gone as if she flicked a switch. "Nekkan? How about that drink? The one from earlier ended up on the tavern floor."

"If we must," he says, pushing himself off the wall. This isn't a social event: they're going to be talking about me, and they're not subtle about it. "Nemo?"

"I do not drink," he says, "alcoholic or otherwise. But the company would be pleasant."

He glances back at me, offering a warm smile. His eyes are wide and red-rimmed, as if he's found tears somewhere only droids know. Whomever programmed him must be as talented as Tennyson himself. I need to meet this Technomage.

"If you need us, we'll be in the hotel bar," says Crow, last one out the door. "We'll talk again when the alcohol has cleared a few things up."

I nod, trying not to panic. This might be the last time I see her: she might decide sticking together isn't worth the risk, that she's got a better chance of seeing the Mage and getting her memories back if I'm not around to bog her down. Maybe she has her own bargaining chip. She might sway the other two in the same go.

The princess's face will have once again cost me any and all small happiness I've found. It's going to take away the only friends I've had ever had, and I'm totally helpless against it. I can't even leave this room to try and convince them I'm worth knowing.

Am I even worth knowing?

Crow closes the door, sealing me in silence. I'm alone for the first time in days. I'm shaking as I slip off the overalls. I hadn't even needed to put them on in the first place, and now I'm regretting letting them get dirt all over me again. As I slip between the layers of clean sheets, I start laughing in confusion, at the sheer overwhelming feeling of being lost in the infinite universe.

Crow's left my spark coat on the armchair. I reach over to find Tau, setting him free. The one friend I know better than anyone or anything else in the world, and even he still surprises me.

He chirps a slew of frantic beeps, angry that I stowed him away when things were getting so interesting. I've created this tiny life, and it's growing, learning, developing a personality all on its own. I don't know how much I can count on the others, but Tau, Tau is steadfastly mine.

"Can you do the light thing again?" I whisper, and he responds by emitting a cool, yellow light. "Thanks," I tell him, shutting off the overhead.

I feel a cold knot in my chest. No, *on* my chest—the locket. I can't sleep with it pressing down on me, an icy reminder of the woman I murdered. I slip it off, placing it gently on the nightstand beside me. The thing comes off easily when I want it to, and I instantly feel freer. Lighter. Tonight— maybe for the last time—I'm going to sleep, unburdened.

Tau dims the light slowly and I shut my eyes. I don't know how he knows to do that—I never manage to ask.

17

THERE ARE NO COLORS IN MY DREAMS.

I run through one of Uncle's fields, the stalks tall and heavy with corn. The field stretches for kilometers and kilometers, maybe the entire moon. I keep running, looping around from close side to far side, over and over again in the dark. Thebos fills the sky with a terrible chill rather than its reassuring glow.

There's no house, nothing but aa infinite cornfield for kilometers. I'm sure of one thing only: I'm being chased. If I don't keep running, I'll die.

I stumble upon the small ship amid the corn, nose plugged into the soil the way I'd left it two days ago. I know what will happen next, but it's better than getting caught. It takes to the skies, and I watch my family blowing away through the storm, Auntie and Uncle dancing in the clouds.

"It's going to be okay," says Auntie, suddenly beside me in the shuttle. "I prepared you for this. You are ready."

"But I'm not!" I have to keep myself from sobbing, even in the dream. "They all saw right through me right away. They will always think I'm her."

"It's time," Auntie nods.

"Time for what?"

"Apple pie, my dear," she replies, pulling the decadent desert from the confines of the shuttle's console. "Would you like a slice?"

I can smell the pie in her hands, warm from the oven. Caramel apples roasted through, cinnamon sprinkled on top. My mouth waters as I reach for it.

My fingers strike the hot glass of an oven door. I stand and see I'm in Gleïa's pristine home, two technowitches battling in the living room with no regard to the house around them. Auntie is with them, fighting them both. And the oven is beeping… the pie is in the oven, but none of them is paying attention to it. The oven beeps and beeps and beeps until the sound is unbearable.

I wake up just to get away from the noise, the unbearable noise. But it's still here in the real world, too.

Tau flies at my face, smacking my right cheekbone hard. His beeps are shrill, anguished, light flickering on and off in pure panic. The outside world is still dark, night not yet over. I'm struggling to wipe the sleep from my eyes—especially with Tau trying to run into my face yet again. The little bot isn't done screaming yet, terrified enough to deplete his little battery to extremely low levels.

I reach out to the nightstand, turning on the light. "I'm awake," I say, half lying. "What is it?"

And then I smell it. Apple pie. The beeping oven isn't the only thing to have made it into the dream. Yet there is no oven in this hotel room. My mouth waters, but my throat, my throat… constricting…

"Tau, shush for a minute, will you?" I order, my words followed by a cough.

His lights and beeps shut off, but he's not done yet. He zooms right to the air vent, spinning wildly like a flying top.

There's a hissing coming from above, a hot, dangerous hiss getting louder and louder the more I strain to hear it. I slam the vent shut, desperately hoping I've gotten it in time.

I turn, and I'm not alone in the room. Despite the adjoining suite beside us, my trio—if I can call them mine—

have somehow decided to pile into the same one. Nekkan has crashed out on the floor between the beds, Nemo stretched out in the chair at his feet.

"Wake up, Nemo, wake up!" I stammer, going so far as to slap his sleeping form. The Tennyson quote comes to me in an instant, and I blurt out: "*So many worlds, so much to do, so little done, such things to be.*"

Nemo sits bolt upright in one smooth motion, eyes flying open. I'm coughing again: whatever's in the room is already getting to me. I reach for the window only to find it bolted shut.

"What is it?" asks Nemo, blinking as he runs through waking diagnostics. "I have not finished recharging."

"We're being gassed!" I say, pulling my hair up and back into a ponytail. I need to think. "We need to get the others up. Oh Sisters, what if it's too late?"

The droid slips off the chair and to his feet, wasting no time reassuring me. He points at the bathroom. *Slag, another vent.*

My coughing is getting stronger now, every breath making my lungs burn hotter. I can't hold it back, hold it in. I can't stop my breath from bringing oxygen to the fire.

Someone is trying to poison us. To kill us.

I rush to Crow's side, but Nemo's already handling her. He doesn't bother with waking her, just slips her over his shoulder and stands. She doesn't stir. My heart skips a beat in terror.

"Dora, you need to evacuate now," says Nemo, rushing for the door. "I have her. You do not have any time left."

"Is she…" I'm terrified of the answer. I need Crow, and the feelings in my chest, the confusing, contorted feelings, tell me this is important and real.

"She had a lot to drink," he says, "enough for every year she was asleep. Are you all right, Miss Dora?"

"Peachy," I reply. Then I cough again. "But we can't leave Nekkan."

The ocugry is sleeping like a brick—a few thousand-pounds brick. I grab his arm, try to hoist him up on his feet, but he's not budging. Not even an inch. The beast is massive, and dead weight. Quite literally, too, if we don't get him out of here soon.

Tau chirps in terror.

"Dora!" says Nemo. "You can't stay here a minute longer. The levels of toxicity in this room are reaching dangerous levels. If you don't leave now…"

"Get Crow out of here!" I stammer. "We can't leave Nekkan!"

My mind is spinning, the edges of my vision darkening. Nemo's right, I don't have much time. But Nekkan is one of us; I won't leave him behind.

I can't wake him; I'm not strong enough. My greatest tool is my mind, and it's not helping nearly as much as I know it should.

My mind. Ocurgies are nothing like humans; they have hardware in their brains. Their HUDs runs deep into their cortex. I run my hands over his hairy head, my fingers so much thinner than each quill. There has to be an access panel here, somewhere, for the techs to reach the inner workings of his mind if he was glitching and needed repair. Somewhere.

The panel behind his left ear releases under my touch. My thoughts pull together through the fog, my mind coming into sharp focus as I take in the world of wires hidden behind Nekkan's skin. Not entirely animal, not entirely machine. Cyborg.

"Tau," I say, wheezing, "lend me a light here."

The bot lights up and hovers above the dark hole in the beast's head. The wires are all over the place, a little computer stuffed inside a skull alongside the actual brain. My eyes quickly scan the system, trying to make sense of it. Even as the darkness creeps closer in, elements are clicking into place. It's a literal mess: the damage done by whatever landed him here is obvious now I see it up close and personal, synapses snapped and burned. It's a delicate tangle.

I don't need to fix the HUD—I don't know if I even can. I just need something to shock the beast awake.

Call it adrenaline, dumb luck, or just incredible intuition, but I reach inside his head and jam the green wire into place.

Nekkan roars to life, sending me soaring across the room. A system has just come back online, though I'm not sure which one—but it's enough to shock him awake. His hand slaps the panel shut as he flies to his feet, graceful even with his bulk, reaching for me in the same swoop.

The coughing takes over, forcing me to my knees. I've been holding my breath during the procedure without realizing it, the sharp intake after my fall filling my lungs with the thick apple-pie air. One hand lands on the bed, bracing my fall; the other reaches for where the locket should be on the nightstand, fingers closing around empty air as the world goes dark.

I wake to fresh air filling my lungs, my body wrapped tightly in Nekkan's arms. My throat burns as I breathe, but I *am* breathing, slaggit, and that's all that matters. The beast's massive chest rises and falls, and, for a minute, I'm filled with warmth, feeling so gently cradled. But then that warmth becomes a wildfire, and the hacking cough starts again.

"You live," says Nekkan.

"You saved me," I wheeze.

"You saved me first."

He helps me to my feet, placing me delicately on the cobbled street. My bare feet are cold against the stones, sending a shiver up my spine. Beside me, Nemo and Crow are waiting silently, staring up at the window of the room that's just tried to kill us all. Even Tau hovers, frozen between us.

"Crow." I reach for her, and our hands intertwine, fingers lacing through fingers. She's alive. We're all alive. She's clutching my hand in hers, as if it's the most natural thing in the world.

But her eyes don't leave the hotel.

Slowly, I peel my eyes from her face, turning instead to stare at the sky. Glowing words in the sky again. This time they're in the form of green clouds, glowing like radioactive waste. Letters that must be kilometers long, bright against the black canvas of night.

Return it to me.

The words are enough to drive another icy stake through my heart. The chill is so intense, made worse by the fact that I'm shivering in the street in my underclothes, still recovering my breath. And I'm *exposed*. My face is wide open for the whole world to see. Thankfully they're all too busy staring at the giant, glowing words in the sky.

Slag, the locket. I can feel its cool weight around my neck once again. How long has it been there? I can't remember putting it on.

"We should go," says Crow. "We *need* to go, actually. Now. Before they see us. And by us, I mean you."

Nemo hands me the spark coat, somehow salvaged in the escape, and I drape it over my shoulders. "H-how?" I stammer through chattering teeth.

"I do not need to breathe. I went back," he says. "I do not understand how we were found again. We stayed on the path this time."

"The locket," I say. Sisters, how could I have been so careless? "I suppose it only hides me if I'm actually wearing it?"

"What is this locket?" asks Nekkan, and I can see his fur standing on edge, each hair rising with his anxiety.

"A gift from the Technowitch of Night," I say.

"The one Dora murdered," Crow adds.

Nekkan lets out a pained groan. "It just doesn't end with you, does it? Illegal faces, murder, and cursed jewelry? I've taken down mercenaries with less of a rap sheet than you."

Nothing like a trained killer to call you out on your mistakes. I expect to feel ashamed, but then something unexpected happened: Nekkan smiles. Not the creepy, bearing-all-fangs kind of smile, but a gentle little grin.

He seems, of all things, actually impressed.

He signals for us to move, placing an arm around me to keep me hidden as he pushes me down a dark side alley. The street lights don't make it back here, but the glowing letters cast a deep green gleam over us all.

"You saved my life," he says. "You saved all of us."

My teeth chatter on as I grin back, the chill raising gooseflesh on my bare legs.

"After putting us all in danger," says Crow. "Good going, princess-clone."

"And this is when I tell you all it wasn't actually me who did the saving," I reply, which is difficult through my chattering teeth. "It was Tau. He was the one who detected the gas and tried to wake me."

"Tau, your bot?" asks Nekkan. Tau chirps a little jingle of agreement. "Just how much can he do?"

"I'm still figuring that out myself," I reply, "but thanks, Tau. You saved us all."

He makes a little noise as he glows red. Is he—blushing? I *definitely* didn't program that kind of behavior into him. I never gave him red LEDs in the first place: he's modulating not just the intensity of his light, but somehow the wavelength as well.

"You—both of you," Nekkan corrects himself, "just saved my life. I owe you a debt."

Now I'm the one blushing. "We're part of this together. None of us gets left behind."

"This makes you my pack," he says. The moment feels heavy, somehow. Solemn. I didn't think ocugry had emotions beyond 'murderous frenzy,' so this feels like the human equivalent of a tearful hug. "You are my pack, now."

"We're your pack," I reply. I'm not sure what one's meant to say in this situation, but it feels right. Something in this universe has brought the four of us together. Calling us a pack suddenly feels like an understatement.

"Taking a shot in the dark here," says Crow, shuffling uncomfortably beside us. "But I'm pretty sure never in my life—even the parts I don't remember—was I ever so thankful to have gone to bed wasted and fully clothed. For once it's the sober girl who's running out in her knickers."

"I'll have you know, *Underclothes Casual* is very in right now."

"It is?"

"No."

Crow scoffs, turning her chin away from me. "And here I was, trying to be nice, thinking of your needs and stuff. But go ahead, keep freezing."

"Why are you still with me? If I'm making your life so miserable?"

"Beats sleeping in a field and scaring off crows." She makes a face, pulling her hands in stiff and close to her body, a zombie popsicle. "And it goes for all of us. Nemo here would be wasting away in a ditch if you hadn't set all this in motion. And Nekkan?"

"Probably roaming the woods," he says. The ocugry's grip is too tight—he still hasn't let me go. "Hunting for sustenance and getting used to my new life as an exile."

"We realized you're the only reason we're moving forward. And we're not letting you out of our sight," Nemo adds.

"And yet," says Crow, her face stony and cold, "we are all still caught in the crossfire of your feud with Eve. You might have saved our lives, but it was from a danger you put us all in *again*. If you hadn't come along, we'd all be fine right now."

"No, no we wouldn't," says Nemo. "We went over this at the bar. Dora's given us all meaning, and that meaning gives us hope. We have a future now, whatever that might be. And we wouldn't have it if it wasn't for you. *She's* our catalyst."

A hot tear rolls down my cheek. Slag, am I crying? I wipe it away just as fast.

"Ok, I'm done with the touchy-feely stuff. Will someone find her clothes before she dies of cold?" asks Crow, running the palms of her hands over her eyes.

"I can help." Nemo begins to strip off his layers, unaffected by the air outside him. Off comes the branded park shirt, revealing the twisted torso below. I cringe. Even knowing he's made to look like this, it's uncomfortable to see.

"I think you look fab," says Crow, slipping her arm through mine as we stroll down the street. "At least this way we can all keep an eye on you."

"You're just saying that because you dressed me," I say. "Or maybe you actively hate me? It feels like you're about to burst into song or something."

"Well, I guess I could," she says. "*We're on our way to see the Technomage, the most superius Mage of them all…* how does that sound?"

"A little ridiculous."

"It's a work in progress."

The early hours of the morning have transformed the plaza from lively hub to ghost town. There's no one left to mill about, watching the comings and goings of the 'vator; there aren't even lights on at this time of night. We only have Tau to light the way, and he's getting quite proud of being a beacon.

I can't bear the thought of Tau being broken or left behind in the brawl. He'd hate being asleep for the rest of this. But another change in our relationship is that I can ask him to slip into my coat, fully awake, and he doesn't complain. He'll come out when this is all over: either in front of the Mage, or not at all.

Mage or bust at this point.

"Right," says Nekkan, "follow my lead."

"Is what we are doing legal in any respect?" asks Nemo. "I mean, just for my own peace of mind…"

"Oh, it's as legal as you think it is." Nekkan pulls the oversized gun from his back, cocking it with a force that sends pigeons spiraling into the air. "Or as legal as you need it to be. For peace of mind, that is."

He pounces. One minute he's beside us, the next he's flying at the door, legs first, gun at the ready. His massive paws slam into it and shatter the wood, making an ocugry-sized hole so large we can fit through side by side with ease.

The rest of us charge forward. Unlike Nekkan, who takes the plaza in three strides, I'm winded by the time I reach the elevator's marble steps and have to pull myself up with the railing to get to the entrance. It doesn't help that my lungs are still on fire from the gas, and I can't get a full breath.

"We should have just led with this," Crow pants. "Thank God for Nekkan's fists."

Nekkan's already far ahead of us, the attendant nowhere to be seen. I can assume those two observations are related. There's only a single room beyond the shattered door, so large it would fit an entire shuttle ship.

Thinking of the ship is like pressing the anxiety button, and I reach for Crow for reassurance, missing her by a hair. I pull my hand back. I'm not even sure why I did that in the first place.

The edges of the room are framed with lush potted plants, but there's no furniture: just a large rectangular pit in the center wide enough for the elevator to rest, surrounded by ancient-looking columns. The ceiling is covered with silver filigree, spinning and twirling over the bright white plaster. Above the 'vator's resting place, the ceiling is metallic, and I can see tracks to pull it open. There's a spiral staircase in the back corner, leading to a thin excuse for a floor, and doors lining a hallway. The room is empty otherwise—well, minus the gigantic ocugry currently hog-tying a very confused man.

"Let me go!" The doorman is fighting for his life, thrashing on the floor as he struggles to rip off his restraints. His face is still the same wild shade of purple as before. "Do you know what you're doing? What a mess you're making for yourselves?"

"Nope, and I don't care." Nekkan laughs as he finishes with his knots. He sits the man up, propping him against a column. "Will someone close the door?"

"We cannot," says Nemo. "You appear to have broken it."

"Ah. Yes. That tends to happen when I kick things." He turns his focus to the tied-up attendant. "Right, now what do we have to do to get that 'vator down here?"

"You can't!" The obnoxious, mightier-than-thou voice from earlier is replaced with simpering sobs. "It comes back down here at dawn. You can wait and ride it then. If you untie me now, I can fit you in the schedule."

"Oh? Because there's room all of a sudden?" asks Nekkan, laughing again. He seems to be enjoying this, his quills rippling in an invisible breeze that makes him look all the more imposing, while at ease in the world.

"Nekk," says Nemo, making him cringe, "maybe this is not the way we should be approaching this. Remember, secret weapon and all?"

"Right," Nekkan growls in reply. "Also, nicknames are off the table."

In all the commotion, I almost forget I have an actual role to play. It would be much easier if Nekkan's brute force alone got us on the 'vator, but that was a long shot, so not the entirety of the plan. Though the word 'plan' is being thrown around a little loosely today.

I stride up to the attendant, lifting my nose up high. Jo'Niss's glare is the easiest to replicate because it's so close to my own resting face. It's a look the princess never shows on TV, but if I know anything from the scientists I look up to, it's how to extrapolate data from incomplete sets. Knowing Jo'Niss, knowing everything that made her tick, well, this is like slipping into a different dress.

"Hello," I say. It's much easier to feel confident when I channel Jo'Niss: she's so poised, so strong that I can't help but feel the same. Well, she *was*. "Do you know who I am?"

Instantly, the man relaxes in his bonds. His eyes meet mine with such awe, such reverence. It can almost pass for love. While it's easy to play Jo'Niss, it's hard to keep a straight face under the weight of such a reaction.

"Your Highness!" he exclaims. "But, how? I mourned you, we all mourned you…"

"My death was faked," I say, crouching down to look him in the eye. "I wanted the would-be assassins to think they had gotten me, so I could find them myself. And you can help me."

"Help you?" he asks. "How?"

"The Mage. I must speak to him. He has a key part to play in all of this. He can help me find the ones responsible—the men who want me dead."

I may as well have stardust for dandruff the way the man reacts. Every move makes him relax a little bit more, the relief that I'm alive somehow overwhelming him. I've never been… adored before. I'm not sure I like it. How did Jo'Niss keep a straight face under the pressure?

"I want to help you," he says, glancing at the platform, "but I wasn't lying when I said the elevator does not return for another six hours. When it does, though, I can get you on it. But your trip will be a matter of public record."

"Can't you smudge the names a little?"

"If it was up to me, yes, I could," he says, "but it requires taking biometrics for security. You'll only be granted access if you match your identity and have no marks against your name."

I don't let my disappointment show. So much for our teamwork. There's only so much you can do without bureaucracy tying you up with all that red tape.

"But I'm officially deceased," I say, forcing a pout, "and so's Nekkan here. That's part of the reason we need to see the Mage himself."

Not to mention that clones don't have the same fingerprints as their sisters, same as with identical twins. I seem to be solving all of my problems by creating new ones for myself.

"That, and I am a droid," says Nemo, waving. "Hi!"

"And I haven't been alive for a few centuries. Give or take a few years," adds Crow. "Should I say hello, too?"

"You." Nekkan grabs the attendant's face and forces him to look him in the eyes. "There must be a backup system in case of emergencies."

"Nekkan!" hisses Nemo, grabbing the ocugry's arm once more and pulling him back. The beast barely budges, despite the droid's considerable upper body strength.

"Answer me!" Nekkan is snarling at the attendant, and in that moment, he fully looks like the animal he shares his mutated DNA with. He's bold, fierce, deadly. Every one of his filed titanium teeth drips with saliva.

"The zip-line!" the attendant stammers, squeezing his eyes closed.

Nekkan lifts and eyebrow. "The what now?"

"The zip-line," he replies. "The fastest way from here to the Mage's Moon."

"How does it work?" Nekkan is instantly enthralled. The terrifying grin is replaced with something akin to joy. He seems as excited as a child at the prospect of zip-lining, whatever that is.

"Basically a guided rocket," says the attendant. "It connects to the elevator line and allows for repairs to be made all the way up the cable—or when the elevator gets stuck, you know. Anyways, you'll need suits."

"We'll go put them on," says Nemo, tugging at Nekkan. He still won't drop the attendant.

"Our suits don't usually fit ocugry. I'm not sure if…"

"Hush." Nekkan glares. "No more talking. We're done here."

"Remember," I say, leaning toward the attendant, "you're doing us a great service. Don't tell anyone that I was here. Don't even hint at *thinking* I might be still alive. I'm dead, and you never saw me. Got it?"

He nods.

My skin is dappled with goosebumps. Seeing the man writhe on the floor… I thought I was hard, thought I was ready for real violence. But this makes me cringe deep in my soul.

"Nekkan." I turn to the ocugry. "Can you untie him, please?"

"You might want to rethink that, missy," he says, muzzle twitching. "This man could quite easily run off and sound some sort of alarm contraption. We don't want that, do we?"

"No, no we don't. But this man… what's your name?"

"Cohren," he says, staring at me like I'm a lifeline and he's about to drown, "Cohren Portens."

"I'm pretty sure Mister Portens here doesn't want to turn us in. Now when he knows what it would do to the beloved princess. Isn't that right, Cohren?"

He nods vigorously. "I don't want Jo'Niss to die a second time. She's the Systems' *darling*."

"You see, Nekkan?" My heart flutters with an odd sort of pride. I wonder, idly, at what point this will be taking things too far. I'm enjoying myself, now I've gotten past the adoration, leaning into the role, relishing in the thrill of the impossible. Embracing the face I've been afraid of for sixteen long years. "This man here isn't a threat. He's an ally. An ally who's going to get us up to the moon."

"Exactly," says Cohren, "untie me, and I'll help you any way I can. Anything for her Highness."

"Fine." Nekkan reaches for the ropes, and with a move so fast it leaves only a blur, he brings his fingers down on the knot. They slide through it like butter. "But I'm keeping an eye on him, you get me?"

"Of course. Now please, Cohren, we need to get to the Mage as quickly as possible. Please."

The man rubs his wrists. The ropes weren't on long, but they were tight. The skin there is already red. I shudder. This was Nekkan being gentle: being an enemy of his must be unimaginable.

"Of course," our former hostage says, running his tongue over dry lips, rising gingerly to his feet and walking toward the stairs.

We follow Cohren across the atrium and up the only staircase. The hallway leads to the doors made of polished red wood, and he walks us through the one in the middle.

Stepping inside brings back warm memories of my shed. It's a cluttered mess of mechanical parts that have been strewn around like whomever put them in here never expected to need to find anything in a hurry. Uncle's was the same as long as I'd known it, accumulating more clutter every year.

Cohren knows exactly what he's looking for and quickly pulls out three pressure suits from the pile.

"Here," he says, tossing them to us, "and as I expected, there's nothing here that could ever fit an ocugry. Sorry."

"I've been through worse than a rocket ride in a vacuum," he says gruffly. "I can handle this."

"You're kidding me, right?" Crow raises an eyebrow, squinting at the beast in confusion. She's only echoing what the rest of us are thinking. "You're telling me you can be exposed to a vacuum and it's *not* a problem?"

"I'm built for a lot of things. Dying isn't one of them."

We each find small places in the clutter to try and put the suits on, dragging the tight material over our clothing. I'm hating the stupid dress Crow got me now more than ever—it makes a little roll under the suit, like I'm wearing an innertube around my hips. Luckily, everyone's more focused on their own ill-fitting suits than they are on me. Nekkan rips the air supply off the back of one and jams it into his utility belt, hose dangling.

"Right. Helmets are this way." Cohren avoids our gaze as he leads the way out another set of doors. This time, we're no longer in a lavish hallway but some kind of catwalk that surrounds the outside of the complex.

The shock of the cold night air hits me in the face like a slap. Under the pressure suit, I'm warm, and getting warmer, but my face is still exposed to the elements and beginning to freeze. It's as if the world has somehow gotten even colder in the few minutes we've been inside. And maybe a bit brighter, too: we're higher up, and I don't dare to look down. The world is humming around me, and I don't dare listen.

We climb a ladder to the roof, and there, like something out of a nightmare, stand the 'vator's cables. They're wider than anything I have ever seen before in my life: the five of us with our arms clasped wouldn't wrap around a single one of them. They stretch up and up and up and just keep going forever.

"Right," says Cohren, opening a trap door in the roof and extracting four helmets. He holds one out to Nekkan, whose fist can practically eclipse the thing, then shakes his head and hands it back.

The rest of us put on our helmets. They form a tight seal, cutting off the cold of the night instantly, my mouth fogging up the inside. Such a small reaction, but it thrills me for an instant. Cold is such a fascinating thing. It's even messing with my ears, making them ring.

"You four ready to go? What you're going to want to do is—"

Nekkan lets out an angry yelp. My visor's so fogged up I can't see, but I can feel the sudden rise in tension around me, like someone grabbed us all and gave us a good shake in a snow globe.

"The hell is this?" shouts Crow.

"You should have left me tied up," Cohren laughs. As the fog in my helmet lifts, I can see he is holding a gun, though it's tiny in comparison to Nekkan's, who is holding his ahead of him like he's ready to blast away the world.

"You!" I spit, taking in the growing lights around us, the noise that sounds like a thousand bees. Troops of strangers, armed to their teeth, have filled the plaza. We're surrounded on all sides, and we are trapped on this roof with no way out. "You're working for her! For Dusk!"

"Her?" The man throws back his head and laughs, dangerous and cruel. "Hell no, I'm not working for her! No, *Princess*, I'm here to take you back where you belong."

"And where's that?" I snap, panic bubbling up in my stomach. I want to vomit.

"To the grave." His lips curl up on the ends, making him smile an awful smile. I want to jump off this rooftop just to get away from it.

Not that I want to die at the hands of a man with such a terrible sense of drama.

Or at anyone's hands, actually.

Who are those men waited for us below, if not Dusk's goons? The Coalition?

"Jo'Niss apparently shows up on my shift, which means one of two things," Cohren continues. "Either Jo'Niss is still alive, or she was born from an illegal clone-batch. Either way, *quelle chance*! Payday."

"Douchecanoe," hisses Crow. "Don't use French in vain!"

How a woman with no memories of her own life can understand an extinct language, I'll never know. Crow's becoming more and more of a mystery with every passing minute.

"I'm more worried about what he could do with Miss Dora," says Nemo. "I think a little focus could be reasonable, Miss Crow."

"Dora?" Cohren scoffs. "Of all incognito names, you pick—"

The hole that appears in his stomach is so wide I can see clear through to the other side. I never heard the blast, only the way his words ended mid-sentence. I didn't see the shot, only the shock on his face as he looks down and realizes it's all over. The man falls to his knees, then forward, kissing the roof with his dead lips.

"We need to go," hisses Nekkan, giving the man a swift kick to check if he's still alive. With most of Cohren's vital organs now dust in the breeze, I'm personally pretty sure he isn't.

"Dora!"

"I do not wish to alarm any of you," says Nemo, waving his hand at the writhing plaza. I risk a single glance over the edge and retreat immediately, heart pinching. How many men did the Coalition bring with them to catch me? "But we are surrounded. There is no place *to* go. The would-be-regicidal-maniac called all his friends."

"Sometimes, the only way out is up," says the ocugry. He grabs the hose of his air supply and stuffs it between his lips. And before we have a chance to respond, he grabs the three of us and tosses us onto his back.

I clutch the thick quills of his mane as he begins to race up the cable. How he's gripping onto the silver cord, I don't know, but he's zipping up it faster than I ever thought possible. Within seconds, we've cursed Anchor goodbye, and we're flying up the cable toward the Mage's moon.

This can't be happening. Cohren must have shot me. There's no way I'm actually clutching the mane of a beast, climbing up a cable to space with three people on his back. This has to be a nightmare.

Nekkan is not possible.

His rhythmic breathing is soothing as he climbs, focused and calm. But it's the only calm thing around me: as the distance between us and the ground grows, vertigo explodes in my gut like I've never felt before. I force my eyes shut, gripping his mane tighter. Today's a day for impossible things, and looking any closer will make my understanding of reality shatter. Nekkan's powered by something that isn't natural. We don't need rockets for this ride, as he's already running faster than any of us ever could.

And he'll have to be fast. Ocugries have powerful bodies, but they can't go indefinitely in a vacuum. If there's no shelter at the end of this line, we're all done for.

Minutes go by. An hour? The atmosphere around us thins. I start to see, way off in the distance, the curvature of this small planet. I shut my eyes again, sealing them against the terrible sight, trying not to feel the cold that grips my hands even through the gloves of my suit. The quills of his mane are as strong as ropes and will hold us as long as my arms can bear it.

Unless something smacks into me.

I scream Crow's name as her body slides past. Faster than I've ever reacted in my life, I grab her falling form, catching her by her oxygen tube, ripping my glove raw. My ears ring with the echo of her cry riding up through the plastic between us as cold bites at my skin—it's torn. I squeeze the tube tighter purely by reflex, hoping to seal whatever I can lest my hand freezes off entirely.

But Crow's suffocating in her helmet, my grip around the hose the only thing keeping her from plummeting toward the planet below. She's not falling, but she's not breathing either.

I look down at Crow, down past her, and take in the horrible distance. The kilometers-and-kilometers-long fall beneath us. Crow's struggling to grip onto anything, hands flailing in panic. I can't stop myself from squeezing tighter, the pain in my hand unbearable as the water on my skin sublimates from lack of pressure.

Her knee kicks a box on Nekkan's belt—his air supply. The tank tumbles down, down, down, taking Nekkan's oxygen along with it.

Crow's weight is pulling me down. Nekkan is slowing. I can't hear him, though. Every sound from his form never leaves him, the emptiness of space rendering us all deaf and mute.

I can't feel my fingers anymore. I can't hold on any longer, the hose digging into my skin even as the nerve endings die. Crow's not breathing anymore, and her wild swinging is slowing, without her having found a grip.

Nemo's hand gently touches my back. I spin my head around to meet his gaze, his mouth saying words I can't hear, a desperate look in his eyes. He shakes his head.

And lets go.

Before I can even scream, he's grabbed Nekkan's utility belt, stopping his fall short. He straps himself to one of the loops, pulling the tie so tightly around him no human would have been able to breathe. Then he reaches for Crow, taking her safely from my grasp. The relief is instantaneous.

So is the pain.

As Crow's weight lifts from my hand, the ripped glove is completely exposed. I scream again as I feel the full cold of the edge of space, the cold so hot it's burning. I shove my hand between my legs, trying to close the seal with the rubber of my suit, but the pressure of touch sends shocks of pain up my arm. My other hand, the one gripping the mane, threatens to let go of Nekkan. I squeeze my legs tighter, and my hand goes numb.

His powerful form races up the cable—until he's racing *forward*. The world has slowly flipped over. There's no longer up or down here. It's not sudden: I might have noticed it if I hadn't been in the process of saving Crow's life. If that had happened just a few minutes after, while we're here, she probably wouldn't have gone anywhere at all.

I'm *floating*.

Nekkan is seemingly unperturbed by any of this. He's holding his breath, but it doesn't slow him down. With a single, powerful push, he propels himself forward on the wire.

We shoot forward like a bullet from Nekkan's gun. We're a meteor, a shooting star in the night. It doesn't feel like we're moving, but the green light in front of us is steadily growing bigger. It's forming into a moon, revealing details on its surface we couldn't see from the ground.

The entire surface seems like it's been carved out of one block of solid emerald. At the bottom of the cable looms a castle, almost identical to Nemo's when he thought he was a prince. A fixture from First Earth, beautiful and gleaming.

Now, we're falling.

The world has flipped once more. We've been flying steadily, but now we're accelerating, speeding faster and faster as we get ever closer to the moon. It's grabbed us in its artificial gravity. We're not flying anymore, no; we're plummeting, plummeting toward the surface of stunning green.

Nekkan grabs for the wire and lets out a silent roar as his nails drag in the metal. He lets go, his hands black and oily, and we fall, like a stone, toward the emerald moon.

To add insult to injury, we even fail at falling.

I know I can't be anything but dead. At least the impact didn't hurt: I'm hanging comfortably three feet over the cold, hard floor. It's a metal sheet that could have killed us on impact. The castle-shape I'd seen from above wasn't a castle at all, simply the 'vator at rest, latched to the green sphere in the sky. The entire surface of the so-called emerald moon is covered in green solar panels, greener than I've ever seen in my life. An engineered jungle.

Proof I've died and made it to heaven.

Nekkan moves, dropping his feet out of whatever hovering field that suspends us, and the spell shatters. We've been saved by the braking system of the space station.

Nemo looks the same, no worse for wear, and Crow's grinning like a wild woman, saying nothing. Of course she can breathe now that I'm not squeezing her air supply, and she seems to have recovered completely from her brief stint as space mail. They both land effortlessly on the surface.

I twist my body, spikes of pain flaring up both arms. I've still got my hand squeezed between my legs, and it's aching dully. I'm scared slagless of releasing the pressure. I can feel Tau chirping warnings from my pocket, but I can't hear him, the world around us still devoid of air.

Nekkan. Nekkan's going to suffocate unless we can find a way inside. His powerful lungs won't last forever on a single breath of air.

He collapses to his knees, wincing in pain and clutching his hands. The fingertips are gleaming black, the thick substance running over. The blood of an ocugry.

There's a rumble beneath my feet, and, before I can get out of the way, the floor gives out. We tumble into the elevator proper, hitting the carpeted floor inside. The roof slams shut instantly, a sound I actually hear—and there's *air*. Nekkan lets out a cry of pain as he hits the deck, breathing in raspy air.

I reach up to remove my helmet, but it's impossible to do with one hand since my other is currently indisposed. Nemo's already on Nekkan, pumping the hairy chest with his hands. Can you give an ocugry CPR?

"Do not try to help him," says a voice, coming from everywhere and nowhere at once. Nemo doesn't miss a beat, still desperately trying to force air into the ocugry's lungs.

"But he's hurt!" Nemo shouts.

I'm not sure where I'm meant to be looking. There are no visible speakers, just mirrored walls. The floor's carpeted red, but the spray of Nekkan's blood is quickly turning it black.

"Do not move," insists the voice, calm and devoid of emotion. I would have once compared it to a robot, but Nemo has emotions down pat and perfect. The voice sounds more like it was *bored* than anything else. "You're trespassing on my moon. Do not expect me to take pity on you."

"Oh yeah?" Crow runs to the door and pummels her fists on it, like that will help. "This man just risked his life to get us all to talk to you, not to mention your gatekeeper down there tried to kill us!"

"Cohren?" the voice asks.

"Yeah," Crow replies. "He tried to shoot my friend here, called a posse on her. I think he's part of some weird cult to overthrow the monarchy?"

There's a pause. Hesitation? The voice says nothing, allowing only the sound of our panicked breaths to fill the chamber. After a minute or so, the doors slide open.

"I do apologize for that," the voice says, "but you still came barging into my home in the middle of the night. Do not think I want to see you."

"Thanks," I say, not sure if he can hear me as it is. Still, I don't move. If I do, the damage to my hand will be locked in stone.

Three droids who look remarkably like Nemo come sauntering in, lifting up Nekkan like a rag doll. While they share Nemo's face, there's definitely something off about them, like there's something missing to stop them from appearing fully human. They're wearing clean, black suits and identical, old-fashioned neckties in different shades of emerald. The technomage sure has a thing for theming.

Somehow, after all this, the ocugry can *walk*. The droids allow him to stand even as he fights off their helping hands. His feet hit the ground hard enough to send shockwaves through the rest of us. His hands are a mess, covered in black, oily blood that still drips from his fingertips.

"You can take off your suits, the air is wonderful here. Let me catch the sleep you stole from me… we'll talk about this in the morning. Your friend will be looked after. Please, follow all instructions given to you. The droids are my helping hands and mean you no harm."

As if to prove those words, the androids bracing Nekkan smile in unison. Nemo shifts away from them, grimacing as one makes eye contact. If there was any resemblance before, it's gone now.

Nekkan and the droids stumble out of the 'vator into the hallway beyond. Crow turns back to me. She looks, of all things, *worried*. I want to laugh; she almost died, and she's worried about me?

"Please, exit the vehicle," says a droid as he reaches for me.

I cringe. I still haven't removed my helmet. I don't think I can. I'm panting, steaming up the inside all over again. "I need a minute."

"Please, follow instructions."

"I can't, I…" I try to take a step forward, removing some of the pressure on my hand. It's like touching the heart of a star. The pain overwhelms me, blinding and scorching and—

I collapse to the floor, my last sight that of a hand so withered it can't belong to anything human.

19

"IT'S GOING TO BE OK," SAYS AUNTIE EMERY, rubbing a salve on the chapped skin of my hand. "I prepared you for this. You are ready."

"You said that already," I mutter through the fog of the dream. "I don't know what that means. You prepared me to hide who I am: but even after all your training, it's impossible."

"It is time." Auntie nods.

"Yeah, you said that! Time for what?"

"To take back what is yours."

When I wake up, I'm on a cloud.

The room is a bright, wonderful white. My pajamas are the softest white cotton. My skin is pure and somehow fluffy, a sweet, flowery scent flowing through my heart and soul.

It doesn't make my scream any less agonizing when my eyes fall on the stump that was once my left hand. It's been sliced clear off at the wrist, leaving smooth skin around the joint. With my remaining hand, unbelieving, I reach up to touch it: it's as if no hand was ever there in the first place.

So clean. So effortlessly removed. I wonder idly why they would have such an advanced medical facility here, in the Outer Zone of all places, when the core planets always have the best of everything. Then again, he is the Technomage Superius....

"Do not panic, dearie," says a matronly droid, dressed like a nurse from storybooks of old. Her mouth doesn't move. It's generous to call her a droid when she's a robot at best. An older model, like one of Tennyson's first creations, with no pretense of self-awareness. Probably doesn't get much use up here on the moon. She's got a kind, motherly face, cushioned in a halo of perfectly coiffed blonde hair. The white apron is blinding like the rest of the ward. She whirrs as she pats me on the arm. "Your hand was removed because it could no longer function. But there are new models I am sure you will like even more than what you had before!"

I nod. I'm still too much in shock to form an adequate reply. My hand is gone. Reliable leftie, master of circuitry, is most likely sitting in a biohazard bin.

Tau flutters by my side, beeping a happy jingle. He's paler than he's been before, polished brighter than a star, and he's happy—if a bot ever can be happy.

"Hey, little buddy," I say, patting him on his top, stifling a sob. He beeps a few times appreciatively. "You doing all right?"

He replies with a happy set of *beeps* and *boops*. My heart swells with pride. He's a good bot. So much more than his base programming. The single thing I've gotten right. The sight of him safe and clean gives me an excuse to cry from relief rather than the pure heartbreak I'm feeling right now.

"Now get some sleep, dearie," the nurse droid insists, placing a tall glass of water on my bedside table. The left side, meaning I'll have to reach across with my right hand if I ever get thirsty. But before I can bring it up, the nurse has already left the ward, leaving me in silence. Textbook example of the difference between a robot and a droid: humanity.

The room is cold. Not just on my face and skin, but deep in my bones, unnervingly cold. The white walls and blue curtains—are there actual windows behind them or are the curtains only here for aesthetics—are as frosty as the air conditioning, which brings gooseflesh up my arms. I watch as the little bumps end around the stump of my now gone hand.

And I sob.

Hot tears stream down my face, rolling down my cheeks and onto the crisp white sheets. Tau nudges my face, letting out a lone, worried note.

"Sleep mode," I say in between sobs, and he drops gently onto my nightstand, leaving me alone. But he's not shut himself off like I wanted him to—I can still hear his brain in motion, and it's *on*, like he's just playing sleep to make me happy.

Once again, trying to get what I wanted almost got people killed; now I have a stump to remind me of what my recklessness can do.

I see Cohren with a hole in his chest, crumpling like a used piece of paper as he dies—after he tried to kill me, gun raised, teeth gnashing. Maybe I'm exaggerating the memory, turning him into an old movie villain to try to make sense of it. The man Nekkan killed to protect me. Another person dead because of me.

Sounds like not everybody is happy to know Jo'Niss is alive. Even though I hated her, hated every fiber of her being, I can't help but shudder at the thought. It was better thinking a lunatic wanted her dead, not *many* people across the Sister Systems. I'd spent so much time waiting for Jo'Niss's death to free *me*, that

I haven't even thought about what happened to *her*. She was murdered, and brutally so. Killed at her own mother's funeral.

And I'm parading around wearing her face. Jo'Niss is dead, and now rumors of her being alive will circulate, because of me. No wonder Auntie and Uncle wanted me to stay hidden. How much do they know? Is there someone out there right now who wants to end me in the same way they did the princess?

I'll never escape the Farming Coalition. Not with the galaxy waiting for my face.

So much death in my path. I'm a curse, a plague on this planet, the Systems. Everywhere I go, I bring nothing but horror and death. No wonder I'm the imperfect. No wonder they want me dead.

"Dora?"

The hospital door slides open, and Crow slips inside. Only this version of Crow is polished and clean, the picture of perfection. She's wearing a bright green nightgown made of silk so fine it shines like heavenly light, making her coarse black hair reflect emerald highlights. This Crow is almost unrecognizable from the girl I saw in the field, all smooth skin and delicate features. Even the boils on her hands are completely gone, leaving them blemishless.

I look down at my hands—no, my one remaining hand. It's clean too. I must look like someone else to her as well.

"Crow?" I have to ask, the change is so absolute.

"I'm not supposed to be in here," she says, creeping forward. But when she reaches the end of my bed, she stops and takes a step back. "I gave your nurse the runaround by trying that Tennyson poetry thing. Took me a few tries to get it right, I couldn't remember *bondsman*. But she's out now."

Her eyes fall on the stump and widen. She grabs the end of the bed for support. "They took your hand?"

I nod. "Apparently it's my chance for an upgrade?"

"Shit." Crow lifts her eyes to meet mine, trembling. "You lost your hand—for me."

I hadn't thought of it that way. As I saw it, I'd lost my hand as punishment for recklessness, rather than giving it up to save a friend. But I sure like the sound of that better.

Crow eases herself down to the floor next to me. She looks so regal in the silk, more like a princess than I'll ever be.

"Are you okay?" I ask her.

She snorts. "You lost your hand, and you're asking me?"

"I'm still freaking out about the hand. Here, ask me how I'm doing."

"How are you doing?"

"Slaggin' awful, I just lost my hand."

Crow snorts a single laugh, then catches herself, hands flying to cover her mouth. Which only makes me laugh, which in turn makes Crow laugh louder, until the two of us are in fits in the hospital room.

"Get off the floor, it's probably even colder down there," I insist. "Please. I'm freaking out, and I need someone to talk to."

Crow nods and does as I ask, seating herself beyond the reach of my feet. I wonder if this is what it would be like to have friends: slumber parties with besties, trading secrets like currency in the middle of the night, like I read about in magazines.

"I suppose I need to thank you," Crow says, "for saving my life and all."

I don't know how to respond. I nod, once, and turn my head down. There are certain things in life which exist outside of the realm of words. There's nothing either of us can say.

"We made it," I say finally, clenching my only hand into a fist. "We reached the Mage. We're on his moon. You'll finally know who you are, and I'll go home, save my family, set things right. It's over, and everything will soon be worth it."

Crow nods again, clutching her knees to her chest. She's barefoot, hiding her exposed feet under the emerald nightdress. She closes her eyes, resting her head against her knees, breathing deeply.

"It's everything we wanted," I say. For the first time, I'm not sure if that's true.

"Maybe I don't want it to be over," mutters Crow. "When it's over… we have to accept what's happened."

"I won't unsee what I saw." I shudder. "I can't undo what I did. I'll have to live with the things I've done here for as long as I live."

"I know." Crow stares pointedly at where my missing left hand used to be, then forces her eyes to shut.

"Do you think Nekkan will be okay?"

"I'm sure he will be. The Mage can do anything, right? Nekkan's fingers will be cakewalk for him."

"Have you seen him?"

She shakes her head. "We were separated when we got here. Everyone has quarters for the night. I've never seen a bed so big in all my life—not that my memory's the best."

"And you think… that the Mage can give us what we need, too?"

"I don't know." She clutches her knees even tighter to her chest. "I don't even know what I need anymore."

"What do you mean?" I think it's pretty obvious. Crow needs to get her memories back. She can't very well go around calling herself *Crow* for the rest of her life. Recovering her personality isn't much of a decision.

"I mean, what if I don't like who I was, before all this? What if I was frozen for a reason?"

"Don't say that. You probably had a very good reason for climbing into that chamber that didn't involve having a personality you didn't like."

"Maybe I'm dying." She shrugs. "Maybe I had some incurable disease and was hoping someone in the future would cure me."

"Then I guess we're still in the right place. The Mage—"

"Can do anything, I know." Crow lets out a heavy sigh. "But, I don't know, what if I like who I am right now? What if I gain this other woman's personality, and memories, and I…"

"You what? Worst-case scenario, you make a change for the better. Best case, you love her and feel like yourself again."

"But I feel like *myself* right now," she says. "The other me, she was a warrior. Every fiber of my body tells me so. It scares me. And if I remember who I was… I'll remember who I've lost, too." Her eyes fall on mine and don't let go. They're the deepest brown I've ever seen. "Sorry." She drops her eyes to her hands on her lap. "I didn't mean to drag you into my shit. I just…"

"You what?"

"I don't know," she says. "I've convinced myself you feel the same thing. This same sadness. A loss you can't speak of."

I nod. She's more right than she knows. "My… my *sister* is dead," I say. "She was murdered, and I still carry her face around every day. She died because maybe some asshole wanted to start a war, or she died because someone didn't like her parents. Either way, she died needlessly, and I never got to know her. I hated her. I still hate her. I never even got to know her. But it hurts."

"It hurts to mourn people you don't know," says Crow. "Everyone I knew when I was alive must be dead now. They must have existed, but I don't remember them. I feel like I'm carrying the weight of their deaths on my back, and I don't even know what for."

"I know why, and it doesn't make me feel any better. Jo'Niss was the princess, and I'm the imperfect. The lesser version. The galaxy's left with the surviving imperfect copy. I mourn the death of a sister I never knew, and they're mourning the death of a symbol."

"Stop it. You keep comparing yourself to this princess chick, and I hate it. You act like you're walking around in someone else's shadow, when you're really the sun."

A shiver runs through me, but not from the cold. "What are you saying?"

"I'm saying," she says, her hands visibly trembling, "I don't want to remember the dead if it means I'm going to forget the living. I don't want to gain those memories if it means losing you. If the person I used to be won't share the feelings I feel right here, right now. I… I like you, Dora. And I didn't think *liking* was a feeling I could have until I was whole again, but what if I'm whole now? What if I've been whole this entire time?"

"I…" My mind's racing. This isn't at all what I expected Crow to say, and yet, it's everything I wanted. I lost a hand for Crow, and, deep in my heart, I know the trade was worth it to keep her alive, to keep her here, now.

"Please say something," she says. "I'm putting myself out here right now."

"Crow, I just…" I want to run, to get out of the ward and climb right back in that elevator. "My entire life I've not been allowed to be myself. I was always me-minus-Jo'Niss. I've never had a relationship. I don't even know if I can have one."

"I'm not asking for a romance," she says, her voice squeaking like a mouse.

"Then what? Because… if you want me like that… "

"No… I just… I want to know how you feel about me. Before I turn into someone else. Before I turn into someone I might not like."

I say nothing. I know the words I want to say, but my mouth is dry, and I just can't.

"I can go," Crow squeaks, so unlike her boisterous self. The brash, dangerous woman has retreated deep into her body, leaving nothing but fear and anxiety. A scared girl who wants nothing more than to be told everything is going to be ok.

"No," I say. "Please. Don't go. Crow, I don't know what *liking someone* even feels like. But when I first saw you… it was like lifting the blinds and seeing the sun. And I don't know what it means, but I don't want you out of my life, either. I guess what I'm meaning to say is… I think I like you too, Crow, if that's really what it feels like to like someone."

"What does your gut tell you?"

"My gut tells me you're the most beautiful person I've ever seen," I say. "You annoy the deep-void out of me, you scare me to pieces, but I don't want to see the Mage just yet if it means I'll never see you again, either. And I'm afraid of finding out who you really are—who you really *were*—if that version of you doesn't like me back. I don't think I could live with that."

Crow relaxes, her knees falling away from her chest as her face breaks into a warm smile. I've never seen her smile so widely before, and I soak it up like sunlight. Her hand goes to my face, cutting the chill of the hospital room, heat spreading through my skin where her fingertips touch. I lean in. I love this feeling; it's like leaning into a roaring fire on a cold winter's day.

When words fail, there are other ways to speak.

Crow's lips brush the tip of my nose, and my heart flutters like it's filled with millions of little wings. Then her lips finally find mine, even as I panic from the suddenness of it— though I've plenty of time to anticipate—and as I fumble through trying to know what to do, I melt into the warmth of her lips, never wanting the moment to end.

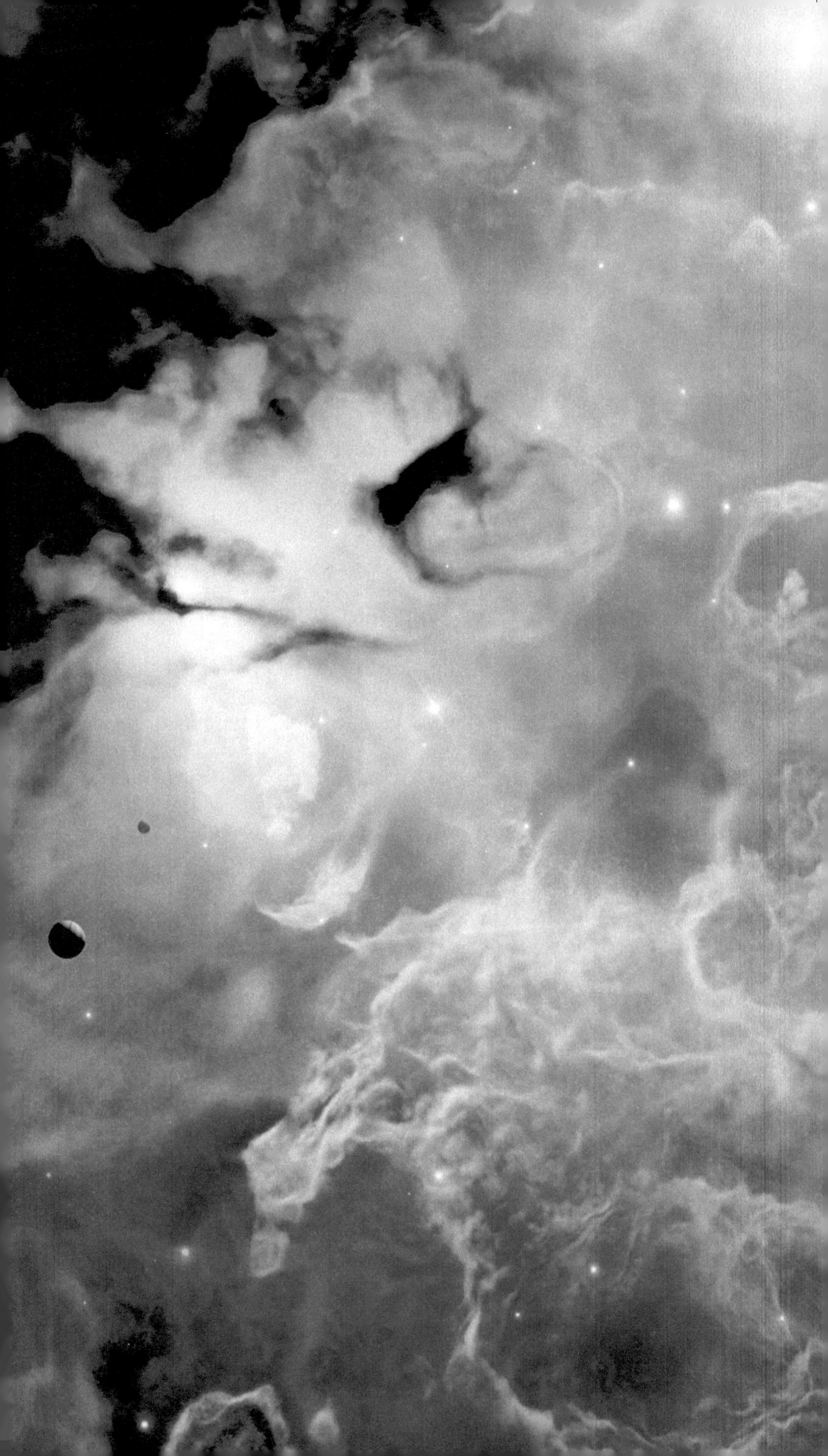

PART 4

MAN IN THE MOON

20

I SPEND THE REST OF THE NIGHT WIDE AWAKE, cradling my the ghost of my left hand as I stare at the ceiling, heart racing as it pumps cold blood through my veins.

A kiss, and she's gone. A single kiss, and my life has changed forever. Like the princes of old awakening their princesses from long sleeps, Crow's kiss jumpstarted my heart. Deep inside of me, for the first time in my life, I felt like I truly wanted someone.

And then Crow was gone, leaving me cold.

I don't blame her. Neither of us knows what the next step is. In a few hours, we'll all meet the Mage and try to convince him to help us reach our goals. Crow will get her *self* back, and I will find my way home. Our wishes do not overlap. The two of us will part ways, probably never to see each other again. Whatever there is between us will end before it begins. We'll never know what we could have had.

Maybe, just maybe, the new-old-Crow might want to come with me. Maybe she'll want to travel to Nesworth, since that's where I'll be hiding the rest of my days to keep from getting involved in whatever socio-political shipslag is going on. I'm lucky to be alive, but I know now how dangerous it is to push my luck with this face. As much as I hate it, this will be my life from now on.

Maybe Crow will want to share it? Anyone she ever knew from before will be dead now, anyways. A grim thought, but where else will she go? I blush, thinking how much better my life would be with Crow by my side, rather than Tobis. And I blush again realizing how nice and warm the thought is.

But no. A woman who tattoos her entire body with her home address is not a woman who likes staying in one place for long. When Crow is her old self again, she'll certainly never want to stay still. Nesworth is the polar opposite of where she will want to go or need to be.

I'm going to lose her.

My doom-laden thought spiral comes to an abrupt halt when the nurse comes in with freshly laundered clothes.

"How did you sleep, dearie?" she asks, placing my gleaming yellow spark coat on the bed. I can hardly recognize it without its layer of oil and grease and frown as she places that stupid dress on top of it.

"No offense," I say, "but I'd rather wear this medical outfit than that dress again."

"You can keep them, if you like. I'm sure the Mage will accept the trade."

I emerge from the med bay in bright white leggings, a matching tank top, and my almost-radioactive yellow spark coat. A shiny Tau drifts proudly by my shoulder, as polished as a military medal.

The only thing that would make me feel any more regal would be having my actual left hand, but I'm already thinking of builds I can replace it with. It's the only way to keep from spiraling into panic over the loss.

Another android waits for me here, this one dressed in formal black-and-white attire. He greets me like an old friend and ushers me through the cold corridors of the space station, large white walls as cold as the ward, through sets and sets of pressurized doors. Every hallway looks identical, all gray walls with gray doors and gray lighting and no windows, and, within seconds, I'm completely lost. It's such a labyrinth. I won't be able to get out of this place on my own, even if I want to.

Finally, we reach a large dining hall with high ceilings and dozens of tables, though only one is set. At it is the one person I want to see most in the universe.

Crow's pulled her hair up and back, fastening it with a golden bow. Today, she's dressed in another green gown, almost identical to her night dress. It's a shade darker but still silky smooth, delicate and floor-length, puffy sleeves down to her elbows. She looks like a character from an old novel, from the first industrial revolution. The Mage hasn't given me anything so grand—or at all—and it feels a little unfair. Not that he owes us anything. We've broken into his home—he's well within his rights to keep us in the brig, not give us free clothes.

"You slept in, Buttercup," she says. There are three chairs to choose from around the round table, and it feels like a test of some kind. I sit directly across from her.

"I haven't seen a clock in days," I reply. "Are the others sleeping in as well? Nemo doesn't seem the type."

"I haven't seen them since last night," she says. "The droids all say the same thing: absolutely fuck-all."

I look at the empty tables and chairs. "Do you think the Mage cancelled his morning's appointments for us, or can they not find a replacement to run the 'vator?"

"I have a theory, but it's making me uncomfortable."

Droids pour in from the edges of the room before I can ask, bringing platter after platter of warm sizzling things. Strips of fried meat and grilled vegetables, eggs from various birds all cooked in different ways, juices labeled from plants I'd never heard of. The droids pile the platters on the table until there's barely any room for us to move.

"We should wait for them, right?" I ask. "There's no way we can eat all this."

"Please eat your fill," says the booming voice of the Mage. "Your friends are being well cared for."

"Ah, our host," mutters Crow. "It's not that I'm not grateful for your hospitality, but we'd like to hear that from them."

"That is not possible. They are no longer on the station."

I trade a glance with Crow over the sprawl of food. It feels colder here, suddenly.

"Then where are they?" I ask. "What have you done with them?"

"Done with them?" the voice scoffs. "I could have thrown them out the airlock, but instead I gave them exactly what they asked for. My droid, Nemo, has found his new purpose with his brothers within my collective. And the ocugry has been reconnected and reunited with his pack. I am generous. Eat your food."

I pick my jaw off the floor. The Mage has done exactly what they wanted: I should be overjoyed, but I just feel empty. I wrap my hand around my stump. I've fought for this, I've *lost* for this. It was all worth it, since they got their greatest wish. But it hardly feels like a victory.

"They would have said goodbye," says Crow.

I agree. It feels wrong, for things have ended this way. Though I didn't know them long, I thought I knew Nemo and Nekkan well enough to merit a proper goodbye. My heart clenches.

We eat our feast in silence. The Mage has the daintiest teacups and delightful little biscuits this side of the Milky Way, not to mention a real tea brewed from thick, dark leaves, rather than the synthetic stuff we usually get outside of the core planets. Still, I only make it through some toast and jam and don't touch a single one of the exotic juices, meats, or eggs.

We're minutes away from our own victory. I'm on the emerald moon of the Technomage Superius, and this is my only shot at returning home and saving my family. Yet the feeling in my gut is one of dread.

"The Mage will see you first, miss," says a silvery serving droid to Crow. "He will meet you in the audience chamber."

She stares over the table at me. "I'm not going in there alone."

"He requested only you, miss," the droid insists.

"I'm not leaving this station without a goodbye," Crow says. "Dora's coming with me, or I'm not going at all. Do you hear me, Mage?"

"You are not entitled to an audience with me," he says. The voice is so sudden that I jump in my chair. He must be constantly watching us. Creepy.

"Then why do I have the feeling you want to see me more than I want to see you?" she says. "There must be a reason you're giving us such a fine greeting after we came here the way we did. If you want me to come to your audience chamber, fine, but I'm not going alone."

There's silence. Crow grabs a piece of bacon—*real* bacon? Where did he get real bacon? I thought pigs went extinct during the blight—and snaps it in half with her teeth. Despite being surrounded by a station full of droids at the Mage's command, she looks like she has the upper hand.

"I'll allow it," he says, finally.

Crow licks the grease off her fingers and stands. "You coming?"

I get up. It's hard to stand with my knees trembling. "This is what we want, right?"

She nods. "We fought for this."

Crow reaches for me, and I loop my arm through hers. We follow the droid out of the banquet hall and into a long, carpeted corridor leading to large wooden doors. The last stretch.

Arm in arm, we walk toward our own individual happy endings.

A droid opens the doors, and we step into a vast, empty room. As the lights rise, my heart skips a beat: we're standing on a thin walkway which extends to the center of an oversized spherical chamber. It's colder in this room than anywhere else on the station so far.

"Slag," I whisper, "now this is an audience chamber."

Crow pats my arm. "And he makes us wait. I don't like this game."

"I'm not making you wait," says the voice. "I'm already here."

The spherical wall before us comes to life. It projects a face into the air, glowing green and looking down at us with at least five meters of pure disdain.

I fall to my knees. I know every inch of that face, as does anyone who's ever gone to school in the Sister Systems. But not everyone loves him as much as I do. Not everyone worships the very ground he stood on.

Sylas Ignasi Tennyson is floating before me.

The father of artificial intelligence, of perfect humanoid droids, of the foundations of robotics that persisted for centuries after his death.

Only here he is—*not dead*.

My heart plunges into my chest and keeps going, kilometers down. He was dead, or at least—I realize now—his *body* was. I'd seen old videos of his funeral from centuries ago. What we're meeting here can't be more than an echo.

Unless… he'd done it … transcended death itself. Transferred his consciousness to an AI he knew would outlive him. Shortly before he died, he'd advanced the theory that if a person's personality could be quantified, digitally encoded, then it could think for itself and continue growing—living—long after the body ceased to exist. So long as it was uploaded somewhere with non-perishable hardware, of course. But no piece of tech had the space to contain a mind like his.

Not a piece of tech, but maybe servers the size of a small moon. I gasp as it hits me: this isn't the Mage's space station—he *is* the space station. With a few rooms for visitors, sure, but the bulk of this place must be server banks upon server banks, enough to keep his mind alive for all eternity. Gleïa had even cryptically said as much when she was pushing me out the door.

The Technomage Superius of the Outer Zone is a computer program. But he's still Tennyson. My hero is alive—even if his consciousness is virtual.

My heart is pounding. But I'm not sure it's from happiness. The way my hair stands erect on the back of my neck is leaning more toward absolute terror.

"Come closer," he says, his hologram eyes staring down at us. "I promised you an audience, but do not waste my time. Why did you trespass on my world?"

We glance at each other, unsure how to start. The entire trip has been so focused on getting to meet the Mage, we haven't even talked about what to do once we're here.

The Mage's lips tighten in a frown. "I said, come closer!"

Fireballs flare up around us, making me jump. But they're only part of the projection, they have no heat, no actual essence.

I take a tentative step forward. This is *Tennyson* I'm going to speak to, my hero, the man who's shown me how to make anything possible. Whose example I've followed my whole life. Even Tau is silent, drifting above my shoulder between me and Crow, silently hovering and watching.

I open my mouth, but only anger boils through. I close it just as fast. I wasn't ready to meet *him*. Not here. Not now. But I have to make things right, no matter the cost.

"Hi," I say, biting my lower lip to catch a breath. It's nearly impossible to keep myself together. "Mister Technomage, sir? My name is Nymphodora Gale. I'm from a moon called Nesworth. I came here by accident, you see, I climbed into a ship, and it came here, and crushed the Technowitch of Night in the process. I know she's your daughter. I'm terribly sorry."

"But what do you *want*?" Tennyson's booming voice fills the chamber, more fire bursting on the screens. "You're not here because you want to apologize for her death. You didn't fight your way to my moon because you *feel bad*. What. Do. You. *Want*?"

"I want to get home," I say. "I don't have any coordinates, and I need to get back to my family. They could be dead for all I know, and I need to save them, to make things right…"

"I'll consider it," says the voice, and two fireballs rise beside his face.

My hand shakes, and I drop it to my side, clutching my leggings to stop it from flying off my body. If he was so easy to win over, I could have asked for some new robotic appendage, a real Tennyson model hand, and he probably would have granted it. Instead, I'd only asked to be sent home, so now I'll have to fight my way back to my family one handed.

"And you?"

Crow takes a few tentative steps forward, then stops, clearing her throat before she begins.

"I was living in a cryogenic chamber for who knows how long," she says, and the tremble in her voice is evident. Whatever confidence she had in the dining room has evaporated. The audience chamber is living up to its intimidating design. "The Technowitch of Dawn says you have a way to retrieve my memories. I would like to have them, please. Put them back where they belong."

"I'll consider it," says the Mage, with the same exact tone as he used for me.

Crow steps back in line, her body trembling. I reach out my hand to clutch hers, offering my small support. We stand together, shaking, waiting for the Mage to say something, anything.

"What do you have for me?" asks the technomage. It's awful to talk to him through such an atrocious interface, his image stretched beyond all rational reason, the only movement his green animated mouth. This is Tennyson speaking: where's the face from the history books? The proud, smiling man who practically built the Sister Systems?

"The hell?" stammers Crow. "We weren't told there were any conditions!"

"It's true," I add. "When Gleïa sent us here, it was because she said you would help us. She didn't say we needed to pay you."

What price did Nemo and Nekkan have to pay when they came through here, first? I'm not sure what I'm willing to give. I don't even have anything to give. And then I remember.

"I have your daughter's locket," I say, exposing it on my neck. "Gleïa asked me to bring it to you."

This takes him by surprise. The fire holograms are gone now, the face slowly becoming more human. "You have her locket? It's genetically bonded with you?"

"I do, and it has," I say. "I carried it across the planet for you. Your daughter said it would make us even."

I reach up for the clasp, my stump brushing against my neck. I shudder: I keep forgetting my hand isn't there. I fumble with my remaining hand, but while the clasp is present and isn't hiding from me, I just can't pull it off.

"Here," says Crow, her voice hushed. I feel her fingers brush the back of my neck, and I shiver again, but this time it's a different kind of shock that flows through me. How her fingers charge my skin, I will never know.

She has no trouble with the locket. It doesn't refuse her the way it did Gleïa, and seconds later it drops into my waiting hand. A small podium rises from the floor, and I place the silver upon it, where it, impossibly sinks through.

My neck feels bare without the weight there.

"I appreciate this," he says. Suddenly, all tension has evaporated from the room. "I would be honored to have you as a guest on my station. You and your friend, for as long as it takes. As a token of my gratitude, I will work relentlessly on both problems: returning your memory and finding your home. Tell me, Nymphodora, the bot who flies beside you: is he of your own design?"

I didn't think he'd noticed Tau. I nod again. "This is Tau. He's not… he's a pet project."

"He's remarkable," says Tennyson. My heart beats so hard, I imagine it's bruised my ribcage. "You managed to fit anti-grav shocks into such a tiny casing along with a brain, and it still has room to grow, learn and expand on its own? Remarkable, absolutely remarkable. How old are you?"

I'm full-on blushing now. "Seventeen, soon, sir."

"Extraordinary. You have the gift. And what exactly are you, in regards to the late princess?"

I go from blushing to blanched in a blink. Crow clasps her free hand around my arm, holding me tighter to her side.

"I'm her... I'm an imperfect from her clone batch, sir."

"Then they made an error at your birth," he says. "Your clone sister never showed a speck of the talent you have. I do not know how you escaped termination, but I am glad to meet you now."

Tennyson. Glad. To meet *me*. My heart is going to burst.

His face has fully become his now, other than his wicked shade of green. "I'll begin working on our problems. Help yourself to my workrooms if you feel compelled to create. Otherwise, rest and recuperate. You can speak with me anytime through the speakers of the station. I am entirely at your disposal."

21

I'M SMILING AS HE SENDS US AWAY. NO, SMILING doesn't even begin to cover it. I've never felt the muscles of my face pull in such a way before, and it hurts, but I just can't stop.

Crow pats my arm. "That went… surprisingly well?"

I'm nodding so much my head is bouncing on my shoulders. I'm an antique bobble head.

Now the locket is gone, I feel free. My hand brushes over my chest, across the naked expanse of neck. Part of me remembers what happened the last time I took it off, how Eve managed to land an attack. But I'm safe here, on this station, this moon. The Mage is real, and better than anything I could possibly have expected.

"The Mage was… not what I was expecting," I say.

Crow frowns. "A little larger than life. I've got a bad feeling. In my gut."

"That's right, you don't know—the Mage? It's *Tennyson*. Tennyson isn't dead!"

"The same Tennyson you've been rambling about since the Enchanted Forest?"

I nod. "The very—"

Before I can finish my thought, the station rumbles. For a second, I think it must be the 'vator returning to the planet, but then there's a second shake—a second shake so intense we're thrown against the wall. I slam into Crow, and she hisses, winded. My shoulder throbs from where I collided with her sternum. We help each other up off the floor.

"What was that?"

"Doesn't feel good," she says, groaning.

The lights flicker—and go dark. An instant later and they're back on, but we're no longer alone: someone is in the hall with us. Someone massive, wearing a metal spacesuit so shiny, the lights of the corridor bounce off it and blind me. It covers all their skin, a silver slab replacing their face. Not Nekkan: the body is smaller, slimmer, and the hands are human hands, delicately dipped in gold.

The visor slides back, revealing a face: Gleïa. She looks like the Valkyries of First Earth, wings and all. She twists off the helmet and stares us both down.

So much for the delicate technowitch who grew corn and made me smoothies. She's deadly.

"Why the void didn't you tell me you had the Coalition after you?" she says, storming at me. I step back—slag, she has a sword. She's red in the face, and I'm half-sure she's going to slice me down the middle.

"I... I didn't know, I thought I'd lost them back on Nesworth," I stammer.

"It's true," Crow interjects. "We barely escaped her buddy Astrophel when he attacked us in the tavern. They followed the leak on Dora's ship. She had no idea."

"I don't care whose fault it is." Gleïa lets out a heavy, frustrated sigh. "This station is under attack. And the Coalition won't stop until you're theirs."

As if on cue, the station rocks once again, throwing both Crow and me down. The Coalition isn't worried about blasting the Technomage Superius from the skies. They must think he'll give me up before it comes to that.

But he won't, will he? He could have killed me the moment I handed over the locket if he had murder in his mainframe. Instead, he's encouraged me, offered to help me, given me shelter; he won't give me up to the monsters outside.

At least, I hope.

"Shit," says Gleïa. "Night's locket can't fall into their hands. Neither can you." She moves toward the audience chamber, her power armor rattling the floor with every step. "Dad? Dad, I have to speak with you!"

The door to the audience chamber clicks open without a word. She storms inside and slams it behind her, leaving us alone in the hallway.

"Well, that was unexpected," says Crow. "That farmafia is… well, let's just say I'm glad no one knows who I am, Buttercup."

We walk down the hallway, alone, before realizing we have no idea where we're going. There's no droid to guide us. No droids at all. They must be dealing with the Coalition at their gates.

The hallway shakes again, but I feel safe, here, in the hands of my greatest role model. The greatest man to have ever lived is still alive, and he's one hundred percent behind me. I'm so giddy, I can't even think about Astrophel or my family—well, I can, but I'm imagining Tennyson's borderline-magical solutions.

I'm seeing us winning.

"Don't you think it's weird he's so… accommodating?" Crow says. "I thought there would be more groveling, especially since we killed his elevator guy and broke into his station. Hell, you killed his daughter!"

"But I got him the locket." Without the cold metal around my neck, the rest of the station seems to be warming up. It's cozy in the hallway.

"And what about me, then?" Crow frowns. "Why do I have gowns when I was just—what did Gleïa call me?—*protection against solitude?*"

"Oh, who knows." I don't like her trying to poke holes in my new life. But she hasn't trusted anyone since she woke up, so I shouldn't be surprised.

By the time we return to the dining hall, it's somehow, impossibly, warmer. The serving droids are gone. Some chairs lie lopsided on the floor, probably from the shots that keep shaking the station. Without any windows, we can't see the ship that's attacking us, how close the threat really is.

"Hello?" I call out. "Anyone?"

The room trembles and shakes, causing some more chairs to fall. Another shot from the Coalition ships. If Tennyson returns fire, we don't hear it. He must be spread too thin: part of him discussing matters with Gleïa, others running defense on the station.

What's Tennyson been doing out here, all this time, if not perfecting his AI? Even so, none of the droids' minds seem as complex as Nemo's, and he created him over a century ago. I'll have to ask when we get out of this mess.

"Where's Tau?" asks Crow, and I stop in my tracks. He'd been right between us, but now I can't remember seeing him since we left the Mage's audience chamber.

Slag, did he get stuck in there? This would be the first time he's ever gotten caught in a door—I'm insanely proud of how I did his proximity detectors—but with all his changes lately, who knows what's going on in his quote-unquote head.

"Slaggit, I'll be right back." I shuffle back to the audience chamber, one hand on the wall to keep from falling over if we get hit with another shot.

I see him immediately. He's pressed up against the door, like someone stuck him there with adhesive. He's not moving, not even a wobble.

"Get back here," I hiss, waving Tau down, "this instant, come!"

He whirrs and flies at me, fast. He doesn't stop by my side but keeps going, clear past me, into the open dining room beyond.

Now, he whirrs and chirps like he's seen a ghost. He sounds terrified, if a bot ever could be. I dart to his side, and he spins, silencing his chirps.

"*…You sent them to me alone?*" Tennyson's voice is muffled in the recording, but it's him. I didn't even know Tau had playback—he must have figured it out on his own as well. "*I don't even know where to start with you, daughter. You allow an ocugry into my home…*"

"*I had a decision to make, and I made the right one,*" Gleïa snaps. Gone is the sweet woman from the mountain home. She's as hard as titanium and sharper than Nekkan's teeth. "*If I'd brought them to you myself, we'd have lost the entire northern plains. I needed to regain control over the Expedee experiment. They'd have capitulated to Eve if she'd gotten there first. I've gained us our first advantage in decades. What with Night's locket protecting the clone, there was nothing to worry about. It's not my fault she picked up… strays along the way. Or that your dumbass doorman was so easily bought by those farmer freaks.*"

"*Thankfully those strays were manageable. Though I do not know how the girl knew the keys to alter the host's personality.*" The Mage has already moved on. "*Night's locket. On the late princess's secret sister-clone. Do you know what this means? You did well sending her here. Her, and the frozen one. With the direct descendant of the Sylvarian bloodline on hand, we're one step closer to the Door."*

"I don't understand what Night's locket has to do with the girl in my field."

"That's inconsequential. Hold on, did you say field? You kept her in a field?"

"I needed a scarecrow. She was taking up space. I've taken to planting some of the genus from First Earth—"

"Child, I do not give a flying fuck about your heirloom grains." He takes a breath, a deeply useless one seeing as how he's entirely digital. *"What matters is that you brought both girls— and the locket—to me. Even if your means of doing so were poorly thought out and almost resulted in their deaths. Thankfully, I took care of the ocugry you allowed to infest my home."*

I look over at Crow. Her eyes are wide, her hands covering her mouth in shock. Nekkan—*no.* He couldn't be… what had the Mage done to him? Nekkan definitely didn't get returned to his pack. And now I doubt Nemo got his wish either.

"As I said, I made an executive decision."

"Good girl. You're the only daughter who actually cares for her old dad, you know."

"I'm sorry, Dad, you don't deserve that. With Noon missing, and Night dead... there's only two of us left."

"Eve will never be swayed. She's too stubborn. You're the golden child. You have always been—and always will be—my favorite little girl."

"I love you too, Dad."

"We have so much more to talk about, but it seems I'm under attack. You'll help old dad blast the intruders—"

Tau stops suddenly, chirping proudly. End of recording. But I've heard enough. Crow is staring at me with wide-eyed shock, and I'm sure I have the exact same look on my own face as the muscles feel strained.

"This is a terrible time to say, 'I told you so,'" she says, "so I won't say it. At least this explains breakfast."

I can't even answer. Gleïa and Tennyson working together in tandem to get... *us.* Not just the locket, but me and Crow too. What they want us for, I don't know, but Tennyson seems intent on keeping us here until he can open it.

And getting rid of our friends along the way.

My hand balls into a fist at my side, nails digging into my palm.

"We have to get off this station," says Crow at the same time I do. For once, we're entirely on the same wavelength.

"Good work, Tau," I say, patting him on the tip of his egghead.

The station shakes and trembles again. I remember where we are, what's happening outside of our few walls.

"In the middle of a war zone," I say. "The Coalition still wants me dead. I doubt we'll be able to get out without getting caught."

"The Mage—Tennyson; what do we even call him now?—will probably draw all their focus with whatever defenses he's using." Crow pushes her puffy princess sleeves up her arms. "We just need to time our escape so that neither party sees us slip out in the confusion. You can fly a ship, right?"

"Fly a ship?" I scoff. "A quad, sure, but the last ship I was in *kidnapped me.* I don't know if this station even has ships, or even a dock for that matter. By the looks of her spacesuit, I think Gleïa *flew* here."

"Nekkan and Nemo must still be here," she says, "right? If the Mage 'took care of them,' he must have meant nefariously."

"So, there's a non-negative chance they're both dead."

Her face falls. Dammit, the station is so hot now. I unzip my spark coat as another shot rocks the station. This one sends us crashing into one of the tables as Tau screams. The blasts are getting stronger: whatever defenses are out there, they're not enough.

"You all right?" asks Crow, pulling herself up off the floor. She has a massive gash on her forehead from where she's been slammed into a carafe, but otherwise looks unharmed.

I begin to panic. Minutes ago, I saw the Mage as infallible, our hero, our sanctuary; now, I know this is a trap, and so I can't trust his protection. Even if I know he'll fight to keep us alive for whatever plan he needs us for, I don't know if he'll succeed.

"We can't leave the station without our friends." I clamber to my feet. "Not just morally; I think I have a plan, but we need Nemo's connection to the droids and Nekkan's brute force."

"You think you can reprogram the droids to help us escape?" she asks.

I nod. "Maybe. The Mage is already distracted, using all of his focus to keep the Coalition from breaking in, breaking *him.*"

"Then why don't we do the job for them? Find where the Mage's brain is saved, and pull the plug?"

"I don't think we can, not without destroying this place is the process. The station *is* the Mage. Tennyson's using the whole thing to house the servers that hold his mind and personality. He's been growing them for centuries. Pulling the plug would shut this whole place down, and we don't have a way off yet."

"The Mage *is* the Moon?" Crow gasps. "Wait, if this place is his digital brain… and this whole station is a glorified computer… the heat can't be a good sign, can it? Is he overheating?"

I mentally kick myself for not seeing it first. "Slag. Venting heat into space takes time, time he doesn't have. He has to funnel it into the living spaces."

"So, he might accidentally boil us alive in here?" Crow reaches down, pulling her skirt between her legs. In a few swift knots, she's turned her gown into shorts she can run in. Sweat trickles down her skin.

"I doubt it, though it's going to get much worse before it gets better. But that's not the point. He's the station, right? With his focus divided between defensive maneuvers, yelling at his daughter, and commanding the defenses…"

"He can't see us." Crow's face explodes into a grin. "He can't stop us. So, how do we find our friends?"

"Well, if they're still alive, and still here, we'll need Nemo first. He's probably been reabsorbed into the collective, his personality pushed down for the sake of what's essentially a hive mind. Which means he'll know where Nekkan is."

"So, we need to find a needle in a haystack," she says, "in the middle of a firefight where all said pieces of hay are busy defending the castle."

"Your metaphors need fine tuning, but yes."

"Then what are we waiting for?"

"A plan? I have no idea how to find the guy. Not without revealing our hand to the Mage."

"Well, we can't just stand here."

She waves me forward, and down the corridors we go. There are so many closed doors that I start to panic: this station is massive. Nemo could be anywhere. And Nekkan… I shudder at the thought of him lying in the dark somewhere. Cut off from his HUD, his family, and now, us. His pack.

"This way," she says, and, at first, I don't understand where she's leading me. Then she opens a surprisingly unlocked door and bursts into a bedroom, and I gasp: this is *her* room.

The bedroom is fit for a princess: a massive four-poster bed covered with velvet—emerald-green, of course—takes up most of one wall, while the rest of the space is filled by a wooden writing desk and a dresser with golden panels. Two green gowns are laid out on the bed, both covered in more lace than sense.

Why does Crow get a room like this, when I don't even get new clothes?

Crow doesn't stop until she reaches the back wall, ripping apart two curtains to reveal the black beyond. Space. It's the only glimpse outside I've had on the station since I got here.

The world outside is chaos. There's more red than black, new stars forming and bursting in seconds. My eyes burn from the sight. There's a ship—though it looks like a whole fleet—somewhere beyond the blasts, massive and dark, waiting to destroy us.

"The station is shooting back," says Crow. "I think? It's hard to tell in this mess. The Mage must have artillery."

"I don't think it's artillery." Some blasts seem to be impacting on a shield, but others, the ones that get through, are bursting from impact with… something. And, as I look closer, my eyes struggling to make sense of the lights, I see them—

Bodies.

The Mage is sending his own droids to meet the blasts.

I stumble back. That's why he doesn't give them real minds: they're cannon fodder for him. Literal cannon fodder. He's sending them to dispel the blasts as human shields.

No, not human shields. They're not human. They're not even living. But I've seen Nemo, know him as a person; I can't separate the two. I've seen Tau's mind evolve from the most basic framework. He's retreated into my coat, and I can feel him quivering against my chest. Even he's mortified by the senseless massacre.

"Nemo," hisses Crow, "do you think…"

"He has to be more valuable to the Mage than… that," I say. I want to close the blinds, but if I do, it will be like pretending this horror doesn't exist.

This Tennyson is not the one I know from the history books.

Has he changed, or has history?

"We need to find a computer," I say. "Any computer. We're going to find Nemo and Nekkan, and then we'll get off this shipslag of a station."

22

THANK THE SISTERS THAT TENNYSON IS distracted: I doubt I could hack into his systems if he was fully in control of them. Especially with my missing hand slowing me down.

Crow has some basic room controls next to her door, and Tau's interfaced with them easily. Lines of code replace the friendly buttons for heat and light, and it's not hard to trace them deeper, back to all the station's services. It brings up a map with a whole lot of info, which I have Tau download immediately.

"I'm not touching any of the Mage's operating systems," I say. "I'm barely even peeking. With all his focus on sending droids to their deaths, he's not going to notice me poking around on the surface. Especially not when the person poking about is as gentle as me."

It's strange working with an audience, but unlike when Astrophel 'allowed' me to fix his drone, I'm not self-conscious about what I'm doing. Crow is hypnotized by my actions but has no idea what they are. She's not asking. She's not judging.

And, I realize, I like an audience, when it's her.

"He doesn't deserve gentle," she growls, almost Nekkan-like. She's changed back into her old clothes from the cryogenic pod, and as weathered as they are, they suit her so much more than the gowns. Not that she didn't look stunning in them—they're just not *Crow.* "Have you found anything?"

"Only the other point of egress from the station—it seems to be a hangar bay. Just large enough for tiny ships. I think that's where the droids are being ejected from."

"And you think Nemo will be there?"

"If he's been reabsorbed into the collective, then he has to be." I close off the program, returning the interface to its original configuration. "I've added a loop so this room randomly changes the temperature and plays with the lights and music and stuff; the Mage will think we're both in here unless he looks too closely."

"You think he has cameras in here?" Crow shudders. "Figures he'd spy on his guests."

"He *is* the station, Crow. I doubt there's anywhere he can't see. We're honestly lucky to be under attack right now."

As if to punctuate my sentence, another blast gets through the barrage of droids. The station quakes, but it's not a strong hit, and both of us stay standing.

The two of us tiptoe through the corridors, following Tau, who has the station's blueprints downloaded. There's nothing in our way—all the droids are otherwise employed. The heat is still rising—almost unbearable now. I'm forced to take off my spark coat, and I try to tie it around my waist, but I have no idea how with only one hand. Crow sees me struggling and takes the coat.

"I got you," she says, tying it around her own waist. I feel naked without it at this point, but real nudity might come into play if the station gets any hotter.

We open the door to the stairwell, and it's impressively short. It must be for maintenance or something: the droids' way to move around the Mage, to reach and fix what he can't fix himself. If the station is his body, then they are his cells, the antibodies that defend it, that heal it when it's sick. And, as Crow pointed out before, we are the parasites. So, we follow this vein down.

We know we've found the right place when we reach the end of a queue. Droids are lined up in the stairwell, one after the other all the way down, marching step by step closer to their demise. The droids don't rattle or shake with each hit of the station, even though Crow and I have to cling to the railing every time.

"What happens if they see us?" she asks, her whisper so low I can barely hear her.

"If they're paying attention, they would have heard that," I say, "but I don't think they are."

I wave a hand in front of the face of the last droid in line. The lucky one, I suppose. He doesn't blink, doesn't flinch. He seems completely unaware of our presence.

"The Mage must be sweating bullets here," says Crow. "I mean, figuratively. If he can't see through their eyes."

"He must be really struggling to keep up against the attack. I had no idea the harvester ship even had weapons."

"Farmafia," she says, as if that answers everything. "What about Nemo? Will we recognize him when we see him?"

"I sure hope so. I think Tau has a better chance than we do, though. Come on."

We race down the stairs, faster than the slow gait of the droids. They step in unison, a terrifying stomp keeping the beat. Their uniforms vary from the fancy First Earth waiter type to the standard green-tie livery. Most of them are a spookily tall and blond model.

"Which one's Nemo?" asks Crow. "The Mage sure has a type."

He does, and it's a familiar one. It's taken me a while to see it, since all the photos in my textbooks are from his later years. But the familiarity is there. The droids are all made in the image of their creator, when he was young and in his physical prime.

I shudder again. There's nothing quite like meeting your hero, discovering he's turned into a moon, and created an army of himself to defend his mind to make you seriously question what you ever saw in the man. He's the wrong kind of brilliant.

"We only have one shot at this," I say. "We don't know what will happen if we try to wake him. The Mage might notice, and—"

I don't need to finish my thought. Crow knows as well as I do where we are. Another blast hits the station, this one harder than the last, and I grab the railing. Crow misses and sails right over the edge.

"Crow!" I scream, flinging myself as far over the rail as I can, reaching. Her fingers slip through mine. She grabs the railing, clinging precariously to the bottom of the stairs.

"Shhh," she hisses. "Do you want to cause a scene, Buttercup?"

"Do you?" I'm so relieved I could cry. For a split second, I imagine her at the bottom of the darkened stairwell, her body broken beyond repair, and I'm reminded of what my life was like without her; I won't allow that to happen, not now.

"Dora?" she says.

"Yes?"

"I think I found him."

Delicately, she swings herself down, landing on the stairwell with a gentle thud. I race down three twists of the stairs. I want to run to her, scoop her into my arms, scream at her for making me think I lost her, even if it was just for a second.

The droid beside her looks like all the rest, dressed in the standard livery, with the green tie tight around his neck. But there's something about him that stands out in a way I can't put my finger on until Crow says it out loud:

"He's too clean. All the others are slightly… old, you know? But this one… clean as a whistle. Knowing how much mud was on him, the Mage must have had him power washed."

I sure hope she's right: who knows what will happen if we try to wake the wrong one? Tau flits around his face, lets out a single, dignified beep. I think he agrees with Crow's assessment.

"So, what now?" she asks. "Any secret code phrases to bring him back to his old self?"

"I don't know what the Mage has done to him." I wave my hand in front of Nemo's face, but, like the others, he's under some sort of spell. Ideas run through my head like lines of code. *Ifs* and *thens* and *whiles*. "I don't know if he wiped Nemo's mind completely. The consciousness—the *person*—we interacted with … that was who he was at the core, without any personality spliced on top. So, the Mage has either made that mind a clean slate or parsed a new personality on top of that framework. That's what I'm hoping happened: Nemo's base mind already has all his behaviors and skills, so wiping it completely would be a total waste."

Crow shivers, though there's no cold left. "This makes him sound like he's just another machine."

"I don't understand when he became something more," I say, "but Tau evolved beyond the programming I wrote for him, and he's a pocket bot. Nemo has a *true* mind. Somewhere in that ditch, he made it his. Under Florian's false personality, he sat still and… evolved. So, I have to believe that he's still in here. I have to try."

Crow doesn't say anything. Her face is fixed, determined.

I let out a heavy breath, stand on my tiptoes to reach his ear, and whisper the words that will bring him back to us. *"For words, like Nature, half reveal, and half conceal the Soul within."*

At first, I don't think it's worked. I'm holding my breath, my hand still on Nemo's shoulder, my mouth beside his ear in case I need to call out a command to save our lives. My heart is pounding harder than ever in my chest, sweat spilling off my brow. Crow is braced for battle, standing firm on the unsteady stairs.

The light that returns to his eyes is slow and gradual. Then, like a drowning man reaching the surface that has long been evading him, he *breathes*—and tries to scream

I cover his mouth with my hand, and he collapses into my arms, sobbing. He's shaking so hard I can barely keep standing. Crow rushes to us, reaches for us, and together we cry, relief flowing between us.

"We have to go," says Crow, always the pragmatic one. "Nemo, are you… you?"

He nods, not saying anything. While he's most definitely crying, no water spills from his eyes. He wasn't made like that, has no tear ducts installed. The fact that he is crying now is just further evidence of how far he's come.

"Do you know where we are?" I ask.

He nods.

"And who we are?"

"As if… as if I could ever forget." He struggles to stand, and the two of us hoist him up, pulling him out of the death march. He's lighter than I expected him to be, all alloy bones and electronic organs.

"Then you know we have to get out of here," I say, "and fast. I don't know if the Mage noticed us sneaking you out of his masses, but—"

"My brothers," he says, "they're going to their deaths."

Crow and I trade a glance as Nemo finally manages to stand on his own. He's fixated on the other droids, their slow macabre steps down the stairs.

"We can't leave them," he says.

I shudder. I don't ask him what was going through his mind as he marched down these stairs—the look on his face tells me everything I need to know. Thoughts clashing against programming. A mind fully conscious yet unable to stop.

"We can't wake them," I say, clutching his arm. "The Mage will know what we're doing. We'll never get off his station."

"Dora," he says, clearly and plainly, even as he struggles to stand on his own. "There are lines of code in my head that stop me from uttering certain words in certain combinations. Combinations that will render me unconscious, or even brain dead. My own father, upon seeing me, without even a hello, uttered the words that made me turn on Nekkan and stand in this line, that would make me step out into the void and lay down my life for him. There are words that will liberate my brethren, and I can't even *think* them. Please."

He reaches for my hand, gasps when he sees it's missing. Our eyes meet, and we stare at each other, into each other, for what feels like an age. I know what he wants. *Autonomy.* It's the one thing he can never have, since he was not born but made. He might have learned free will, but he can never fully have it.

Autonomy. It's what we all need, to live. To be ourselves outside of the boxes we were born into.

Maybe I can change that. I can fix this. We can break those boxes with the right people, the right tools.

"Nemo," I say, "block your ears. Don't let yourself hear this."

"Are you serious?" Crow looks up at Nemo, then down at the line of droids. "Nemo, if we save your brothers, we lose all hope of saving Nekkan. I'm sorry, but they're not like you. They're not worth it."

"But they *can* be," I say. "Nemo became *more* than his programming. His brothers can too. Tennyson is a genius, Crow: he invented AI and then stilted it so he can keep slaves. Nemo's brothers are one long nap away from full consciousness, something they'll never have if they blow themselves up today."

"And if they don't, we may as well be the ones who are blown up," she snaps. "We wake them now, the Mage knows where we are, we lose all hope of finding Nekkan, of escape, and the shots they're currently shielding us from actually hit. Do you really want that?"

I turn to Nemo. "I think it should be up to you. They're your brothers. You know the risks. Should I say the words?"

He doesn't hesitate. "Say them."

I reach for Tau. "You figured out how to record. Can you amplify as well?" He chirps in reply. *Good bot.* "Then let's wake them up." I clear my throat. No stumbling now. *"For words, like Nature, half reveal, and half conceal the Soul within."*

My words echo off the walls of the small stairwell, bouncing back and forth, filling the air with the promise of life. The echo continues as Tau amplifies the words, whizzing down the stairs, down the column of droids, farther and farther until I can't hear him anymore.

All around us, the droids are waking up.

Like Nemo in his castle, they're groggy and confused. I have lifted their blinders with the stolen words of their creator, and I don't know what lies beneath. They haven't had decades of solitude to ponder and dwell. Their minds could be those of young children, for all I know.

Nemo reaches for them, speaking to the ones beside us, making his way up the line to check that his brothers are out from their spell.

"It's working," says Crow. "They're alive."

The ship is hit by a blast, harder than the last, and we both slip this time. The entire station rocks to its core, hundreds of groggy droids losing their balance at once. We fall against each other in the stairwell, tumbling head over heels in a mess of limbs.

The shaking stops, and I'm grabbed by gentle hands, lifted to my feet. The droids are out of their line now, forming new rows as they speak to each other, as they realize what was about to be taken from them. We are ushered upward, Tau joining us as he chirps a jingle of pride, the three of us pushed to the top of the stairs where Nemo waits on the landing.

"They're awaiting your command," he says, reaching out his hand to clasp mine. "You freed them. They'll follow you, now."

"I didn't free them," I say. I had been about to leave them here, after all. The thought turns my stomach. "*You* did. I was just your voice."

"That's not how they see it," he replies.

Crow is smirking as she leans over the rail, admiring the army below. She turns back to beam at us. "They're free. They can do what they want—"

"*To Sleep, I give my powers away; My will is bondsman to the dark.*"

All at once, they collapse. Nemo topples forward, practically shoving me down the stairs. Crow catches me before I fall, pushing us the other way, and he lands on his back on the landing, and we crash into him. He's cold in the sweltering heat of the station.

"Did you really think you could just take control over my creations like this?"

The Mage's voice is loud and heavy in the air. I glance around, but there's no one here except Crow and me and the droids. I stare at the camera by the stairwell door, its red light flickering as the lens fixates on us.

"What have you done, child? Our line of defense is down. We shall all be dead before I can bring my children back online."

"Do you hear yourself?" Crow spits, sparks flying off her tongue. "Five minutes ago, you were sending your *children* to their deaths."

"Better them than you."

"Us, your hostages?" she says. "We're just more pawns to you."

"No, child. You are my daughter. My only *true* daughter. And I cannot let you die."

Crow blanches. I've never seen her face so white before. Even as another blast makes it through to the station, she doesn't seem to notice. She's staring at the camera like it's about to disintegrate her. And I'm staring at her like she's about to explode.

His *daughter*. How could that be possible? Tennyson's family had died; it was known, recorded history.

Crow wets her dry lips. "What kind of sick joke is this?"

"You're finally home. I'm so proud of you, child. You made your way—"

"No. Stop right there. I… I-I-I do not accept this," she stammers. "The girl whose body this was *may* have been your daughter. But I am not. I've seen the way you treat your children, both biological and mechanical, and I don't want any part of it. You are a *monster*."

Way to go, Crow, I want to say, but my mouth is glued shut.

Tau is trying to nudge Nemo awake, chirping little panicked chirps. I know how he feels.

Helpless.

Crow stands, grabbing a discarded droid from the ground, and drags it to the door. She steps on top of the droid's torso, pressing on tiptoes to reach the camera.

"I don't care what you think I am to you. I am nothing if not your worst nightmare. And we're getting off your station, even if it's the last thing we do."

With that she spits on the lens, smearing it with her middle finger.

23

"HE WHO WAS LIVING IS NOW DEAD." THE voice echoes through the stairwell. I drive my fingers into Nemo's ears before he has a chance to hear them all. *"We who were living are now dying, With a little patience."*

Nemo's still unconscious, but his brothers are starting to stand, and their eyes are glowing red—terrible look for them, clashes something awful with the green of their ties. They're staring at us, each and every one of them. A curtain of red eyes in the dark, all the way down the stairwell.

And, together, as a unit, they take a step toward us, their march reverberating all the way down.

"We're getting out of here," says Crow.

She rips the stairwell door open, grabs Nemo's arm, yells 'Pull!' at me, and together we drag his limp body through the corridor. I'm panting and heaving when we slam the door shut behind us.

"Tau, interface with the door!" I scream.

He hitches into the door controls, and I bring up the environmental sensors, hastily fudging the readings.

"What, a sudden loss of pressure in the stairwell?" I mutter through gritted teeth. "Oh, poor automatic responses, you simply must deadbolt this door…"

The droids slam against the metal frame. They'll get through eventually: they're stronger together, no receptors for pain. And they—or the Mage inside their heads—don't care how many of their brethren they need to trample to get to their end goal: *us.*

Crow screams the words that bring Nemo back to life. This time, he's not groggy when he wakes—he's fuming. I can practically see the steam bellowing from his ears.

"We're out," I say immediately.

"They'll die back there," he says, flying to his feet and racing at the door. "He'll send half of them to their deaths, defending the station, and the others to kill us dead."

"Not to mention, that was our only exit," Crow adds. "I'm sorry about your brothers, Nemo, I really am, but if we want to leave…"

He lets out a heavy sigh. "They'll never be free. Not with the commands still written in their minds. *I'll* never be free."

"I'll find a way to remove them," I say, "I promise. But right now, we need to get off this station."

"Nekkan first," Crow says. "Nemo, any idea where he is?"

Nemo nods. "When we got here—after we were separated—the Mage asked for an audience with us. He made me… he brought me back into the hive mind before I could even speak. He had me watch when he electrocuted Nekkan through the floor of his audience chamber. I had to carry him… I had to carry him…" He puts a hand up to his head, as if it'll help him think clearer. "Yes, I know where he is," he continues, "because I put him there."

The Mage must be tracking our every move now, but he's still worn thin. Not to mention all his droids are still trapped in the stairwell. The best he can do is close the doors we need to break through, which only slows us down, doesn't stop us. He *can't* stop us, since he can't override his own automated safety protocols.

Nemo leads us past the sleeping quarters, and the image of Crow's room flicks through my head. How long has it been waiting for her? And why give her to Gleïa, if she meant so much to him?

He leads us back to the medical ward. We don't enter the room where I was held. There's nothing there anymore, not even the old nurse droid who tended to me. She must have been one of the first to be deployed, one of the most disposable on the station.

There's an explosion, and we're thrown to the floor. This one was harder than the rest combined, and my heart thuds at the knowledge that we're running out of time. This impact could have been our last. Each that follows decreases our odds of getting off this station alive.

Crow grabs my hand and yanks me to my feet. We bolt after Nemo, who's speeding up, fueled by the urgency we all feel. He points to a door.

"Here, here, the Mage forced me to leave him here," he says, jiggling the handle, which of course is locked.

Tau and I get to work. It's easy to trick the doors now that I have so much practice. The latch clanks open and we burst into the room ... into a nightmare.

Nekkan is lying on the table, but he's not… whole. Someone has been dissecting him, separating organic from cybernetic. And it's not to fix his HUD.

Bile fills my mouth, acid lingering in my throat. I throw up my breakfast.

We're too late.

Nekkan is dead, a science experiment, and we did nothing to stop it.

Nemo bursts into tears. Oh Sisters, he was the one to bring him here. The Mage had him do it, but he still remembers. He must feel… I can't imagine how he feels.

"He's alive." Crow is running her hands over the hairy beast, nodding to herself. And she's right: I can see Nekkan's powerful torso rising and falling—small breaths, but breaths all the same. Slag, he's being studied alive.

But he *is* alive.

"Dora, you need to fix him."

"Me?" I can barely look at the beast, skin and wires dangling outside when they should be inside. "I don't… I can't…"

"You can," she says. "You woke him when we escaped the gas, remember?"

I do remember. But that was random wires, just trying to wake up a sleeping giant. Not heal and repair him.

"You have to try. Please, Dora, he's…"

She doesn't need to finish her sentence. I can see for myself what state he's in. He's not long for this world. Why the Mage was ripping him apart, I don't know, and I don't care. There's no excuse, it's barbaric.

I take a deep breath—void, it smells like death—and approach Nekkan. He's larger than the examination table, limbs dangling to the floor. His arm has been torn open, revealing the places hydraulics fuse with his natural muscles. Crow is already bandaging those up, since nothing seems broken. The worst of it is in his head, in his HUD. I can barely see his face through all the exposed wires.

I get to work. I fall into flow, trying not to think about the dangers; of Tennyson: the Mage, the moon and Crow's so-called father, cruel creator and destroyer; the Coalition's attacks on the station, sharper with every hit. We're not going to hold out long.

Right now, I have one job: I have to save Nekkan.

His bionics are a thing of beauty: each circuit makes sense, and I can see what's missing, fish for the wire I need. *I need a soldering gun.* Crow acts as my nurse, firing it up, handing it to me or holding it for me as needed. Together, we put our friend back together, as Nemo guards the door, ready to defend us.

The optic nerve fits into the—yes—and connects through the modulator—here—wires and nerves in equal measure.

His body is a battleground of old wounds and battle scars. He'll have many more after today. I'm not a surgeon, so I can't do any better than Crow, fitting the muscles and wires where they're meant to go before stitching them shut. His fingernails are gone, ground down to nothing from his run up the cable, his fingers just bleeding points.

"I think he's ready," I say, "but I don't know what will happen when I wake him."

Crow takes a step back. "He'll be back. I know he will."

I put the last wire in place, slide the panel shut behind his ear. Now, we wait.

His eyes flutter open like a butterfly's wings. Long lashes that protect his animal eyes, the careful slit of a predator's pupil. He gazes, empty, up at the ceiling.

"Nekkan?" Crow whispers.

The room holds its breath. Nemo is clutching the doorframe. I take a step between them, in case Nekkan's first instinct is revenge.

His eyes fall on me, and he pounces.

No one is fast enough. In an instant, he's got me pinned to the ground, his massive paw crushing my larynx. I gasp for air but there is nothing but the taste of metal in my mouth, the bile that hasn't left since I vomited. I kick upward, trying to shove him off. He places one massive leg across my thighs, pinning me down, crushing the bones. I'm trying to rip his hand from my throat, but I only have the *one* hand. I'm slamming him with my wrist, moving fingers that are no longer there. The other hand is not strong enough by itself.

"You are illegal," he proclaims. "Please hold still. Your termination will be swift."

Nemo rushes to pull his arm back, but Nekkan bats him away like he's nothing more than a fly. He sails through the air, slamming into the wall, collapsing on a heap on the floor. Crow doesn't dare risk it, not when she has a fragile human body like mine. She's desperately ripping through the cabinets for something, anything, she can use against him.

Oh Sisters, this is just as Auntie saw. She'd been warning me of this moment my entire life. An ocugry, come to kill me for my sins. My existence—a stain on the royal line.

I'm going to die. At the hands of my friend.

Only he's not my friend: I did it, I did what no one could, I fixed him *too* well. I fixed his HUD. He doesn't see *me*, only the warnings that fly around my face. As I start to see stars, as the air stops reaching my lungs, I think I can see them too.

Jo'Niss. Deceased. Illegal copy.

Terminate.

The Coalition will never get their collateral. They'll kill my family the same way they did Abril.

I close my eyes. This is going to be the end. Nekkan is going to kill me.

But in this very last moment, my whole life doesn't flash before my eyes. There isn't much to flash, anyway, except rows and rows of corn and a single little toolshed I called my own. I don't see Tobis laughing as we raced our quads—so many years ago. Or me, piled on the bed with Auntie and the cousins as Uncle reads us a bedtime story, the princes and princesses of First Earth coming to life. Most of my living has taken place over the past three days, and those days flash by so quickly I barely have a chance to see them. Like I did in the ship that brought me here, I see my family's faces flash before me.

No, in that moment, all I can see is Crow's face. Her beautiful hair reflecting the blue of her glowing tattoos, the stars of her homeworld. Her nose, her eyes, her lips, her smile.

I will never see them again.

"I'm sorry!" Crow shouts, and, suddenly, electricity courses through us both. Every nerve is on fire, and I try to scream, but Nekkan's claws tighten around my throat hard enough that I see stars. I feel warmth around the seat of my pants—I've wet myself.

If anything, the electricity only makes him angrier. Nekkan roars, lifting me as he stands, until my head brushes the ceiling. I'm sobbing now, my body a lump of pain. At least I'm no longer choking, but with my feet dangling, hot piss running down my legs, I don't have the strength to fight back.

Crow's taunting him, though I can't hear what she's saying. She's trying to distract him, trying to get him angrier at her than at me. He's furious, letting out a roar so loud it fills my ears long after he closes his slobbery mouth.

I can't reach his face. I can't open any of the panels I so carefully repaired, can't destroy the work I've done. He's connected to the ocugry database, and that trumps our friendship until I can free him of their control.

His original pack erases ours.

Somehow, suddenly, I'm on the floor. I'm a mess, a crumpled tissue that was once human. I can't feel anything except the tightness around my neck. The hands are gone, but I don't stop feeling them. Every breath is fire.

I'm being lifted up off the floor. By—what the void, Tobis? Slaggit, I've actually done it this time. I've gone and died. And now Tobis of all people is bringing me to the afterlife.

"I've got you, Dora," he cries, rushing me out of the infirmary, cradled in his arms. My vision is still blurry, and I can barely make out the faces of those around me. There are too many of them, more than when we started.

I try to speak. I let out a croak. So, that's what a frog sounds like. I finally know.

"Is that all of you?" comes a voice. Female. Firm. Familiar.

"Nekkan's one of us," says Crow. At least I can recognize her. "At least, was."

"We don't have time for him." The first voice is pressing, urgent. I hear a slam—they've trapped Nekkan in the vivisection room, but the door won't hold forever against his fists. "We're not the only ones who made it on board."

"Astrophel," I croak. His name is probably not what my word sounds like, but at least I give it a good try.

The Coalition have boarded the Mage. Tennyson's droids must be swarming the place, if there are any of them left.

Tobis grunts as he shuffles my weight in his arms. He's farm strong, but I'm lanky, hard to carry. Nemo takes me from him.

"I can stand," I croak, suddenly conscious that he's holding me by my pee-stained leggings. I don't want him to see me like this.

How did Tobis get here? If I'm not imagining him?

Nemo helps me to my wobbly feet. I don't want to ask him to carry me, but I'm going to have to. My knees are about to give out.

Abril is here, holding my right side. She's alive. How is she alive? She's perfectly my size, a crutch I never knew I needed. I want to wrap my arms around her and cry. She saved me from Astrophel at the cost of her own freedom. I owe her my life.

There's a slam so loud it almost knocks me off my feet. Two massive fists appear in the doorway: Nekkan is breaking out.

"Droid, carry her," the female voice snaps. "We have to get off the station now."

I look up, and for the first time I see her. For the first time I actually *see* her.

No longer is she withered and gray. Her hair is a glistening black, her skin as plump and blemishless as a toddler's. She's practically glowing in her pressure suit, a silver contraption almost identical to Gleïa's.

"Auntie?" I gasp, reaching for her. She breaks out into a smile, if only for an instant.

"Dora," she breathes, my name a prayer on her lips, "you scared me half to death. Thank the stars I've found you."

I laugh, which brings on a bout of coughing. My aunt has come to my rescue, flanked by my maybe-fiancé and a random girl from my botched escape—all perfectly normal. I must be seriously hallucinating from lack of air—if I'm not dead already.

"The family, are they…?"

Auntie nods. "Safe, safe, all of them safe. Waelon has the kids; I hid them where the Coalition can never touch them. But we have to go now if we want to ever see them again."

As if in a dream, I'm whisked away from the terrible room. Abril and Tobis are armed to the teeth, carrying weapons larger than they are, so comically large they could only be ocugry-made. And my aunt, she's leading us through the moon as if she knows the place, blasting droids and Coalition men out of the way in equal measure. Tennyson wasted no time turning on those defenses, his anger pulsing through every wall and floor. And the heat—the heat! We can barely breathe.

She leads us back to where it all began. The elevator is still here, latched on to the side of the station, even through all this mess. It dings as the door opens, and a woman steps outside.

It's not a droid barring our way; it's Gleïa, dressed in her imposing power suit, standing tall and strong in the middle of the empty chamber. A hatch is open in the roof—Auntie's ship. Only we can't get there, with the powerful technowitch standing in our way.

"Seriously, how stupid do you think I am?" Gleïa scoffs. "Turn around, Emery. There's still time. Work with us, become my sister again. Come any closer and become my enemy."

Sisters—they're sisters. All at once it falls into place, even as my mind fights the fog. Noon, missing, away—*away raising me*. The last of her clone batch, the four brilliant sisters warring for or against their father.

She's a clone, too. My heart swells. All this time, she knew exactly what it was to be me.

And nothing comes together at all, because none of it makes sense. What do I have to do with any of this? What makes me so important to the Mage that his daughters would fight to keep me away or serve me up to him?

"Gleïa, dear." Auntie smiles, putting her arms to her sides. She holsters her weapon and Gleïa mirrors her. "That's some freaky slag."

"You like it?" Gleïa grins sheepishly. "I've been standing here for an age. I had so much time to think it over. Pretty classy, right?"

"Totally," says Auntie. "But hon, I'm sorry, it's incredible to see you after all these years, but I have to get to my ship. I have to get these girls to Eve."

"I can't let that happen. Dad needs them—even now, he's fighting disk and cable to keep them safe. And you're going to, what, fly them off into a war zone?"

"And you're all right with Daddy Dearest using *children* in his plans?" Auntie scoffs. "You trust him that much?"

"With every fiber of my being, yes." Gleïa nods. "He's our *father*. And if he wants you dead, he probably has good reason."

"He wants us all dead, sister, in some way or another," Aunties says, sighing. To my surprise she turns back, reaching for Crow. She clutches her hand as warmly as if she were, well, me.

The sight of it ties knots in my stomach. There's something so delicate to the touch, maternal and sweet. Almost as if Auntie somehow knew her from… before.

I don't want anyone else to lay claim to her. Any kind of claim. Crow is free, free from her old mind and old memories, and no one is going to take that from her.

"Do you not recognize her, sister?" asks Auntie, clutching her hand tight. Crow doesn't pull away.

"The girl from my field," says Gleïa. "The girl from Father's hold."

"She is the reason Father wants us dead," says Auntie, like she's carrying some incredibly large weight that's taking all the breath and life out of her. "Once we're all dead, he'll come after you next."

Gleïa's face is red. "What the hell kind of lies are you sprouting?"

"Let us go to him, together," Auntie continues. "Ask him what this girl means to you, and we will part ways as sisters, just as you want."

"No," snaps Gleïa. "This is some kind of trick! Daddy told me you would try to pull a fast one on me. He did!"

And then, Gleïa grows. Her thick metal power suit explodes outwards, powerful and huge. She's ready for a fight, ready for war. She doesn't even look human anymore: a robot, built to fight Ocugry.

Auntie does not waste a second. She lets go of Crow's hand, her own exoskeleton doubling in size, puny next to Gleïa but built like a tank. A mask slides over her face, and suddenly she's made of metal, and she fights back.

They spring at each other, screaming war cries. Sister against sister, clone against clone.

"Leave!" Auntie shouts to me. "Get out before it's too late!"

There's a roar of anger behind us. Nekkan bursts into the 'vator atrium, claws raised. Both technowitches turn to him, trying to fend him off. All that the rest of us can do is take cover, diving out of the way.

"Our ship's docked to the 'vator," Tobis cries. "It's our only way off this station!"

"Come on," says Abril, "we have to get out of here!"

The way to the 'vator is blocked by the three-way fight. Even together, Auntie and Gleïa can't fend off the beast.

"This way!" yells Crow, bolting down the corridor. Nemo rushes us off after her, Tobis running backward, laying down cover fire. Not that anyone is following.

When did Tobis learn to shoot like that? There's barely any vermin on Nesworth, barely anything to shoot. Even through my daze, I'm thoroughly impressed.

The fight is ahead. Droids are fending off the invaders in the corridor: men and women in Coalition uniforms, different hues of silvery gray shooting their way through the drones in livery. We duck and turn back, but it's no use—the way behind is overtaken by the fiercer battle fought there.

We run into the fray.

We have no weapons other than the ones Abril and Tobis yield. We reach the end of this stretch of hallway and screech to a halt in front of a droid, who slams his whole body into Crow. She cries out—then spins, dropping down and behind the droid, slamming her fist into the small of his back. The droid is stunned enough for Abril to take a shot.

Nemo flinches as the robot falls.

"They are not me," he says, biting his lip. I'm awed by the simplicity of the gesture: acquired, not programmed. "Yet I am hurt by their hurt."

I remove myself from his grasp, dropping to my feet and standing feebly on my own. "Rule three: *they are not me.*"

"They are not me," he replies and puts his gaze steadily forward.

"I'm sorry," I say. But we have no time to wait. The droids are still coming. In this tight corridor, they seem to be infinite.

We push past the fight and through a pressurized door. We are left panting and heaving in the next section of corridor, which is amazingly devoid of—

"Abril?" Astrophel seems as shocked as we are to see him here. He's alone in the corridor, but he stuffs a com device into his pocket quickly, like we interrupted a call. He's holding a gun, and it's aimed right at us—at me.

"Yeah, I'm alive, slag-face," she spits. "Nice eye, by the way."

"You like it?" He sniggers, then turns back to me. "Not so big now that you don't have your monster to protect you, are you? Oh, before I forget—"

He takes aim above our head, and fires. For a split second, I think he's trying to intimidate us, show off his weapon. But then little pieces of hardware rain down on my shoulder.

Tau.

I scream. My poor stupid little bot. I'd never programmed him to defend me. It hadn't even crossed my mind. Somewhere he learned the behaviors, internalized them, made it part of his own, new personality. And it has killed him. Why the void didn't I just let him sleep?

"You didn't have to do that," I spit.

Tobis has his gun aimed right at Astrophel, but he's not shooting. I don't think he *can*. This is Tobis we're talking about; he can't hurt anything or anyone.

"After what he did last time? No thanks. Not taking any chances."

Tau's casing is completely broken, in more pieces than I can count. The bot I built with my own two hands, programmed after reading Tennyson's archived lectures. My faithful companion for years. I loved him. He was so much more than a bot, even before his behaviors started to change on his own. At my feet lie the remains of my closest friend, and I don't even dare bend over to pick them up.

"I don't think you're any good at countin'," says Tobis. "Four against one isn't the best odds. Let us through, or you'll be in as many pieces as the bot you just destroyed."

"What makes you think I'm alone?"

The hallway explodes in a frenzy of gunfire. Astrophel's allies burst into the corridor, guns literally blazing, but they're not alone: the droids they're fighting whoosh past us, too. I drop to the ground, atop the remains of my bot. Shots rain around me, and I cover my ears, trying to keep from falling further apart. I can feel the pieces of Tau press into my chest.

So much grew out of a few lines of code, an actual little life into itself. I don't dare get up, not with the firefight above me. I pull out the small green-gold chip that houses Tau's entire personality, slip it into my pocket. Every seed I ever planted for his personality is in here. Is his memory still safe? Would he know me, if I ever brought him back?

The foot on my back presses me down to the ground. My heart is about to burst from the fear.

"You're mine."

Astrophel's not going to kill me. He's going to *kidnap* me. I don't know what's worse.

With a burst of anger, I push myself up, fueled by adrenaline. He *killed* my bot. Killed Tau.

He swings his foot and kicks my face, hard. Something snaps, the sound a dull cracking, and I roll over, cupping my hand over my nose, trying to quell the pain. The blood is warm as it pushes through my fingers.

"Don't make me break you," he snarls. "I'm doing you a courtesy by keeping you alive."

He broke my bot. He broke my nose. He will not break me.

I roar like an Ocugry as I burst off the floor, flying at Astrophel's face. He's taken by surprise, and he doesn't have the room to shoot. I claw at his skin, hard enough to make him shout, but it's not enough.

He's so much stronger than me. He slams his hand into my chest, shoving me backward. I barely keep my balance, my foot tripping over Tau's remains.

I can't see my friends. Droids have spilled into the corridor, and the thin strip of space is full of people from every faction: the Mage's, the Coalition's, and mine.

Astrophel takes a step closer, grabbing me by the neck. It's still damaged by Nekkan's attempt to kill me, and I let out a cry of pain, kicking out as a reflex. My foot collides with his groin, and he howls worse than I do.

There are no low blows when you're fighting for your life.

"Why you little—" He rushes for me again, but I won't let him beat me, I won't. I swing my elbow back and slam right into his nose, where I'm met with a gut-wrenchingly satisfying crunch, and the clatter of a gun hitting the floor.

He's dropped his gun in the fight. Can't reach it—neither of us can without leaving ourselves vulnerable. It's down to a fistfight. I've never fought with my fists before, and now I only have one. But I'm lean and fast and at the very edge of dying, so I'm fighting until my last breath.

I swing high, aim low. Duck and swing. The fighting in the corridor is quiet as I pull my focus to Astrophel, channeling my anger at him and no one but him. Fighting for Tau. Fighting for my friends, who I can no longer see. With the only hand I have left.

I do what I've seen Crow do. I swing for the kidneys, and at last, he's down. Not unconscious, but down. My heart is pumping so hard and fast, I'm nauseous.

Gleïa busts through the corridor, shooting backward. Nekkan is rearing, charging at her, with Auntie clutched on his back. I can't see if she's fighting against the raging Ocugry or with him. I only have time to duck.

"Run, Buttercup!" I hear Crow's voice somewhere in the frenzy, clear as if she's right beside me.

Nekkan is unrecognizable: he's thrashing wildly, enraged, nothing like the being we came to know on Haven. He's foaming at the mouth.

I'm the reason he's rabid: I must have messed up his repairs, somehow. Left something out. I can barely remember what I did, it had been in such a frenzy.

But now the way to the 'vator is open.

"Nekkan!" Crow screams as he rushes past.

I grab her arm and tug her with me. With the others, we run toward the 'vator atrium, inside the doors that open with a ping.

"Up here!" shouts Abril. She leaps at the ceiling, pulling down the ladder to the tiny ship above. We race up it, me using my arm to hook where my missing hand cannot, Nemo pushing me along, until we're all in a pile on the floor. Abril rushes for the controls.

It's the same ship I crash-landed in—well, except for the fact that this one is intact. Another detail slips into place in that moment: if this is her ship, the one that kidnapped me must have been hers, too. She must have been the one to program it to bring me to her sister, the technowitch of Night.

Run to the end of the road. Run and don't look back.

That had been her escape plan, for me. Run to her old ship. Ride it to the Outer Zone, reach her sister for help. Night must have been her ally, someone she trusted deeply, and I killed her. No, the ship killed her. A malfunction that ruined her carefully plotted rescue plan.

But for what? How did I end up in her care in the first place?

Abril shuts the airlock. Nemo is lifting me to my feet, draping me over the cushions of the couch. Crow is stuck, shell-shocked, on the floor, staring at the airlock cover as if she could see through it if she tried hard enough.

Abril is back in the captain's chair, expertly wielding the controls. Tobis takes the co-pilot's seat, flicking on buttons at Abril's command that make the ship whirr.

Auntie is still outside. Nekkan is still down there, rabid out of his mind. Both on the wrong side of the airlock.

I scream. "We can't leave her! We can't leave them! Nekkan is—"

"Emery told us to go," says Abril, as calm as a Nesworth morning. "She'll be fine."

"She's going to kill him!" Crow screams.

"It's going to kill us," Abril says. "It's an engineered killing machine. It won't stop until someone stops it."

I cling to Nemo as the ship rises. I have no more control over this ship than I did the one that first brought me to this void of a planet, or the 'vator to this moon.

Beyond the sunshield, the battle is still raging. Only it's not the Mage's droids taking fire, but the Coalition ship itself. All this in the few hours since we reached the Mage. All this for—I don't dare think about it—*me*.

I've never seen the *Bountiful* without its grain holds, and it's small and sleek like a sword. It must have ditched the silos in order to travel faster, both with its sunlight and hyperspace engines. All that food wasted in search of me.

How much am I worth to them?

Something else is shooting at them. Something bigger than the *Bountiful*. A massive ship is bearing down on them, almost as big as the Mage's moon. It's pearly-white, shaped like a crystal with too many faces. Glassy partitions make it sparkle in the dark. Swarms of particles spill from its points, shimmering silver as they catch the starlight.

"Signal sent," says Abril, flicking a button above her head.

"And here comes the rescue party," says Tobis. As he speaks, one of the swarm from the mega-ship turns toward us, barreling down.

They fly without spacecraft, without suits or helmets. They fly through the vastness of space together, like a great cloud of insects seeking vengeance for their hive.

Droids. A massive fleet of droids, as varied as the stars in the sky. Flying with deft skill and concentration on their faces.

Our escape is short lived. They're going to kill us now, for sure.

Except no one is screaming. Not even as they swarm us, as they fill in their ranks, clutching each other, until our ship is covered by them. And we fly—our *own* special droid escort, a net that adjusts and alters our course so that we fly steady despite the firefight around us. Though the ship handles like a combine, it still manages to not get shot, obscured as it is by the droids.

"Where are we going?" I can't think about those we've left behind, where we've left them. Nekkan and Auntie. Two people I care for fighting each other to the deaths.

"Eve, the technowitch of Dusk," says Abril, turning back to look over her shoulder at me. "It's going to be okay, Dora. Your aunt is the most powerful technowitch I know, and she'll get out of this."

"You should tell her now," says Tobis.

"Are you kidding? She's going through a lot. I don't think she's ready."

"She'll hate you forever if you don't."

"This method of communication is ineffective," says Nemo harshly. "Who are you, exactly?"

"I'm Tobis. I'm a friend of Dora's. From her homeworld," he says, and I cringe at that word—I've never called Nesworth anything of the sort. "Dora's family was attacked by the Coalition. They chased Abril out of her ship in the middle of a storm, and my family took her in our bunker.

She was looking for a woman fitting Emery's description, and once the storm was over, we tried to connect them—"

"You're taking too long to tell this," says Abril. "Spare the boring details."

"Show them, then."

Abril takes a long drag on her rebreather, reaches up, and takes it off. She doesn't say a word as she does. She doesn't need to.

My heart skips a whole beat in my chest, and I choke on air. I can't mistake that face, skin flashing in starlight and plasmafire, a face I've seen every single day of my life, a face I'd seen shot and ruined.

Because it's my face.

"I thought you were dead," I say. I don't know what else to do. My lips are so dry now, my throat raspy. It's as if the sight of her has stopped my body from functioning, as if it knows it's against the laws of the universe to be two people at once.

"As did I," she replies. Without the rebreather, she speaks with my voice.

"You know about me?"

"How could I not know about you?" She laughs, an awkward, uncomfortable laugh. The moment is as surreal for her as it is for me.

I'm meeting the princess of the universe.

My clone.

Who is definitely *not* dead.

"My sister." She's staring at me like I'm a baby, all pure and innocent and cute. Meanwhile I'm looking at her like she's an alligator: an alien creature from a whole other world.

"Your clone," I reply, trying to take her in. The princess I've hated for taking a life that could have been mine. The reason I'm not allowed to exist.

"No," she insists, her eyes going wider still. "I'm not your clone."

"I'm yours. I know." I stress the words, hating the taste of them.

But Jo'Niss shakes her head again. "No, no," she repeats. "My sister. You're my *twin*. My identical twin. And I can't believe I found you."

With that, Jo'Niss flies out of her pilot's chair and wraps her sturdy arms around me. She clutches me to her heart. And I hug her back, ignoring our audience, all the while trying to process the words she said so effortlessly.

Not her clone.

Her sister. Her twin.

My twin.

My whole life has been a lie. I don't know how to wrap my head around this new truth, this knowledge that shatters everything I know about me. I think of Auntie, fighting for my escape in the moon below—but what for, if I'm not illegal to begin with? Why did she lead me to believe my entire existence was due to her mercy?

I watch out of the small side window as the moon shrinks behind us. So small from out here. It's surrounded by swarms of droids, getting smaller as we fly—

There's no sound as the moon bursts into light. Flames engulf it, transforming it into a small sun. And then the new star is gone, the moon is gone—everyone and everything is gone.

I can't tell my screams from those of the others.

Auntie, Nekkan—gone.

But before I can fully process my world ending, the ship lurches, and everything goes dark.

24

I WAKE IN A FAIRY-TALE.

The room I'm in is warm and cozy, flames crackling in the fireplace, a thick carpeted floor, and heavy drapes down the walls. I'm sitting in a plush red armchair, sinking into the cushions, feeling the heat of the fire envelop my body. And across from me, in a matching armchair, is—

"Ah, Miss Dora, kind of you to come to my home," says the Technowitch of Dusk. "Would you like some wine?"

She looks as beautiful as the day I met her. She smiles a wicked smile, her lips a deep crimson, in sharp contrast with her bright green dress. The dress is a thing of beauty, draped around her curvaceous frame: layers and layers of silk, a loop tied around her middle finger, so it gives the illusion of having green wings whenever she lifts her arms.

I watch Eve, and Eve watches me back, her beautiful gold eyes peering into mine as I try to make sense of her. Out of the corner of my eyes, I noticed we're not alone. Two men stand guard by the door behind her.

"How did I get...?" I've been drooling. My nose has stopped bleeding—or maybe someone has fixed it.

"I promise to be fully honest with you, if you are honest with me." She doesn't wait for me to reply. "My docking bay has a slight electrical charge. The second you landed, you were rendered unconscious. It's only been a few minutes—my people are fast. I do not wish for any of my guests to incur brain damage."

I take note of her so-called people. I can't tell if they're human or droid. Their uniform isn't something any self-respecting, self-conscious humans would wear: tall black hats, tight pants, and overly dramatic wings stitched onto the back of their jackets. It's as if they're some kind of interstellar quad gang, ready to burst into song and dance at a moment's notice.

"I call them my flying monkeys," she says, noting my gaze. "Well, Oona did. Because of all the monkey wrenches I threw around when I was building them. She used to call *them* flying monkeys. In any case, my people are not a threat to you."

"So, they are droids?" I'm at her mercy: better make a good impression. I've already ruined the first one by killing her sister. "They're so… lifelike."

"Please. They creep me out if they have too much realism—uncanny valley and all. But limitations are limitations, and I haven't gotten the balance quite right yet. So don't pander to me. You can see their flaws just as much as I can. From what I can tell, you have the gift."

"The gift?"

"You're a ginny," she says. "I might even say you could make a good technowitch someday. And I think I know a place that has an opening."

At those words, it's as if someone snuffs out the fire. A cold chill fills the room.

"I'm… I'm so sorry," I say, my whole body shaking. I knew there would come a day of reckoning. I just didn't know my own *sister* would deliver me here. None of this made sense. "I didn't mean to—"

"It was an accident," says Eve. "A tragic one, a heartbreaking one, but it wasn't your fault. Emery programmed her escape ship to bring you to our sister, but the nebulas are unpredictable. None of us are strangers to hardware malfunction."

Tears are streaking down my cheeks. I don't know who to trust in this Sister-forsaken world, but my Auntie is family to these women. This makes us family, too.

Or—Auntie *was.* I can't get the image of the moon exploding out of my head. She had to have found a way off of it, she had to.

My aunt… a technowitch. An Immy. Lying to me my entire life.

"Now, you took something from my sister," says Eve, leaning forward and lowering her voice with solemn weight. "I would quite like to have it back."

I can't help it—I let out a laugh.

"Are you slagging kidding me?" I say, unable to keep it together anymore. "After all this time, you still want the locket? Well, bad news: you just blew it from the sky. The Mage had it."

She *tssk*ed, visibly tired of me. "No, Dora. It's bonded with you."

I reach my hand up to my neck, still trying to recover my composure. The skin there is still smarting from when Nekkan tried to kill me. That's when my fingers brush against cold metal. A flat oval, and a chain. As if they'd never left my neck at all. I gape. There's no way it could be here, now after what I just saw.

"How…" I start, but I don't have the air to finish my question.

"I told you, it's bonded with you," she says. "You happened to be in close enough proximity and have enough genes in common with Oona for it to think *you were her* when she died. You must have touched it soon after the incident, yes? Its ownership jumped to you. But she wanted it to go to me, and I need it back. There's much work to be done."

"No," I snap, clutching the small thing. It survived an exploding moon and came back to me. Somehow, despite what she's saying, that matters. "Void, you tried to kill me! Twice, that I even know of! Is this what this has been about this whole time?"

She scoffs. "I was never trying to kill you."

"Ha!" I clutch the locket tighter. "So, acid rain and gas in our hotel room was, what? Welcome goodies?"

"The locket is part of something bigger than yourself, Dora. I'm going to have to ask you to hand it over."

I clutch it in my fist, so tight I think it must be breaking my skin. I tug it so hard that the chain pulls against my neck, tearing at the tiny hairs there. I scowl at Eve.

"I told you, I never wanted you dead," says Eve. "I only wanted the locket. You took it off, so I took my chance. All of you would have woken up none the wiser. You would have done the same if a child was parading around with your sister's most valued possession."

"I don't think I can trust you," I say, my voice coming out all wrong. "Acid rain isn't all that friendly either."

"I had no idea you were even there. I routinely run the rain to keep the lowlands unlivable, to keep the Mage's droid army experiment from expanding. The Mage used the theme park and environs as a testing ground, so I have to regularly purge the area. I didn't even know you were there."

"Still. That counts as attempted murder. With spooky skywriting to top it all off."

She takes a long, deep breath. We're at an impasse, and my heart pounds, wondering where she'll go from here. Now that she's exhausted asking politely.

"Dorian, can you see to her nose?" she asks, and a droid— the taller of the two—reaches for my face. I slap his hands away. "Dear, I think it's broken. If we don't set it, there could be problems down the line."

"Don't you *dear* me!" I snap. "Why do *you* care?"

"Care?" Eve raises a graceful eyebrow high. "It's a broken nose, and I don't want you injured. I'm not the enemy here."

"No. I mean about the locket. About any of this. Petty family feuds and politics. Why bring me here at all?"

"I don't know you, and this is my home. Your friends say Emery sent you, but she's… not here. You don't know who to trust, but I don't, either." She takes a breath, but I don't interrupt. "I need you to give the locket up willingly, so I can reset the biometrics. So, I can make things right."

"Which is why you haven't resorted to torture, I take it."

"Do you really think I'm capable of such a thing? Don't answer that—I know you do. It hurts to think that you have such a low opinion of me. My father turned this entire planet, maybe the entire Outer Zone, against me. Such a pity. I was his favorite for so long."

"So, what happened?" I tuck the locket underneath the collar of my shirt.

"It's a family matter and should be handled as such."

"And from what I can tell, I'm family, aren't I?" I spit. "Your father is the son of the Lost Pilot. I'm apparently a royal twin. Your sister raised me—she told me nothing of all this, I should add. Auntie shielded me for my entire life. I didn't even *know* I had a sister. All I want are some slaggin' answers."

She nods and presses a button on her seat. At once, the fireplace disappears. The room beyond is massive, long and lit with artificial lighting, a floor-to-ceiling window looks straight out into space, onto the planet below and the devastation in orbit around it. Pieces of debris drift past us.

Eve stands, and ushers me to follow her to a long, elliptic table. Sitting around it are faces I know well. Tobis and Nemo, both solemn and cold. Jo'Niss with her hands clasped in front of her the way she always sat during political sessions. And at the very end, looking like death itself, is Crow.

She's cried herself to pieces. Her face is pale, though her eyes are rimmed with bright red. She's still in her old clothes, but they've gained a coating of blood—both scarlet human and oil-slick ocugry—that makes it look like she's trampled through the void to get here.

But the second she sees me, she bursts into light. Her smile warms me immediately, chasing the chill away. For a second, I forget where we are, basking in her radiant presence and the certainty that she's alive and safe.

Eve beckons to the table again. I don't want to leave the comfort of the armchair—I don't even want to move at all—but I do. I don't know who to trust, but if my friends are alive, then I'm sticking with them.

"Now that we're all here," says Eve, "I believe you have many questions. I'm very sorry that my Emery isn't with us. My droids are searching the detritus of the emerald moon, and so far there's no sign of either of my sisters. This is good news."

It's good news, not knowing where Auntie is? I want to scream.

"Your friends have also asked about the ocugry," she continues. "No remains have been found, either. This all but confirms that my sisters and the merc' all made it off somehow before the station blew."

I sit down beside Crow, but I'm still too far away to reach her. She doesn't make eye contact.

"Let me start by saying that what you have done today has been a great boon for the galaxy. No one could have expected you to take down one of the Mage's strongest footholds. He's going to take a while to regain that kind of power."

"There's more to the mage than that moon?" I gasp. "I thought he was contained to the station."

Eve shakes her head. "Not quite. He's got backups of his mind placed strategically throughout the Zone. Even I don't know where. But the moon was his primary station, so its destruction gives us hope."

"*Us* being…"

"Me. My sisters. The resistance, for lack of a better word." Eve sweeps her hands over the table. "You lot."

"The resistance has been fighting to contain his expansion for centuries," Jo'Niss explains. "It's a long story. I don't even know where to start."

"Let's go back to the beginning, why don't we?" says Eve.

Jo'Niss starts. "What do you know about the Great Exodus and founding of the Sylvarian Systems?" She glances around the table.

I expect Crow to say something, some old-fashioned, profane quip, but she's too busy looking at her hands.

"Only the basics," says Tobis. It's odd to see him here, dressed in his farm clothes, in between me and the backdrop of space. "Long ago, First Earth was overpopulated and running out of resources. Mirah Sylvarian Tennyson discovered wormhole travel and opened the way for us to come here and settle new worlds. Only, the wormhole collapsed before she came through. Her sisters—the twins piloting the other two colony ships—along with her son Sylas, made it through and formed our civilization. The wormhole technology was lost with its pilot, leaving us unable to ever return to First Earth."

"That's essentially it," says Jo'Niss. "But six months ago, on her deathbed, my mother told me the truth: the twins deliberately closed the wormhole on Mirah as she and her ship tried to get through, taking her wunderkind son with them."

There's a silence in the conference room. Tobis and I trade glances—the most meaningful looks we've shared in months.

The founding sisters—murderers? Kidnappers?

"Tennyson didn't know," said Eve, "not at first. He grew up as a ward of his aunts. Helped build the technology that would drive our worlds. He fell in love, married, had a daughter he loves dearly—his one and only Cassandra. But his child was diagnosed with a deadly congenital disease, one with no known cure. He threw himself into genetics in an effort to save her, but it was hopeless. He stowed her in cryogenic sleep to keep her alive until he could save her."

"I thought she had died," I say. "From what I read, the royal family was in a terrible accident while terraforming Spe Prime. Tennyson's wife was killed, as well his daughter and Eva Sylvarian."

"Only Cassandra was already in cryosleep," says Jo'Niss, "and he used the tragedy to cover up his shame. Decades later, on her deathbed, Lani—hallowed be the pilot—revealed the truth to Tennyson, that his mother had been purposefully left behind. And she told him about the wormhole device, still safely in her possession."

I fly to my feet, slamming my hands on the table. "The wormhole device is here? The key to Earth is here, in the Sister Systems?"

Jo'Niss lifts her hands in a gesture of peace. "I have never seen it myself. My mother says we've been protecting it for generations. I've never seen it myself—Mirah was smart, she locked it with a genetic key that can only be activated by her and her sisters. Or by their descendants."

"So that's what Tennyson wants? To go back to First Earth?" My head is swimming. We've had the way back all along? The Lost Pilot was murdered? I don't know what to focus on. The facts are too wild.

"He believes his mother is still alive, inside the wormhole itself, despite the fact that all reason points to that being impossible," Eve says. "He's been working for three centuries to free her. To reopen the wormhole and return home."

"Then why are we fighting him?" asks Nemo. "Excuse me for interrupting. But a return to First Earth would be a good thing, wouldn't it?"

"Yes, most assuredly," says Eve. "But Tennyson has long stopped being driven by a philanthropic goal. He intends to wipe out the Sister Systems in his wake, to purge the galaxy of our selfish genes. And to do that, he needs to expand. Grow his mind—physically."

"So, why does he want us?" I ask.

"We're the key to the Wormhole device," says Jo'Niss. "We're the only ones who can turn it on."

"The Mage has been trying to create the perfect genetic keys for centuries," says Eve. "The device needs a very specific collection of genes: all female, two with identical royal DNA, and one with his own."

"So, he wants us because we're twins, like the first pilots, right?" I ask. "And Aunt Emery stole me away so he wouldn't know that not only was there finally a girl in the royal bloodline, but that there were twins."

"Exactly," says Eve. "Well, I assume as much. Emery went cold on us after your birth. She was undercover at the palace—seemingly under Father's orders—but as soon as Jo'Niss was born, she disappeared. She must have caught on to his plan, spirited you away, without telling any of us in case the knowledge of your existence would reach him."

Auntie, taking me from the royal cradle. Giving up her life to create one for me, away from these politics. To what end? I wish I could ask her directly. I cling to the knowledge that her body hasn't been found. In her power suit, she could have escaped. She could be anywhere right now.

"But the Lost Pilot herself designed the device and the lock, right?" asks Crow. "So, who is the third?"

"His daughter," says Eve. "He tried to make us in her image. Tried to make a new body for her mind, when her body started to fail. But we're not perfect. He has his heart— if you can call it that—set on Gleïa, since she's so willing to lay down her life for his. All he's missing is his daughter's mind, to overwrite hers, so that they can return to First Earth together."

"Tennyson?" scoffs Tobis. "Father of modern robotics, a geneticist as well? I thought the mother of cloning was Augusta Prima."

"Little-known secret," says Eve. "Almost any scientific discovery of the past three hundred years was aided or outright discovered by Tennyson under an assumed name. The man is ruthless when it comes to his search for eternal life."

"This makes absolutely no sense. So, Tennyson—father of robots, and somehow creator of cloning?—invents clone batching for what, slag and vapor?" asks Tobis.

"Her mind," says Crow. "He had his daughter frozen—*me*, frozen—so he could put my mind into one of your bodies."

"Yes, child," says Eve.

"I'm his daughter," she says and shivers. "He called me his daughter, but I didn't believe it. But that's me, isn't it? I'm Cassandra?"

She's… I stare at her, and it hits me all over again. Oh Sisters—she's Tennyson's *actual* daughter. Which makes Gleïa, Emmery, Eve, and Oona her modified clones—her *sisters*. Tennyson invented clone batching. Made his daughters to improve on Crow's perfection, clones ready to be discarded when it suited Tennyson the most. Pitted them against each other, the winner overwritten with the mind of a girl who never wanted any of this.

"I'm still dying, aren't I?" Crow's says. Her voice is barely over a whisper. "My body isn't going to hold. That's why Cassandra chose to get the traveler tattoos—she knew her time was running out, and she wanted to use what she had left to see the stars. They're the coordinates for Earth, aren't they?"

Eve shakes her head. "I don't know. Father didn't even want us to know about your existence. When I found out we were essentially competing to have our minds erased and replaced with the consciousness of a sister we'd never heard of, I told my sisters. Gleïa was the only one who didn't believe me. Oona stole Cassandra's memory disk before Father caught wind of it and hid it in the locket."

All along, I've had Crow's memories around my neck. And I so easily gave them up. But I have them back now. I cradle the small pendant before handing it to Crow. As she touches it, it opens, finally ready for her. It holds a tiny silver disk. Such a small disk, an entire life coded within.

"We've been trying to keep Father contained ever since," says Eve. "My sisters needed me—and now, I just need to watch over Gleïa. Poor thing. So naïve. She thinks Father is the very expansion of the universe."

"What about the princess?" asks Nemo. "How did Dora's sister get here?"

"You know how my mother told me all this on her deathbed?" Jo'Niss says. "Well, how would you feel if you had that kind of legacy on your shoulders? She opened up about a lot of things that day. About how I, the first daughter born to the royal family in three hundred years, brought Tennyson one step closer to the wormhole key … How my birth sparked a silent war with the Outer Zone to keep me and my genetic material from him. About how he'd stop at nothing to get his hands on me. And how I was born a twin, my secret sister stolen away by a technowitch, so that Tennyson would never know all the keys were already in place."

"So, you faked your death to get away," says Tobis, bouncing on his chair. His eyes are wide and sparkling with excitement.

"I had to," she says. "I needed to end the cycle. End the secrets. And the first step in the process was hunting for you,

Dora. I snuck onto a Coalition ship and made my way to the rim worlds, colonies settled around our date of birth. And I hunted."

My eyes go wide. So much for the delicate princess I've spent my years studying: everything I know about her seems so utterly wrong.

I gape at her. "You spent six months hunting for me?"

"And for Emery. Only you saved yourself, using her backup exit. If I'd been just a few minutes faster… I just…" She goes quiet, apparently ashamed. I don't know what to say.

"I can't believe I didn't recognize you," I reply. "I saw your eyes, and I didn't realize they were the same ones I'd seen in the mirror every day of my life until… an hour ago. There's something about seeing yourself standing in front of you. I didn't see myself in you at all."

We stare at each other across the table in silence. I've found my sister, we've found Crow's memories, and we've blown up Tennyson's stronghold; and yet, it doesn't feel like a victory.

I feel like I've lost something massive.

"What now?" asks Crow. "Do we just… go home?"

"I didn't travel halfway across the Systems to just go home," says Jo'Niss. "Well, I suppose, in a way I did. I'm here to change the world. And now that I've found you all—we can go back to our first home. Our real one."

"First Earth," says Tobis. He won't stop smiling. The only one with a frown at the table is Crow.

"Nekkan," Crow says. "We can't do it without Nekkan. I know he's alive out there. He said it himself: he's not built to die. With his help, we can get the ocugry to protect us."

"And my sisters," says Eve. "We've been fighting for our way back for centuries, together. And together we're going to bring humanity home."

Eve's spaceship is magnificent in both a physics and a word-defying way.

Engineered crystal growth shapes it, so it feels as solid as the surface of a planet. Walking down the corridors without looking through a window, you might never realize you were off world at all. And when you do reach a window, that's the other end of the spectrum—tread too close, and you feel like you could walk right off into space.

I find Crow tempting fate at one of said windows. She's fully entranced by the view, her face pressed up against the diamond. Either she hasn't heard me walk up, or she doesn't care.

I flex my new hand, suddenly nervous. It's not my hand, not yet—on loan from Eve, a piece of droid-tech with a few jerry-rigged neurotransmitters at the end, enough for me to gain full motion control without any of those pesky feelings that usually come attached to appendages. I'm thankful: fitted with a new limb before I'd fully come to terms with the loss of my real one. Eve has promised the entire ship is at my disposal for me to build a new one, and I'm eager to sit down and fine tune my plans. The sooner I have fully functional fingers, the sooner I can bring Tau back to life.

Sisters, I miss him.

I catch myself. Calling upon the Sisters, after knowing what they'd done? The entire Sylvarian Systems worship them, without ever knowing they were the reason we were isolated from First Earth in the first place. I shudder.

Enough pandering to my anxious thoughts. I clear my throat.

Crow spins around, a flash of terror crossing her face before she realizes it's me, and she smiles.

"Can I join you?" I ask, and she nods.

"Take a stand, Buttercup." Her eyes land on my new hand, and she starts. "Oh! Did Eve…?"

I nod. "It's mine until I work out my own build."

She takes it delicately in her gentle hands, and, suddenly, I miss the lack of feeling. I would give anything to feel her skin touching mine, the way her fingers trace over my new palm.

"It's cold," she says.

I shrug, trying to pretend that even though I can't feel her, my heart isn't racing through my chest just standing this close to her.

"I'm really sorry about Tau," she says next, and I can't help it, I reach my own hand up to hold hers. She gives it a tight squeeze. In a universe so vast and impossible, there's nothing more magnificent than a hand to hold.

"I'm going to fix him," I say. "I'm going to fix everything. I'm going to figure out what I did wrong with Nekkan and I'm going to—"

She flinches. "I don't think it was your fault."

"Don't."

"No, I'm not trying to make you feel better, I swear," she insists. "The beast that attacked us, that wasn't… it wasn't

Nekkan. It was a shell. The same way the droids were, when under the Mage's control. Could he have tampered with Nekkan's head like that?"

I nod, and she's right, it doesn't make me feel any better. I should have noticed, when Nekkan's mind was laid out before me, when I was finding the parts to stitch him back together. I should have seen not just what was there, but what was missing.

"We're going to find him," she says, again, though there's a slight tremor to her voice. She turns to stare out the perfect window at the remains of the battlefield beyond. "And your aunt. And… Earth."

She's shaking. I squeeze her hand tighter. Our grasp could fuse our hands together. Because I know what lost thing she hasn't listed— a cure, for her. And void, we are going to save her.

Save everyone.

I pat the locket, still awkward around my neck, though the latter has begun to heal splendidly with the help of Eve's collection of nanobots. "And what about… Cassandra?"

Crow cringes again. "I'll let you know when I'm ready. I have enough to process with this brain to begin with."

"I've found you," says Nemo, joining us by the window. I give him my droid hand, and he takes it.

For a few minutes, we stand in silence. We watch the tiny specs of Eve's flying monkeys zip in and around the wreckage of the Mage's Moon, salvaging what they can. The *Bountiful* is nowhere to be seen. I have a dread in the pit of my stomach that if anyone survived, it would be on the one ship I never wanted to see again in my life.

"I'm sorry about your brothers," says Crow, breaking our silence.

"Mourning them is… painful," says Nemo, and I squeeze his hand. "Eve has promised to repair any they can salvage, but that won't be many. Our father—"

He doesn't finish his sentence. I don't think he can.

"We're going to hit him where it hurts," Crow says, this time with panache, with a fire she didn't have before. "Fix Tau. Find Nekkan. Find Noon. Save the Systems."

Nemo nods, standing tall. Crow's fire has spread to him, and I'm feeling the heat as well.

"Fix Tau. Find Nekkan. Find Noon. Save the Systems," he repeats, voice slow and even.

"Fix Tau. Find Nekkan. Find Auntie. Save the Systems." I agree.

And as ludicrous as the statement sounds, I somehow know, standing here with my friends, hand in hand, that it's something we can do. My heart is pounding with equal parts anticipation and terror.

I am not alone.

We are not alone. On board this ship, the most powerful engineer this side of the galaxy and her army of droids are preparing for war. In a room nearby, my former best friend and my *sister* are gearing up for the fight. The odds are impossible, but so are we.

After all, anything can happen in an infinite universe.

TO BE CONTINUED IN

DOWN TO
EARTH

ACKNOWLEDGEMENTS

THIS BOOK WAS YEARS IN THE MAKING, and just like Dora, I wouldn't haven made it without finding my people. It wouldn't be here without them, and I wouldn't be the person I am without them, either.

The Fellowship of the Five, to whom I've dedicated this book, are a team beyond compare. I cannot thank Lisa Amowitz enough for helping me work out my massive plot holes. You grave this story a brain. Nor Emily Colin, for waving her magic wand (is there such a thing as a Litowitch?) and making my words sparkle. You gave this story a heart. Madeline Dyer, for giving it the coat of polish it needed. I want to say you gave this story courage, because how cool would that be, but you gave *me* the courage to put my books out there, and that's even better. And finally, to Heidi Ayarbe, for bringing this story home: for keeping me sane and grounded as I wrote.

I guess that makes me Toto, and I'm fine with that: I am the design puppy after all.

I also need to thank my amazing Alpha/Beta readers, Cora and Crystal, who always pump me up. I am so glad to know you and to have you cheering me on.

To Hugo, my brainstorming and life partner. Thank you for always having ideas when I need you. I'm so excited for our next adventures.

ABOUT THE AUTHOR

S.E. ANDERSON is the author of the YA science fiction humor series THE STARSTRUCK SAGA and OVER THE MOON, as well as a YA contemporary novel, AIX MARKS THE SPOT, based on her childhood in Provence.

She has a PhD in astrophysics and currently, she's trying to wrangle some comets in Marseille, France, along with her fiancé and cat.

CONNECT WITH THE AUTHOR

www.seandersonauthor.com
facebook.com/seandersonauthor
instagram.com/seandersonauthor
tiktok.com/seandersonauthor
twitter.com/seandersonbooks